Electric Blue

Dr. Chris Harz

For information about quantity discounts or reproducing parts of this book, please contact:
Phantom Ranch Productions
22546 Saticoy Street
Canoga Park, CA 91307, USA
Or email at: chris@drchrisharz.com

ISBN 978-0-9903284-0-7

His snorting throws out flashes of light; his eyes are like the
red rays of dawn.

Firebrands stream from his mouth; sparks of fire shoot out.

Smoke pours from his nostrils as from a boiling pot over a
fire of reeds.

His breath sets coals ablaze, and flames dart from his mouth.

When he rises up, the mighty are terrified; they retreat
before his thrashing.

The sword that reaches him has no effect, nor does the spear
or the dart or the javelin.

Iron he treats like straw and bronze like rotten wood.

Arrows do not make him flee, sling stones are like chaff to
him.

A club seems to him but a piece of straw, he laughs at the
rattling of the lance.

He makes the depths churn like a boiling cauldron and stirs
up the sea like a pot of ointment.

Nothing on earth is his equal— a creature without fear.

He looks down on all that are haughty; he is king over all that
are proud.

–Job 41:25 ("Leviathan")

Dedication and Acknowledgements

Many thanks are due to the members of the Topanga Writing Group and West Side Writers, whose encouragement and feedback were essential, as well as to Sarah, John and Mary, my support system, and the many other friends, experts and colleagues who provided insights.

Thanks are also due the people of Anguilla, St. Martin, and St. Maarten, whose kind and generous spirit is reflected in the beauty of their islands.

This book is dedicated to the real-life fossil hunters who have found—and painstakingly recreated—the remains of the ancient monster featured in this story, which is not generally known to the public, and to the many other researchers of the primeval who keep scientific discovery alive and vibrant, and changing from year to year. It is because of them that generations can *Ooh* and *Ahh* at these amazing animals, in museums and books and films that seem to describe creatures from a different universe. Their dedication turns dusty bones into a living history of the wonders of our planet. A question posed in this novel is, "Will wonders never cease?" I hope the reader agrees: "No! They never will!"

Chapter One

The hummingbird hovered outside the window of the Pelican Restaurant, the feathers of its back scintillating bright emerald green. A flash of neon violet-red glowed on its neck as it craned its head forward to take a long, deliberate sip from a trumpet-shaped, peach-colored hibiscus blossom. The hummer was framed by the mid-morning sun, which poured through the open wall like a blessing, suffusing everything it touched with an orange-gold glow. The Caribbean sky formed a calm aqua-blue background over the *swoosh...swoosh-swoosh...swoosh* of waves depositing foam over blindingly white sand.

David smiled at the shimmering sprite's antics, and inhaled the fresh ocean air. Being a treasure hunter certainly had its good side, he reflected. Here on the island of Anguilla he was treated like a celebrity, with a long line of men buying him drinks and young women who wanted to drink with him. His smile morphed into a frown and his shoulders slumped as he thought about the reality of his situation. His treasure hunting days were about to come to an abrupt end if he didn't find more money. He barely had enough to pay his crew through the end of the week. After that, his many new friends here could disappear as rapidly as the hummingbird before him, which, finished with its draught, vanished into thin air.

He leaned forward in his chair, took a deep sip from a giant coffee mug, and added a little more milk from the cow-shaped creamer on his table. Intoxicating odors of grilled red snapper and shrimp drifted across his nose from the kitchen, but he had no appetite for Chef Patrick's famous cuisine.

His smile returned as a smooth finger ran a languid path along his right ear. A sultry whisper of, "When we get togeddah again, eh?" tickled his earlobe, followed by a girlish giggle.

"Soon, Liza, soon," he responded, clasping and releasing her manicured hand before she glided toward a table at the back wall, to gossip and giggle with her girlfriends.

David stole a nervous glance at his watch. AJ was late for their meeting. He hoped his friend had the funding he so desperately needed. He'd known AJ since they were both in the Marine Corps. When David told him he was looking for gold in a sunken U-Boat near Anguilla, AJ had shown great interest, and said he knew collectors of war memorabilia. His contacts were willing to invest, and wanted none of the gold that German Naval records indicated was on the sub; they only wanted its documentation and records. That investment had kept him going, but was about to run out.

The Pelican's door creaked on its hinges, and David swiveled to see his friend making his usual grand entrance, working his way through the restaurant like a conquering hero who had just returned. His strikingly handsome black face was punctuated by a bright white grin as he stopped at tables to exchange a ritual of hand bumping and slapping, and greetings peppered with the local patois. He finally reached David's table, picked up a chair, and sat in it backwards, resting his muscled forearms on top. The mesmerizing grin grew even wider as he said, "Well, I've got news."

David's insides churned—he knew his friend would like nothing better than slowly drawing out what he had to tell him.

"Did you get the money?" he blurted out.

"Well...maybe," his friend replied.

David gripped the table tightly. "How much?"

AJ became serious. "I got you another quarter million, enough to keep going till the storm season starts."

David exhaled slowly. He realized he'd been holding his breath. "Thank God. We're so close. I know we can find it."

AJ held out a restraining hand to David, who had started to rise out of his chair in his excitement, "But—there's a condition attached, a major one."

"What do I have to do?" David half whispered, sinking back down.

"You remember those dinosaur bones you found while hunting for the sub? The ones you sent your friend in the museum?" AJ replied. "That's how we came up with the tie-in. The money from this investor group is for science, to fund a research team to find more of those bones. You have to take a team of two paleontologists along on your ship and help them."

David looked astonished. "Paleo...paleontologists?" he stammered.

"Yes. They're scientists who look for dinosaur fossils," AJ offered helpfully.

"I know what paleontologists are," David scowled. "But...I'm under a tight schedule. I can't afford to baby-sit bone hunters while I'm looking for..." He bit off the rest of what he was about to say, and looked quickly around. He knew that if word got out about what he was searching for, he would soon have an army of divers crawling all over his operation.

AJ drew closer, and spoke quietly. "Listen. My investors have different pots of money. Sometimes they can just write you a check, like they did the first time. Other times, they need to run the money through different channels. This time they chose to run it as a, er, donation to the Museum of Natural History in New York." He paused. "You actually gave them the idea when you sent those fossils to the Museum."

David looked thoughtful. "Well, I guess it makes sense. Your investors can't lose. If we find what we're looking for, they get their historic wartime documents. If not, they still get a high-profile tax write-off."

AJ looked at him slyly. "I can see there's no fooling you, is there? But don't worry. The paleontologists won't be any bother—you're both hunting around in the same area for different things, so you might as well help each other. And she and her assistant have their own diving equipment and Zodiac boat, so they won't slow you down."

David's head jerked up sharply. "She?"

"Yes, she," AJ replied. "She's an Australian, doctorate in something called cyber-paleontology, whatever the hell that is, and she's explored in this area of the Caribbean before. She applied for a research grant, and my sponsors donated the money—on condition that she shares it with you." AJ pulled an envelope out of a jacket pocket and laid it on the table. "So. Are you in?"

David took a deep breath. "Well, if I have to babysit a woman bone hunter, I guess I'll just have to put up with it. When do I meet her? Is she as old as the bones she's hunting?"

AJ took a few moments to place his breakfast order with the waitress and get a cup of coffee before answering. "You can meet her this very morning. She's giving a lecture on what she's looking for at a paleontology convention in Philipsburg in St. Maarten at eleven-thirty. I would guess you could still make it..." AJ looked at his watch, "...if you catch the next ferry over there. I've arranged a pass for you at the National Conference Centre."

David jumped up and threw a few bills on the table. "I'll be back by tonight. Let's celebrate then." He looked down at the way he was dressed, in shorts and an oil-stained T-shirt, and said, aghast, "Oh, no! I don't have time to make a run out to the ship and change clothes!" He looked at AJ accusingly. "And I'm wearing one of your T-shirts."

AJ broke into a huge grin. "From one of my best customers. *The Shady Lady Gentleman's Club*. They go through a lot of champagne."

David sighed. "Oh, well. She'll just have to take me as I am."

As he started to walk away, he stopped and whirled around, looking back at AJ. "By the way, what's her name?"

AJ smiled mysteriously behind the dark wraparound sunglasses he wore. "Bettelman. Doctor Erika Bettelman."

After David had left, AJ walked to his car and got out a satellite phone with an extra-long antenna. He flipped it open, speed-dialed a number, and flipped a switch marked CRYPTO. "OK, the deal is on," he said. "Go ahead and transfer the money from the Maritime Intelligence account."

Chapter Two

David pushed his way through the throng at the 75th Annual International Society of Paleontology Convention in the main hall, and found one remaining seat in the front row. As he glanced at the crowd, he caught the eye of Reginald Fowler, the Lieutenant Governor of Anguilla, and David returned both his smile and friendly hand wave.

The lights dimmed as an older gentleman at the podium began to introduce the next speaker, with pompous throat-clearing and much shuffling of paper. He finally concluded with, "... and without further ado, here is Dr. Erika Bettelman, to discuss *Possible Genetic Adaptations of Mosasaurs*."

The audience, which overwhelmingly consisted of older men who looked like they were themselves fossilized, vibrated their hands in polite applause. They started to stir as a young, blond woman in a conservative dark ochre pants suit walked purposefully toward the podium. She had obviously toned down her youth and femininity with glasses and hair that was severely pulled back. David saw her mouth twitch slightly as she looked out at the audience; she appeared to have reservations about her colleagues. She wore black pumps with high heels, but appeared not to be used to them. She wobbled slightly when walking, and finally stumbled on the carpeted stage, eliciting a few snickers from the audience.

Erika waited a moment while her assistant, a skinny young man in a black T-shirt, connected her laptop to the projector. She started up, slipping in and out of an Australian accent.

"G'day, ladies and gentlemen, fellow colleagues. I'm Erika Bettelman." She was evidently very nervous, and almost choked on the words. She hastily swallowed a mouthful from a bottle of water on the lectern, and then clicked on her mouse. The title slide of her briefing was displayed on two wide screens. "Since I see members of the press in here, I'll try to explain this in laymen's terms as I go along. For a sound bite, you could say the animal I'll describe was the most dangerous, most aggressive killer the earth has ever known."

David discerned the ongoing nervous edge to her voice. Erika looked at her laptop or the screens behind her, avoiding eye contact with the audience.

"I'm a cyber-paleontologist, which means I use 3D computer generated models of an animal to illustrate how it probably moved, to give us clues about both its structure and behavior, especially when we have only parts of it in the fossil record. It was early work in cyber-paleontology that demonstrated that the great dinosaurs like T. rex did not drag their tails as was once thought, but walked upright and held their tails up for balance—and to use as weapons."

"My topic today concerns the order of Mosasaurs, and some recent discoveries I came upon. Let me review briefly."

A click revealed a painting of a Mosasaur, which looked like a giant ocean-going crocodile, but with flippers instead of legs, and a much larger and longer mouth and tail.

"The Mosasaur was one of the first saurians ever discovered, in 1780 near the River Meuse, or Moos, after which it was named. Its discovery preceded that of dinosaurs by quite a bit, and made sensational headlines. Its nearest modern relatives are the Komodo Dragon and perhaps giant snakes like the python."

A click revealed a photograph of a fearsome-looking animal, with the legend, *Komodo Dragon, Length 22 feet* beneath it.

"After the originally land-based animal decided to make the lakes and oceans of our planet its home some 180 million years ago, its four legs broadened into flippers, and its tail lengthened to propel itself rapidly through the water. Mosasaurs had flexible, double hinged lower jaws, so they could swallow huge prey in one gulp." Another click revealed a picture of huge open mouth with a hinged lower jaw, taller than the figure of a man standing next to it.

"The animal was a master of adaptation. Although it breathed air, it adapted to swimming for long periods underwater. It has been found in every area of the world, from shallow lakes to the deepest ocean, and ranged from small mollusk eaters with broad teeth for grinding..." another click showed a painting of an animal eating a large underwater snail, with the legend *Mylasaur, 4-6 feet long* underneath, "...to a group that included the giant carnivorous Tylosaur, which ranged from 40 to perhaps as much as 70 feet long. It dominated the oceans of the world, as the apex predator of the Cretaceous seas. It is sometimes called the Tyrannosaurus rex of the ocean. But it was larger than the T. rex, about four times as large, and could likely have eaten one for lunch if they had met."

Another click revealed a charging Mosasaur's jaws engulfing a giant shark, above the title, *Tylosaur attacking a Megasaur.*

"Mosasaurs were powerful swimmers, with the ability to jump completely out of the water like dolphins," she noted. "We've found in their stomachs the remains of large pterosaurs, probably seized while flying low over the water looking for fish."

"We've always believed," she continued, "that Mosasaurs disappeared during the K-T extinction, the great dying, around 65 million years ago, when all the dinosaurs died. The theory is that the sun was blocked by the detritus that resulted when a giant meteor hit the earth. But many animals such as sharks—which are also very adaptable—survived. A number of researchers have described the Mosasaur's disappearance as a quandary, including Richard Ellis in his popular book, *Sea Dragons*."

Erika paused. "You'll now see a short computer animated film on the evolution of this remarkable group of animals, generated by my associate, the ace animator Moshe Kirshbaum. " She waved toward the front row at her assistant, who smiled shyly at the compliment.

The video played with bright graphics and thumping background music. David thought of how this must contrast with the soporific deluge of words—with only a few black and white photographs of bones—that a typical presenter in this hall would inflict upon his audience. His attention was disrupted by the nonstop commentary from the second row. He turned to see an extremely corpulent gentleman with several layers of chins in the middle of that row, conducting a running commentary for a coterie of young sycophants. His discourse was periodically interspersed with a laugh that sounded like a donkey braying, and was accompanied by a fine spray of spittle that hung suspended in the air.

After the video concluded, Erika turned back to the microphone. "I've left copies of our paper at the back of the auditorium. I'll let you pick one up and read at your leisure. But now, I'd like to talk about something entirely different." There was a stirring in the hall, and a clearing of throats. This was, clearly, out of the usual.

She beamed as she touched her laptop to call up the next slide. "These are recent discovered fossil remains of what I believe to be a Mosasaur from this part of the Caribbean." Photos showed different views of fossils that David recognized as the ones he had found while looking for the sub.

"I've uncovered similar fossils in previous digs in marine layers that I believed to be less than 65 million years old, but the evidence was inconclusive. These remains, however, could be revolutionary, if they are indeed from a Mosasaur. The rock strata they were found in are almost certainly only 30 million years old."

This proved entirely too much for the bulky gentleman in the second row. Grasping the lapels of his tweed jacket, he let out a braying laugh. "30 million years! Ha! Why not just say they're still running around outside on Van Hoek Avenue?" His coterie started to snicker, as Erika's face grew red.

She clicked through several more slides, starting to stammer. "The skeletal structure is similar that that of a large Tylosaur." Several slides flashed by, showing photos of the subject fossils compared side-by-side with those of known Tylosaur parts.

The second row emitted another painful laugh. "Pah! With those small bits and pieces, that could be a whale or dolphin or almost anything else. What nonsense!"

Erika tried to regain her composure. "However, there is one interesting difference."

The members of the audience craned their necks forward to get a better view as Erika shone the red beam of a laser pointer on several photos. "These impressions in the fossils could indicate electroplaxes, electric organs. Note the similarity of these features..."–click—"...to the electric organs in modern electric eels and stingrays."

"Electric!" The mountain of human being in the second row started to shake like a giant pyramid of Jell-O. "Electric organs! And this is what passes for science nowadays!"

Erika paused, and appeared to be lost. "If, er, if..." She stopped, leafed desperately through her notes, and started up again. "If these, er, remains are from a Tylosaur, and if these are electric organs, it means that our friend the Mosasaur came up with yet one more adaptive trick. We know from the body structure of sea-going Mosasaurs that they were adapted for diving into the ocean depths, to a thousand feet or more, like modern whales and porpoises. The problem is, there is no light at that depth, so how could the Mosasaur find anything to eat? Whales such as this one..."— a click showed a sperm whale seizing a giant squid in the depths of the oceans —"do this by echolocation, which allows them to find prey in total darkness with high frequency sound waves."

A picture of an electric eel hooked up to wires in an aquarium appeared on the screens. She continued, "Electric eels have a similar problem: they have to find prey in muddy water. They do this by electrolocation, sending out electric fields, as shown in this animation."

An animated video started up, showing how the field from an eel was disturbed by the presence of a fish it was seeking, allowing it to locate the fish. Erika looked somber. "The electric field has a second function: it can kill the prey after helping to find it. The charge from a 4-foot eel can kill a fully-grown man instantly, and a 6-foot eel can kill a horse. Imagine what the charge from a 60-foot

Mosasaur might have been like." As the audience tried to visualize this sobering scenario, Erika continued.

"Using electrolocation and deep diving could have allowed Mosasaurs to live past the K-T junction, by feeding on large prey such as giant squid swimming at great depths, without being dependent on fish near the surface of the oceans."

The gentleman in the second row was beside himself at this point. He started rocking in his seat, openly guffawing. "Electric!" he shrieked. "Electric! She's gone totally over the top."

Erika furrowed her brow, a movement David found charming. "This is all speculative, of course. It's a hypothesis I am now pursuing by dives in the Caribbean to find additional fossil specimens."

"No, this is not a scientific hypothesis," spat the gentleman in the second row. "This belongs in the category of poppycock and superstition!"

Erika looked at her audience, knowing she had equally intrigued and irritated them by presenting apocryphal data. She continued, the nervousness in her voice becoming ever more evident as it occasionally started to crack.

"Lord Shrewesbury appears to disagree with me. But look at all the ways animals have adapted. No one believed they could change color, until chameleons and octopi showed they could do it easily. And we all know that hypotheses can transition to fact overnight. When the first coelacanth..." Another mouse click caused a picture of a large, ancient looking fish to come up on the screens, "...was pulled up from the ocean by a fisherman in 1938, it astounded our community, because it was thought to have been extinct for 80 million years."

"In summary," Erika continued, now rushing desperately onward, "I believe that some Mosasaurs with deep diving and probably other adaptations managed to live for far longer than we give them credit for. If I'm successful in finding more evidence for that, I'll be back at the next conference and report on it. Thank you for your attention."

Erika closed her laptop with a snap, disconnected the cable that led to the projector, and walked determinedly off the stage to scattered applause, ignoring the dozen or so questioning hands raised in the air.

David caught up with her in the lobby. "Dr. Bettelman—hold up a minute!" She turned and focused slowly on him, giving his wrinkled and stained shirt and short pants a quick once-over. Her eyebrows arched down into a frown, and then her mouth dropped open in disbelief as she read the "Shady Ladies" logo printed over a picture of amply endowed and barely clad females on the front of the shirt.

David reddened. "I'm sorry. I didn't have time to change. My friend—my so-called friend—AJ Simon only just told me this morning about your conference, and I—"

Erika's eyebrows shot up. "Blimey, you're the treasure hunter."

David put a finger up to his lips. "Please, let's keep that quiet. Yes, I'm David Kilmer. Pleased to meet you."

They shook hands somewhat awkwardly, with Erika extending only a few fingers, and then jerking them back quickly. She looked at her hand as if it was contaminated. Several audience members started milling around them, maneuvering for a place next to Erika, trying to get her attention.

David almost stuttered. "Look, Dr. Bettelman, is there a place around here where we can talk?"

Erika considered this a minute. "Yeh. We can have lunch at my hotel. It's right down the street." She took another look at his oil-stained shirt and sniffed the air. "It has an outdoor terrace."

David bit his lip. "I said I was sorry."

She looked at him coldly. "It is what it is, I guess. OK, let's go."

As they turned to leave, Erika waved off her gathering would-be retinue with a breezy, "Sorry, I've got to run. Catch me tomorrow," and then added under her breath as they walked out of the Convention Centre entrance, "...if you can!"

David smiled at her as they walked rapidly down the street. "You're less than fond of your fellow scientists," he noted.

Erika's Australian accent thickened with the emotion of her response. "Yeh. Half of them are old blockheads that have been doing the same crap for the last 30 years, and the other half are probably just trying to get into my knickers. They can kiss my arse. None of them has an iota of respect for a woman." She looked darkly at the scantily clad female on the front of his shirt. "Not that you would understand!"

David sighed. "I said I was sorry. AJ gets these by the dozen, and I use them when I work on the ship." He started again. "Is that why you ignored all the raised hands after your presentation?"

Erika flushed. "Too right, that. I've been through that before. Instead of asking a real question, they start pontificating on their bloody stupid points of view, to try to show how fucking smart they are. Once I just totally lost it, and told some old fart that he should at least finish up his so-called question with a question mark at the end!" She wrinkled her nose. "Like I said, fuck 'em."

Her brows darkened. "And the worst one of them is the chief arsehole, bloody Lord Shrewesbury. I'd love to kick him in his ballocks, if I could find them in that mountain of fat!"

David stared at her and grinned. "You don't beat around the bush!"

Erika looked at him sternly. "Look you, I grew up in Australia, where we still know the difference between truth—straight dinkum—and pure bullshit. I hope you're not one of these politically correct Yanks that tries to be so pure that butter wouldn't melt in his mouth, and then blows smoke up your arse. I don't have time to waste!"

David bristled. "Hey, hey. Back up. I'm not the one you're mad at. I'm just an innocent bystander."

Erika smiled contritely. "Sorry, mate. You're right, I'm just pissed off at those hypocrites in the hall. Tell you what. I'll buy you lunch." She gazed at his shirt again. "Looks like you may not be able to afford it, anyway." She glanced up at stairs leading to the lobby of the hotel they had just arrived at, The Carlton. "And here we are!"

They chose a table next to the front railing of the terrace, and sat back and looked at each other. David saw a tall, young, athletic-looking woman, perhaps just shy of 30, with a piercing gaze, dishwater-blond hair that would hang to her shoulders if it were not so severely pulled back, no lipstick, and a slightly weathered look that included freckles and skin peeling from a sunburn. The corners of her generous lips curled upwards, like a dolphin. He thought she must have a great smile, if she ever let herself go. Her shoulders were hunched up, as if she was constantly ready to defend herself.

Erika saw a 30-something who was strongly built and very sloppily dressed, with messy, dark hair that curled over a broad forehead. A deep tan set off flashing white teeth and sharp incisors that reminded her of a wolf. He looked vaguely roguish, but had a tinge of sadness around the eyes. He had not shaved for days. The stubble hid a dimple in his left cheek, which appeared whenever his mouth curled in a wry smile, which it did often.

She leaned forward, and her stern look put a "V" into her eyebrows. David tried to match her mood, but was distracted by trying to decide what kind of gem her greenish-hazel eyes reminded him of. Her voice jolted him back to reality.

"Look, Mr. Kilmer..." Erika started out.

David held up both hands, and averred, "Please, make it David."

She hesitated. "All right. David." He noticed she did not offer to reciprocate. "I'll put my cards on the table. On the one hand, I'm grateful to you for discovering those fossils and sending them to my associates at the museum."

David nodded assent. "I spent a lot of time there when I was young. I got to know some of the curators, and stayed in touch with them over the years. When our vacuum hose sucked those fossils out of the sand I sent them to Benjamin Wasserman..."

"...who called me," Erika finished for him. "Benny knew this was my area of interest, and that those bones could confirm some discoveries I've made elsewhere in the Caribbean. Like I said, thank you for that. What I'm not so happy about is that the grant I've been chasing for over a year finally came through last week, but with this hook on it, that I've got to give over half of it to you and sail around on your boat like a bloody passenger on some fucking cruise line."

David felt himself reddening. "Listen, I don't like it any better than you do. AJ just laid all this on me this morning. I've got only two months at most to explore for— what I'm looking for— and I have to accommodate you and your assistant on board. I'm just as unhappy playing social director of 'The Love Boat' as you are being a passenger."

Erika glared at him. "If you're really that upset about it, mate, I'll just shit-can the whole thing and fly back to Sydney."

David held both hands up in the air. "Whoa, whoa! Back up. Listen, what I really hate is—"

"Personal hygiene?" she finished the sentence for him.

He bit back a reply, and took a sip of water from a glass instead. He scratched his forehead with a thumb, leaving an oily smear on it.

She glanced up. "Are those eyebrows, or are you trying to grow a mustache up there?" she asked.

David let out a deep breath, and said, "We're both looking in the same area. We're both diving and using a vacuum pump to look for relics. It makes sense that we should help each other. You bring funding and two extra sets of eyes that can help me look for... my stuff. I've been diving and exploring in this area for two years, and know the ocean floor, the currents, the whole lay of the land. I've got all the maps, and made corrections to them. I plotted GPS coordinates, including where we found your fossils. I've got a ship and equipment and a crew and contacts on shore that would take you months—and a lot of money—to gather. We can work together. After all, we are both ... professionals."

Erika let out an audible sigh. "Yeh. Well, OK. Like you say..." she eyed his stained T-shirt and shorts with a sarcastic glance, "We are both ... professionals."

She glanced at her watch, and then at David. "All right, enough chit-chat. When do we professionals start getting to work? My assistant Moshe and I have our equipment here already. We can be ready as soon as the Conference ends tomorrow night."

David answered stiffly, "That would be fine. Be at the Ferry Landing in Anguilla at noon on Friday, and I'll pick you up and bring you to the ship." He took a deep breath. He looked at his hands and noticed how dirty they were, from helping to repair a fuel filter assembly earlier that day. "Sorry about my hands. It's from—"

"—dragging your knuckles on the ground?" she finished sarcastically.

David's nostrils flared. "Where was all this bravado when you were giving your presentation? You looked like you were going to pee your pants."

Her face flushed a bright red and she grasped the edge of the table so hard her knuckles whitened. "I don't have to explain myself to you. What conference have you ever been to? The rag picker's convention?"

David's eyes narrowed. "*You're* talking about fashion? Where did you get that baggy suit, from a 1940's detective movie? And who dressed you—a blind Sunday School teacher?"

She fumed. "A troglodyte like you wouldn't know fashion if it bit him in the ass!"

He shot back, "And you almost fell out of those Minnie Mouse shoes!"

"So says the thing the cat dragged in!"

He took a deep breath. "I apologized. Why are you so angry?"

Her eyes blazed. "Why am I angry? After you show up like that to my presentation and humiliate me in front of—"

"—in front of people you don't give a shit about? Do you realize how ridiculous that sounds?" he shouted.

She was about to reply, but he stood up suddenly as a waiter approached. "Never mind," he told him. "I'm not hungry any more."

David looked down at Erika and spoke slowly and deliberately. "OK, princess, I was looking forward to lunch and talking, but you're not even listening to me. You're talking to some other bunch of guys who pissed you off. I don't know if they're old boy friends or what, but it's too damn crowded here." He threw a 50 euro note on the table. "Here, I'll buy them a drink. They probably need it, the poor bastards. I'll see you Friday." With that, he turned on his heels and walked away quickly.

David muttered, "What's wrong with me?" to himself under his breath as he jogged down the stairs and onto the sidewalk. "Why did I get so upset? She had stage fright, and was defensive about it—no big deal."

He shook his head to clear it. "Oh, well," he said, "the hell with her. I'd make a deal with the devil himself if it'll finance me for another two months. Once I find the gold, and have a hundred million in the bank, nothing else will matter." He mentally reviewed the things he had to do over the next two days— buying fuel and supplies, paying the crew, and getting the MRI equipment repaired and re-calibrated. He thought about the money, and the possibilities that lay ahead.

"I should be celebrating right now," he thought as he jogged down the sidewalk. "Why is my stomach tied into knots?"

On the terrace, Erika rose to say something, but settled back down in her seat. She glanced at the waiter, who was looking at his feet. "Can you tell I work with fossils because I'm not very good with people?" She sighed and tapped her plate with a chewed-down fingernail. "Never mind the food, just bring me a glass of red wine. As quick as you can." As the waiter moved away, she called out to him, "Hell! Bring the whole damn bottle!"

She looked over the balcony as the figure of David as he disappeared down the street. "Well, that went well," she said. She looked down at her shoes. "Christ! They do look like they belong on Minnie Mouse!" She exhaled slowly and shook her head. "Bloody men!" she said.

Chapter 3

Erika arrived by ferry in Anguilla Friday precisely at noon. As she got out of the Customs Area she was met by David, who pulled up in a battered dark red Jeep that had seen better days.

"Hi, Princess!" he called out cheerfully as he took her bags. "I decided to give the chauffeur the day off. I'm afraid you're stuck with me, instead." He tossed her bags into the back of the Jeep, and opened the door for her. "This is your royal coach." He waved his arm around at the bright blue sky. "It's a beautiful day, the sun is shining, and the sky is as clear as the Virgin Mary's conscience."

She looked at his outfit, a clean dark blue polo shirt over a pair of beige cargo pants. "You look almost respectable. And you've even washed—or at least irrigated the top layer of dirt."

David smiled at her as he swung onto his seat. "I'm sorry I was impolite when we first met. Maybe we both just had a rough morning."

She looked him up and down. "You look like you've had a lot of rough mornings."

He grinned. "You just don't stop, do you? All right, if that's how it's going to be. Hold on, princess. Time to get going."

"My assistant Moshe will be coming on the next ferry," she said as she fastened her seat belt. "He'll grab a cab to the docks."

"We'll drive down to the Global Explorer in a short while," he said as he put the car into gear and eased onto the road. "It's a U.S. Navy ship that got retired long ago, and I was able to get a reasonably-priced lease on it. It's nothing fancy, not like the yachts you're probably used to, but it is rock-solid even in high seas. The equipment you sent is on board, including your Zodiac and diving gear. We'll go there as soon as we've made a stop at Government House."

In response to Erika's questioning glance, he said, "We're picking up some paperwork from Reginald Fowler, the Lieutenant Governor of Anguilla. He's sort of in charge here, since the Governor is always hunting grouse or something in England. I've found it's best to let him know everything we're doing, so he can keep Colonel DuBois, the Chief of Police, off our backs. DuBois is a real piece of work. Tries to hassle anything he doesn't own a piece of, and is totally paranoid."

Erika looked puzzled. "Surely the police wouldn't bother you if you're not involved in anything criminal?" She arched her eyebrows.

David shook his head. "Unfortunately, no. Island police are famous for being easygoing, but if there's a bad apple like DuBois, he has a lot of opportunity to grab you and do you in—all it takes is one of the crew getting drunk one night, or sneaking out behind the local saloon to smoke a little ganja. That's why I usually keep them on board, and keep the ship anchored far out in the harbor, away from prying eyes."

They pulled up in front of a large white building with Grecian columns and a marble sign stating "Government House." David looked at Erika. "Since you're so concerned with how people look, I think you're going to love Reginald. He looks like he stepped out of the pages of *GQ*. Every hair in place. Educated at Eton. Just your type." Erika gave him a hard look, but held back her retort.

They walked up the white marble stairs and down an airy hallway with wicker furniture and walls burdened with portraits of stiff-looking government officials. They entered a room occupied by an elderly secretary with pince-nez glasses.

"Good afternoon, Gladys," said David cheerfully. "We have an appointment with the Lieutenant Governor."

The secretary nodded her head in the direction of a door. "Go right in," she said, "He's expecting you."

They entered a much larger, wood paneled office, and David made introductions to the person sitting behind an elaborately carved cherry-wood desk. "Dr. Bettelman, I'd like you to meet the Lt. Governor, the Right Honorable Reginald Fowler."

The person behind the desk quickly got up and came toward them, a bitter smile on his face. "No, I'm afraid only the Governor gets the 'Right Honorable' title. I just get to do all the labor." The bitterness disappeared as he came up to Erika, and was replaced by a display of brilliant white teeth.

"What a delightful surprise. Welcome to Anguilla, Dr. Bettelman!" Fowler beamed at her.

Erika smiled back at him. "My pleasure, Lt. Governor. Please call me Erika." Fowler took her hand and shook it warmly. "And you must call me Reginald, or Reggie for short."

David noted with annoyance that Fowler was impeccable as always, wearing an off-white raw silk Seville Row suit, and without a single hair out of place. "The man has no sweat glands," he thought to himself, but outwardly he said, "Did everything go all right with the paperwork?"

"Of course," Fowler replied while he grasped David's hand and then led him to his desk. "Here's the permit to explore and claim salvage rights within Anguillan territorial waters, signed and sealed."

David turned to Erika. "Up till recently I was far enough away from Anguilla itself that I didn't need a permit to claim salvage rights to the ship I'm looking for. But lately I've been looking in an area near a small island that belongs to Anguilla." He walked over to a wall map, and indicated an island Northwest of the main island. "It's this area just east of Dragon Island, so I thought it better to get a permit."

He added ruefully, "The permit also allows you to explore for fossils that you might find in Anguillan waters. The only difference is that we get to keep all of any animal remains we might find, whereas I have to give half of any gold coin or bullion that I find to the Anguillan government."

Fowler put a placating arm on David's shoulder. "Now, you know that the Government needs to get its cut. Some nations would have demanded *all* of the salvage rights for themselves."

David looked at Fowler. "I know that, Reggie, and I'm not ungrateful. Thank you for your help."

Fowler continued, "Even more important, that island is now called *Paradise* Island, and nothing else!"

He took Erika's elbow and steered her to a map on an adjacent wall. "Here's an overview, with photographs of the new Paradise Island development. It's a luxury resort, with huge pools with waterfalls. It will eventually have night clubs and a casino, as well as several fine restaurants. It has a sheltered lagoon for boating and swimming, and is protected by a shark net. The resort has a modern marina capable of berthing over 200 boats and yachts."

"Over here is a private airport," he said, tapping the West side map with a riding crop. "Here are the tennis courts and riding stables." He looked appraisingly at Erika. "Do you like to ride horseback?"

"Oh, yes, I do," Erika enthused, "I had my own horse in Australia, and used to ride in competitions as a child."

Reginald grasped her forearm. "Why, that's wonderful," he said. "You must come visit so we can ride together! Do let me have your card." He produced his business card with a flourish. "Here's mine."

David turned to look out of the window, his irritation rising as he mouthed an exaggerated imitation of Reginald's British accent, "Oh, you simply must come visit..."

Reginald continued, accepting and briefly glancing at Erika's card as she handed it to him. "The whole project is designed to increase tourism and employment for Anguilla and this part of the

Caribbean. The grand opening ceremonies are in two weeks, and you're invited, of course." He glanced sideways at David. "Both of you."

Erika and David thanked Fowler for the invitation, and then David shook hands, picked up the paperwork and started to leave. Erika remained behind a few moments longer to talk privately with Fowler, and then joined David in the hall.

As they walked down the hallway, Erika turned to David and said, "He seems really nice. Sure got pissed off at you calling it Dragon Island, though."

He gave her a half-smile in return. "It's been called that for centuries. There are a lot of legends about it, including one that says you can hear the dragons howling if you go close enough. It used to be inaccessible—a lagoon with steep cliffs formed from an old volcano. Several divers and spelunkers have disappeared in that area, and most people stay far away from it."

One of her eyebrows shot up. "Spelunkers?"

"Cave explorers. There are a lot of caves on the island, including volcanic lava tubes, like there are throughout the Caribbean."

Just then, one of the doorways in front of them opened and a uniformed figure emerged and stood there imperiously, hands on hips, and spoke with exaggerated pronunciation, "Ah, Mr. Kilmer. I need to talk with you." He drew himself up to his full 5-foot-6, bouncing on the balls of his feet. His dark face was rendered even darker by oversized gold-rimmed aviator's sunglasses.

David came to a stop and scowled at the man. "What do you want, DuBois?"

"That is *Colonel* DuBois to you," the man snarled at David. "And who is this?"

"This is Doctor Bettelman," David replied. "Not that it's any of your business."

"Whatever anyone does on Anguilla is my business," DuBois replied with narrowed eyes. "Whatever threatens this country is my business."

"This is not a country," said David. "It's an island that belongs to England."

"For the time being," replied DuBois. "We will have our independence soon. Then we will be free."

"Free to—" David started to say, and then stopped himself with an effort. "What is it you want?"

"Colonel." DuBois said.

"What is it you want, *Colonel*?"

"Your passport, please," DuBois replied. David searched in his pocket and handed it to him.

"Your visa is about to expire. That is against the law. The minute it expires, I will personally escort you out of here."

"I'll get it taken care of," said David, snatching back his passport.

"And may I see your passport and visa now?" DuBois said, turning his attention to Erika.

"No, you may not," she shot back. "It was looked at when I cleared customs. You have no reason to ask for it again—just to annoy me."

"You think you can talk to me that way because you're white and I'm..." DuBois started.

"Don't pull that shit on me. My great gram was an Aborigine. And whatever pussy complaints you have, your life was paradise compared to what she went through. So I'll tell you again. Leave me the fuck alone!" She glowered at him.

His nostrils flared. "I will not tolerate that kind of disrespect to this uniform," he said.

"I don't give a shit about the uniform," she said. "It's you I disrespect."

His eyes turned wild. "I'll have you..."

"You'll have me what? You're going to throw a visiting scientist in jail? That will be the end of your tourist business on this island, and my attorney will have your arse for lunch."

"Anything else really important demanding your personal attention besides annoying tourists?" David asked.

"No, you are free to go. Just watch your step," DuBois said, holding himself back with an effort. He turned and stalked back into his office.

"What's his problem?" Erika asked as they continued down the hall and emerged out the front doorway into bright sunlight.

"Just throwing his weight around," David answered. He sighed. "You may have just set back our relationship with the Colonel even more." He looked behind him. "Now every crew member will have to watch his step, whether having a drink at a bar, or while spitting on the sidewalk."

She looked contrite. "I'm sorry. I just hate that kind of macho arsehole. Did I really mess it up for you?"

"What the hell. I guess it's OK," he answered. "In a way I'm glad to see you're a bitch with other people. I thought it was just me."

She took up the challenge as they walked toward the car. "I haven't been that bad to you, now that you've actually bathed." She sniffed the air.

"I'm so glad I'm living up to your standards." He waved his passport in the air. "I'll have to remember to get my visa extended by Fowler tomorrow."

Erika turned her head. "So Reggie is someone you really trust?" she asked.

"Trust?" David asked scornfully. "No, that would be too strong a word. I don't really trust anyone, with very, very few exceptions."

Erika turned to him as she got into the Jeep. "Blimey, mate. What was her name?"

David reddened slightly, but kept his eyes on the road while he drove. "It was both a *her and* a *him. She* was my wife, Gloria—now my ex-wife—and *he* was my business partner, Mel. I had one of those country-western-song experiences one week. You know, where your world comes crashing around your ears all at once. I came home early from a trip to find them going at it big-time in the kitchen. It was pretty spectacular. She was lying on top of the butcher block counter."

Erika tried hard to keep from laughing. "The butcher block?"

"Yeah. And this from Miss Hygiene-everything-spotless. I found out she and Mel had been an item before the two of us got married, and they continued on afterwards. Darryl was also in charge of the books, and had sucked all the money out of the firm. I had to declare bankruptcy to get out from under it all."

"My God," said Erika. "What did you do then?"

David replied sourly, "Well, after I filed divorce papers I headed for the nearest bar, and tried to drink the West side of New York dry. Then one day my Nana made me an offer. She had lost something really valuable in Rome during World War 2, stolen by the Gestapo. She offered to finance a search for it. I checked German records, and discovered it had been put onto a submarine that was lost while carrying that item and a bunch of other valuables to the island of Anguilla. I got a boat and a crew together, and started exploring down here. Eventually AJ came in as a second investor."

Erika looked at him, puzzled. "A German U-Boat carrying treasure?"

David nodded. "It wasn't that unusual. German U-Boats met with Japanese submarines in this area and exchanged cargo. The Germans provided technology such as radar sets, and the Japanese paid for that with strategic materials such as tungsten, or sometimes hard cash or gold. One Japanese submarine, the I-52, met up with a German U-Boat with 2.2 tons of gold as payment on board."

"Wow. So you're looking for a U-Boat?" Erika asked.

"Yup," was his rejoinder, "I think we'll find it soon. In the past, we've found only little submarine parts here and there, but in the last two months we've gotten major sections of what I believe was this particular U-boat's conning tower, and the edge of a number. I believe it may be the number of the boat we're looking for, the U-307."

"Is your Nana your only family?" Erika asked as they started to pull up to the wharf.

David replied, "She's not really my grandmother, she's my great-aunt. But yes, she's the only family I've got. Along with Bucky."

"Bucky?"

"You'll meet him."

When they walked onto the Global Explorer, David dropped Erika's bags on deck and gave her a quick tour of the ship, showing her the bridge, the Electronics Room with its computers and displays, the Conference Room, a small gym with exercise equipment, the dining area and kitchen, and the SCUBA equipment room and air pumps.

He picked her bags up again and carried them down a hallway. He opened a door at the end of it. "Here you are," he said, waving his right arm around the cabin. "The best room on the ship. Hope you're comfy."

"Yeh, it's OK," she noted. "A bit Spartan, but I've had worse."

"Spartan, eh?" he asked. "It used to be a military ship. I'm afraid it only has a normal toilet, not one of those things that shoots warm water up your butt!"

She laughed. "My butt will survive nicely, thank you."

"It gets cold at night," he noted. Let me know if you need extra blankets."

"I guess I could always call Reggie Fowler up," she said coyly. "He looks like he could keep a girl warm at night."

David tried not to show his annoyance. "Good luck with that. Right now I have to do a quick final check, after which we'll get underway. Let's meet in the Conference Room at 8:00 tomorrow morning."

Erika started unpacking. Within ten minutes she heard the thrumming of diesel engines. She went outside and stood at the rail, listening to the blub-blub-blub of the ship's exhaust as

Anguilla grew smaller in the distance. She moved a deck chair into a shady spot, and sat down to read a book on reptile adaptations.

As she was finishing the book, she looked up suddenly. It was late in the afternoon, and the sun had started to shine in her eyes. She saw an island with jagged cliffs in the distance, and assumed it was Dragon Island, now trying to change its identity to Paradise. They were passing a dive boat with a bright red flag with a diagonal white stripe, displayed to show that divers were about to go down. She saw a group on deck getting ready to dive, and waved at them. Several waved back cheerfully.

Chapter 4

On board the boat, the dive master gave his group one last admonition before going into the water. "You're about to dive in an area that's usually off limits," he said. "There are strong and dangerous currents around here. A number of divers have disappeared. Today seems to be OK—our readings show that everything's calm below. But stay alert, and close to each other." He added, "The good news is, the reefs around here are pristine and full of life. The wall we'll be diving on is incredible."

One by one, the divers grabbed their face masks with one hand and jumped into the water with scissors kicks. They gathered as a group about 15 feet down, glancing anxiously at the dive master. He looked at each of them, and nodded when he got "thumbs-up" signs from everyone. As the divers followed him deeper, they looked in awe at the incredible spectacle. The wall of coral extended from 40 feet below the surface straight down for over a thousand feet, seemingly into infinity.

The small group of SCUBA divers kept tightly together. They followed the dive master's brightly colored wet suit, his yellow and red and black stripes challenging the bright neon colors of the myriad fish darting in and out of the crevices in the coral wall.

One diver, however, a young woman with curly flame-red hair and a bright yellow bikini visible under her diving gear, separated from the group, following a large gray and silver grouper that lazily wended down the wall. Fascinated by the 500-pound fish, the diver slowly propelled herself along behind it, neglecting both her group and the readings on her depth gauge. She strayed ever deeper along the wall, which appeared so uniform that it blurred all clues as to depth or position.

She had heard that groupers of the type she was following started life out as females and then became males; she smiled as she contemplated what such a life would be like. She was further distracted by a group of Swiss Guard Basslet fish darting around the coral next to her. Their alternating red and gold stripes reminded her of the uniforms of the Swiss Guards during a trip to the Vatican. A six-inch Bluehead drifted into her view, showing off an impossible color combination of a neon-blue head preceding three black and white stripes, a lime-green body, and an aquamarine-colored tail.

Suddenly, the young woman stopped swimming, momentarily confused. She felt a sudden surge of foreboding danger. She glanced at her instruments, and shook her head in disbelief. Both her compass and her depth gauge were gyrating wildly. The values of the digital displays were jumping up and down the scale. Only her air pressure gauge, with its mechanical readout, seemed to make any sense. She turned around to look for her group, and saw them as vague blobs of dark blue hundreds of feet behind her, and dozens of feet closer to the surface. Her heart was racing, and her short, repetitive quick breathing echoed in her ears.

She sensed something below her, and snapped her head down quickly, sending a cloud of bubbles out to rise above her. She stared in horror as the disembodied head of the grouper floated in front of her, streaming blood and tendrils of pink tissue behind it like a skirt. Her eyes flew wide open as she tried to focus on the reef below the grouper—it seemed to be moving toward her!

She blinked her eyes twice in consternation, but the picture remained the same. A wide section of the reef was undulating and approaching her, its colors and shapes shifting like a 3D psychedelic display. She screamed loudly into her mask, and in total panic whirled around and fled back in the direction of the group, paddling her flippers as fast as she could, and wildly flailing her arms to try to pull the water past her. Her erratic motion caused her to crash into the reef at full speed, and her tank emitted a loud and resonating clang. Stunned, she looked behind her once more, moving her head in little jerks to and fro, like a frightened bird, her heart like a trip hammer in her chest. The oppressive sense of something closing in on her was suddenly gone, as was whatever had caused the reef to sinuously change shape like green-blue taffeta candy.

She glanced at her gauges, which were calmly displaying, "101 feet" and "NE 27 degrees." She glanced back toward the group and saw her dive master coming toward her at full speed, a worried look on his face. He stopped in front of her and glared at her sternly, pointing at his depth gauge and then motioning in circles with his finger to show his displeasure at her for having ventured so deep and so far away. She meekly followed him back to the group, anxiously glancing over her shoulder every few yards.

Far below her, a monster from the dawn of history swallowed several hundred pounds of grouper as if it were a snack. It had returned from an unsuccessful hunt for giant squid thousands of feet down in the black depths of the offshore drop-off, and was still ravenously hungry. It turned slowly, changing the colors of its body as it got deeper along the wall, until it finally came to a huge circular opening, almost 600 feet deep. With a swish of its gigantic tail it propelled itself away from the coral wall, and used its back flippers to turn its body in place. It glanced up the coral-covered, almost-vertical hillside in front of it, moving its head slowly left and right. Sensing nothing directly above, it pointed its head into the darkness of the opening. Its massive body, the length of two school buses, seemed to take forever before the last of it disappeared into the cavern.

Chapter 5

As Erika walked into the ship's Conference Room with Moshe at 8 a.m. the next morning, she saw David with several other men. One wall was lined with large LCD screens showing 3D pictures of the ocean floor, with markers and overlays. Rows of collapsible chairs faced the monitors. David greeted her with a cheery, "Good morning, princess," and then made the introductions.

"Erika, Moshe, let me introduce you. This is Shawn, the computer alpha geek and electronics technician. He's also the radio and radar operator. He's responsible for these displays."

"Bob and his assistant Ben are in charge of the diesel engines, and steer the ship when I'm tied up. Bob is also an expert welder, in case we find the sub in large pieces and have to cut it up. Larry is in charge of the diving equipment, and is also an experienced diving instructor. Dr. Werner Zinni, here, is our ship's physician, assisted by his son Mark. Everyone on board is an experienced diver, like on Cousteau's ship, the *Calypso*, and everybody has learned to work the suction pump and screens. We take turns being the cook when we're not diving. Finally, Nick Collins back there keeps us shipshape by cleaning and painting and whatever else needs doing."

The men nodded at Erika and Moshe, who nodded back and then took seats. David pointed one hand at a screen, and the display changed from showing the ocean bottom to presenting a 3D schematic of a large German submarine, titled "U-Boot, Typ IXD."

She noticed that he wore gloves with small electronics packs on the back. The thumbs and first two fingers of each glove had different colors of LCD lights. As he pulled his hands apart, the view zoomed closer. It reminded her of the gesture control interface in the sci-fi movie, *Minority Report*.

David moved one hand so that the screen changed to a top view, showing each of the compartments of the sub. "This is what we're looking for, a large German U-Boat they called a *Milch Kuh*, or milk cow, since it was used more for transporting goods than for hunting allied ships. It was larger than a regular U-Boat, with a longer cruising range, almost 24,000 miles. It had storage tanks for supplies and extra fuel, which it would hand off to other U-Boats in the area. According to German records, our boat, the U-307, left its dock at Saint-Nazaire in France in May of 1942, and arrived in this area by June."

He pointed to an icon on a second display, which showed a map of the Atlantic, with a line drawn from the French coast to a point in the Caribbean just North of Anguilla.

"We know that it docked with a Japanese submarine, and then proceeded to Anguilla to deliver money and other goods to pay the Axis spy network in the area. From the 4th of June through the 6th, the sub underwent a severe tropical storm. When the storm died down, it surfaced and gave its location, at about here." A point on the electronic display map glowed neon green.

David moved his hands apart, and the display zoomed in on the map. "During the night of the 6th, the U-307 ran into trouble. It sent a short signal giving its location and indicating that it was under attack. It was never heard from again."

He paused. "The strange thing is, there were no allied planes or warships in this area at the time. We can conclude that the U-307's crew either made a mistake, or that it became another victim of the curse of the Bermuda Triangle."

The men grinned nervously at one another. They had all heard of the curse, which had sent hundreds of ships and planes to the bottom in this part of the Caribbean, often with no plausible explanation.

David continued. "If we plot a straight line between the last two transmissions of the U-307, and continue on that line for another 5 to 20 miles–remember, the boat was running submerged at that point, so it was only doing 5 or 6 knots–and assume she sank at that point, we have the general area we've been searching in." The display showed a dotted line between two points, and then a green grid with map coordinates appeared over the area.

He twisted one wrist, and white overlays of X's and O's appeared, as well as one colored icon. He pointed at the X's and O's.

"This is where we've found traces of metal and other materials that we believe came from the U-307. Note they form a more or less straight line–allowing for drift from currents and storms–that runs about five kilometers from East to West. We believe the U-Boat is located somewhere on the Eastern side of this line, which is where we are now." David pointed at that area of the map, and the icon of the ship glowed bright green.

He swung to the colored icon at the left side of the line. "This picture of Barney the Purple Dinosaur indicates where we found your fossils, Erika and Moshe. Sorry we didn't have a better graphic available."

The men chuckled as Erika interjected. "Actually, a Mosasaur is not a dinosaur. It's a different kind of reptile, which lived at the same time as the dinosaurs, and was bigger than many of them. But I have a question. Why only to the East?"

David, puzzled, was caught off guard. "Huh?"

Erika continued. "You said you're only looking at the Eastern end of your line. Why not the Western end?"

David explained patiently. "We've looked over the Western end. It's a series of reefs and steep underwater hills, with very little sand on the bottom. If there was a boat there, it would be out in the open, and we'd already have noticed it. Besides, the prevailing current runs strongly from West to East, so that's where the boat— or the wreckage from it—ought to be."

Erika persisted. "But, still..."

David sighed dramatically, and then grew impatient. "Listen. Your purple dinosaur is at that end, so you'll be exploring there with one of the Zodiacs and the small vacuum pump when you need it. If you see anything that looks like a submarine part, please let us know."

Erika's face took on a hard set as she seethed inwardly at being patronized. David did not notice the mental daggers she sent in his direction, and motioned at a third display, which showed colored lines overlaid on a 3D picture of the ocean floor. "Here are today's dive plans for each team and each shift."

He concluded with, "OK, everybody. We should be starting up the main vacuum pump within an hour or so. Let's suit up and find us a U-Boat!"

He came up to Erika and Moshe as the others left the room. "We'll need you to file a dive plan each day from now on. Where do you plan to dive today?" He leaned to his left and tapped a button on a printer. A minute later he handed her a printout of the map of the ocean floor, along with an ink marker pen.

She drew a dashed line along the Eastern part of the map. "I want to get an initial overview of the area you found the fossils in. I'll go along here, starting..." she glanced at her watch, "at around 9:00." She drew another dotted line that ran in parallel, about 200 yards North of the first. "And Moshe can check out this area here."

David shook his head. "No good. First, I can only spare one person to go with you today, Larry. You'll have to stay closer together so he can watch both of you, no more than 50 meters apart. And he won't be available until 10 at the earliest."

She shot him a look of contempt. "We don't need any bloody babysitter. And I'll dive when I like."

David's eyes narrowed. "Not from my boat, you won't. On land you can do anything you want. But here you follow the rules, to the letter. And the rule is no one dives without someone watching over them. There are no other options."

The color rose in her cheeks. "And if I refuse?"

He met her gaze. "Then I'll call a boat to come pick you up and you can leave."

She rose and thrust her face within inches of his. "Then I'll take my part of the money and do my own expedition."

He answered without flinching. "Too late. It's already in the bank and obligated."

She staggered backwards. "What? That can't be!"

He answered levelly. "But it is. Check the contract you signed. Failure to follow the ship's safety rules forfeits all claims on your part of the funding. I can assure you that I, er, the person who wrote it made it air tight."

Her hands balled into fists as she hissed at him. "You ignorant..." She gasped for air. "...arrogant bastard!"

He looked at her with a thin smile. "That's *Captain* bastard to you, princess."

She spat back at him, "That's *Doctor* princess to you. I mean..." She panted, confused, and so angry she could barely speak.

David ignored her, and looked at Moshe. "Let me guess. Technion?"

Moshe nodded with a smile. "Yes. Then the Army."

"Israeli Army, electronics?"

Moshe nodded again. "After that, an uncle invited me to work for him in the film industry, and I learned special effects and 3D virtual worlds."

David gave him a thumbs-up. "Nice. I've worked with the IAF." He jerked a thumb at Erika. "Do you think she could fight in the Israeli Army?"

Moshe nodded emphatically. "Oh, yes. She'd be fighting all the time. The question is, would she be fighting the enemy?"

"Moshe!" She looked at him in shock.

David laughed. He took the marker pen and drew two dashed lines much closer together. "You can start this at 10 if you want. Good luck." He nodded at them and left.

She stared at Moshe, daggers in her eyes. "How could you?"

Moshe shrugged. "It's true. You would explode the first time a man gave you orders."

Larry came over to the two of them. "Excuse me, Dr. Bettelman. The Captain isn't just trying to be a hard-ass. This is a dangerous area. It's got riptides, sharks, and...God only knows what else. We've heard of divers disappearing suddenly. Most of the regular dive boats avoid it. We're also afraid other groups may get wind of this and move in on us. If that occurs, there's no telling what might happen. So far no one's gotten hurt on this expedition. He wants to keep it that way."

She breathed heavily a few times, and then glared at Larry. "Fine! You're the babysitter. We start at 10?"

"Roger, that," he replied.

Chapter 6

Erika and Moshe transferred their gear to their Zodiac. Larry fired up the outboard motor, and they sat watching the bustle of activity on the ship as they pulled away from it. After about 20 minutes, Larry looked at his GPS locator and nodded at them. "We're at the coordinates. Let's drop anchor and I'll show you where we found your fossils. Please follow your dive plan and I'll stay in back of you."

Erika, Moshe and Larry leaned backward from the side of the inflatable boat and splashed into the clear green-blue water. Larry led the way to a distinctive small seamount that had outcroppings of coral circling it. He spoke into the microphone in his full-face mask. "This is where we found them. We were sucking sand along this shallow depression, and came up with those bones—and a few smaller pieces we didn't bother to keep—in the filters from the vacuum pumps. You may want to just look around the area for a day or so, and then use the suction pump to go through anything that looks interesting."

Erika answered, "Good idea. OK, Moshe, you ready?" Moshe gave the thumbs-up sign, and soon he and Erika were scanning the bottom, stopping to fan away the sand from anything that looked unusual.

After swimming for a few hundred yards, Erika looked around and checked her instruments. It was about 10:30 a.m., and she was in very clear water at 82 feet. She noticed with satisfaction that Moshe was working the controls on his dive computer. Since he was a whiz at math, and always accompanied her on dives, she generally let him take care of the diving tables, figuring out the safe working time on the bottom each day.

She was glad of his company, and even that of (she had to admit to herself) Larry. She looked back to see him following them, his head swiveling from side to side as he carefully scanned the area. Most of her digs had been with larger teams on dry land, and she still felt a little lonely and overawed when she started an exploration underwater. There was so much ocean to cover, and the sea had many dangers—rogue currents, moray eels, sharks—that she did not have to worry about on land. She knew that once she really got into it, these concerns would go away, and the feeling of being in an alien landscape would abate.

Moshe's voice crackled in her earphone. "Looks like we're on a plateau. There's been considerable erosion, so we've got a decent chance of finding something uncovered or at shallow depth. If there's anything here."

Erika noticed that Moshe had started sketching on his underwater iPad, filling in terrain details. He kept checking compass headings and GPS coordinates as he did so. He also took panoramic photos with a small camera attached to the iPad, and attached these electronically to the digital map. They had overlaid rough squares on the map so they could cover the ground with consistency.

They swam about 100 feet apart, fins moving in unison, heads swiveling left and right, saying little, occasionally using a fan or one of the other tools they had brought with them in their belt packs to clear an area of sand or dead coral.

"Let's just swim today," Erika said. "Tomorrow we'll use the aquasleds, so we can cover more ground." She was about to add more when she noticed an odd piece of what appeared to be coral sticking out of the sand. It resembled a small stalagmite. She tugged at it absently, and it came free in her hand. She looked at the bottom of the chunk, and her heart started beating faster. She showed it to Moshe.

"What does this look like to you?" she asked him, though she knew what the answer would be.

"The vertebra of a large reptile," he replied. "I would guess the tail section of a...something." He turned the item over in his hands. "This is definitely fossilized bone tissue," he said, excitement rising in his voice. "Could it have belonged to a Tylosaur?"

"It's too eroded to really tell," Erika replied. "Let's look around for the rest of him." They scanned the area for another half hour, till the air in their double tanks started running low. They found a half dozen more parts of what they hoped was the tail section of a Mosasaur, an animal that was perhaps 20 feet long. "Pity none of these are connected to a whole skeleton, but at least it's a good start," she commented.

Moshe carefully photographed each fossil and marked its location on his digital map before they picked it up and placed it into their sacks.

Erika and Moshe surfaced next to the Zodiac after carefully stopping and resting at the prescribed depths, and then headed back on the ship to rest and regroup. They were both as excited as school children by this time, and Larry smiled tolerantly as they gave him a quick layman's synopsis of what they had found, before lapsing back into the jargon of their profession.

Chapter 7

Erika and Moshe continued diving and exploring for the next three days, recording the location of anything they found. The relatively shallow water allowed them the luxury of long bottom times. They ate with the crew at the end of each day, and fell into an easy camaraderie, although Erika was careful to avoid speaking with David. She became increasingly irritated that he took this in stride. To her annoyance, he would hold long conversations about 3D animation with Moshe, and often sat next to her, acting as if she didn't exist.

On the second evening, as David was expounding on his view of how computer animation could best be used to illustrate concepts, she could take it no longer, and broke her vow of silence. "How do you get to have an opinion on this?" she asked. "Do you have a degree in computer science?"

David shook his head. "No, not really."

She continued to vent. "Did you even graduate high school?"

He seemed to think about it a moment. "No. Actually, I didn't."

Her look of triumph fell flat as he continued his conversation with Moshe as if she hadn't spoken. "I think that a blended mix of 3D animation and models works really well, like they did in *Jurassic Park*."

On the last dive of the fourth day, Moshe noticed an oddly shaped piece of coral at the bottom of a shallow ravine. He cleared the area around it, and noticed it was tubular in shape and quite large, perhaps a foot in diameter by three feet long. Judicious use of his pick and hammer to remove chunks of coral revealed that it was a long metal tube, smooth along the sides and torn and ragged on both ends. It took both of them to drag the item up to the surface and manhandle it onto the Zodiac.

Larry's eyes flew open the moment he saw what they had found. He tapped it to make sure it was metal, and then immediately reached for the digital radio set, but Erika laid a restraining hand on his arm.

"No," she told him. "Don't tell anyone yet."

Larry blurted out, "But—this is fantastic—that looks just like a section of periscope! This is the biggest piece of metal we've found to date! It's..." He was so excited that his voice failed him.

Erika interrupted him by gently prying the radio set out of his fingers and switching it off. "I thought that's what it looked like," she said. "Well, I'd like to break the news to Mr. Smart-Ass Kilmer myself. Perhaps he'll think twice next time before he gives me his condescending bullshit."

She puffed out her chest and made an exaggerated imitation of David. "No, Erika," she intoned pompously, "you just don't understand. The currents here are West to East. There couldn't be *anything* at *this* end of the area." She turned to Larry, and smiled sweetly. "You've got to promise you won't tell him before I do."

Larry sighed. "O.K. But I don't really want to get into the middle of this."

Erika's super-sweet smile never wavered. "Hey," she said. "You've been on this hunt on and off for over two years. An hour more or less isn't going to matter. Besides, we found this, not any of you."

Larry capitulated. "All right. I'll be sure to tell him that when he rips my head off." He paused a minute. "He's really a nice guy, you know, but he's been under a lot of pressure. He knows he's got people counting on him, and time is running out. If he doesn't find the sub in the next two months, before the hurricane season starts, it'll be all over for him, and for the rest of us. We'll have thrown over two years of our lives and a lot of investment money down the drain."

"Don't worry," Erika reassured him. "I won't be too hard on him."

When they arrived back at the main boat, the others had also shut down for the day, and were just finishing cleaning off their underwater equipment and putting it away. Erika walked up to David as her two companions tied the smaller boat alongside and brought a large package covered with a tarp on board. "Well, hello, Captain Kilmer," she said sweetly. "And how did your exploration go today?"

David looked both exhausted and disappointed. "Nothing much. Actually, exactly nothing. What looked on the magnetometer like hunks of man-made metal just turned out to be lumps of raw iron ore. We did a lot of searching and digging for nothing. How did you do?"

"Oh, not bad," Erika replied brightly. "We have to clean them up, but it looks like six fossil samples, including two entire vertebrae. They could be part of a Mosasaur, and if they are, it might be a brand new species."

David brightened immediately, and grabbed her hand and shook it with both of his. His excitement was palpable. "All right!" he shouted. "I'm so glad to hear that. This is wonderful! Could I see them?" He grinned at her wholeheartedly. "Will you still talk to us when you become world famous?"

His genuine excitement took some of the wind out of her sails. "It's hard to feel sweet revenge when he's being so bloody nice," she thought to herself. However, she revealed none of this outwardly as she prompted him with, "Follow me!" and led him to the tarpaulin. When she pulled the tarp back, it revealed several small bags of carefully packed fossils, as well as the large metal tube they had found.

David sank to one knee, and the blood drained from his face. He reached out a hand to carefully caress the pitted metal surface, which still had traces of blue-gray paint on it. "Where did you find it?" he asked softly. "Did you mark the place where you discovered this?"

"No, we just picked the frigging thing up willy-nilly, like we do everything else," Erika replied loudly and sarcastically. "You know what a slap-dash lot we are. We can barely tell East apart from West!"

David turned slowly to her, and the contrite look on his face almost made her regret her sarcasm. "What?" he asked slowly. "Oh. I'm sorry. I didn't mean to..." His voice trailed off as he looked at Larry. "Is this what I think it is?"

Larry nodded. "It's got a lot of crud inside that we need to remove, but I'd bet my left nut that I saw optics in there."

David seemed to recover his energy in a single bound. He sprang to his feet, turned to Erika and gave her a hug that lifted her off her feet. "You're wonderful!" he shouted. He set her down and impulsively kissed her full on the mouth. He then grabbed Moshe's hand and pumped it up and down. "And you, too! Thank you both."

He turned to the men standing behind him. "Well, what are you waiting for? Let's get this thing into the equipment room and take it apart!"

Chapter 8

Later that night, Erika walked to her room, and saw a note taped to her cabin door. She opened it to read, "Please join us on deck at the stern of the ship."

She folded the note and walked to the back, to see David sitting on a chair, tilted back with his feet up on the railing. He was smoking a cigar. He jumped up as she approached, and looked at her anxiously.

"Yes?" she asked warily. "What do you want?"

"First, please sit down," he said as he pulled a deck chair with cushions out for her. He looked around for a place to get rid of the cigar, when she stopped him.

"Can I see it?" she asked. He handed it to her and she looked at it. "I'm impressed," she said. "Romeo y Julieta. And Cuban. I expected El Ropo, made from horse manure. Do you have another?"

He looked at her. "You smoke cigars?" he asked.

"Yeh," she answered. "It shocks my conservative colleagues to the very core of their beings. I first saw women smoking cigars at Tivoli Gardens in Copenhagen, and started getting into it as a way to relax and take in the scenery."

David produced another cigar from a wooden box and handed it to her, along with a Colibri butane lighter. "Before you light up, I have something for you," he said. He bent down to a silver bucket and emerged with a chilled bottle of Veuve Cliquot Grande Dame champagne in one hand and two glasses in the other.

He set them down on a small table. He bent down again and emerged with a large form that he held gently with both arms. She looked closer. It was a large, smoky-gray cat, with an extra-long tail. It had a hand-made white flag stuck in its collar, made from a long swizzle stick and a paper napkin.

She smiled in spite of herself. "And who is this?" she asked.

He looked down at the form in his arms with obvious adoration. He scratched its head, which caused the cat to purr loudly. "This is Bucky, my family. He's named after Buckminster Fuller, one of my heroes. Bucky, meet Erika."

She was enchanted. The cat had an expressive face, with cream and beige markings accenting huge gold-green eyes, which had black trails beneath them, reminding her of a cheetah. The subtle tiger stripes around his cheeks matched those on his body and tail.

She looked at David in surprise as he held Bucky up to her, waving the flag. "Bucky and I are offering a white flag of peace," David said. "Or, if you like, a time out. Do you accept?"

Erika lost an inner struggle to remain stern, and broke out in a wide grin. She stroked the cat's silky head, and took the homemade flag from its collar, considering it. "What's a 'time out'?" she asked.

David smiled. "It's a term from sports. It's when the normal rules don't apply, when you don't have to be antagonists, when you can just safely say or do what you feel. It's a temporary truce."

"Well, I guess," she finally said. "If it's Bucky that's asking me, and if it also includes champagne worth 100 bucks a bottle, I'll go for a 'time out'."

He set the cat down gently on a deck chair, handed her a glass, popped the cork and filled her glass quickly while holding it at a slant. He then filled his own. As he clinked glasses with her, Erika asked him, "How long has Bucky been with you?"

They both sat down, and the cat came to lie on his lap. "He's been with me the whole two years we've been exploring. Sometimes, after weeks of finding nothing, he was the only thing that kept me sane." He watched fondly as the gray cat sneezed, and then wiped its wet, cold nose off thoroughly on his shirt, after which it stuck its head in the hollow below David's shoulder.

He said softly, "That's his safe place. It's a sign that—"

She finished the sentence for him, "—that he totally trusts you. I know. I had a cat named Sweet Pea when I grew up, a Calico. She was nowhere near as big as Bucky, or as, er, attached." She chuckled as the big cat let out a series of guttural growls, moving its head around in small circles in utter joy and contentment as David scratched its tummy. "Hey!" Erika said. "Maybe I'd better leave you two alone."

David laughed. "No, no, we're just friends." He watched as she leaned over and let Bucky sniff her fingers. Apparently having passed muster, she was allowed to scratch his cheeks and behind his ears. When she stopped for a moment, he got up from David's lap, walked onto hers, and plopped himself down. David tried looking stern. "Damn. Bucky likes you. That means I have to be nice to you."

"Don't bloody well force yourself," she said sarcastically.

David responded cheerfully. "No, no. I've found Bucky is a far better judge of character than I am. If he says you're good, you're good."

As he refilled their glasses, she asked, "I take it your examination went well?"

David nodded. "We discovered optics inside, stamped Zeiss Ikon, 1940. I emailed the description and part numbers to a friend of mine who's an expert. They match what would have been used in a periscope of this type of boat, manufactured in 1941."

He sipped his champagne appreciatively, and looked through the glass to study the silvery trail the full moon left on the calm ocean surface. "It doesn't mean it has to be U-307, but the chances are good. There were not that many 'milk cows' support U-Boats of that type in the world at that time, and U-307 appears to be the only one ever lost in this area of the Atlantic."

Erika drained her glass. She looked at him quizzically. "So, what's next?"

David turned serious. "What I really want to do is dive tomorrow," he said. "I hate to lose diving time. But the weather forecast is for heavy rain, and ocean turbulence. We won't be able to see anything. Since it's Friday, we might as well take the weekend off. I need to pick up more supplies, anyway."

He took out a map and pointed to it. "We plotted the location where you found the periscope on the map, and it's at the extreme Western end of the trail of debris we've found so far. I still don't understand it. The sub should either have ripped itself open on coral or burst on the bottom. In either case, it would have drifted with the currents to the East in the last 70-some-odd years."

She thought a moment and said, "Well…"

He leaned over and looked into her eyes. "Well, what?" he said. "I'd like to hear your thoughts on this."

Erika played coy. "Now, far be it from me to enlighten you, when you've done all your research and analysis. And after all, I am only a woman…"

"No, no," he said, desperately heading her off from this course of conversation. "That guy that was unwilling to listen was a long time ago—many, ah, hours ago. I've already apologized for that guy. This is the new David in front of you, the one you converted, the one who's willing to pay attention."

"Well," she said, taking a deep breath. "Let's see. I need a visual to explain this."

"We can use the 3D computerized display with the gesture recognition gloves," David offered.

She shook her head. "Too bloody complicated. I need something physical, like sand. Do you have any sand around here?"

Moments later, she knelt down next to Bucky's kitty litter pan.

Its owner was clearly puzzled by all this attention. "Meek, urk?" he commented.

Erika used the scoop lying next to the pan to rearrange the sand. She looked up at David. "It always pays as a scientist to look at your basic assumptions. You know, when you take the word 'assume' apart, it's really three words, as in, 'This can make an ASS out of U and ME.' Do you know there is almost no one who won a Nobel Prize for science after their 30's? Even Einstein, though he got his award late in life, got it for work he did in his 20's."

David looked at her curiously. "Why do you suppose that is?"

She looked out the window at the ocean, and said quietly, "I think it's because as people get older, they no longer question their basic assumptions."

David looked puzzled. "And what basic assumptions have I made?"

Erika cocked her head to one side, played with her hair with one hand, and looked at him, challenging. "Why don't *you* tell *me*?"

David thought a minute, flustered. "Well, I've assumed we'll find the sub underwater, of course. It's unlikely that it learned how to fly. I assumed we'd find it in this area. I've assumed it's in many pieces by now, and that those pieces have all drifted from the original point of impact. And I assume no one else has found it, because it's covered with sand."

"Let me ask you something else," said Erika, as she continued molding the cat sand into a miniature replica of the ocean floor below them. "Here on the right side we have a flat ocean floor with an increasingly sheer drop-off. Here's where you found your little bits and pieces." To emphasize the point, she picked up a few bits of Bucky droppings with the scoop and dropped them onto the right side. "And what does the terrain look like here on the left, to the West?"

"Well, that's obvious," he replied. "It's very hilly, even mountainous. There are sea mounts and walls of coral and hills of volcanic origin, including..." he pointed out of the cabin's window to the distant horizon, where a large island and a string of small islets could be seen in the moonlight, "...that chain of islands, which includes Dragon, excuse me, I mean Paradise Island." His eyes suddenly flew open. "You mean to say that some part of the sub might be lodged in the side of a hill, instead of at the bottom?"

"I'm not implying anything," she replied smugly. "I'm just saying that maybe you need to look at places other than what's directly below you. That's something I've learned as a paleontologist. Sometimes I scrutinized the ground at my feet for days, and then I look up and see what I'm looking for embedded in a ridge way above my head."

To emphasize the point, she dug the scoop into the hill she had made in the cat sand, emerging with a generously long sample of Bucky's droppings. "There!" she said, triumphantly waving the scoop with the dark, torpedo-shaped object on it. "Do you see?"

"Let me follow this logic train," David said sarcastically. "You're saying that because you found some cat poop in a hill of kitty litter that I should start looking..."

He stopped himself, and gazed at her radiant face as she beamed proudly at her prize. Her porpoise-mouth smile lit up the entire room. He felt a sudden sharp pressure in his chest as he looked at her, as excited as a 5-year old, and the bitter reply died in his throat.

He resumed, "Er, what I meant to say was, that's a fantastic idea. I'm willing to explore there as soon as we get back on Monday. We'll take the sleds, so we can go over the whole area in a couple of days."

"But," he added. "On one condition. You let me take you to dinner tomorrow night. In gratitude for finding the periscope."

Erika looked at him. "I don't believe in dating anyone I work with."

"It won't be a date," David said. "I'll ask AJ and Leah to join us. It'll be purely professional."

"OK, if you put it that way." Erika looked down at the plastic scoop, and dropped her proud discovery into the nearby trash bag. She sipped her champagne as they walked back to the stern of the ship.

David looked at Erika as she re-lit her cigar while leaning against the railing. The sight of her standing in the moonlight, the night breeze playing softly with her hair, increased the tightness in his chest. He felt a sudden tug on his pants leg, and looked down to see Bucky standing on his hind legs and pawing at him. David smiled and picked him up in one swing. Bucky immediately plopped onto his left arm, draping himself over it like a leopard on a tree branch. David was glad of the distraction.

"Well," he said, his throat suddenly dry. "I guess it's time to get some sleep. Thanks again for the periscope, and for all of the insights."

He stroked the cat gently, and unconsciously pulled gently at its tail. Bucky, who was happy to be in the arms of his master, was more than willing to put up with such indignities. David repeated, "Yeah, time to hit the rack. Tomorrow will start early. Good night."

"Good night," replied Erika. "I'm going to finish my cigar and then turn in."

David started to walk away and then turned back to her. "You know, I just thought of something. This animal of yours, this Mosasaur. It kind of looks like a giant eel, or a sea serpent, right?"

Erika half-smiled. "I guess you could say that. It's streamlined like an eel, and also has flippers and a long, flexible body. It's just broader, and much, much bigger. But, yes, you could say it looks something like an eel. Or a sea serpent. Why do you ask?"

David replied thoughtfully, "Well, it's this country that we're in. It's named Anguilla, a name it's had for a couple of centuries. Anguilla is Portuguese. It's the Portuguese word for... eel. And before that it was named Malliouhana by the native population, which means 'arrow-shaped sea serpent.' Isn't that strange? Well, good night." He turned, and left.

He did not see the shocked look on her face. She shuddered involuntarily as she felt cold shivers running up and down her spine, as if someone were walking on her grave. She could not for the life of her understand her reaction, but she also could not bring the shivering under control.

She turned to the railing and tossed the rest of her cigar into the ocean. "That's it for me, tonight, then," she said softly, and headed to her cabin, where she burrowed under the blankets to try to stop the shaking, and to get warm again.

Chapter 9

The sun was low on the horizon on Friday by the time David finished securing the ship for the weekend. He had arranged to meet Erika for dinner at the Cap Juluca Restaurant at 8:00 p.m. At 7:15 he found himself in his cabin, still dripping from the shower as he stared at the inside of his closet, feeling as nervous as a high school student getting ready for the prom.

"Well, Bucky," he told his friend, who stood next to him and also stared into the closet, as if he were trying to help him decide, "it doesn't look like we have a lot to choose from. We have one good suit. From the old days."

He took the suit off the rack, dusted it off and tried it on. He noticed it fit rather loosely.

"I guess I've lost weight in the last two years," he told the cat, who sat down on the floor to watch the proceedings. "And we have four shirts." He pulled the shirts out and sniffed them, one after the other, while Bucky raptly watched his expressions. The fourth one, a blue safari shirt, appeared to be the cleanest, or perhaps just the least malodorous. He dressed quickly, and then looked down in response to the, "Rowr-meep?" David sat on the bed and patted the spot next to him. The cat jumped up, sat down beside him and looked at him gravely.

"Maybe I'm just being overly optimistic, Bucky, but I think this woman has...possibilities. She's smart, and she's fit, and she's natural, and she tells you what she thinks instead of dancing around it, and, well, you know. You like her, don't you?"

The cat seemed to consider this a moment, and let out an, "Urgh."

"Yeah, I know," replied David. "I've managed to piss her off a couple of times, and she thinks I'm just a shiftless ill-mannered low-life, but hey—who ever said the course of true love runs smooth?"

He paused. "Maybe the best thing about her is that she has no resemblance to Gloria whatsoever—and being the exact opposite of a rich stuck-up New York socialite bitch ex-wife is probably the best qualification for a woman I can think of right now."

The cat got up and bumped his head against David's elbow. "Sorry, buddy, no time to take you for a walk right now," David told him. He glanced at his watch, then into the corner of the room. "You've got food and water and a more or less clean litter box, and...I've gotta go. Wish me luck!"

David passed through the portals of the Cap Juluca at 5 past 8:00. He handed a bag with two wine bottles in it to the maître d'. He took a moment to gaze through the Moorish arches, framed by pink-colored walls, to admire the long crescent of shimmering white beach that the restaurant commanded. He looked around and noticed the place was packed. He saw Erika at a table near a window. He waved at her, and she waved back. He approached her table, and gathered up his courage to give her a quick peck on the cheek–which she returned, he was happy to see.

He gave her an appreciative glance. She was dressed in a short black skirt and a white silk blouse that showed some midriff (which was flat and fit, he mentally noted). "Hi!" he greeted her. "You look really nice. Did you put on the sexy miniskirt just for me?"

"Oh, this thing?" Erika replied deprecatingly. "A shopkeeper talked me into this today. I put on some girly-girl stuff every once in a while. But no high heels!" She held up one tanned leg to reveal a black Nike sandal at the end of it. "I'll return the compliment. You certainly clean up well, shaved and scrubbed and wearing grown-up clothes. Too bad they didn't have that suit in your size at the Goodwill store. Bargain hunting?" she asked, grinning wickedly.

David smiled back, a little uncertainly. "Not much hunting. It was made for me by Hugo Boss in Duesseldorf, for around 3,000 Euros."

She snorted in disbelief.

"But, thank you," he continued. "This has been such a busy day. It looks like we'll have everything we need ready by Monday morning, so we should be ready to sail again at 8." He waved the sommelier over to their table.

"Ca va, Jacques?" he greeted him. "Je besoin ma bouteille de Laurent-Perrier, s'il vous plait." The man disappeared.

"Did I just hear you speak French?" she asked.

"Mais oui," he smiled. "I used to travel a lot on business, and had clients in France, so I took some classes."

The sommelier reappeared almost immediately, and filled their glasses with chilled, pale yellow champagne. David clinked glasses with her. "Here's to success." She drank some of the bubbly fluid.

"Mm, yum," she said. She looked at the glass. "Lots of bubbles," she remarked.

"Yes, and very small, as they should be," he remarked absently. "Listen, I know I'm being selfish about all this. I'm all excited about my find, but that doesn't help you any. You're losing two days out of your diving schedule."

Erika sipped more of the champagne. "No, no, I'm happy," she replied. "I've spent most of the afternoon talking to colleagues and sending them digital pictures, and we're all in agreement–the fossils are almost certainly a Mosasaur, and possibly a brand new species. If that's true, I'll get to name it! It's good enough that two graduate students are being sent down here to help me, which is great, because students do all the slave work. I'll be able to sit back on the ship and drink umbrella drinks while they're down there rupturing their ear drums and doing all the digging. And once they find something I'll scoop in and claim all the credit for it!"

David chuckled. "Somehow, knowing how hard you work, I doubt that very much," he commented. He raised his champagne glass to her. "Here's to the new species. What will you name it?"

She raised her glass as well, but hesitated. "I don't know. I hadn't really thought about it all that much."

David smiled. "How about Big Mo?"

She laughed, and her face lit up, with her lips curving into the dolphin smile. "Big Mo?" she asked.

"Yes," David replied. "It's short, and it's descriptive. Not one of those long Latin nightmares. Big Mo is also the name of a famous American battleship, the Missouri. Consider it a working title until you find something better."

Erika grinned as she clinked her glass against his. "All right, then. Here's to Big Mo!"

A pretty young mulatto waitress approached the table, and beamed when she recognized David. "Hello, David. How are you?" she asked him, smiling.

David, temporarily taken aback, mumbled his reply. "Oh. Hi, Doris. I didn't know you worked here."

"Oh, yeah," she replied, "Just on weekends. Nice to see you..." She let the words hang in the air. "...again."

David quickly introduced the two women, who gave each other analytical once-over glances.

Doris smiled sweetly, and asked, "So, what would you like?"

David placed their orders as Erika looked on, enjoying his discomfiture. After the waitress left, Erika grinned wickedly as she looked at him expectantly. David stammered, "Ah, she and I used to date a while back. But that was, ah, months ago."

"Well, I'm glad you get along so well with the locals," Erika replied, her voice dripping with honey. "It looks like you fit right in."

"Yes," David retorted. "They're very... friendly." He quickly decided to get out of the cul-de-sac, and looked at Erika. "So, what's your life like in Australia? Are you married, do you have children?"

"No children, no," Erika replied somberly. "But I did get married once, bejesus."

She stopped, but David pressed on. "What happened?"

She looked down at the table. "I got married. It didn't work out."

He asked again, "And then?"

"I met a few other blokes. They all started as friends, but as soon as we got close, they left. That's it."

He chuckled as he tilted his head to one side while looking her in the eye. "You should have warned me about how long this was going to be. The beginning and the end were OK, but it was definitely starting to drag in the middle."

She laughed as she reached across the table to punch him in the arm.

He started laughing, as well. "I'm just saying, keep the main points, and get rid of all those details."

She kicked him under the table.

"Ow! Do you know what this means?" he asked.

"No, what?"

"It means we need another bottle of wine." He called over the sommelier.

"Ma bouteille de Château Montelena." He held up one of the inexpensive-looking wine glasses on the table in front of him with disdain. "Et Jaques, deux verres de Riedel, tout suit, s'il vous plait."

Within a few minutes, their old glasses disappeared, replaced by large, thin-sided crystal filled with light gold-colored wine. The bottle appeared in an ice bucket.

He looked at it. "I brought a couple of bottles in with me. The corkage fee is a lot less than the cost of the wine they serve here."

She noticed that his dimple was more pronounced now that he had shaved, and that she had started to stare at it. To take her mind off that, she looked at the wine in the glass with suspicion. "What did you bring?" she asked. "Boone's Farm, vintage March?"

He ignored her as he carefully swirled the wine in the glass and held it up to the light. "Nice straw color, good legs."

He sniffed it. "Layered, complex nose. Honeysuckle, tropical fruit, and a hint of citrus, with a faint vanilla tang of French oak." He took a small sip. "Apricot. Something tropical—star fruit, with a little papaya. Faint butterscotch in the background." He closed his eyes. "Bright tartness in the aftertaste. Nicely balanced."

She smirked sarcastically. "Oh, yeh. Sure it is!"

He swirled it again. "This is one of my favorite Chardonnays, from the Napa Region. Montelena won as the best white wine at the International Wine Competition in 1976, a blind tasting of top wines held in Paris. That rocked the wine world, because up to then everyone assumed that only French wines were that good. It established California as a premier region overnight."

He took another sip and expressed an appreciative smile. "And this is the wine Company that did it. One of its neighbors, Stag's Leap, won as the best red wine."

"You're putting me on," Erika said. "You're really into wine?"

"You mean, how could low-level trailer trash like me be a wine snob?" he replied.

"Something like that, but I wasn't going to be that honest about it," she said, starting to smile.

"I was interested in it, so I took some classes, got my WSET Certification, and visited wineries when I traveled on business," he replied.

"I'm glad you got some kind of education," she said, wrinkling her nose at him.

Doris brought them their seafood appetizers, artistic arrangements of oysters and red-boiled shrimp in nests of cracked ice on square white plates with blue borders. She leaned down and told David, "There are some fans of yours in the corner who'd like to say hello."

David looked over at a corner table with a family of locals sitting at it. Two teenaged girls were waving to him. "Excuse me, I'll be back in just a minute," he told Erika, and walked over to the table to embrace and chat with the girls.

Erika walked around the corner of the bar into the rest room. Within a few minutes she was standing at the long marble sink, washing her hands, when she noticed Doris next to her, doing the same.

"My God, how many women does he have around here? And how young is he dating them?" Erika asked her.

The waitress looked puzzled. "He met those girls at the hospital while they were sick. He comes in many nights with Bucky, his cat. We call Bucky the therapy cat—he seems to have magic healing powers. And David reads to everybody and tells them stories, especially the kids and the old people. That's where I met him."

Erika returned to the table at the same time as David sat down again. "My, my, I was starting to think what a pervert you are, and here Doris tells me you're a regular nurse Nightingale."

David was about to reply when a middle-aged, intense-looking gentleman with a Van Dyke beard and wearing a hounds-tooth suit and knit tie approached their table and bowed, followed by a slender woman and a bored-looking teenage girl.

"Guten Abend, Herr Doktor Doktor Kilmer. Wie geht es Ihnen?" the man asked, and offered his hand.

David shook the proffered hand, half-rising to answer. "Ganz prima, danke. Let me introduce you. This is Doctor Erika Bettelman. Erika, this is Mr. Wolfgang Katzenberg and his wife Kristina, and daughter Melanie."

There was a lot of hand shaking all around before the man, who appeared not be sweating in his suit in spite of the tropical heat, bowed again, and said, "My pleasure. Nice evening to you both," and the family departed.

Erika stared at David with a bemused look. "This is getting worse and worse. What was all that about, eh?"

David replied offhandedly, "Oh, I met them in a bar. They're German tourists on vacation. He works in..."

"No, no," intoned Erika, not to be put off. "What was that 'Herr Doktor Doktor' all about?"

"Oh," said David sheepishly. "We exchanged business cards, and I gave him one of my old ones, when I was a partner in a law firm, and he saw the 'J.D.' after my name. And, er, in my spare time, I also got doctorate in business at night school, a D.B.M. In Germany, if you have two doctorates, they call you, 'Doktor Doktor.'"

She sat back open-mouthed, then shook her head and gave him an appreciative look. "An attorney. And a Doctorate in Business. So you're not really the shiftless no-class tosser that you look like, eh?"

"Well, it was just that I hadn't had my new business cards made out yet. The ones that say, 'Treasure hunter who's likely to wind up selling pencils on a street corner,'" he said with a lopsided grin.

Erika looked at him with mock suspicion. "Did you pay that guy?"

David hung his head. "You found me out. I wonder if I can still get my 50 dollars back?" They both grinned at each other, and their eyes locked for a moment.

She shook her head to clear it and lowered her eyebrows. "You told me you didn't even graduate from high school."

He nodded. "I didn't. I was in a hurry, got enough credits to enter college at 16, so I never attended graduation. Signed up with the Marine Corps in college, and they paid to put me through law school. After I did my tour, I joined a law firm in New York, and eventually started my own."

She suddenly stared at his suit. "Don't tell me—you weren't kidding? That thing really cost 4,000 Euros?"

He nodded. "Yes. Custom-made silk and mohair blend, by Hugo Boss. I guess I've lost weight since then."

She shook her head as she looked down at the table. "You know what this means," she said.

"No. What?" he replied.

"It means it's time for another bottle of wine. You order. I love watching you go through all your foo-foo." When the sommelier appeared, David looked at the wine list and ordered a Mollydooker Shiraz. It appeared quickly, with new crystal glasses.

David pointed at the bottle. "This got 90 points from the *Wine Spectator*. It's Australian, so you can feel at home." She imitated him exactly as he swished the wine around the glass three times, breathed it in deeply, took a tiny sip, and then swished it around the glass three times in the opposite direction. He looked at her making fun of him, and they both broke out laughing.

"And why do you like this one so much?" she asked.

He chuckled. "To tell you the truth, I just like the name and the outrageous label."

Their meals arrived, grilled grouper with steamed vegetables for David and a rare steak with pommes frites for Erika. She sawed off a large chunk of pinkish red meat, speared it with a fork and waved it in the direction of David's vegetables. "Steamed veggies and healthy fish! Are you sure you're not gay?" she asked.

He laughed. "Maybe it's still a remnant of how I learned to eat in the posh restaurants of New York. You know, where they serve you a tiny portion of something with a foreign name and then charge you triple for it."

He used his fork to point a piece of grouper at her steak. "That looks like a meal for a truck driver. Are you sure *you're* not gay?"

She cut him a hard look, but saw that the laugh lines around his eyes crinkled. She shook her head and chuckled, "No, I'm just..."

He helped her finish the sentence, "...Australian!"

She nodded and continued, "Yeh. Except for a one-time drunk exploration with a girlfriend in university, I decided not to go that route. I've stayed with men, no-good wankers that they are."

He grinned again, and mentally noted that she seemed mesmerized by the dimple in his cheek.

He said, "You were going to tell me more about your social life."

She made small circles with her glass, then looked at him. "You first," she said.

He grew somber. "For that I'll need more wine," he said, refilling his empty glass. He looked out the window at the ocean. "I grew up really poor. East Germany when I was very young was a terrible place, desolate and paranoid. Everybody informed on everybody else. Someone told on my father. The next day he was taken away by the Secret Police, and the last we saw of him was his sealed coffin. My mother and I fled East Germany to come to New York City, and she worked as a cook in rich people's houses. We lived in the servant's quarters. I never really had a home. At that time I swore I'd never be a servant again, and that I'd get my mother out of having to take crap from rich assholes. Once I left the military after law school, I went after cases like a house on fire. I didn't care about what I was doing, as long as I won and made money."

He paused a moment, and stared into his glass. "The Buddhists have a saying," he continued. "Whatever you resist, you become. So I became a rich asshole. I married a snotty old-money socialite, and poured money into a condo on Park Avenue. I put my mother into a nice home, but then never took the time to visit her. I kept telling her I'd see her someday soon. And then one day she passed away, and 'someday' never came.

Erika looked sympathetic. "I'm sorry."

David sighed. "Friends of hers called. I was on a business trip, as usual. She had had a heart attack on a trip with a seniors group. I took a couple of days off and drove up to finally spend time with her, but she passed away before I arrived. I never even got to say good-bye."

He glanced at the ocean, touches of pain evident in his face. "Suddenly it seemed like I was too late for everything. I drove directly home and entered my condo to the sound of heavy breathing and moaning. I walked into the kitchen to see my wife spread out on the counter, with my business partner Mel busily devouring various items of food that were..." he hesitated a moment, "...distributed on and around and in her."

Erika let out a low whistle. "This was what, food fucking? Is that what you do in New York?"

David bit his lip. "Well, *we* had never tried that. In fact, we really hadn't had a lot of sex that year. She always came up with some excuse." He shook his head. "One of the items was a Mars Bar, I remember. And she'd told me she hated chocolate!"

Erika burst out laughing. "I'm sorry, I..."

David waved off her apology. "That's OK. Now the whole thing seems funny. I should have seen it coming. But at that time I was devastated. Gloria was everything I wanted, or so I thought. She was upper crust, and her family had houses everywhere. We were invited to lots of posh parties. I deluded myself that I finally had a home. That I belonged. But, of course, I never did."

He took a deep breath. "It got worse. When we started the divorce, I got an accounting of my assets. Mel had always taken care of the books. He had robbed the company blind, and piled up tons of debt. In fact, he'd been false-billing, for work not actually done. I was lucky not to wind up in jail. I was in hock up to my eyeballs, had to sell all my assets, and my professional name was mud. My clients disappeared overnight."

He looked directly into her eyes. "After declaring bankruptcy, all my so-called 'friends' melted away. I tried drinking the bars on the West Side dry for a week, but, strangely, that didn't seem to help."

He brightened. "Then Bucky came into my life. He found me one night, in a cold, dark alley next to a bar, where I was, er, resting, and adopted me. I'd never had a pet, so it was a new feeling. Someone loved me, no matter what, and wanted nothing in return, except a little kibble and water."

"That sounds awfully good to me," Erika commented. "Does he have a brother?"

David laughed, and clinked his glass with hers. "If I find out he does, I'll fix you up!"

Erika was about to reply, but was interrupted by AJ walking in. He was with a very pretty woman with milk chocolate skin that set off a white suit with short sleeves and bell bottom pants. She wore her hair in short corn rows. Her generously wide mouth revealed large, even teeth that sparkled bright white whenever she smiled, which was often.

"I'm sorry we're late," AJ said contritely. "We had some urgent work to finish up." He nodded at Erika and turned to his partner. "Erika, this is Leah. She's my assistant."

They shook hands, sat down, and both ordered grilled swordfish. Two more wine glasses appeared and were quickly filled.

David motioned at AJ. "AJ is one of the most successful wine and spirits distributors in the Caribbean. He's always traveling, and seems to know everyone."

"How did you and David meet?" Erika asked AJ.

"We met in the service," he replied. "I'd gotten into some trouble after a Special Forces operation, and was being court-martialed. David got me off. I'm still trying to figure out how he did it." He looked at David and raised his eyebrow.

David bit his lip. "I'd figured out what the case was really all about. The boss of the senior officer of the court was a Vice

Admiral, an old Southern cracker, and AJ had dated his daughter. He was bent on getting AJ thrown in the brig. Unfortunately, the Navy treats Admirals like gods. It was impossible to get around him."

"I've never heard this part," Leah chimed in. "What did you do?"

"Damnedest thing I ever saw," AJ replied, shaking his head. "In the middle of the fifth day of the trial, the Admiral was going on some diatribe when four SPs—Shore Patrolmen, Military Police— came in and arrested him. They had gotten a tip and found incriminating evidence on his office computer, really vile stuff. Like many religious zealots, he was a hypocrite. They put him in cuffs and led him out."

David laughed. "The court suddenly became a lot more flexible. The prosecutor decided to dismiss the case. AJ got off with a slap on the wrist."

Erika's eyes bored into David. "What a coincidence."

David looked at her. "I wouldn't plant evidence. I might have, er, discovered it by unorthodox means."

AJ continued, "An even greater coincidence was the TV camera crews showing up that same day."

Erika shook her head.

"After that, David got quite a reputation," AJ noted. "He became 'Killer' Kilmer. I think the Marine Corps was happy when his term was up."

"I wasn't about to let AJ get framed," David said. "Unfortunately, it ended his career. He came from a long line of military heroes. His grandfather and father have rows of medals on their chests, and brag about them all the time. I think AJ's biggest wish was to get at least one award, so he could hold his head up."

AJ sighed. "It makes for embarrassing silence from my side at the dinner table when the family gets together."

"Where is your family from?" Erika asked.

"Stratford-on-Avon," AJ replied. "My folks have an estate in the country. I have dual citizenship, British and US."

"I have a father just like yours," Erika said. "Nothing was ever good enough for him. He didn't even come to my graduation because my work wasn't worthwhile in his eyes. If I ever get famous, he's going to rue the day." She turned to Leah. "How about you?"

"I had a wonderful childhood," Leah said, beaming her wide smile. "We lived on the outskirts of Pittsburgh, on the edge of a forest that I could explore. My parents were both professors. We had great discussions at the dinner table. The only time they freaked is when I wanted to take a year off after high school, to travel. They're workaholics. Jobs are sacred. Leaving a job or taking time off puts you in league with the devil."

They fell into an easy companionship as they finished their dinners and ordered warmed-up Martell XO cognac for dessert. The amicable atmosphere in the restaurant was suddenly interrupted. David noticed that several tables of locals were no longer chatting, and that the room had gotten quieter. He looked toward a corner, and made a subtle motion to AJ. Two police officers had taken a table, and were looking at the diners with pinched, suspicious eyes.

"What's wrong?" Erika asked.

"There are two guys in the corner that are checking everybody out," David answered. "The tourists aren't noticing it, but the locals are. They've stopped talking, for fear of being overheard."

"Do those guys belong to DuBois?" Erika asked, turning her head to observe them.

"Yes," AJ answered. "And their uniforms are looking more and more military, which worries me. Those two both have Captain's bars on their uniforms, and a bunch of medals on their chest. They're not even real. Those are US Navy medals. They probably got them in some war surplus store, or from EBay."

He turned to David. "Listen. We were planning on going down to Auntie's. Want to come?"

David rose up eagerly. "Sure would," he replied. He looked at Erika. "Would you like to come and meet a great lady and good friend, and pick up on some local color? Aunt Marie's the leading voodoo and Santeria priestess in this part of the Caribbean."

Erika looked briefly at her watch, then smiled. "Yeh. Sure, why not?" she replied. She finished the wine in her glass, and then stood up and took David's arm with, "Lead on, maestro!"

As David and Erika walked out behind AJ and Leah. David whispered into Erika's ear, "Isn't she great? If she didn't have a crush on someone else, I would have chased her down long ago."

Erika snorted. "She's much too good for the likes of you!"

"I know that. But she trusts me, and I'm great at marketing," he replied.

Erika whispered in his ear, "That person she's got the crush on is AJ, isn't it?"

He nodded. "Oh, yeah. If I could bottle the sexual tension between those two, I could solve the world's energy problems!"

Chapter 10

AJ drove like a madman in the lead car, a red Jeep Cherokee. After they left the outskirts of town they ran out of pavement, and jounced along a rutted dirt road that was surrounded by overhanging pepper trees and lush greenery that reflected in the tunnel of light thrown by the headlights.

Erika was thrown against David as the car went through a particular deep hole in the road, and David put his arm around her to steady her. He became aware of every square inch of her that was touching him, and found it difficult to concentrate on his driving. They crossed a rickety bridge, and emerged into a clearing with a bonfire in the center. Several dozen people were gathered around it.

As they parked their vehicle and opened the car doors, the sound of drums assaulted their ears. They joined AJ and Leah and walked toward an imposing elderly lady seated in an overstuffed easy chair on a raised platform. Her black face beamed as she saw them approaching.

"AJ, David, Leah, I see you," she intoned, and held up her arms to hug them.

David introduced Erika. "Erika, this is Aunt Marie. Marie, like Marie Claire, the voodoo queen of New Orleans, who was one of Auntie's ancestors."

Aunt Marie grasped Erika's hand in hers, and looked deep into her eyes. Erika had a strange feeling of being pulled in by that gaze, almost like being sucked into a vortex, although she felt safe and secure. For a moment the sounds of the drums and the people around her seemed to fade away into the distance. She swayed slightly on her feet, and was starting to fall forward when Aunt Marie released her hand and smiled warmly. Slowly, Erika became aware of her surroundings again.

"You been looking for something for a long time, child," Aunt Marie said, kindly. "You'll find it soon, but you will be in great danger when you do."

Erika found she had a hard time focusing her eyes as she listened to Aunt Marie's voice. "I don't think so," she replied, absently. "What I'm looking for has been dead for millions of years, so I don't think..."

She stopped in mid-sentence. Her mouth fell open as she noticed the sizeable silver pendant suspended around Aunt Marie's neck. Its bright, dazzling reflections contrasted with the dark chocolate color of the ample bosom. The serpentine form could have been a dragon, or perhaps a snake with leg-like appendages. "What is that?" Erika asked in amazement.

Aunt Marie looked down and grasped the charm and turned it from side to side. "This is an ancient god, child. Perhaps not a god as you understand the word—you might call him an angel, or a messenger. This is *Mokele-Mbembe*, the lord of the seas and the lakes. The people around here know him a long time. Some have different names for him. The Mayan people, down South of here, they call him Quetzalcoatl, the Rainbow Serpent. The old people of these islands, they call him the God of Lightning and the Serpent of the Sea. But in Africa he was known for thousands of years as Mokele-Mbembe."

She looked solemn. "Many people afraid of him all round the Caribbean. When he angry, he makes storms and lightning, an' he make people disappear. Not just people, but whole boats, an' airplanes too. Earlier tonight we pray, we make offerings an' ask that he leave all of us here alone, but take revenge on our enemies."

Erika was speechless. She reached out one hand to the pendant almost unconsciously, then, realizing what she was doing, quickly withdrew it.

David noticed the look on her face. "What is it? What's the matter?" he asked.

Erika spoke slowly. "That...that pendant she's wearing. That's a very good likeness of a Mosasaur!"

Aunt Marie shook her head. "I never hear him called that. But you be careful. Mokele-Mbembe, he kill more than one person from these islands. I asked him to kill the cousin of that snake DuBois. The two of them come here from Haiti, and the cousin started shaking people down. He disappeared one night, along with his boat. DuBois don' watch out, he gonna disappear too!"

David took Erika's arm and steered her away gently. "I'll bring her back later," he told Aunt Marie. He brought Erika to a long rough wooden table with a giant metal tureen with reddish liquid in it, took a ladle, and filled a plastic cup, which he handed to her. He filled three more, for himself, AJ and Leah, and then explained, "This is Auntie's special secret punch. We've never found out what's in it, but we know to be careful with the refills."

The four of them clicked their plastic cups together and drank the fruity-tasting concoction. Erika watched the people around the fire, fascinated, as additional drummers started up. The deep thrumming resounded from the dark forest around them and seemed to come from everywhere.

Erika and David sat on a log near the edge of the circle and watched as AJ and Leah mingled with the others, who all seemed to know them. "The belief in voodoo, also called hoodoo or Santeria, is strong in the islands," he told her.

"Aunt Marie is one of the most famous practitioners in this part of the world. Lots of people come to her, to ask her for favors, or to heal someone who's sick. And it's true that some people she's gotten pissed off at have disappeared. I've been one of the few outsiders, meaning persons not from this island, who's been allowed to watch one of her banishing ceremonies. She brings out several statues, including a larger version of that amulet you admired so much, and they conduct a voodoo mass, somewhat like a Catholic mass. If there is someone that has become persona non grata because they've hurt one of the believers, a chicken is sacrificed and the blood is sprinkled on a replica of that person. And at the end, Auntie and everyone here chants 'Be gone!' nine times and then she throws the doll into the fire. And very soon, that person is no longer around."

He put one arm around her to reassure her. "Don't worry. She does that only very rarely. Mostly we sit around and discuss what's stopping us in life—like how the past can keep us prisoner, and how to break free of it. Aunt Marie has studied a lot of the wisdom of the Mayans and American shamans and African wise men."

He continued. "But nobody messes with Auntie and Mokele-Mbembe, not even our new police Colonel. Now, this tonight..." he pointed at the circle of people around the fire, some of whom had started dancing vigorously to the drums, "...is not one of those ceremonies. This is just for fun, and to pay our respects to Auntie."

The music picked up, and a couple of fiddles and a concertina joined in to enliven dancers whirling around a large circular area next to the house. As the music grew louder and more insistent, more of the crowd joined in. Some of the women started shrieking as they whirled in mad circles, and men started shouting and twirling, and jumping up and down. Several of the men took their shirts off, and one woman removed her blouse, revealing pendulous breasts barely contained within a rose-colored bra. AJ and Leah were among the dancers now, dancing passionately but at a careful distance from each other.

Erika's face flushed as she responded to the ancient rhythm and the sight of bodies as they surged against each other in time to the music. On an impulse, she set down her drink—it was her second or third by now, she wasn't sure which—and rose unsteadily to join in. David felt the blood slowly rising to his head as he saw her lose herself in the music, hands raised above her head, hips pumping, head tossing to and fro, eyes closed tightly. He rose as if in a trance and sidled up to her, facing her, slowly joining in the rhythm. After a while he noticed that both of them were perspiring freely, the heat from the fire and from the dancers around them adding to the warm and humid night air, which seemed to flow like thick liquid around them.

Sometime later–David had no idea how long–he moved closer to Erika, his legs touching hers, and put one arm around her waist to draw her closer to him. She did not resist, but her eyelids flew open and she looked at him with wild, unfocused eyes. He moved one hand around the curvature of her butt and drew her even closer. She melded into him, both bodies moving as one to the wild throbbing of the drums and other instruments that continued non-stop, one rhythm blending into another.

By now both of his hands were encircling her bottom, and he could feel the outline of her panties as her miniskirt slid up toward her waist. On the periphery of his vision he noticed appreciatively that said panties were white with frilly borders and a pattern of little blue hearts. Both of them were caught up in the heat of the moment, and it seemed perfectly natural for their faces to come together very closely, almost touching. David's lips brushed lightly against Erika's as they continued moving in time to the music, as her pelvis ground against his gathering arousal.

She put her arms around his neck and pulled him in closer. They were locked so tightly together that when they both swayed in one direction at the same time they almost stumbled into the fire. They reluctantly broke free and faced each other, both breathing heavily, absently wiping the sweat from their faces.

David's voice seemed to be stuck in his throat. He managed to say, "Let's...go somewhere."

"Okay," she said meekly, and followed him as he grasped her hand and led her toward the car.

He stopped suddenly. "We'd better say good-bye to Auntie," he said.

They found Aunt Marie in her house, a rambling structure with many halls and doorways. She was inside a large room, earnestly talking with AJ and Leah. Her faced brightened when she saw David and Erika. "Come in, children, come in," she beckoned, and they entered.

Erika looked around her in wonder. The house was full of candles. There were dozens of them burning in the ceremonial room they were in. The air was redolent with musky incense. Statues of different gods—or perhaps Catholic saints—stood in shrines against the walls, each one bedecked with necklaces of beads and flowers.

Erika was riveted by one such shrine, and walked over to it, her eyes wide and unfocused. The statue pictured not a human, but a stylized animal. It was a much larger and more finely detailed version of the pendant that hung around Aunt Marie's neck. Half in a daze, Erika ran a hand over the statue, her fingertips tracing the unmistakable outlines of the long broad tail, the broad flukes and the massive elongated jaws of a Mosasaur, perhaps a Tylosaurus. "If not that," Erika said quietly, "it's at least first cousin to one."

"I notice you've taken a fancy to Mokele-Mbembe," said a voice behind her, and Erika whirled around.

She reddened when she saw Aunt Marie's beatific smile, and asked her, "Aunt Marie—Auntie—have you actually ever seen anything like this?"

"No, not really," Aunt Marie answered sadly. "Three, four times, maybe, I saw flashes of lightning at night on the horizon. That could have been him. That's my dream. I always ask him in my prayers, let me see you once, real clear, before I die."

"Why does lightning remind you of him?" Erika asked her.

"Why, child, he's the god of lightning. He can kill his enemy or confuse him wit' lightning, just like it comes from the heavens."

Erika ran her eyes over the statue once more, appraising its pastel colors. "Why all these colors, Auntie? You've got red and orange and yellow and green and blue and violet here."

Aunt Marie smiled gently. "Like I told you, the Mayan people called him the Rainbow Serpent. He can be all the colors there are. He can change color, come up on you, you never see him till…" Aunt Marie made a sudden clapping motion with her hands, and Erika shrank back. "…he right on top o' you, an' den' it too late!"

Aunt Marie laid a hand on Erika's arm, and told her warmly, "I like you, so I'm gonna give you something you need. Don' go away." She disappeared into a side room, and re-emerged a moment later with a silver amulet on a leather thong, which she proceeded to tie around Erika's neck. "I call the blessing of Mokele-Mbembe and all the spirits down on this," she intoned, solemnly touching first the amulet and then the top of Erika's head. "You meet up with Mokele-Mbembe, this will protect you."

"Thank you," Erika said, just as solemnly.

They bade farewell to Aunt Marie and walked back to the car. Just as they reached it, Erika's cell phone buzzed, and she took it out and tapped its screen to see who was calling her. "Oh, hi," she spoke into it. She looked at her watch. "No, I didn't get a message. He's been waiting for me at the airport? I didn't know that. Sorry. I'll be there in 10 minutes. Bye, Reggie." She ended the call.

"I–I'm sorry, David," she said. "But, as I said earlier, I have another...a previous appointment. Reggie...Reginald Fowler offered me a complimentary room at the Paradise Island Resort for the weekend, and I promised I'd take him up on it."

"Paradise Island?" David asked, bewildered. "But there's no way to get there. The last boat left hours ago."

"There is a way," Erika insisted. "I have a helicopter waiting for me at the airport. I dropped off my suitcase earlier today." Then, when she saw the crestfallen look on David's face, she added, apologetically, "I promised. I can't go back on my word. I'm sorry!"

They got in his car. David slammed the door as he got in. He drove the few miles to the airport at breakneck speed.

"Are you angry about something?" asked Erika.

"No, that's quite all right," David replied bitterly. "I should've known better. I'll know my place in the future. You won't have to worry about me...bothering you again!"

"That's not fair," Erika shot back. "I told you I promised. I didn't know it..." she glanced at her watch, "...would turn out to be so late." She turned toward him, and her face was a mix of emotions. "Look!" she said sternly, "Like I said, it's not a good idea to be...dating...while we're working together. I've found it...can lead to problems."

They came to a screeching halt in front of the small airport's single terminal. Ahead they could see the helicopter, with a pilot leaning against its side, reading a paper in the aircraft's lights. He recognized Erika, and climbed in the helicopter to start up the engine.

"Thank you for dinner, and everything, David. I had a really nice time," Erika said, trying to lighten the mood.

David walked around the car and opened the door for her. "It's fine! Don't worry about it!" he said bitterly, almost biting off the words.

She got out and started hesitantly walking toward the helicopter, then stopped and turned. "Thanks for everything. It was...wonderful."

"Yeah," David replied, trying to smile but doing a bad job of hiding his disappointment. He hesitated a moment, and said, almost sadly, "I guess the miniskirt wasn't for me, after all." He climbed into his car, slammed the door and roared off in a screech of tires.

Erika took a deep breath, and let it out in a sigh. "Bloody men!" she said, exasperated, as she turned and walked toward the waiting helicopter.

Chapter 11

After Marie bid farewell to the last of her guests, she came back into the house, where AJ and Leah were waiting.

"Let's go downstairs, I need to transmit some stuff," AJ said. Marie closed the shutters of the room's windows, and then AJ helped her pull back a rug, revealing a door in the middle of the floor. He opened a concealed combination lock, and pulled open the door to reveal a staircase going into the basement.

"This is probably the most secure place in this part of the Caribbean," he thought as they descended the stairs to the room below. "No one would dare mess with Aunt Marie." Aloud, he said, "Aunt Marie, you know the Agency appreciates your help. Are you sure you wouldn't like to be put on the payroll?"

"No thank, you, child," she replied as she turned on the lights. "I'm happy to help, 'cause I know it can help this island. But I don't want to be a paid informant. I want to do it because it's right."

"Let's talk," AJ said, motioning to the table in the middle of the basement room. He handed a sheet of paper to Leah. "You can transmit this list in the meantime. Tell them I'll put the videos in the diplomatic pouch in St. Maarten tomorrow."

Leah moved to a computer on one side, logged in, and started filling out a form with data. "Did we get anything interesting?" AJ asked.

"We got a few good ones," she replied. "We got a US Congressman doing pillow talk with a hired friend. A French Minister in a pouf in Martinique. A possible drug trafficker speaking in Spanish. And a German Senator going at it with a hooker."

AJ smiled. "I'm not sure that's such a big deal in Germany. Was she one of our contractors?"

Leah grinned. "It wasn't a she. It was a he."

AJ nodded. "All right. Go ahead and put the memory disks in the sealed bag and lock it."

"I'm going to lose her help for a few weeks," he told Marie. "Leah is on assignment at Paradise Island Resort. She got in by getting a job as a hotel receptionist. With her there, we should have an idea of who's coming and going in that place."

"Good, good," Marie said. "But be real careful, child. I also got a member of my parish in, as a chamber maid. They've been real careful in hiring. They seem to be importing people from far away.

And they're bringing in lots of security people, from Haiti and Jamaica, with automatic weapons."

"What kind of guests do they have?" AJ asked.

"So far, they've been real respectable, VIPs from the area. But I hear they're planning to invite very different guests in the future, the type they need all those guards for. It could turn into a real pirate den."

AJ sat down at the table. "And what's going on in Anguilla?" he asked.

Marie shook her head. "It's getting worse and worse," she said. "DuBois is bringing in more and more policemen, tough men from the slums of Haiti, where he's from. I don't like the looks of it. He's taking over the island—everybody's afraid of him."

"Where's he getting the money to pay for all these hired guns?" asked AJ.

"Nobody knows. My niece is in Payroll for Government House, and she says they're not getting paychecks from any regular government funds. There are about 30 of them here now, and no one knows how many more at the Resort. They keep to themselves and pay for everything in cash. They live in a bunch of trailers on the north part of the island."

"Is there anyone we can still trust on the police force?" AJ asked.

"Your friend, Sergeant Baisley, and maybe a handful of others. They've replaced a lot of the older guys, one by one."

AJ tapped his fingers on the table. "He's built a private army," he muttered.

"He may be tapping into some of the investment money for the Dragon Island Resort," she said. "What they're trying to call Paradise Island. Why Fowler thinks he needs so much security for a resort, I don't know."

Marie took one of AJ's hands in hers. "One thing's for sure. DuBois is spending a lot. That means he's hungry. If David finds his treasure, that'll be like red meat in front of DuBois and his sharks. We should warn David of what may happen."

"I thought of that," AJ replied bitterly. "I asked my station head, Bedrosian, and he absolutely forbade it. He doesn't want us to blow our cover. No one is to know that someone may be trying to take over that island as a haven for drug runners, or that we're keeping an eye on it."

Marie patted his hand. "If David does find the treasure, I know you'll find some way to help him. You're old friends, right?"

AJ nodded. "He saved my butt. When I heard he was looking for that U-boat near here, I got the Agency to invest some money in his venture."

"What are they hoping to find, some kind of historical war documents?" Marie asked.

OJ smiled ruefully. "Yeah, historical is right. The Agency wants to know who the spy was that the U-boat was coming to pay off. He ran a whole network spying for the U-boats, letting them know what kind of ships were coming and going in the Caribbean and along the Atlantic seaboard."

"Really?" Marie asked. "Was the network successful?"

AJ nodded his head. "They were so good at sinking American ships that the Navy and FDR lied to the public, ashamed to reveal the real numbers. It was also a thorn in the side of the OSS, the predecessor to the Agency. And the CIA has a long memory."

He mused, "In a way, they're having the same problem now. Some group is organizing drug shipments, and they seem to know exactly where and when the US Coast Guard is patrolling. They're either avoiding those routes or offloading the drugs and hiding them in some safe harbor. Our agency and a bunch of others have a whole task force looking into that."

Leah stood up from the computer. "OK, everything's transmitted."

"Thanks again for your help, Marie," AJ said. "Be careful. I don't like the direction our peaceful little island is heading in. If someone took over under the pretense of 'freeing the people,' this could become a real haven for bad guys in this part of the world. And they could hurt you."

Marie smiled. "Ain't no one going to mess with me. Don't you worry. The people of this island will get together and stop DuBois."

They walked up the stairs into the living room, and replaced the rug over the trap door. AJ and Leah made their good-byes before driving off. Marie went to a corner of the house that had been set up as a shrine, and lit a candle. The candlelight provided flickering illumination of a larger version of the fierce animal that Erika now had hanging around her neck. Marie sat in a rocking chair in front of the shrine, closed her eyes, and rocked slowly back and forth and hummed to herself as she said a silent prayer.

Chapter 12

David had reached the ship by the time the helicopter flew overhead in the direction of Paradise Island. He did not know it, but the aircraft's lone passenger had her face pressed against the window, staring down at the lights of his ship.

He walked up the gangplank and stomped on board in a foul mood. It did not improve until he sat on his bed and Bucky sidled up next to him. David threw his jacket into a corner of the cabin with irritation, but his eyes softened as the large cat crawled into his lap and urged him to scratch his face by rubbing it against David's belt buckle. David complied, laughing. "Oh, Bucky! Thank God for you. Why can't you be a woman?"

He paused as the cat looked at him, head cocked. "OK, maybe I fucked up tonight. I don't know. It probably doesn't matter—it looks like she'll be with someone else now. He can probably give her a lot more than me. But it's too bad."

He looked down at the cat, who flopped over on his back and stuck all four legs up in the air, paws bent. David scratched his tummy, and the cat arched his back and purring in total ecstasy.

David sighed, and told him, "OK, OK. I'm over it." He smiled down at his friend. "What would I ever do without you? I don't think I could stand being alone...that alone." He looked around his cabin. "I'd probably have to get a television."

Bucky jumped off his lap and walked to the door, looking back expectantly.

"OK, I got it. Let's go out. It's still early."

They left the ship and got into David's Jeep. Minutes later, they pulled into Johnno's Beach Bar parking lot. David opened his door and told the cat. "Let's go."

Bucky did not move. He let out an "Urr."

"What?" David asked him. The cat repeated his guttural growl.

"We can't go in here? Not even for one drink? Not even after the day I've had?

"Urr!"

"Where else? Don't tell me..." He looked at Bucky in exasperation. "OK, but only for ten minutes. Then we're coming back here!"

He got back into the car, and drove past Sandy Ground Village, past Road Bay, up Buntin Hill, and into the parking lot of the Princess Alexandra Hospital in the township of The Valley.

He picked Bucky up on his arm and strode into the lobby. The receptionist behind the desk, a young woman with a *café au lait* complexion set off by her starched white nurse's uniform, immediately brightened. "Hello, you two!" she said. She keyed the microphone in front of her.

"Therapy cat is at the front desk," she announced. As an afterthought she added, "And David." He rolled his eyes as she laughed.

Four nurses and a doctor gathered around them as if they were celebrities. Each bent over to pet Bucky.

"I don't suppose anyone is still awake?" David asked.

"Oh, yes," a nurse with the nametag of Molly Jordin said quietly. "Mrs. Goodfellow. She's in bad shape. It looks like she's passing on tonight. She's in a lot of pain, but she won't let doctor give her any medication. She says if she's going to go, she wants to be awake for it."

"Aw, that's too bad," David said sadly. "She's been such a nice old soul. What room?"

"Number 12," Nurse Molly replied. "We've contacted her son in Kingston, but haven't been able to reach him. It'd be terrible if she passed away all alone."

"Never fear," David called out. "The Bucky Team is here." He strode down the corridor and swung into Room 12, where a very old lady was lying in bed. Her face looked like it had the maximum number of wrinkles possible for a human being. A small procession of tears marched down one of the deeper wrinkles. She turned her face toward the two of them, her eyes focusing slowly, and then broke into a trembling smile.

"And how are we this fine evening, Agnes?" David asked cheerfully, letting Bucky jump onto the bed.

The withered old face turned toward the ceiling. "It looks like I'm going to see St. Peter tonight," she said slowly. "I'm hurting so bad, and I'm so afraid and alone."

"What do you mean, alone?" David said heartily as he pulled up a chair. He waved in the direction of the nurse, who had just entered the room with a slender, solemn-looking Indian doctor. "We have Nurse Molly here, and Doctor Chopra, and me, and Bucky. You've practically got a mob. Any more and we'd get the police called in on us!"

Bucky sidled up and settled tightly next to her as she started stroking him. He started a deep, rhythmic purr that could be heard all the way out in the hallway.

"Are you sure I can't get you any medication, Agnes?" the doctor asked, concern in his voice.

"No, no. I'm OK now," she said, stroking the cat from head to tail, stopping to scratch him behind the ears. The purr, impossible as it seemed, got even louder. "I've got my therapy right here."

Chopra turned to the nurse. "I wouldn't believe it if I hadn't seen it so often. If I had ten more like him, I could fire the anesthesiologist!" They both left and walked out into the hall.

In the room, David sat in a chair and looked around for reading material. "Since I can't purr, let me make myself useful by reading something," he said. "How about the history of Anguilla?"

He picked up a travel brochure and moved his chair next to the hospital bed with a loud scraping sound. He put one hand on top of the old woman's, noticing the dryness of the skin and the many age spots, and how cold it was. He started reading, holding the book with his other hand.

"Anguilla was first populated three or four thousand years ago. One of the first people were the Arawak Indians, who called it 'Malliouhana,' meaning 'arrow-shaped sea serpent.'"

He paused. "It's like I was saying just the other day. Sure is a lot of stuff about sea serpents and dragons and giant flying snakes around this island," he remarked. "Pretty spooky."

He continued. "Life on Anguilla was always hard, due mainly to a lack of fresh water. Settlers tried to grow sugar in the 1700s, but that didn't work, so they tried cotton, importing African labor to work the plantations. The island was so poor that the slaves got a couple of days off each week, so they could grow their own food to feed themselves. After Emancipation in the 1840s, things got so bad from draught that the British suggested that Anguilla be abandoned, and everybody be moved to British Guyana."

He turned to the old lady. "Did you know all this, Agnes?"

"No, David," she replied gently. "But keep on reading. I like the sound of your voice. Thank you so much for coming, especially so late at night."

"Don't thank me, thank Bucky," he replied.

She smiled at him. "You look sad. What's the matter?"

He shook his head. "Nothing, really. Maybe I just learned a lesson in whom you can trust."

"You have a hard time with trust," she said, speaking slowly.

He nodded. "I seem to keep bumping into that."

"When was the time...you...couldn't be trusted?" she asked in a wavering voice.

"It was my fifth birthday," he replied immediately. He stopped for a moment, surprised at himself, but continued. "I saw a cowboy movie on East German TV, and told my father I wanted to go to the land of the cowboys. He told me he was planning a trip, that we had a distant relative, a lady in New York City. I was so happy, I told the mailman about it the next morning. That evening..." He bit his lip.

She laid a withered hand on his. It felt like parchment.

"That evening they came for him, and he looked at me with a terrible pain in his eyes. I said good-bye, thinking he'd be back in a couple of hours. I didn't realize good-bye would mean...forever."

She said gently, "I'm sorry...David..."

His voice choked. "He had terrible claustrophobia, and tried to escape. They killed him." He hesitated. "I didn't mean to betray him. I only wanted to see...a cowboy. I was...five."

"Hush," she said gently. "David, do me a big favor. Get rid of that word 'betray'. And forgive yourself, like I'm sure your father has. I'll see him soon, and I'll make sure of it."

She patted his hand feebly. "Promise?"

He bit his lip and looked at her. "I can't really refuse, can I?"

"Thank you," she said, smiling slowly.

He stroked her hand gently. "It's been such a great honor to know you. Thank you for all the little cakes and treats that you sent."

"You're welcome," she replied. "How are you...otherwise? Do you have a nice girl you care for?"

"No, Agnes," he replied, doing his best to appear cheerful. "I can say with all honesty that at this moment you're the only girl in the world for me!"

"Then I'll go meet St. Peter..." She stopped for breath. "...with a great, big smile on my face," she said.

The effort was a lot for her, and she closed her eyes and labored for breath for a while. She didn't stop smiling, or stroking Bucky's fur, though each stroke became slower and lighter. David continued reading from the brochure. After a half hour, the stroking stopped, and then the breathing. Bucky's steady purring ceased abruptly.

David stood up and bent over her, carefully watching for signs of movement. He leaned down and placed a kiss on her forehead. "St. Peter will be proud to have you," he said, and picked Bucky up on his arm.

He met Molly out in the hall. "She's passed on," he said gently.

"Thank you so much for not letting her be alone," Molly said.

"I told you," he said. "It wasn't me, it was Bucky." He looked down at his companion, now settled comfortably on his forearm.

He hugged Molly with his free arm, and walked out the front doors into the clear and chilly night air. He looked at his watch, placed Bucky in the passenger seat, and got into the car. He pulled out of the parking lot quickly. As he drove, he heard commentary from his passenger.

"Urr!"

"You're saying that was something I needed to learn?"

"Eep!"

"You think you're so smart!"

"Murr!"

"Oh, blow it out your fuzzy butt!"

He pulled into the parking lot of Johnno's Beach Bar a few minutes later, hissing in frustration as he saw the doors being locked.

"You see what you did?" he asked the cat, who merely blinked his eyes.

Just then, he heard a cheerful voice. "Is that you, David? Do you have Bucky with you?"

The doors were speedily unlocked, and he was admitted into the bar by Sarah the bartender, who ushered him to a seat. She touched David's shoulder. "Thank you so much for being with Mrs. Goodfellow."

David shook his head. "Is there anything on this island that everybody doesn't know about immediately?"

Sarah smiled, and handed him a six-pack of Red Stripe. "I've closed the register, and am about to close up, so this will be on the house," she said.

David thanked her, and headed for his car. He heard a familiar voice, and turned to see AJ. He asked, "You and Leah left Auntie's?"

AJ nodded. "Yeah. She had stuff to do and it was getting...hot. How about you and Erika?"

David recounted what had happened, and said, "Johnno's closed. How about sharing my six-pack? We'll show you our secret spot."

AJ clapped him on the shoulder. "I'm in! I'll follow you."

They drove East, up a winding road that led to a little white church on top of a hill. David parked his car and led the way through the graveyard next to the church. They stopped by a tree that overlooked a steep cliff leading to salt ponds far below, lit with bright silver streaks by the moonlight. He sat down, and Bucky settled into his lap. AJ sat next to him, leaned back against the tree, and accepted a cold bottle. They could faintly hear the surf crashing to the West.

"Well, so much for Erika," David said as he looked out into a nighttime sky that was generously sprinkled with stars. Bucky sneezed, and wiped his nose on David's arm, to a response of, "Oh, sure. Feel free to use me as your snot rag."

AJ chuckled. "Don't give up. And don't get all jealous. Be happy. That's the best revenge."

David nodded. "I'll remember that." He paused. "AJ, if you could have anything, what would you want?"

AJ thought a minute. "Probably the Medal of Honor."

David's head snapped over. "What?"

AJ smiled ruefully. "I know that's impossible. But something like that. To make my father proud of me." He sipped his Red Stripe. "When I was young, I was kinda wild. But he always stuck up for me. He got a lot of shit from his family about that, since he was lily-white British, and he'd fallen in love with my mom, a native from this island."

David also took a sip. "Don't you give up, either. I know the outfit you work for gives out some great medals. You could get one."

AJ's head snapped left. "What do you mean, the outfit I work for?"

David laughed. "Please! I figured that out a while ago."

AJ said, "All right. What's the thing you want the most?"

"A home, for me and Bucky. I've moved from place to place all my life. Even my New York condo was in the name of my ex. I want a place I can call my own. I'm tired of being a Gypsy."

AJ pulled a fresh Red Stripe out of the box, and held it up. "All right. Here's to us getting our impossible dreams!" They clinked bottles together.

AJ looked around. "So this is your private place, huh?"

David nodded. "We come here at night to talk. Some of the people in back of us are old friends from the hospital. They never disturb us."

Bucky pulled himself up on David's arm, and burrowed under his shoulder, making him laugh. "All right. I'll stop feeling sorry for myself." He looked at AJ and shrugged his shoulders. "Actually, my biggest fear is losing him. What would I do without him?"

Chapter 13

Erika arrived at Paradise Island's small private airport in just over an hour, and was immediately whisked off to the resort area in a silver Mercedes. As she entered the hotel, a bellboy met her at the door and took her past the reception desk directly to her room, a suite on the top floor that faced the ocean. She heard the gentle *swoosh* of the surf as she opened the sliding glass doors. The balcony was over 20 feet wide, with chairs and tables and recliners. She left the door open so she could hear the soothing sound of the ocean, and fell into bed, exhausted.

She slept late, and woke to the sound of the phone buzzing. She was lying on a king-sized bed in her underwear. It was warm enough that she had thrown the covers off during the night. To her right side, the sun poured in from the open sliding glass doors. She picked up the receiver and was greeted by Fowler's cheerful voice. "Good morning, Erika! I trust you slept well?"

"Oh, yes, I did. Thank you," she replied.

"Come down to breakfast if you feel like it, and then I'll give you a tour of the facilities," he offered.

"Sounds great," she replied. "Can you give me 30 minutes?"

"Wonderful," he answered. "I'll send someone up to escort you."

After showering and dressing she went down to the start of a magical day. Fowler played the gracious host: he rose when she entered, made sure the breakfast she wished was delivered promptly, and ensured her every wish was quickly granted.

Several of the organizers of the International Paleontological Society Conference were guests at the table, and Erika noted with bemusement the deference they showed her—as an extension of the respect they paid to Fowler. Instead of being critical of her, as usual, they hung on her every word, as if she were Moses just returned from the mountain. Fowler explored the concept of opening a small museum on the island, with a section dedicated to ancient marine reptiles, and grants for explorations. She made suggestions, and Fowler complimented her on the creativity and soundness of her ideas, as the learned gentlemen at the table bobbed their heads in approval.

After breakfast, Fowler gave her a tour of the island on an electric golf cart. He showed her the open end of the lagoon, and noted, "That long metal gate across the gap extends underwater, and serves as a shark net to keep swimmers and our performing dolphins safe." They rode through gardens of native plants, looked at stables with a riding ring, circled around eight tennis courts, and then drove through the resort itself, with splendid pools and restaurants and high-end shops, all newly constructed. Fowler asked if she'd like to play tennis, and she agreed, delighted. He insisted that she pick out a racket and outfit at the Pro Shop.

The man behind the counter laughed when she offered to pay for the equipment, and gently returned her credit card. "Please, Miss," he begged her, "Don' make me look bad in front a' the boss."

Fowler played competitively, and they tied in the end, each having won two sets.

"You play very well," he complimented her with a flashing smile. "Let's leave the deciding game for later, shall we? You should always leave something for later," he teased, and winked.

She laughed, and winked back, and they went on to have a light lunch on the terrace, listening to the surf crash in the distance as a five-piece music group played Chopin for them. After lunch she let herself be talked into choosing another outfit from one of the stores, before changing and riding another cart down to the stables. She chose to ride English style, and picked out a Steuben saddle and a hunting bridle to adorn a tall roan gelding. They rode along the lagoon, and jumped over ditches, and she laughed out loud as they galloped through the surf, and he laughed with her.

After a nap she put on her best black dress and went down to dinner, and Fowler met her as she came down the staircase. He was dressed in a stunning designer tuxedo that she was sure cost the equivalent of at least one of her monthly paychecks. He complimented her gallantly, kissed her hand like a chevalier, and took her arm as he accompanied her to the dining room.

A butler announced their entrance. All the men at the long table in the private dining room stood, and he introduced her. The guest list was outstanding, and included many of the movers and shakers of the neighboring countries. Fine wine and food courses flowed by in a dizzying array. She knew that she was probably drinking too much, but it was all so good, and all so dazzling, and everyone was so nice to her, that she really didn't care.

After dinner and a spectacular flaming dessert there was dancing to the music from a 10-piece orchestra. Reginald swept her around the floor and told her what a great dancer she was, and she told him likewise. When the music slowed down he held her close and she nuzzled into his shoulder, tipsy from the wine and overjoyed with the glow of the day.

Later, when he invited her to his Penthouse Suite for a nightcap, she said yes, and rode up with him in a glass elevator that faced the sea. She was looking at the gently breaking surf on the lagoon shoreline when a mental image of David suddenly appeared to her, lying in the moonlight with Bucky on his arm. The elevator stopped with a soft ping, and the doors opened with a sigh of air. She forced the image of David out of her mind with a shrug and the thought of, "Bloody hell with him _and_ his cat!" and turned to follow Reginald.

He pressed his palm against some sort of security screen by the side of the doorway, and two beautifully carved walnut doors opened up before them with a soft hiss. He put his arm around her and guided her into the suite, and then turned and locked the doors behind them with a definitive click.

Chapter 14

Monday morning opened with industrial-gray cloudy skies, a rising breeze and a slight chop on the water. Erika arrived at the Global Explorer punctually at 8 a.m., exiting from a white Mercedes. She declined the help offered by the chauffeur, and carried her own suitcase on board, passing David talking on his cell phone while supporting the irrepressible Bucky on his left forearm.

"Good morning, you two," she called out cheerily.

"Good morning, Princess," he replied, somewhat less cheerfully, as he turned off his cell phone. He looked her up and down. "Looks like you got a nice tan over the weekend," he remarked carefully, keeping his voice neutral.

"Yeh. It was great," she replied, keeping her eyes hidden behind her new oversized Yves St. Laurent sunglasses. "That's a really beautiful resort out there. The development company was able to buy the whole island, so hotel guests can go anywhere."

"Yeah," David answered off-handedly. "The new owners pulled a few strings with the government to buy it. I know they had to spend millions on tons of dynamite and dozens of Caterpillar tractors, to widen the entrance to the lagoon, level the land around it, and build the resort and marina. The island used to be a bird and wildlife refuge. I guess the birds and wildlife all had to relocate, to somewhere they could afford."

He looked at the sky, ignoring her sudden crestfallen look. "I hope this weather doesn't get much worse. Go ahead and get settled in. We'll be underway in 20 minutes. We'll use aquasleds today instead of diving off the Zodiacs."

He turned away from her and activated his cell phone. Erika started to say something, but, seeing his back was turned to her, shrugged and walked off to her cabin. David turned to look after her, turned off the cell phone, and glanced down at the cat spread-eagled on his arm.

"Well, I think we handled that rather well, don't you?" he asked his feline friend, who replied with, "Gurr-meep."

"Yes. I thought so, too," David replied, "We've entered the 'just friends' part of the relationship. Well, I guess she and Fowler belong together." He then made the final arrangements for departure.

Several hours later, they arrived at the GPS location where the periscope had been found. The sea was calming down, with a slight breeze from the West. The water was clear, and ranged in color from azure to deep blue. Erika noted that Dragon/Paradise Island was much closer now, riding high on the horizon. They all gathered on deck, and checked out their diving sleds, which resembled jet-skis, but were lower and electrically powered. Each Kawasaki XLT sled had a short windshield, motorcycle-type grips and a seat long enough to hold two adults, who would ride bent forward so as to be more aquadynamic. There were storage compartments under the seats, and straps on the sides to attach spear guns and other equipment.

It had been decided that David, Erika, Moshe and three of the crewmen would make the first run together, on six of the brightly-colored sleds. The Kawasakis were lowered into the water by a sling. Each person jumped into the water from the diving platform, found the proper sled, climbed on, and started it up.

"Don't forget to keep a sharp eye on the depth gauges on your sleds' dashboards," David spoke into the microphone built into his mask. "When your sled gets up to speed, it's easy to go up or down a couple of atmospheres' worth. Better not take chances with the bends."

Erika and Moshe grunted in answer. David could not tell whether it was out of respect or annoyance. They slowly approached the spot where the periscope had been found, and stopped for a moment. Erika and Moshe played with the controls until their sleds hovered just above the bottom.

"Let's stay abreast, and keep moving in an Easterly direction," David continued. "You two," he indicated the two paleontologists, "please also keep an eye out for anything metallic, and we'll let you know if we find anything bony. We have enough air and battery power to go around a section about five kilometers on a side each day. We'll enter anything we see on our electronic maps, and also put down marker flags, so we can come back and take a closer look later on."

They proceeded to map out the area of the square throughout the day, diving as long as they could with double tanks, returning to the ship to rest while the next shift took over, and then getting back into the water again.

Chapter 15

Later that night, David sat in his customary chair on the rear deck, his feet up on the lowest rung of the railing. Bucky was draped over his legs. David was smoking a Rocky Patel cigar, and waved it in the air as he made points in his discussion with Bucky, who responded periodically with alternating grunts, *meeps* and growls.

"Is this a closed party, or can anyone join in?" asked a voice from the side. Erika appeared, wearing a gray sweat suit with "University of Melbourne" on the chest, and looked down at his glass. "What kind of swill are you drinking tonight?" she asked.

"Not good enough for you, I'm sure, princess," David replied coolly.

Erika removed the bottle from the second chair and sat down while looking at the label. "Glenmorangie single malt, 12 years old, with a secondary aging in Madeira barrels," she read appraisingly. "Hmm. Not bad. I had you figured for Old Crow or some kind of moonshine."

David was about to make a retort, but Bucky rose up from his perch and jumped into Erika's lap. She smiled down at him and scratched behind his ears. He purred rhythmically.

David sighed. "Shit!"

Erika looked at him. "What's the matter?"

David looked down at the cat. "I had it all planned out. I was going to be all pissy with you, and ignore you as much as I could. For at least the next month. I was going to say things like, 'Why don't you get your boyfriend to do that for you?' or 'How come your rich boyfriend doesn't give you that?' But now..." he waved at the cat, "Bucky adopted you. So I can't stay mad. Damn. I was really looking forward to it."

He looked at his bottle of scotch and offered it to her. "Would you like some?"

"Sure. Let me just get a glass, thank you." She rose, forcing the cat to jump back on David's lap, and ran off. She returned moments later with a cut crystal tumbler, and poured herself a generous shot. "Mm," she said, as she savored the amber liquid. "God, this tastes good."

She fished a cigar out of David's cigar case, cut off the top, and lit it, settling back as she blew smoke rings in front of her. "Ah," she said. "I needed that."

David sighed again as he looked at the cigar she was smoking. "Sure, smoke my best Cubans, too. Make yourself right at home."

He looked down at the cat, who had sauntered back over onto Erika's lap, and looked sternly at him. "Traitor!" he said.

Erika leaned back in her chair, putting her feet up on the same rail that David's feet occupied. "So what do you two do when you're back here?" she asked. "Just stare out into space?"

"Not at all," David replied. "Sometimes I read aloud to Bucky. We have serious discussions. And we play music." He leaned over to pick up a ukulele. It was made out of beautiful Koa wood in shades of salmon red and light yellow and dark gold. "We specialize in show tunes and rock," David added.

"So, do I get to hear one?" she asked.

"Sure," he replied. How about some Nickelback?

Someday, somehow,

She joined in, in a clear, strong voice,

Gonna make it alright.
But not right now.

They finished it together, laughing out loud.

She looked out into the distance in the fading light. "So we're all right, then?"

"Yeah. I guess so. Damn it." he replied, smiling ruefully in the darkness.

Chapter 16

On Thursday, the teams started diving at 9, and continued for most of the day in alternating shifts, taking advantage of outstanding weather and clear water. By the time they came back on board at the end of the day, all of them were cold and exhausted. Wearily, they sat around the deck pulling off their diving suits and equipment, and slowly went through the motions of rinsing their hardware with fresh water and putting it back on racks in the Equipment Room.

They had found various clues—some fossils, a few pieces of metal—but nothing breathtaking. David talked to Erika.

"It's time for us to go back to the Eastern part of the search area. I can't afford to spend any more time here."

"How about just a couple more days?" Erika pleaded. "I like having both of us searching in the same area. Better to keep off sharks and things."

"All right," he said gruffly. "But that's it. After that, we split up."

Later that evening, Erika finished typing up a report, and closed her laptop with a snap. She grabbed a light jacket to ward off the evening chill, and headed toward the stern of the ship. She could hear singing. She peeked around the corner and stood there for a few moments, watching.

David's laptop was connected to a projector that showed Karaoke videos on a white wall, with his back to the ocean. He reclined on a deck chair, and was in the middle of Enya's *Caribbean Blue*, singing and strumming along on his ukulele. Bucky perched on his legs, letting out an occasional "Mawrr" in time to the music. She smiled and shook her head at the incongruous sight, and then stepped forward to join them.

She plopped herself into an empty chair and looked down at a bottle of Oban Single Malt. She picked up an empty crystal glass from a small table. "You were expecting me, eh?" she asked.

"No. Sometimes Bucky has a sip or two," he replied.

"You're teaching that cat bad habits," she retorted.

"What other bad habits can he really get into?" David asked. "He's neutered. The state you'd probably like to see every man in."

"It's what you all deserve," she replied. She poured herself a generous helping of scotch.

David shut down the computer and projector, and turned his chair so it faced the ocean. They talked about that day's dives, and plans for the next. The level in the bottle had dipped dangerously low when David said, "You never finished telling me about your social life as you grew up."

"It's not that interesting."

"I told you about mine. Your turn."

"All right," she relented. "I grew up in a little town in the country, far West of Sydney. My father was a supervisor in a mining camp. He was hard on us, me and my brother. I think he was lonely–my mother left when I was little."

"There wasn't much to do in our town. When I was in high school, the only recreation on a Saturday night was to get a six-pack and jump into the back seat of a pickup truck. I got really drunk one night and a couple of blokes talked me into making out with them, because we were really close friends and all. The next day my 'friends' immediately told everybody that they'd scored. We didn't even do it, we only fooled around some, but nobody believed me. After that, my reputation was mud, and my friends turned on me. I couldn't wait to get to get out of there. In college, I dated a few guys. Got my heart broken once by a guy that I thought was a friend that turned out to be a real master at lying. I tried not to repeat it."

"Finally settled for a nice, boring bloke in graduate school, and said 'Yes' when he asked me to marry him. After a while, he made me crazy. He was so predictable. I noticed I was happier away from him, somewhere on a dig or doing research. Eventually, we called it off. I started coming to the States a lot, and working with the Natural History Museums in New York and Washington, DC. I studied ancient marine life because I loved the ocean. I got my doctorate, and applied for a post-doc grant about a year ago, to study fossils in this area. I finally got the award—but had to share it with this madman. You! And that's about it."

David cut the tips off two Cuban Cohibas and handed one to her. "So you've been a tad sensitive about men and whether to trust them ever since, eh?" he asked as he lit it for her. "And you think all men are either milquetoasts or bastards?"

"Pretty much," she replied. "Except for Reggie. Maybe he'll break my streak of bad luck."

"I don't think luck is how it works," he replied. "Have you ever met somebody that seemed really different and terrific, and then turned out to be just like the others?"

"Yeh. Too right," she said. "So what do I do?"

"Let's ask Aunt Marie," he said. He reached for a satphone and speed-dialed a number.

"Hi, Auntie. We have a problem. Erika thinks all men are bastards and not to be trusted. Can you help her out? I'll turn on the speakerphone so we can both hear you."

They could hear Aunt Marie chuckling on the other end of the line. "Many are. But you should discover that with eyes wide open, instead of already having already made the decision going in."

"You haven't met some of the blokes I have," Erika said.

"Oh, yes, I have, child." Marie replied. "But it's what you bring to it. You gotta trust somebody."

Erika frowned. "But there are people you obviously can't trust. Like DuBois."

"Yes, you can. You can trust him—to be himself," Marie said. She added, "So, how about it, Erika? Can you let it go? Honestly"

"I don't think so," Erika responded. "It may not be possible."

Marie's voice sounded like warm honey. "As impossible as a little bird flying backward? Have you watched the hummingbirds you see all over the island?"

Erika took a sip of scotch. "Tell you what, Aunt Marie. How about I come meet you next time I'm in town, and we talk girl to girl. I'll bring the wine."

Marie said, "I'll look forward to it. I'll make my special rum cake."

Erika said, "It's a date." David said good-night and disconnected. She looked out at the ocean for a while, then at her empty glass, then at the bottle sitting on the deck to David's left, and said crossly, "Are you going to hog that whiskey the whole bloody night?"

The next day started uneventfully. David decided it was his turn to accompany the two paleontologists. He trailed behind and above them in his aquasled, glancing at them every few moments while scanning the walls of the underwater valley they were passing through. He saw a 5-foot tall sunfish suspended in the water to his right, a few dozen feet from the ridge, and idly motored over to look at it. He looked at the silvery disc-shaped body, which reflected the sun's rays shining through the water. Its dorsal and ventral fins were extended at a straight vertical above and below the body, and gave the fish a unique appearance, as if it had been compressed in a giant waffle maker. As he got closer, the fish twisted its body rapidly from side to side and shot off. The sudden movement loosened a small avalanche of silt and rocks from the side of the hill.

David was about to turn back when he noticed an unusual pattern emerging. He turned off the aquasled and dismounted, holding it by a nylon rope as he swam up close to the hillside. He clawed off some rocks and sediment, and the water became turbid as more of the hillside slid into the valley below. What he saw looked like a set of prison bars, about a dozen large slats of dense material. He swiped at one end with his gloved hand. The vertical bars continued on into the hillside. He finned himself backward and hung in the water, looking at the pattern.

"Hey, Erika. Can you hear me?" he asked loudly.

"Yeh. You're breaking up a little. Where did you go?"

"I'm behind you a hundred yards, and about 10 yards up. Could you come back here, please?"

"All right," she said with a trace of irritation in her voice. David backed up more. The form in front of him became clearer.

"What is it?" she asked as her aquasled approached. Moshe was a few yards behind her.

"Come here," he beckoned.

She got off her sled. He grasped her shoulders and turned her around, putting his hands over her mask to shut off her vision.

"I haven't got time to play games, David," she said. "We were just looking at a stratum that had some promise. It..."

"Stop being such a tight-ass," he replied. "And get that condescending, professorial tone out of your voice! Now, take a deep breath."

He pointed her in the direction of the hillside. "If you had the bones of one of your beasties in front of you, what would it look like?"

"Well...all right. The head would be in front, of course. The jaws would be partly open, and the neck twisted—muscles contract when the animal dies. The head would be followed by the ribs, which would continue for several dozen feet."

"What do the ribs look like?"

"They're curved, but they're so long that from the side they would look almost vertical. They—"

He took his hands away from the front of her mask. "Like that?"

Her eyes started to focus. She swam closer. "It couldn't be. It is. But it couldn't be. Oh, my Lord!" She gently touched the row of ribs of the fossilized animal in front of her, one after the other. "It looks like a Mosasaur. A very large one. It might even be a complete skeleton." She turned to him. "How did you..."

"I was just doing a little investigation," he said modestly. "I remember a Discovery Channel show where they found a whole T. rex in the side of a hill. So I checked this hillside, while you two were playing in the mud below." He decided to omit the fact that he had come across the fossil totally by accident.

Moshe chimed in from the background. "This is still the same layer we've been looking at, around 30 million years old. If it's really a Mo, it means you've proved..."

"No!" She cut him off. "Don't say it. Don't jinx it. Let's excavate first." She turned toward David and touched his arm. "I don't know what to say. This is..." She lifted up first her mask, then his, and kissed him full on the lips. They pulled their masks back on, quickly clearing them of water.

"This is so exciting!" she exclaimed. "This is—is that your hand on my butt?"

"Yes, it is," he replied cheerfully. "This is where you throw yourself at me. Second base, at least. Though we may have to wait till Moshe leaves."

"You're incorrigible!" she replied, laughing, as she pushed him away. "But, seriously, thank you." She turned back to Moshe and her tone became more businesslike. "Let's get started on photographing the site. If there are any loose fossil parts, we can take those with us for analysis. Once we get topside, we'll have to call for help with the dig. We've got a major project here."

Later that night, David was sitting on his usual deck chair, with Bucky on his lap, when Erika came to join them. She presented a bottle of Cline Zinfandel, noting, "I got some wine lessons from AJ. This is a rich, fruit-forward California wine. Did you hear me use a wine term, 'fruit forward'? Actually, it's too good for the likes of you." She filled his glass and then hers before collapsing onto the chair. "Good Lord, I'm tired."

He smiled at her. "All right, since you've bribed me with something really decent, we might as well do something besides singing and chatting on these evenings. Since it looks like you'll have some big news to present at your next conference, let's work on your presentation."

"No, no. I'm too tired," she whined. "Maybe some other night..."

He was relentless. "No, right now!" He pulled her up to a standing position, and returned to his chair. "OK, Bucky and I are your audience. Let's hear you give a 5-minute version of what you'll present." He looked at his watch. "Go."

She started, "G'day, ladies and..."

He stopped her. "Lose the accent and slang. Say, 'Good afternoon, honored members of the Society, ladies and gentlemen...'"

Reluctantly, and with much theatrical sighing and rolling of her eyes, she started up again.

"Good afternoon, honored members of the Society, ladies and gentlemen. I am here to present my findings on...what?" She stopped as she saw David whispering to Bucky. "What are you telling him?"

"I'm telling him you get distracted too easily," David replied. "Keep going. The show must go on, no matter what happens in the audience."

She started again. She was some three minutes into her speech when David stopped her.

"What's your concept of communicating?" he asked.

"What?" she replied, confused.

"Communicating. You know, the 'C' word. What you're supposed to be doing right now. What do you think it's really about?"

She thought a minute. "Why, I guess I have some knowledge and I'm trying to transfer it to the audience."

David shook his head. "Sorry, wrong answer. You can't transfer knowledge. You can only transfer information. We audience members have to recreate that within our own backgrounds and experience to form knowledge."

"So?" she shot back.

"So right now you don't care about whether we can recreate what you're throwing at us, or not. You're just shoveling it like dirt onto a coffin. How about you give us the info so that we really care about it, so it's meaningful to us?"

She looked annoyed. "What would you know about giving scientific presentations based on research?" she asked him.

"I've done more research of professional literature than you've dreamt of," he replied. "It's how I used to spend every day and weekend. And I wrote peer-reviewed articles, and gave presentations. And I won in court, over 95% of the time. And I got paid about $1,000 an hour to do it."

Her eyebrows shot up. "A thousand US dollars an hour?"

"Yes," he answered, looking pointedly at his watch. "That's what I would charge for this. What you're pissing away right now."

She looked contrite. "I didn't really mean to...I'm just tired and I thought..."

He grinned wickedly. "You know, that act would really have worked on me while I was trying to get into your pants. But now, I'm immune. Tough love, baby. Start from the beginning. Go for five minutes. And I want ten times the energy!"

She started again, and went through to the end. He demanded a repeat, with more dramatic hand motions and facial expression. After the third take, he applauded and poured a generous glass of wine for her as she collapsed onto her chair. He grasped her hand as he clinked glasses with the other and told her, "You did good today. In more ways than one." He held on to her hand for a few minutes, and she did not snatch it away.

The following night she came to the same spot and smiled as she saw that David had set up a several cutouts next to him, so that they looked like a row of audience members. "Ah, how nice. I see you've brought friends. They probably have more personality than you do."

David had a notebook on his knee, and waved with a pen. "Enough chitchat. Take it from the top."

She rolled her eyes. "Oh, God. What's next?"

Erika found out what was next on the following night. As she turned the corner at the stern of the boat, she saw David's laptop and projector set up, displaying a bright picture against the white wall, which served as an impromptu screen. She was astonished to see that the image was of hundreds of audience members sitting in rows, moving, talking to each other, coughing and making a hundred other noises, all of which were played by two stereo speakers set along the wall.

"So tonight I have a whole audience," she said.

"Yes, you do," he replied. "It was created by Moshe. He's a genius with Computer Generated Imagery and animation. Don't they look life-like?"

"Oh, yes," she said sourly. "He's very good at fooling you into thinking something's real, when it's not."

"I see you brought your notes. Start from the beginning. And with some energy, please."

She started out, but found herself distracted by the audience noises. "My throat's really dry," she said, reaching for a wine bottle. David pulled it away. "Nope. Not till you've completed tonight's lesson. Let's go."

She started again, and misspoke a couple of the words, and then got lost in her notes. "Damn it to hell," she moaned. "Why is this so hard?"

"You know what the biggest fear that people have is?" he asked her. "In survey after survey?"

"What, fear of flying, or fear of falling?" she replied.

"No, fear of public speaking," he answered. "What you're feeling right now. What we're going to work on. What you're going to master."

He pointed to two of the CGI audience members on either side of him.

"Don't look at the whole audience. Lock eyes with a couple of people in the front rows that look friendly, one at a time. Look at that person as if she or he is the only one in the room. What are you feeling right now?"

"Terror," she replied.

"You're thinking too much about what you look like. You're afraid you'll look like a fool, right?"

"Oh, yeh. Too right!" she replied, biting her lower lip.

"Good. Now start hopping up and down on one leg and do your presentation. Start now."

"What?" she asked, not believing her ears.

"It's a technique you're going to use. You no longer have to worry about looking like a fool. You're now guaranteed to look like one!"

"You're doing this just to humiliate me!" she said heatedly.

"No, it's academically sound. It's called exposure therapy. I did my Psychology Master's degree dissertation on it."

She stared at him.

"What are you waiting for?" he said impatiently. "Start hopping!"

She shook her head firmly. "No. I can't do this."

He shrugged his shoulders and looked at Bucky in the adjacent chair. "Not surprising. She's a wuss. I told you."

Anger crept into her voice. "I'm a what?"

"A wuss. New York expression. A cross between a wimp and a pussy."

"You're calling me a bloody coward?"

"No. Much worse! A wuss dreams of one day becoming a coward!"

Her eyes narrowed, and she glared at him. Different emotions flitted across her face. She complied, hopping on one foot, then the other, as she started again. "What I am presenting today is..."

"Don't look at me," David said. He pointed to the CGI figures on the screen behind him. "Look at the friendly faces in the audience."

She made a face and stuck her tongue out at him.

"That won't help you," he noted. "Also, could you be a little more enthusiastic, please? Let's try doubling it."

He glanced down at Bucky, who was now reclining on his lap, and staring intently at her. David looked her directly in the eyes. "The monster, here, and I are counting on you," he said. "Take it from the top."

Chapter 17

Thursday started with David hitting the snooze button on the alarm clock to get another 20 minutes of sleep. Unbidden and undeterred, the unstoppable Bucky marched over his chest, brushing his long and bushy tail across David's face until he sat up, laughing.

"OK, OK! I give up!" He shrugged into a pair of jeans and a T-shirt and walked out on deck, with Bucky leading the way. He went into the galley to grab a quick cup of coffee, and brought it with him as he sat down on a deck chair. He took a deep breath as he enjoyed the vision of the sun beginning to blaze in red-gold bands on the horizon. Bucky jumped on his lap, demanding to be stroked with a free hand as they watched the sunrise together.

"G'day. You two are early risers," commented Erika, coming up to them in last night's sweat suit.

"Not voluntarily," David replied, looking grumpy. "I love sleeping in. But Mr. Oh-boy-it's-morning here has to get up at the crack of dawn, and insists that I join him."

Erika looked at the cat fondly. "Good on ya. I saw you have a little gym set up. I'm going to go work out. Cheers!" She left, with both David and Bucky looking after her.

David rose. "Might as well make my rounds," he said to the cat. "Come on." Bucky followed him closely, swiveling his head from side to side in unconscious imitation of his master.

Later that morning, David drove a bright yellow aquasled next to Werner, who played wing man on a turquoise sled. Another team with Mark and Larry was exploring a hundred yards away, and they could see Erika and Moshe working on their hillside in the distance. They were scanning the bottom as they moved at about 100 feet depth along the side of a sheer ridge that rose to within 20 feet of the surface. David suddenly got a reading on the portable magnetometer mounted on his sled.

"Hold it!" he said. "I'm getting something." He moved the control for the instrument. "It looks like there's some kind of metal somewhere on this ridge. Let's take a look," he suggested.

They proceeded along the side of the ridge, at slightly different depths, scanning for clues. David checked his instrument. "The reading's getting stronger. But it's not on the bottom, it seems to be inside the mountain," he said, disappointment evident in his voice. "Probably just some kind of mineral deposit."

"Ah, what the hell," Werner said. "Looking at a hillside instead of only below it seems to have worked out for Erika. Let's take a look, just to break the monotony." They scoured the side of the hill slowly, occasionally reaching out to poke or pull at some feature or irregularity.

Werner started describing a small cave he had found, when suddenly he gasped, "Whoa!"

"What's the matter?" David asked, coming closer.

"Look at this," Werner whispered. "From a few feet away it looks like one of the many small caves in this wall, but when I shine my flashlight into it, it seems to go on forever."

"Really deep?" asked David.

"It looks like it might get wider further in," Werner replied.

David shone his light into the opening as the two other teams approached, sensing something was going on.

Erika asked Moshe to hold onto her aquasled, and approached the tunnel, asking, "What's up?"

"We've found what may be a tunnel," Werner replied. "See? The coral we see here is just a shallow coating that's concealing a larger round cave."

"Round?" she asked. "It's like, literally, round?"

"Unfortunately, it's pretty narrow. I don't know if we can get in," Werner noted.

"Let me take a look," Erika said, crowding in. She stuck her head into the opening and looked around with her flashlight as shed said, "I can get in here, if I take off my tanks. As soon as I'm through, one of you hand them to me through the opening."

She took off her vest with its attached air tanks. She took an extra-deep breath through the air valve in her face mask, and then handed her equipment to David. She swam through the opening, and turned around to take the vest and tanks that David pushed after her.

"Are you OK?" he asked.

"Yeh," she said, her voice blurry until the microphone in her mask was cleared of water. She swam around on the other side of the opening. "It really opens up in here."

"Let's expand the opening," David said, and started to hack at the coral with his diving knife. Werner and Mark joined him, and for the next ten minutes the only sound was that of hard breathing from the strenuous effort. They managed to expand the opening so that a diver could easily swim through it with SCUBA jacket and equipment.

"This looks like it keeps going for quite a while," Erika said. "Let's see where it leads. Maybe there's an old Spanish ship's cannon in here that gave you that metal reading."

"All right," David sighed. "We'll take the time to take a look, if it'll make you happy." He turned to the others. "Moshe, Larry, can you hold onto our sleds, please, while we go inside and check this out?"

He turned to follow Erika, who had already started to swim further forward. Swimming closely behind her with his flashlight gave him ample opportunity to check out her long legs, with tightly muscled thighs that were perfectly outlined in her skin-tight Body Glove neoprene diving suit.

"Keep an eye out for moray eels," Erika said. David jerked his head back, away from his guilty pleasures. He bumped into Werner, who was following close behind. "Oh, sorry," he muttered. "I was distracted."

Werner grinned, "Yes. And it wasn't eels that were distracting you."

They swam past the opening for about 30 feet, after which they merged into a much larger cave, which extended to the left and right to distances their flashlights could not penetrate. Erika played her light along the wall of the cavern.

"You see how smooth the sides are?" she asked. "We've come through the coral into a volcanic lava tube. Actually, that's not so strange. This whole area of the Caribbean is riddled with them. They often have smooth round sides like this, and can extend for hundreds of miles."

"It looks like something erupted out of here," remarked David, looking back at the opening they had come from.

"Think again, mate," Erika retorted. "Maybe something erupted *into* here. Let's check the other side of this cavern. It looks huge."

"It looks several hundred feet..." David started to say, and then an object in front of them started to take form, illuminated by the combined beams of their three flashlights. He gasped, and then exclaimed, "Holy shit!"

David swam up to it slowly, not daring to say anything for fear it might suddenly disappear. Then he came suddenly to life, and started pointing at things.

"Look! This is a propeller! And here's the drive shaft, bent and broken, but it's there. And these are—were—diving planes. It's..." He took a deep breath and expelled it, releasing a cloud of bubbles that sparkled in the reflected beams of the flashlights. "It's the ass end of a submarine! In fact, it's the stern end of a U-boat. A large U-boat." He turned to Erika. "That would explain the metallic readings I was getting. But how the hell did this thing get in here?"

"Excellent question," said Werner, treading water next to them. "It looks like it was barreling along at full tilt and crashed right into the side of the mountain, coming to rest right here."

"But how did it get so deep into a solid mountain?" asked David.

"Because it's not so solid," Erika replied. She shone her light behind them. "That wall back there is very thin, and the boat pierced through it. It looks like it then went through this cavern, and got stuck in a side tunnel."

"Like a cork in a bottle," David breathed.

"Yeh," she replied, "Like a bloody cork in a bloody bottle."

"We could probably explore this cavern and look for other tunnel openings on the left or right," commented Werner. "We might be able to come around on the other side of the boat."

"Not right now, we're not," David replied. "We're not going any further without proper lights."

He grinned sheepishly at Erika, who was suspended in the water only a few feet from his face. "I have a touch of claustrophobia. Caves give me the willies. We'll order lights and power supplies, and come back as soon as we get them. We also need some serious oxyacetylene torches to open this thing up. I never dreamed we'd find the U-boat still in one piece, more or less." He shined his light back at the boat. "Let's take a quick look inside, to see what we can see."

About 20 feet of the sub hung out in the space of the cavern; the rest of it was hidden in the tunnel it had burrowed into. They could see there were long, wide rents on the left side of the sub, and parts of the interior compartments were exposed. They probed through the gaps in the side with their flashlights, illuminating ghostly remnants of what had once been rooms filled with colors and bustling life, but now reduced with a uniform gray coating on everything. The only life forms were a few small fish that stared back at them with wide-eyed reflections of the lights.

"We appear to be in the rear torpedo room," David noted. "U-boats could fire to the rear as well as to the front." He held up a hand to the others. "Stay here, and let me go forward. That way you can help me if I get stuck on something." He disappeared through a bulkhead, flippers waving slowly behind him.

He reappeared a few minutes later, breathing heavily. "I had to push a lot of junk aside," he explained. "This compartment and part of the engine room in front of it are ripped open. But the hatch to the forward compartments is sealed. We'll have to go in to St. Maarten and get torches, and a lot of tanks. And stationary lights for the work crews, and lights with batteries and automatic sensors to turn them on for the tunnels around here."

He motioned to Larry. "You and I will start ordering as soon as we get back on the ship. I hope nobody listens in to our signal. We'll have to go ashore for a couple of days to pick everything up. Some of it will have to be expressed in from Miami," he said. He tapped notes on his waterproof tablet.

David halted before they entered the passage back into open water. "Let's talk just a minute while the others can't hear us." Erika, Larry, Mark and Werner looked at him expectantly. David continued, "Don't mention that we found the sub to anyone else on the ship. We'll tell them after we've picked up the equipment in St. Maarten and returned here. From then on the ship stays here—we can't let anyone go back on shore and talk about this."

"You really don't trust anyone, do you?" Erika asked, a tinge of sarcasm in her voice.

"You got that right, lady," David replied.

Later that night, David and Bucky were at their usual spot on the stern when Erika approached. She threw herself into a chair next to them. "Oh, man, I'm bushed. What a day." She looked down to see a bottle of white wine cooling in an ice bucket. "Wow, Gainey Reserve Chardonnay. Yum. I can really use some of that," she said, reaching for the bottle.

"Uh, uh," David replied, pulling the ice bucket out of reach. "First we have our lesson. Go up and give me a presentation about Mosasaurs and make me care about them."

"But I'm totally tired," Erika howled.

"Doesn't matter. You may be totally tired on the day you do your next presentation. You still have to give it your best. The show must go on."

Slowly, muttering under her breath and rolling her eyes like a teenager, she got up and stood in front, facing them. "What do you want to know?" she asked shoulders slumping melodramatically.

"What's so great about this Mosasaur?"

"You don't make presentations like that to the Academy. You have no idea of what scientific presentations are about. You have to..."

"Fuck the Academy," David retorted. "In this economy, you're not going to get much in the way of research grants for the normal shit the Academy loves, and you know it. Your only chance is with

TV or documentary makers like the Discovery Channel or the BBC." He added as an afterthought, "Or maybe the SyFy Channel."

Since she still hesitated, he prodded her. "Why have you wasted your whole life studying this useless animal?"

She glared at him, visibly annoyed. She was about to make a retort when he tapped his watch and said, "I'm the Discovery Channel. You have 5 minutes. Make me care."

She gathered her thoughts. "The Mosasaur was a historic animal. It started as a small land reptile, about one meter long, and went to the ocean when dinosaurs made the land too dangerous."

"Its comeback was something to behold. Within a few million years it spread throughout every region of the ocean, as well as into lakes and rivers. It adapted to its prey. In the shallows, it remained small, and developed grinding teeth to break and chew mussels and other shellfish. In the open ocean, it developed long, sharp teeth kill its prey. In the lakes and rivers it grew into just about every configuration in between. No other animal has ever covered the globe like the Mosasaur, and done it so successfully."

David stifled an exaggerated yawn. "Everybody knows that the rulers of the seas were the giant sharks, like the Megalodon and the Ginsu. Lots of sharks have been found with Mosasaurs in them. Your precious animal was just Spam lunch meat."

"Yes, it was," she replied angrily, "For a while. That's when it was still small. Within 5 million years, it grew to massive proportions, larger than a Megalodon. After that period, it was *Mosasaur* stomachs which were found with *sharks* in them. Not only that, but they were apparently able to leap totally out of the water—lots of Mosasaurs have been found with pterodactyls inside them. Since pterodactyls usually cruised some distance above the waves, that must have been a hell of a jump."

"They still wouldn't compare to the real kings of the sea, the plesiosaurs," David responded. "A short-necked one like Liopleurodon would probably beat the crap out of a Mo. And the long-necked plesiosaurs, the ones that looked like the Loch Ness monster, with rows of teeth like daggers, would've been invulnerable. They could use that neck to strike your Mo like a snake, over and over, long before the Mo could get close to the animal's body. It had no chance."

"That shows just how little you know," she shot back, her face starting to color a bright pink tinged with red. "The Mosasaur developed something no other animal had. The ability to saw through the toughest bones, including the neck of your precious plesiosaur. Its lower jaw had a hinge at the back, like an elbow, so it could move front to back, independent of the upper jaw. It worked like a huge razor-sharp saber saw, against the vulnerable part of the plesiosaur, that long neck. We have fossils where such animals were literally sawed in half."

Her nostrils flared with her anger. "Sharks have never been able to do that. Their jaws are wide, but not very deep. They hit something and take a bite out of it, and then back off, hoping it'll bleed to death. A Mosasaur like a 50-foot Tylosaurus did no such thing. It went in like a warrior, ripping through its enemy's body with those reciprocating jaws, not letting go till it had won. It was the most advanced killing machine the world has ever seen."

"You're telling me this monster's mouth was like an 8-foot chain saw with teeth over 7 inches long?" David asked in mock horror.

"That's exactly what it was. Nothing like it has been seen before or since. Compared to that, your Tyrannosaurus rex was a Cub Scout."

"Wow," David replied. "That's amazing. Now I'm really surprised and interested."

"You damn well should be!" she answered heatedly.

"Good, good. That was much better," he said. "You might want to use that 'T. rex of the Sea' term more often. The Press will love it. You forgot to mention the teeth on the roof of their mouths, so they could pull prey down their throat like a devil's assembly line."

Her eyes narrowed as she looked at him. "The teeth on the roof of the mouth..." she started.

"Yes, the ectopterygoid teeth," he offered helpfully.

"How the hell do you know about the bloody flaming ectopterygoid teeth?" she demanded heatedly.

"I told you," he said as he bent down and removed the Gainey wine from its ice bucket, and removed the cork. "When I was young, I was in the Museum of Natural History a lot. I learned a few things. But do you ever listen to me?" He filled a glass with straw-colored liquid and offered it to her.

He settled back in his chair, with one arm behind his head. "OK, we managers of the Discovery Channel are sold. We love it."

She held the glass between two fingers and looked at it. "I should dump this all over you. But I'm dying of thirst, and it's way too good to waste."

She sat down hard in a chair, facing away from him. "You're mean and duplicitous, and a real son of a bitch and I hate you!" she said heatedly.

He smiled as he took a sip from his glass, and poured a little into a dish for Bucky.

"By the way," she said. "My close friends call me Rika."

Chapter 18

The next day was Saturday. The Global Explorer was anchored within Great Bay in St. Maarten. David was on his way to meet up with AJ and Leah in Marigot after running a few chores in Philipsburg. He kept a small white Toyota in the harbor parking lot, since he spent a lot of time on the island, which was split in the middle. The North (Saint Martin) belonged to France, and the South (Sint Maarten) belonged to Holland. Marigot was on the West Coast of the French sector, and had a Farmer's Market every Saturday. This is where they had agreed to meet at 11.

He parked the car, took out the cat carrier with its passenger, and walked up to AJ and Leah. To his surprise, he saw that Erika was with them. "What are you doing here?" he asked her. "I thought you'd be at the Dragon-and-Paradise Resort today."

She shook her head. "Nope, no go. I've been stood up. Reggie says the Resort is off limits today, 'cause they're having a meeting of investors. They're also doing construction, putting in lights and other stuff to get it ready for the Grand Opening in two weeks. So I guess you're stuck with me today."

David looked at her appraisingly. She had on a powder-blue-colored polo shirt with the Global Explorer logo, blue jeans and Nike Air running shoes. She glowed with good health, and her sun-streaked hair was tied up in a ponytail that made her look like a teenager. "I guess I can suffer through it," he said. "OK with you?" he asked the cat carrier. "Mii-urk," the cat carrier answered.

He grinned at AJ and leaned over to kiss Leah's cheek in greeting. She was dressed in a flowered white sundress that contrasted well with her light-milk-chocolate skin, with brightly colored bangles on both wrists and strapped sandals on her feet. AJ had on a tight black T-shirt that showed off finely chiseled musculature, and stylish black jeans that contrasted with old-fashioned penny loafers without socks.

They walked through the colorful Farmer's Market on Boulevard de France, stopping to look at the homegrown produce, tropical fruits, handicrafts and spices for sale, backed by smiling salespeople. The air was heavy with the scent of fresh vegetables, overlaid with the enticing aromas from mounds of spices and roasted coffee beans piled on the vendors' tables. They passed a kettle drum band, whose rhythms added to the exotic atmosphere. The three colorfully clad musicians broke out in wide, bright infectious smiles.

Towering over them, across Marigot Bay, was Fort St. Louis, which had been built in 1767 in honor of the ill-fated French King Louis XVI. It offered a panoramic view of the island and the sea surrounding it, for anyone energetic enough to brave the steep climb to the summit.

David took Bucky out, and left the carrier with someone he knew at one of the stalls. Bucky rode proudly on David's left forearm, surveying all that went by with great interest. David bought a bottle of local spice sauce from a middle-aged woman who had a red scarf on her head and a body that generously filled a blue muumuu patterned with yellow flowers.

AJ joked with Erika, "Hey, you ought to try some of this hot sauce." He pretended to think it over. "Or maybe not. They probably have nothing sharper than ketchup in Australia, eh?"

She gave him a stern look. "A lot you know! We have pepper sauce that would take your flaming head off!"

David opened his pint bottle, which had hand-painted flaming peppers on the side. He poured a sample of an evil-looking scarlet concoction onto a large corn chip that he took from a bowl on a table.

Erika grabbed it eagerly and wolfed it down. The look of satisfaction on her face was soon replaced by one of horror. "Mother of God!" she mouthed. "What is that, battery acid?" She waved her hand at her mouth, desperately trying to cool it off as she whipped her head around to look for water. She ran to a stand selling water and grabbed a bottle.

"That won't do it much good," warned David. "It only spreads the heat. What you really need is milk or yogurt." He picked up a bottle of liquid yogurt from the stand and paid for both drinks.

Erika ignored him, and seemed to inhale most of the pint bottle of water. "Aaaaarghhh!" she yelled. She had lost the ability to form words. "Buwing! Ith thill buwing!"

David calmly pried the top off the yogurt bottle and handed it to her. "This would have been the logical solution."

She gave him a wild-eyed, evil look as she took it from him. The relief showed on her face after the first swallow. "Ohhh."

"I tried to tell you," David said, pretending to look offended. "But do you ever listen to me? Nooohh..."

She tried to speak, but was unable to. All she could say was, "Oogh."

"You see, the acting agent in the hot sauce, capsaicin, is oil based, so the water just spreads it," he expounded pedantically, mimicking and exaggerating Erika's tone when she was in her professorial mode. "Dairy products contain casein, which binds to this active ingredient and neutralizes it."

Since she was still unable to speak, David continued to expostulate. He held the hot sauce bottle to his nose and took a whiff. "And you would want to neutralize this, because it contains Scotch Bonnet peppers, also known as habanero, with a Scofield rating of around...oh, 10 million units or so. Wouldn't you agree, professor?"

"I really hate you," she stammered, staring at him fiercely. Tears streamed from her eyes. Then, noticing that Leah and AJ were doubled over with laughter, she amended her pronouncement. "I really, really hate all of you!" She sniffed as she finished the last of the yogurt. Then, unable to hold it in, she starting laughing herself, helpless in the moment.

As she wiped the tears out of her eyes, she gave David a sharp look. "Were you making fun of me?" she asked. "I'm not that pedantic! Am I?"

"No, you're not," he retorted. "You're much worse."

She punched him lightly once on the arm, and then again, and he made "Ow! Ow!" noises as he danced away, carefully balancing Bucky on the other arm. "Take it back or you're a dead man," she threatened.

"OK, OK, you're not that bad. There's hope for you," he recanted, laughing.

She hooked her arm in his as they started walking again. "All right, mate, you're forgiven," she granted.

With harmony restored, they wandered back through the market, enjoying the riot of colors all around them. They snacked at Lolo stands, the local name for outdoor barbecues, and then ate lunch on the waterfront at Le Belle Epoque Brasserie, sitting outside under an umbrella with a view of the bay. They laughed and talked and ate salads with fresh lobster. They toasted each other with a refreshing, crisp, La Crema Chardonnay that was the color of lemon drops.

Leah looked up from her salad to see a hummingbird feeder outside the restaurant with three hummingbirds perched on it, raising their heads up and down as they sipped the sweet red nectar. "Look," she said. "Hummers. They're gorgeous!"

"Yes, they are," David agreed. "The Native Americans hold them as sacred. They believe that because hummingbirds fly backwards, they can help people forget the past. Instead of being stuck in it." He looked at Erika. "That would be good for you. Get rid of all that man-hating and sarcasm built up in you."

"Oh, yeah, you should talk," she retorted. "You're the one with the trust issues he can't forget."

She turned to the others. "I know one thing *I'd* like to forget. Yesterday the son of a gun managed to slip a replica Mosasaur tooth into the stuff we brought up in the diving bag. Moshe and I got all excited, till we saw it was made in China." She glowered at David.

He tried looking scholarly. "I did mention that preliminary investigation indicated it was probably from the Plasticene Era!"

They all laughed, even Erika. "He's impossible, but I put up with him," she said. "He reminds me a lot of my brother Kevin. He was my best friend all through childhood, especially after my mother left. I miss him terribly."

"What happened to him? Did he die?" Leah asked with concern.

"Even worse than that," Erika replied. "The wanker got married. His wife started popping out kids like candies from a Pez dispenser, and he became totally domesticated. Whenever I visited, she hovered over him, waving rug rats around in the air. I couldn't get two sentences in a row with him. And he put up with it!" She shook her head. "God, I miss him." She picked up her glass and took a sip. "How did you and AJ meet, Leah?"

Leah glanced at AJ with a soft smile. "I had just finished my Master's Degree at George Washington U., and was celebrating with friends at Mr. Smith's bar on M Street. AJ was running a wine tasting session with clients, and invited our group to join him. I told him I was job hunting, and he invited me to interview with his company. They hired me the next week."

"What was your Master's in?" Erika inquired.

"Police Science."

Erika laughed. "Interesting background for marketing in the liquor business."

"Yes. It is," Leah agreed, and quickly changed the subject. "How did you get into paleontology?"

"I have a theory," David volunteered.

Erika snorted. "Oh, this ought to be good."

"Since God apparently turned normal human emotions into a no-fly zone for her, I think she looked around for something she could relate to, and bought one of those pet rocks. Probably carried it around everywhere, named it Rocky or something. Then, when it died after a month from lack of warmth and total neglect, she looked around for a field with other rocks in it. And discovered paleontology, where you can get paid for cozying up to fossils."

Erika turned to Leah for support. "You see what I have to put up with?" Leah whispered something into her ear, and they both laughed.

David turned to AJ and whispered. "Doesn't she have the greatest laugh? Deep and throaty, like Cameron Diaz."

AJ whispered back. "You keep claiming that you and her are just friends, huh?"

David responded, "Yeah. Didn't you hear her? I'm like her brother."

Leah looked at the two of them and asked, "What are you two reprobates whispering about?"

Both of them shrugged their shoulders and answered, "Nothing," at the same time, and then broke out in guilty laughter.

As they got ready to leave, David said, "Back in a minute," and disappeared into the kitchen.

"What's he doing in there?" Erika asked. "Hustling the waitresses?"

"He's thanking the cooks and the staff personally," AJ replied. "Even the waiters. He usually does that."

"Why?" Erika asked.

"Because he used to be one," AJ replied. "It's how he worked his way through college."

When David came back, Erika slipped her arm through his and walked next to him.

He looked at AJ. "She's being nice to me. What's wrong?"

"Stop being so defensive," she said.

He laughed. "All right. But I know I'll pay for it in the end." He looked at her with a crooked smile, and said, "You should come with a warning label."

She said nothing, but smiled mysteriously.

They drove in AJ's car to the Butterfly Farm on the East Coast of the island, and ran around like children on holiday, making goofy faces and flapping their arms up and down. They took photos of each other standing in front of bushes covered with thousands of wings beating with blazing neon colors. Leah had a butterfly settle on the tip of her nose, and she stared at it cross-eyed, as her three companions dissolved in helpless laughter.

They stopped at a large new shopping complex located below Fort St. Louis. They walked past Gucci, Ferruci, Yves St. Laurent and other major brand name shops before they found one within their price range. After they entered, AJ and David settled back onto a beige leather couch and sipped coke and rum from plastic cups while the girls tried on a variety of fashions.

Erika came out with a loose beige knitted dress that was gathered in at the knees, accessorized with a bright multicolored scarf and a wide lime green belt. "Does this make my arse look fat?" she asked the two men.

David sputtered. "Oh, God, does it ever! It makes your ass look like it needs its own ZIP code!"

He ignored Erika's dark and evil look as he turned to AJ and expounded, "Isn't it great to be with women when you're not trying to get into their pants?" He turned to the girls, trying to look apologetic. "Oh, sorry. I meant to say women whom you're not 'in relationship' with?" He fist-bumped with AJ, who grinned. "You can just tell them the truth and not worry about getting cut off—I mean, getting them emotionally upset."

Erika turned to Leah. "I used to think he was a boorish, egotistical, totally selfish troglodyte with his head up his arse. Then I saw him with Bucky, and thought, 'Maybe he's not *totally* selfish.'"

David turned to AJ. "See? She's as tough as jailhouse steak." He stood up and approached Erika to look closely at the baggy knit dress that she had picked out. "Just as I suspected, you're hopeless. You look like a Martian trying to fit in at a Romanian wedding."

She started to reply, but he held up one hand, palm out, for silence. He marched past the nearby racks, staring intently and flipping through jackets. "You need a sports jacket. Let's see, Navy blue, perhaps." He picked a jacket off its hanger and threw it to her. "When you're traveling, always go dark. A light colored outfit like that knit job you're wearing is just begging for coffee to jump on it."

"And to go with it, something lighter and livelier," he muttered to himself as he walked down a row of skirts. "Ah, here it is! Electric blue." He picked up a bright blue, moderately-short skirt and threw it to her. "Try those on."

Leah and Erika looked at each other in the dressing room, trying on their next round of clothes. "You know, those two are having way too much fun," Erika said. "We need to take them down a peg."

"Speaking of going down, how are things going with Reggie?" Leah asked, grinning.

"Who?" Erika asked innocently, as she adjusted her thong underwear before pulling the skirt up.

"Don't ask me who!" Leah chided her. "You've spent a whole weekend with him. How are things between you two?"

"Great," Erika replied. "He's really nice. Super connected. Has traveled a lot. Great dinner table conversation."

"And..." Leah prompted. "And..."

"Well, yes, he's a good kisser."

"And..."

"And a great dancer. And a good kisser."

Leah laughed. "He seems strung awfully tight. I can see him wearing a tie with his pajamas."

"He's a proper English gentleman. Table manners you could write a book about."

"I have my suspicions about those 'proper gentlemen.' I think they're often proper on the outside, and real perverts on the inside." Leah changed her tack. "How about David? You seem to get along with him really well..."

"I like him, but I don't go out with people I work with. And to tell you the truth, I need friends more than lovers. My life is littered with friends whom I got intimate with who then got all funny on me and disappeared."

"I noticed that red thong you're wearing. If you're not seeing Reggie today, is that for your 'friend' David?"

Erika's face blushed bright pink. To take the heat off herself, she went on the offensive. "How about you and AJ?" she asked. "I sense sparks flying in the air between you two." She raised her eyebrows. "Have you ever...?"

"No, we haven't," Leah replied with regret. "And, unlike you, I'm not going to dance around it. I'd rip his clothes off and do him in a minute if I got the chance. He's kind, and he's smart, and he's damn hot. But..."

"But?"

"But he says we can't do anything if we're working together. It's against Company policy. And I can't quit the job and be unemployed. My parents would kill me!"

Erika laughed. "Aren't we the pair!" She looked in the mirror. "Krikey! This looks damn good!" She looked at Leah putting on a bikini, and said, "What the hell!" as she pulled the skirt up a couple of inches.

Leah was first to exit, wearing a Hawaiian-print bikini with cover-up. She pretended to be modeling on a runway, and walked straight-legged to the two men, twirled, settled back on one hip, and then walked back again. Both men wolf-whistled their appreciation.

"Woo-hoo!" AJ shouted. "Is that thing legal?"

Erika came out next, wearing the outfit that David had picked out for her. The skirt was now quite short, and displayed a fair amount of suntanned thigh as she walked.

She did the same model's walk that Leah had done, but stopped in front of David and looked down at him, swinging her hips.

"Well?" she asked.

David's brow remained furrowed.

"Hang on, hang on," he said. "You need shoes to go with that."

"I'm wearing shoes," she said petulantly, looking down at red pumps with very high heels.

"No, no, not those come-fuck-me shoes," David muttered. "Your feet are too wide for them, and you sway from side to side in those heels. You look like Minnie Mouse after five martinis. Let's see, what's your shoe size?"

"I'm a 9," she said firmly.

"OK, then, that means she's a 10," David said to himself. He went to a rack and picked up a pair of sandal-style black leather shoes with moderate cork wedge heels and high leather straps. "Here. Put these on."

"Are you sure you're not gay?" Erika asked, as she looked at him skeptically.

David chortled. "No. I just spent a lot time shopping with my ex, Gloria, who dragged me around New York stores with her. I have a pretty good memory, which is useful for a courtroom lawyer. I learned to recognize basic styles. Tommy Choo, Ferragamo, Manolo Blahnik, Yves St. Laurent, Christian Louboutin. I've won court cases because I could tell the jury how much the cry-poor defendant's outfit and jewelry cost. And all my clients were dressed appropriate to their juries." He waved an arm at her outfit. "This is a basic clean Chanel look. And that skirt color is great. Electric blue really suits you."

Erika sat down to put on the shoes, causing her skirt to ride up.

"Wow," said David. "Red undies." He turned to AJ. "If only they were for me. But alas, we know they are not." The two put their arms around each other, pretending to comfort one another with melodramatic sobs, ending in laughter.

Erika stood up. "If you two are finished making fun of me..."

David untangled himself from AJ and walked over to her. He looked down at her shoes and made a turn-around motion with his hands.

She complied, rotating in place. He nodded. "OK, looks good. Try walking in them."

She did so, and he nodded in satisfaction. "Perfect. They have a lot of support, and the heel looks sexy but is not too high. You should be able to climb stairs in them, up to a podium."

He put his finger to his mouth. "One more thing."

He went to her handbag and rummaged around in it. "You wear reading glasses when you do your presentation, don't you?"

She was about to say "Yes," when he pulled the case from the purse. He extracted the glasses and handed them to her.

He smiled at her. "OK, go back and come out again. "Like they say in Hollywood. Once more with feeling!"

She returned to the dressing room and remained in there for several minutes, checking out her hair in the mirror. She then took a deep breath and came back out again, and all three of her companions stared at her. She radiated sex and power and confidence, all at the same time.

"Well?" she asked, unsure of the meaning of their silence.

"You look magnificent, Rika," David said, his voice hoarse. He looked down as Bucky made a "Meep, urk," sound. "Bucky says you're going to take over the whole room as you enter. You're as electric as the blue in that skirt!"

"Yeah," AJ added. "Power Ranger meets naughty librarian!"

Erika looked at David with wonder. "Really? I look good?"

"You look... You're a wonder," David replied, his throat dry. He composed himself. "Tell you what. I'll make you an offer."

She looked at him suspiciously. "Which is?"

"I'll buy that outfit for you. It'll be my gift."

"Really? And what do I have to do in return?"

David hesitated. He swallowed. "Don't...don't wear it for anyone else. Just put in on when you do your next presentations. OK?"

She nodded, taken aback. "Yeh. Sure. Thanks very much. I love it."

He turned to AJ as the two women walked back into the dressing room.

"Her next presentation should be a knockout," he said cheerfully.

AJ looked him straight in the eye. He shook his head from side to side and laid a heavy hand on David's shoulder. "Oh, man. I didn't realize. You got it bad. You're really screwed!"

David regarded him scornfully. "You should talk. When Leah came out in that bikini, your tongue was hanging out so far you could've used it for a necktie!"

AJ looked rueful. "It doesn't matter what I feel. I can't date someone I work with, especially when I'm her boss. My employer absolutely doesn't allow it."

David chuckled. "We're quite a pair, aren't we? Oh, well, I'm having a really good time. You take what you can get." He looked up. "Here they come."

They spent the rest of the day exploring, and decided to eat dinner at the Claude Mini-Club, where AJ knew the owner. The restaurant was built to resemble a tree house, built around the trunks of huge palm trees. The décor was Haitian, with the vibrant colors and music of that troubled country. They sat down around a thick primitively carved wooden table, on a terrace that opened out onto the sea.

David toasted Erika with a glass of Cline Pinot. "This is a great Pinot Noir, I think you'll like it." He held the glass up in front of her face and started to recite, speaking slowly and earnestly.

"It's a hard grape to grow. It's uh, thin-skinned, temperamental, ripens early." He lowered the glass and laughed. "You two should get along really well." He stopped laughing and yelled "Ow!" as she kicked him under the table.

AJ took up the recitation, looking into Leah's eyes and speaking in a low, seductive voice. "Only somebody who really takes the time to understand Pinot's potential can then...coax it into its fullest expression."

Leah laughed. "Are you two playing characters from the film *Sideways*? Which one of you is which?"

David shrugged his shoulders. "Well, there goes our big seduction scene. They're onto us. That's what happens when you go out with smart women."

They were interrupted by a waiter, who replaced the candle holder in the middle of their table. He smiled nervously and left.

A bottle of Nuits-Saint-Georges arrived, and Erika tapped the label with a chewed-on fingernail. "Saint George reminds me of something. When the first Mosasaur was found, in 1780 next to the river Meuse in Belgium, people couldn't figure out what it was. It was suggested that it was an ancient dragon, of the kind that St. George was famous for fighting."

Leah looked at her. "Remarkable, how your Mosasaurs seem to be tied in to all these legends of dragons and flying snakes and sea serpents. And caves. Those dragons always lived in caves. You would swear there were still some around, with so many stories about animals that look like that."

Erika shook her head. "I think people just dug up giant fossils and made up tall tales to explain them."

Leah took a sip of the wine. "That makes sense. But it's amazing how these legends are everywhere. Aunt Marie told me that there've been sightings of Mokele-Mbembe all over Africa, wherever there's an ocean or a really big body of water with caves near it."

AJ said, "Right here would be a great place for it. There are more caves in the Caribbean than anywhere else on earth, both above and under the water. The Arawak legend has it that gods lived in these caves and held mankind captive. Man eventually escaped from them and became free."

Leah continued. "I heard you say these monsters could jump up in the air, and shoot out electricity. Isn't that what dragons did? Except they would have called it 'fire' long ago, because they didn't know about electricity."

A guttural growl interrupted their train of thought. David looked down at Bucky, who was resting in his lap. He smiled as he baby-talked to the cat. "Is somebody hungry? Is my monster feeling neglected?"

Erika raised her eyebrows as she listened to David's speech. "Where did you get that from? Talking with hookers in a pouf?"

David shook his head. "I've found that baby talk can disarm even fierce opponents." He turned to AJ. "Remember, that time your uncle's big-ass Rottweiler came charging out? I talked like this to him, and it kept us from getting eaten alive!"

AJ nodded. "I'm his witness."

David continued, "But there you have the problem with intelligent, sarcastic women. As soon as a man gets a little...soft, they have to jump on him. I pity any guy that's Erika's friend and then tries to get schmaltzy with her."

Erika snickered. "Schmaltzy?"

He retorted, "It's a perfectly good New York term. It means to let your guard down, try to get a little intimate, romantic. AJ, help me out here."

AJ leaned forward to emphasize his point. "I agree. When I'm with that kind of woman, I feel like the Starship Enterprise in the middle of Klingon territory. I can survive, but I have to keep my defensive shields up all the time."

Erika clucked her tongue. "You know that schmaltz is just nonsense that guys use to take advantage of gullible women and get in their pants."

AJ looked at her and imitated a *Star Trek* voice. "This is the Captain speaking. Scotty, get me maximum power on all shields."

David put his glass down with a thump. "Let me demonstrate. Leah, what would you say if I told you that you look great today? By the way, you do. Absolutely radiant."

Leah flashed a blindingly white smile. "I'd say 'thank you.' And you look very gallant today, as well."

"Now," David continued, turning to Erika. He softened his face, and seemed to be swooning at her. "Whenever I think of you, I feel like bells are ringing."

She looked at him levelly. "Bells... You mean, like a garbage truck backing up?"

He swept his arms at the others, who were laughing. "Ladies and gentlemen, I rest my case. You see, she just can't help it."

She snorted. "What's wrong with a good round of give-and-take? Can't you men handle it?"

AJ answered. "It's great between friends, but sucks when the guy is trying to get a little action. It would feel like sticking your dick into a meat grinder." He turned to Leah. "Pardon my French."

Erika was about to retort when they were interrupted by the sound of her cell phone. She looked at it with curiosity. "Odd. Almost no one has this number."

She held it to her ear, and her eyes widened. "Reggie! Great to hear from you. Where are you?"

She listened, and then said, "That sounds like fun. Hold on. Give me a minute." She searched for the Mute button on the phone and pushed it before looking at the group. "Reggie came back to town early. He just invited me to dinner at the Dutch Ambassador's house. I guess I could go, since we haven't started ordering or eating anything yet. Is that OK with you guys?" AJ and Leah shrugged their shoulders. She looked directly at David. "Would you mind?"

David looked her directly in the eyes. "Of course you can go. I have no claim on you." Before she could start to say anything, he added, "But..."

He picked up Bucky and turned him to face her. "Look at him. He'll be disappointed and miserable. You'll break his poor, fuzzy little heart."

She looked at the cat, which let out a plaintive "Me-yowl." She pushed the Mute button again. "Hi. Reggie? I'm so sorry, It turns out I'm tied up already tonight. Will I see you tomorrow morning? Yes? Wonderful. I'm looking forward to it." She turned the phone off and put it into her purse, and scratched the cat's head. "I couldn't disappoint you." She gave him a quick kiss and then stood up. "I've got to hit the Loo. Leah?"

Leah joined her, and both women departed for the Rest Room.

AJ glanced at David, who looked self-satisfied, and said, "Let me get this straight. *You* don't have to tell her how *you* feel. You never have to stick your neck out with any of that emotional stuff. You just say, 'That's how *Bucky* feels.'"

David nodded vigorously. "Yeah. It works like a wonder. And if things go wrong, I can just blame him for it."

AJ looked down at Bucky. "Amazing how he always speaks up when you need him."

"That's easy," David replied. "Look. When I scratch his tummy here, he makes this *urk-urk* sound." Bucky quickly complied.

AJ shook his head. "Man, I get all tongue tied with that emotional shit. I have *got* to get *me* a cat!"

Chapter 19

Outside the restaurant, a white Toyota Land Rover was parked with two men in it. The window was rolled down, revealing that one of them had headphones on, and was watching the volume dial on a small handheld digital recording machine.

"I think that damn waiter forgot to turn up the volume on the microphone," he growled. "I can barely hear them over the background noise."

A cell phone rang, and he took off his headphones to answer it.

"Well?" DuBois asked. "Have they mentioned anything about finding the submarine?"

"Not yet," the man replied.

"Let me know when you have something," DuBois replied, and the line went dead.

The girls rejoined the men at the table, and they drained the rest of their bottle of wine. All four of them decided on the Seafood Buffet, and stood in line while scooping generous helpings of lobster and fresh fish and colorful steamed vegetables onto large square white china plates. All four chattered non-stop, and the laughter increased in volume as they heightened their experience with white California wines, moving through the Sonoma region from North to South like a conquering army.

"What's everybody doing tomorrow?" David asked. "I've got an early flight to Miami to pick up equipment and fly back with it in the evening. I don't want to take a chance on having the wrong stuff show up here."

"Do you need any help?" AJ asked.

"No, I'm good. I've got Larry and Ben going with me to help carry stuff. The waterproof video cams and lights with long runs of cabling are going to be heavy. Bob is taking the ship to San Juan to pick up the acetylene torches and tanks; we can't ship those by air."

Out in the street, the man activated his cell phone and hit the "Return" button. When DuBois answered with a curt "Yes?" he said, "They just talked about picking up lights with long runs of cable, and acetylene torches. And the ship is going to Puerto Rico."

"Damn!" DuBois replied. "They found something. If they're getting lights, they're either planning to work at night or they're going into caves." He thought a moment. "Keep listening, and let me know if they say anything else. Then get back to me. We need to check out that site before they get back with their ship."

"OK. Out," the man replied curtly. He put his headphones back on, and stared through the open walls at the two couples in the restaurant.

AJ continued the conversation at the table. "Leah and I have to meet some customers in Montego Bay," he said. "We'll be back in a couple of days."

"Reggie is picking me up tomorrow morning to go to the Resort," Erika replied. "I'll be back in plenty of time before you sail Tuesday morning."

"So you'll be working on your tan while the rest of us are slaving," noted David.

"Not really," she replied. "I've got a lot of work to get done. I've got to hit the books and do background research for my presentation next month."

"Where will that take place?" AJ asked.

"In New York City, at the American Museum of Natural History," she replied. "You're all invited, of course."

"Will you tell them about your Big Mo?" David asked.

She nodded. "With the caveat that it's not fully excavated yet, and the findings are only preliminary."

"Will there be dancing girls?" AJ asked, teasing.

"No, I'm afraid most of the members are so old they fart dust," Erika said with a frown.

"In that case, we'll probably stay here and watch all the really exciting bits on YouTube," Leah replied.

"How are things going at the resort?" AJ asked.

"I think the construction is almost finished," Erika replied. "They're putting in all the lights this weekend. They're still hiring people, so they're not fully staffed yet."

"Is DuBois on the island a lot?" Leah asked casually.

"I wouldn't know, Erika replied. "I heard that he's off doing something else this weekend." She dropped her voice. "Reggie told me that he doesn't really trust him, that he's up to something. He doesn't like DuBois being at the resort if he's not there to watch him."

"When will regular guests be coming in?" Leah asked.

"The Grand Opening is in two weeks," Erika said. "Reggie said they're already booked for months. There aren't that many rooms available, and they're trying to make the place pretty exclusive. Room rates are exorbitant, five or ten thousand US a day."

"You mean they're trying to keep out riff-raff like us," David said.

"I'm sure they want to keep out riff-raff like *you*," Erika answered him, grinning. David noted her eyes sparkled in the candlelight, and glinted on her porcelain-white teeth as she smiled. He noticed the direction his thoughts were moving in, and forced himself to look away.

The light drizzle outside turned into a sudden downpour. They heard fat raindrops splattering on the roof. Behind the restaurant, car tires made sizzling sounds while navigating the shiny wet blacktop road. Bucky jumped up on the table and looked out at the rain disconsolately. David fondly pulled on his long, bushy tail.

"Don't worry, monster," he said. "I picked up your cat carrier. You won't get wet."

Bucky sneezed loudly, twice. Everyone said, "Bless you." He turned to David and crawled onto his arm, wiping his nose off thoroughly on his shirt sleeve in the process. David looked at him in mock sternness and rolled his eyes up dramatically as he asked, "Is that all I am to you, just a big snot rag?"

AJ looked around the table, grinning. "I think the riff-raff are having a great time. What could the guests on the island possibly have that we don't have here?"

Chapter 20

The rain clouds did not extend as far as the Paradise Resort, which was bathed in moonshine. About two dozen guests were in high party mode, in a roofed-off recreation area that had been built on top of the lagoon. It featured a bubbling, above-ground Jacuzzi, two long bars, and cushioned couches and love seats covered in pearlescent leather and arranged comfortably in circles. An open gas fireplace in the center shot up flames, and Tiki torches were arranged around the perimeter, creating a South Seas atmosphere. The lagoon in front had underwater lights which turned it a radiant turquoise. The lights extended under the transparent glass floor, which caused the illusion of walking on top of the water of a giant aquarium.

The partygoers were in the midst of maximum intoxication with minimum clothing. One of the drug lords attending had laid an ounce of his wares onto a glass table, where three young women were using razors to lay out long lines of the white powder. A fourth was using a hundred-dollar bill to snort one of the lines.

A small round stage with a brass pole in the center of it had been set up on one side, and a redhead on it gyrated to a booming version of "Lo Que Paso, Paso," which also played on two 60-inch video screens nearby. A short, portly man with a crown of dark hair encircling his head attempted to stuff bills into her thong. Two waiters walked around with bottles of Cristal, refilling anyone who waved an empty glass.

A young man with a short, neatly trimmed beard slowly sank deeper in the Jacuzzi. A thin, anxious looking man with a wispy beard, was speaking to him anxiously. "This cannot be a good idea, my prince. Our guards are searching everyone to make sure there are no cameras of any kind in here, but I cannot be sure."

The man in the tub waved his arm around, drunkenly. "You worry too much, Ali. Join the party."

The man shook his head. "No, my prince. I cannot. I will go outside and keep an eye on the guards." He bowed and left, walking backwards for the first 5 feet. The young man smiled and looked down. A brunette appeared out of the bubbling water, gasping for breath, and carefully picked a hair out of her teeth.

One of the nearby men reached out for a young blonde walking by and pulled her onto his lap. She shrieked, but then settled down and put her arm around his neck. He nuzzled an extremely enhanced, Portobello-mushroom-shaped breast, which popped out of its lacy baby-blue bra restraint. As he came up for air, she looked at him drunkenly. "Hello. I'm Rosa. Who are you?"

"You can call me Juan," he replied, starting to undo her bra from behind her back.

She did not resist. "Who are all these other guys?"

His eyes left her cleavage for a minute to look around. He nodded at various people around them with his head.

"That guy on the couch getting head is from Miami. His name is Armando or something. You wouldn't believe how much money he throws around. The gal with him stars in a telenovela. The fat guy pawing the stripper is head of a police department in Venezuela. We call him El Puerco behind his back. The two sitting on the couch trying to do a human sandwich with the bottle blonde are the Marcos brothers. They're with a group that runs product to the Northeast. The guy pouring Cristal on the black lady in the pink boyfriend panties and licking it off is with one of the cartels. He's the CFO or something. The bearded guy in the Jacuzzi with the lady playing pearl diver is somebody's guest or business partner in the Middle East. The girl with the raccoon-makeup eyes riding the guy on the floor and yelling "You're so big!" is an actress. Not a very good one—she doesn't even have the rhythm down right. The guy's a nobody, somebody's assistant. But, she hasn't discovered that yet. The guy next to the fireplace who's rolling weed is Roberto. I think he's a producer and director."

"A director?" she asked, perking up. "You say his name is Roberto?'

"Yeah," he said. "I'll introduce you as soon as you've done me." He looked toward the corner of the area. "And the guy on that far couch, who's getting a lap dance from the redhead while talking on his cell phone, is named Ricardo. He's high up in some big cartel."

"Does he own the cartel?" she asked.

"No, I don't think there is a head of anything here. I think they're all directors or managers working for the real high rollers, and were sent here to see if this is really a place where we can do anything we want."

On the far couch, the man named Ricardo pushed the girl away from him impatiently. He walked out of the area, beckoning to one of his bodyguards. "I've got to find a place to talk. It's so loud I can't hear myself think," he told him in passing.

They walked down the path surrounding the lagoon in darkness. The main lights were not yet lit. The only illumination came from rows of twinkle lights that ran up the base of many of the trees.

The guard stayed respectfully at a distance as Ricardo finished one call and started another.

Deep in the lagoon, the female Mosasaur circled warily, followed by her two offspring. They had emerged from the tunnel that led into the mountain caverns a few minutes before. Her keen sense of hearing resulted from a long-leverage bone in her inner ear that amplified sound over 40 times. She could hear porpoises squeaking, and decided to investigate. She ran into a double iron fence circling an area for trained animals in a corner of the lagoon, beyond which three porpoises huddled in terror in a distant corner. She could have jumped the fence, but was distracted by the unfamiliar sights and noises of what had once been a quiet lagoon.

She cruised the surface rapidly, moving her massive tail to propel her to speeds well over 20 knots. Her two young offspring, each 15 feet long, could barely keep up. Suddenly they heard a voice, carried succinctly over the water from the walkway. They approached slowly, and saw two men, one of them speaking. The female turned toward her male offspring, and signaled him with short bursts of electric clicks.

Ricardo was on his third conversation. He was screaming into the phone, threatening to kill someone if he did not deliver on time. He heard a sudden rushing sound, and jumped back in surprise as an enormous animal charged out of the water and snapped at him with a long jaw full of razor-sharp teeth, missing him by inches. A wave of water rebounded from the concrete walkway, dousing him. He called out to his bodyguard. "There's a crocodile here! The damn thing almost bit me!"

The bodyguard approached, pulling the strap of his Heckler & Koch MP5 submachine gun off his shoulder and flicking off the safety. He stood there for a minute, wondering why the animal was remaining still and not chasing after Ricardo. Instead, it gave a short flick of its head and then turned sideways. The bodyguard took careful aim and was about to pull the trigger when there was a sharp snapping sound, followed by an arcing blue flash through the water. Ricardo started to say something to the guard, but instead snapped into a macabre, jerky dance. His eyes flew open and then started to bulge outwards. They gradually emerged from their sockets, looking like hard boiled eggs with painted-on pupils. His arm jerked up spasmodically, throwing the cell phone over 30 feet into the lagoon. It sank quickly, passing by the left eye of the 70-foot long female.

The guard started to back up, and turned to run. He ran off the walkway, away from the water, until he reached the base of the cliffs circling the lagoon, about a hundred feet away. He stopped to look back, and saw the strange animal illuminated by the cheerful twinkle lights while tearing great chunks out of his erstwhile master. "At least I'm far enough to be safe," he thought to himself. He was unaware that the distance was little more than one body length of the monster gathering speed in the lagoon.

The giant female launched herself out of the water, hit the ground and wiggled her body twice, covering the distance to him instantly. She twisted her head slightly to seize him in her massive jaws. The lower jaw pulled back and forth twice, sawing his body between two rows of 9-inch teeth with serrated edges. He separated cleanly, his upper and lower body dropping to either side of her mouth. She seized the upper body, the face still wide open in incredulous surprise as she forced it down her gullet. She snapped up the legs and lower body in one gulp, and then turned around in a rolling motion.

A few undulations of her long body, aided by her four giant fan-shaped flippers, and she was back in the water, where her young offspring joined her with a splash.

Back in the party area, the redhead had joined Roberto and was puffing on one of his creations. She was joined by Rosa, who had completed her other duties. Roberto told them he produced porn in his spare time. He set about posing the two ladies in creative and stimulating positions, backing away periodically to kneel down and look at them through a simulated camera viewfinder formed by his two thumbs and forefingers.

No one asked after Ricardo or the bodyguard until the next morning, when the room service maid asked whether they had checked out. A quick check by the front desk showed that most of the guests had left that morning. It was assumed that he must have hitched a ride with someone.

Many of the guests at the resort were the type that came and went suddenly, without alerting others to their plans. Whereas the yachts and aircraft entering into the resort were scrupulously searched to make sure their passengers were invited guests, the guards usually gave exiting vehicles barely a second glance. When several more guests departed unexpectedly over the next few nights, no one became concerned.

Chapter 21

On the Global Explorer, the four friends had a nightcap. They were exhausted from their adventures, but did not want the day to end, as yet. When Leah found out that David and Erika sang Broadway tunes on many nights, she decided the four of them should try it. The play they chose was *Mamma Mia*, and they sang the ABBA songs, interspersed by hoots of laughter. Some of the ship's crew joined them as audience, and whistled and applauded after each song.

They had finished three songs when David suggested *I have a Dream*, the song that began and ended the show. All four of them launched into it. David gave a subtle sign, and gradually AJ, Leah and he stopped singing and sat in the deck chairs, leaving only Erika to continue.

She never wavered, and even hit some high notes on the, "I believe in angels," parts, and then finished with a heartfelt, "I have a dream!" at the end.

The listeners applauded. David rose and put his arm around her shoulders, and said, "Ladies and gentlemen, can you believe it? She used to be shy. When I first saw her, she was almost peeing into her more than amply wide pants." He reacted with an "Oof!" as she dug her elbow into his ribs, but continued, undaunted, "And just look at her now!"

The other crewmembers murmured words of appreciation at Erika, and then wandered off, leaving the four of them alone.

Bucky let out a loud, "Mauwr."

David translated. "That means he's proud of you."

Erika looked at Bucky, and said, "Aww!" She kissed him on top of the head, and then got up. "I've got to go pee."

Leah also rose. "I'll come with you."

AJ looked at David after the two women had left. "Bucky says he likes her. Bucky says he's proud of her. You just go ahead and say whatever you feel, and then you claim Bucky said it?"

David grinned. "Yeah. You just need to know how to scratch the secret spot on his tummy."

AJ whistled. "That's great. Can he do any other tricks?"

David nodded. "Sure. Watch this. Pretend that one of us just farted." He looked sternly at the cat. "Bucky! How could you!"

The cat, which had been looking up at them, suddenly looked down, as if in regret, and put one paw over his nose. David laughed, and fed him a couple of small cat treats out of a tinfoil bag.

AJ considered all this for a moment, and then asked earnestly, "Could I borrow him sometime?"

The two women returned, and the four continued in conversation for a few minutes. AJ whispered something into Leah's ear and they both rose. "We're going to leave you two alone," AJ said. "We have work-related issues to talk about. Good night." They waved their hands, got waves from David and Erika in return, and departed for other parts of the ship.

Erika made the "T-for-time-out" sign. Looking out at the ocean, she murmured, "I really had a great time today. Thanks for that, and for the time you've spent on my lessons. No matter how much I bitch, I'm really...moved by it." She took a breath, and made the sign again. "Whew, I had to get that out. OK, 'time back in', back to normal, again."

David turned to her and smiled, though his face looked tired, and his eyes drooped slightly. "Thanks for telling me. Speaking of lessons, now is as good a time as any. Get up there and give me a 5 minute pitch about why the Discovery Channel should sponsor you for a documentary." He removed his laptop and projector from a locker and quickly set them up and turned them on. The computer-generated crowd came to life on the wall behind him, and rustling-crowd sounds came from the speakers.

Ignoring her protests, he propelled her forward, and said, "Go! And give me the same energy you put into that song."

Erika looked away for a moment, and then started up. She spoke energetically, and her excitement was palpable. She used colorful and descriptive terms, such as "the T. rex of the seas" and "the most efficient killing machine that's ever existed." She used her hands to make each point, and her facial expressions became increasingly animated.

David reached over to push a button on the laptop, and the simulated crowd started laughing loudly. She continued, undiminished. He pressed another button, and the crowd started booing, and several members noisily headed for the exit. She halted for a heartbeat, but then went on. She finished in five minutes flat, flushed and out of breath.

David sat silently for a minute. Then he said, with a faint smile, "Not bad. Not bad at all!" He rose, and the cat crawled immediately onto his forearm. "Lessons are over. G' night."

Her face flashed in irritation. Alcohol had dulled her perceptions, and she had misheard him. "It's over, and good-bye? It's over, and good-bye?"

He looked at her, puzzled. "What?"

"Since you didn't get in my pants, you're telling me good-bye and just blowing me off?"

He held up his free hand. "Whoa. I'm not blowing you off. I was saying good night, not good-bye. I've had no sleep lately, and it's been a long day. I'm falling asleep on my feet."

He looked directly into her eyes, lifting his forearm with Bucky on it up to eye level. "The reason we helped you was not to get...to get anything. It's because you're *family*. Bucky chose you. And that means we'll always be your fans, in that front row, cheering you on." He sighed wearily. "And now, good night." He placed Bucky on the ground, and the two of them walked off, the cat's tail waving from side to side like a metronome.

Erika felt a tear forming at the corner of her left eye, and wiped it away. "No fair," she said petulantly. "You didn't say 'time out!'"

She sat and gazed at the moonlight's reflection, a long silver ribbon on the anthracite sea rippling in front of her. She lit a cigar and puffed on it thoughtfully for a few minutes. Then she rose, threw the cigar into the ocean, and walked toward David's cabin. She knocked softly. Hearing no reply, she tried the handle, and found it was unlocked. She opened the door and entered the room, stating, "Hey. I'm sorry I went off. I just wanted to...thank you for what you said, about me being..."

She stopped as she saw David, lying on his bed, illuminated by the moonlight. His shoes were on the floor, but he still wore his pants and T-shirt–he had fallen asleep in his clothes. His right arm was flung to the side, and Bucky lay across it. The cat raised its head slightly toward her and flicked one ear as Erika stood next to the bed, looking down at them. She remained for a moment, and drank in the scene, listening to the soft susurrus of their breathing. Smiling, she reached for the blanket at the foot of the bed and covered both of them up to their shoulders.

The cat slowly and deliberately reached out his right paw, and rested it on David's chin. He blinked both eyes, twice. David's deep breathing stopped for half a heartbeat, but then continued. A strange feeling came over her. Her chest seemed to suddenly squeeze together, and she couldn't breathe. She remained a moment longer, and then hurriedly tiptoed out of the room, closing the door quietly behind her.

She rushed for the back deck and gulped in a lungful of fresh sea air. Slowly, she returned to her seat, put up her feet, and lit another Romeo y Julieta. She puffed it silently, watching the smoke rings rise in the moonlight.

Chapter 22

Police Colonel Daniel DuBois was not fond of the ocean, and he hated the very concept of diving. He did not even like snorkeling, as he felt uncomfortable and out of control underwater. The sea at this moment looked even more foreboding than usual, as the morning sun was hidden by a solid blanket of gray. He had brought six divers with him that would explore underwater for him. He checked his maps and GPS readout once more, and turned impatiently to Police Lieutenant Barker, his second in command, who was already suited up.

"Are you sure this is the right spot?" he asked for the third time in the last hour. "I haven't got all day to wait while you..."

"For sure, for sure," Barker reassured him. "Our guy on Paradise Island has been watching them. He got the coordinates within a hundred yards. And he said they marked every spot with flags, so they could find it again." He looked at DuBois. "You sure they found the submarine?"

DuBois nodded. "We listened in on his phone calls. He ordered cutting torches with lots of tanks. There can only be one reason for that. He's also ordered lights with power lines. He's either doing night diving or he's found caves he's going into."

Barker scanned the horizon. "You're sure they ain't coming back for two days?"

"Yeah, that's what Kilmer told his crew before the ship left. Let's get started!"

Barker nodded, and the six divers went off the diving platform, in three teams of two men each, each team with a sled. Underwater, they spread out to cover a westerly direction, carefully checking out each yellow flag they saw anchored on the bottom. It took them less than an hour before they found the flag that marked the entrance to the cave, and only another 20 minutes to do a cursory check inside the cave and then return to the boat, decompress and get back on board. DuBois was already pacing back and forth.

"We found it!" cried Barker as he took off his equipment and dropped it on the deck. He described the break in the coral wall and the three underwater passages, one of them blocked by the submarine. "We found the back end of the U-boat. It looks like it's ripped open, but it doesn't look like anyone's done any work on it yet."

"So it's in a tunnel?" DuBois asked.

"Yeah. Good thing we brought lots of flashlights."

"Did you look inside? Did you find anything?" DuBois inquired eagerly.

"Nah," answered Barker. "We stuck our heads inside, but we were a little low on air, so I told everybody to come back. We'll go back after an hour's rest."

The rest period was spent arguing over diving tables, with DuBois taking the position that the divers should ignore the safety rules for resting and detoxing after multiple dives, and Barker and the other divers arguing that they should follow the guidelines. Finally, DuBois played his trump card.

"Here it is," he crowed. "I promised you $500 a day, in US dollars, and a $10,000 bonus for whoever finds a safe with valuables in it. I'm willing to increase that. Find the safe in the sub, and you get $20,000..." he pointed a finger at one after the other, to heighten the effect, "...each!"

That ended the discussion on dive tables. The three teams were back in the water immediately, and returned after an hour with news.

"Here's what we found," Barker said, while pulling off his gear in front of the impatient DuBois. "This sub is wedged in a tunnel, pointing due West, with the butt end sticking out. You can get into that part, but it seems to be the engine rooms, and there's no safe there, or valuables of any kind."

He drew a diagram of the sub and the tunnels on a wooden seat with the blade of his diving knife. "To the left and right of the sub's stern are two other tunnels, around 100 feet high, with really smooth walls, like tubes. We went into both of them. The one to the right goes down pretty steep, and we gave up after we hit 200 feet depth and it just kept going on down. The one on the left goes up slightly. After about a mile it branches off into other tunnels."

He tapped the sketch of the sub with his knife. "At the front of the engine rooms are reinforced doors, securely shut. We'd need major equipment to cut through that and whatever's behind it in less than two days. That's probably why Kilmer is on shore right now, getting that kind of equipment together. We need it, too."

"No good," said DuBois, shaking his head. "That would take too long. Can you get around to the front of the boat?"

Barker pointed to his sketch of the left tunnel. "Up here, after about a mile, is a tunnel on the right that seems to run back East. That seems to be our best chance. If we can get around to the front of the sub we should have a shot at getting to the Captain's quarters, where the safe probably is. The front end has to be totally busted up, so we should get inside easy. It'll take a while to reach it. There's a strong current in the tunnels, so we have to watch the battery levels on our sleds. *And* we're going to be careful!"

He turned to DuBois, who was just opening his mouth to comment.

"There's lots of animals in those tunnels," Barker said. "I'll be damned why they're there, but they are. We saw a manta ray, and a leopard shark that was at least seven feet long." He looked nervous. "That shark zipped right by without noticing us, like he was being chased by something. If there's anything bigger than seven feet in there, I want to be ready for it."

He turned to one of the men. "Coleman, you take in a group of four. Take two of the sleds, keep your spear guns out and ready, take plenty of extra flashlights, and check out where that eastbound cave goes. When you get back, me and Sonny will go out. That way we get a little bit of rest in between dives, and in those tunnels the six of us would just get into each other's way, anyhow. And we need to recharge the sleds."

"But hurry," added DuBois. "Can you radio back when you've found something?"

"Not really. We can talk to each other in the tunnels for short distances, but the radio waves won't penetrate out," Coleman answered.

The four men lowered themselves into the water, and then started off on the two sleds. They hesitated a moment at the mouth of the tunnel, savoring the last moments of natural daylight. Then, one following behind the other, the two sleds entered the passage and headed up the left tunnel.

At the first tunnel branching to the right, Coleman scratched an arrow into the wall, in a spot he hoped would not be noticed by anyone else. They continued, checking their compass readings often, since their GPS receivers no longer worked. Occasionally, some fish barreled past, and they moved aside to let them by. They proceeded without incident, though the going was slow because the tunnel did not go straight, but curved erratically.

Several tunnels branched off to the left, but they ignored them, only stopping to mark arrows next to them so they would not take one by mistake on the way back. They continued in the main tunnel for five or six miles. Suddenly, to their amazement, the tunnel rose and they saw air at the top. The tunnel was now over 100 feet high, with at least 20 feet of air on top. They continued until the tunnel widened into a cavern, with stalactites hanging from the ceiling, and occasional small islands rising from the water. They heard what sounded like a waterfall in the distance.

"Let's pull up on this dry spot," said Coleman, and the others followed him, carefully pulling their sleds up on a dry, sandy beach some 30 feet long that butted up to one of the cavern walls. Coleman pulled his face mask off and carefully sniffed the air.

"Smells kinda funky, but it seems OK," he commented.

The others pulled off their masks and mouthpieces and looked around, shining their lights around the cavern, although they could not pierce the blackness of its far reaches.

"Where the hell are we?" asked one of the men, who had the nickname of Jocko. His mouth fell open in utter amazement as he turned around. The lights set off sparkling reflections when they hit parts of the walls, reflecting in all colors, sometimes so brightly that they were painful to the eye. "Are we in some kind of diamond mine?"

"I don't think so," said Coleman. "I bet these are underground crystal formations. I've seen one of these before, in a cavern on Jamaica. We must be in a cave in one of the islands around here, either Dragon, er, Paradise Island, or one of the four small islands near it."

"Wait a minute," said Jocko. "I just noticed something. Turn off your flashlights for a minute." The others did as he asked, and waited for their eyes to adjust to the darkness. To their astonishment, they saw light glimmering along the cavern walls, a blue-green shimmering phosphorescence that looked as if millions of fireflies had settled on the rock surfaces. The light was not uniform—apparently whatever was creating the illumination liked some areas better than others—but it was bright enough so the three men could see each other, and could walk around without flashlights.

"What de fuck is dat?" asked the ever-erudite Jocko.

"It seems to be some kind of plant that gives off light," answered Coleman, peering closely at the wall nearest them. He scraped off some of the material, which had a texture similar to lichen. The plant material stuck to his knife, which now gave off a dull glow.

"Okay, this is all very nice," groused Jocko. "We can rest up a few minutes, and save some air and battery time. But how de fuck do we find the tunnel to the sub?"

"We go back to where we entered this cavern, and look to the right," answered Coleman. "Just keep going along the wall till you find the first tunnel. Here, Jocko, if you're so eager, go back over there." He turned to the fourth man. "Nick, go with him. Rolly will stay here with me. Leave the sled and just swim with your flippers. When you find it, come back and we'll take the sleds."

Jocko grumbled, but pulled his mask back on, inserted his mouthpiece, and slid into the water, with Nick following. Soon all they could see of them was the beam of their flashlights underwater as they traced back the route they had come.

Suddenly, they heard a loud squeaking, which echoed off the walls of the cavern. The two men stared at each other.

"What do you think it is, Rolly?" Coleman asked his companion.

Rolly answered, "Sounds like a dolphin–same kinda whistle. It seems to be coming from back in the cavern, toward the left."

Coleman thought a minute, and then told him, "I'll go check it out. You stay here and wait for Jocko and Nick."

Coleman dragged the sled into the water, got on, and slowly steered it toward the source of the sound. The cavern seemed to keep going on forever. He guessed it must be many miles long, located under some island mountain range. He felt a breeze, and looked up to see a rift in the rock face above him. "Must go all the way to the surface," he mumbled to himself.

He heard hissing to his right, and shone his flashlight in that direction. He saw several hillocks with steam coming from them. One of the mounds was ringed by crystals. The sparkling colors that reflected from his flashlight beam were spectacular. He was lost for a moment as he watched his beam hit a crystal that acted as a prism and turned his white light into a full rainbow, running from ceiling to floor.

He suddenly remembered the impatient DuBois, and tore himself away from the light show, pressing on toward the squeaking sounds, which came from an island that rose above the water to a height of about 20 feet. He propelled his sled toward a sandy beach, and dismounted to pull the vehicle fully on land. He noticed a mound in the middle of the island, with long, deep furrows leading up to it, as if someone had used an old-fashioned plow here.

He approached the mound and looked over the top. It was hollowed out inside, and appeared to be some kind of nest, about 30 feet wide, constructed of sand and coral and other materials he could not identify. He stared as he saw what looked like a pair of crocodiles in the nest. Both of them had their mouths wide open, and were emitting high, keening cries. Each animal was about four feet long, with long snouts lined with needle-like teeth.

"What the hell are you guys?" he asked his captive audience. "Cave crocodiles? Shouldn't you be in a swamp or something?"

He shined his light over one animal from head to tail, and saw a remarkable phenomenon. Although the animal was initially a dark gray, its color changed as he played his flashlight over it, first to light gray and then to bright white, as if it was trying to replicate the color of his light.

He leaned far over the side of the nest to touch one of the animals on the snout, asking it, "Are you the momma and the poppa in this nest? Do you have any eggs or babies?" When he tried to push the animal aside to see the bottom of the nest, it snapped at him, scraping his skin and drawing a drop of blood.

"Don't do that!" he said harshly, and smacked the animal across the snout, one-two. The animal shrank back in fear, and started a crying ululation that sounded like it was terrified. Coleman laughed.

His laughter ended abruptly as he heard a low staccato rumble from across the cave, rapidly increasing in volume. Frightened, he shone his light across the surface of the water, but could see nothing, and the sound suddenly stopped. As he stared at the area in front of the small beach he became aware of a strange underwater glow, as if the lights had been turned on in a swimming pool. He turned off his flashlight so he could see the glow more clearly, and noticed that the light was rising up, displacing great volumes of water that roiled away from it.

He shouted in horror as a gigantic animal broke the surface, and with a mighty push of its flippers hauled itself onto the shore. It looked like the two he had seen in the nest, but much bigger. It might be as long as a whale, he guessed, though not as broad. He backed away and turned his flashlight on full power and shone it on the animal, which surged forward onto the land.

The beam of his light revealed a horrible sight. The upper torso of Rolly protruded from the beast's jaws, the man's eyes reflecting his flashlight like two dancing fireflies. His arms flopped around like the limbs of a marionette whose strings had been cut. Coleman could hear the snapping and crunching of bone and gristle as the creature quickly finished chewing on Rolly, and his torso slid inexorably down its gullet.

Coleman backed up and stared in horror at the creature in front of him. In his mind it appeared that the creature's jaws were longer than he was. He shone his flashlight directly into its eyes, and the animal blinked, shocked by the sudden bright light.

"Get back, you fuck!" Coleman screamed at it, and for a moment it looked like the beast would do just that, as it turned to one side to avoid the light. But just then one of the two animals in the nest let out a shriek, and the giant in front of him— deep in Coleman's brain he now surmised, correctly, that this must be the mother, and the two in the nest were her offspring—spat out what was left of Rollo and turned its full wrath on him.

Coleman stood transfixed, like a bird hypnotized into immobility in front of a snake. The giant undulated toward him in great bounds, and emitted a shrieking roar that deafened him and made his hair stand on end. He finally turned to run, but by then the Mosasaur was upon him. In the last second she twisted her head to maneuver her jaws sideward, and Coleman felt the sharp teeth penetrating his ribs with a pressure of several tons per square inch. The pain was excruciating, as he felt himself being shaken to and fro like a rag doll, until his backbone snapped like a dry wishbone, and he tumbled into nothingness.

Further down the cave, Jocko emerged from the water at the beach where the four had first landed, and pulled off his mask and mouthpiece. "Good news," he called out. "I think I found the tunnel! Nick disappeared on me, though—did he come back here?" He laid his equipment on top of his aquasled and turned around.

"Rolly? Coleman? Nick? Where the fuck are you guys?" he shouted. He then yelled their names over and over, his panicky voice resounding from the cave walls. "Rolly-olly-olly-olly! Coleman-oleman-oleman-oleman!" He saw that one of the sleds was still there, but found no sign of his companions.

He checked his watch, and noticed with a shock that it had been over two hours since they had left the boat. He turned off his flashlight to conserve power, knowing he would need it on the long trip back to the boat. He started talking to himself, and panic crept into his voice. "I'll wait for ten minutes for them to get back. That's it! After that, I head back on my own."

His stomach clenched tight at the prospect. "Wish I'd paid attention to those damn directional markings on the tunnel branches. If I take a wrong turn, I'll be lost..." He was too afraid to complete the sentence.

He sat down heavily on the sand. He heard no sounds except for the far-off dripping of water and the sound of his own ragged breathing. He looked around in the semidarkness, feeling the crushing mass of earth and rock above him. It seemed to press down so hard that he felt it squeeze his chest. He broke out in a sweat as he felt the walls starting to close in on him.

With a final expletive of, "Fuck it!" he stood up and got ready to go. As he lifted up his diving jacket with its double air tanks, he saw a strange underwater glow approaching. Thinking it might be the lights of his companions, he dropped his jacket and went eagerly down into the water until it came up past his knees. He saw that it was not a flashlight as he first thought, but appeared to be a wide, even source of light coming directly at him.

When the object suddenly broke water in front of him, it took his breath away. His voice died in his throat. A vision from hell rose up, towered above him, and then landed back in the water with a resounding splash, sending fountains spurting in all directions. Giant jaws opened and seized him, and pulled him into the water.

To his amazement, he found that although he was being held by rows of sharp, curved teeth, they did not break his skin, and he was being carefully held and transported above water level to somewhere in the back of the cavern. He had visions of trained killer whales that grasped their handlers gently, and gave them rides around a lagoon. He started hoping against hope that this was some kind of killer whale or giant dolphin, and would take him to safety, and he would make it home again.

The Mosasaur reached an island and surged onto it while still delicately holding on to Jocko. It glided up the land with an undulating motion that resembled the Australian crawl of human swimmers. They approached a large nest. She gingerly lowered him into the nest and let him go, and Jocko's relief was overwhelming.

He started babbling his gratitude with, "Oh, good, thanks. I'm fine...whatever you are, and I..."

He stopped abruptly. In the opalescent light from the cavern walls, he saw two much smaller versions of his transportative animal in the nest next him. If he hadn't been so frightened he would have been fascinated. The two animals emitted sparkles of lights along their flanks, and their skins changed color right in front of him, from a dark gray to a pale green. For some strange reason, Jocko got the feeling that this meant they were happy.

Snapping back to the danger of his situation, he whispered, "Okay, this is nice, but I gotta go!" and started to climb out of the nest.

The Mosasaur pushed him patiently back with the merest nudge of her jaws, and settled down to observe. One of the juveniles approached Jocko as he started to rise again, and bit him in the leg with needle-sharp teeth.

He yelled, "Ow! You little shit!" as he kicked the animal in the snout with his other leg. The baby let out a wailing screech–

"Sounds just like that prisoner whose hand I slammed in the cell door last week," Jocko thought fleetingly–and released him, changing color to a pale red in the process.

He scrambled out of the nest and almost made it to the water when the mother Mosasaur whipped around and bounded after him, grasped him by both legs, and dragged him back to the nest, ignoring his protests. As she lowered him into the nest this time she bit down hard, and Jocko heard bone splinter and felt red-hot pain shoot up his back in excruciating waves.

He screamed, first in pain and then in horror, as he noticed he was suddenly paralyzed and could no longer move his lower body. First one, then the other babies came up to him and started to devour him alive, methodically ripping off parts of his clothing and then seizing chunks of his flesh, which they chewed with happy, chortling grunts.

His last sight was of the mother Mosasaur propped up on the side of the nest, calmly looking down at her feeding offspring. One of the offspring grasped Jocko's face in its jaws and he heard a squishing and his vision faded. He could no longer tell what was happening to the lower part of his body, but heard the sounds of chewing and grunting and snuffling grow ever louder in his mind during what seemed like an eternity, until all feeling faded and his last mental image was of the icy claws of Death reaching out for him.

Back at the boat, DuBois grew increasingly nervous as he glanced at his watch. He snarled, "Those jack-offs have been gone over two hours. What the fuck are they doing?" He turned to Barker. "How long does the air last?"

"About an hour and a half, maximum," Barker replied, gravely. "Something must have happened!"

DuBois turned on him savagely. "Well, what are you waiting for? Go find out why they're taking so long!"

"I... I'm not so sure," Barker replied as he drew back toward the other diver, who was losing enthusiasm by the minute. "I don't like the looks of this."

"What are you, cowards?" DuBois screamed. "You've got sleds and spear guns. What could possibly happen to you down there? You've all dived hundreds of times, you told me! What do you mean, you don't like the looks of this?"

"Dis whole area bad, mon," blurted the other man. "Nobody—no fishermen, nobody—go near Dragon Island!"

"It's just local superstition!" DuBois said, eyes narrowed.

"No it's not. That big island and the little islands next to it," Barker said, as he pointed to the land masses on the horizon, "used to be called the Dragon Islands. The old people swore that dragons lived there. Nobody went on 'em. The few that tried it usually disappeared. Some figured it was the coral, but others, like Aunt Marie, said it was because of Mokele-Mbembe, the sea dragons that live on those islands."

He narrowed his eyes. "That's why them guys were able to buy Dragon Island so cheap." He pointed at the nearest of the islands. "It's 'cause none of the locals wants any part of it."

"I don' care 'bout no old-people superstitions," DuBois shot back. "You two get down there right now, and don't come back without something to show me! I jus' send you right back, otherwise."

DuBois took a Smith & Wesson .357 magnum revolver out of his holster, laid it on the seat next to him, and glanced at it significantly. He then looked back at the two men. "I'm gonna be real disappointed, you don' come back with those guys, or better yet, find Kilmer's treasure. Real, real disappointed!"

Slowly, reluctantly, the two divers entered the water, mounted their sled, and drove to the tunnel entrance. They entered it and headed left, as the first group had done.

DuBois paced back and forth on the boat, smoking one cigarette after the other. He put on a headset attached to an MP3 player and listened to a playlist of songs that a local teenager had ripped off the Internet for him.

To calm his nerves, he smoked a spliff of ganja that he had found in the backpack of one of the men. This was a measure of his agitation, since normally he never touched the stuff, priding himself on always being in total control. After a while, relaxed by the effects of the ganja and the calm rocking motion of the boat, he fell asleep on one of the deck chairs.

He awoke with a start and noticed three things: he was out of cigarettes, having powered through two packs of them; he was out of music, having played through all 80 songs on the playlist; and he was almost out of sunlight, as it was already evening. There was no sign of any of the men.

He paced up and down the length of the boat, alternating between anger, frustration and fear. Finally, he shrugged his shoulders.

"Fuck this!" he shouted. "Let Kilmer and his guys deal with whatever's down there. After they find the treasure, I'll just come and take it away from them!"

With that, he started the engines and headed for home, improvising a story to explain the disappearance of the six men. He kept the bow pointed steadily toward Anguilla Harbor, which began to show its lights in the distance.

Chapter 23

By Tuesday morning, the ship was back on station at sea. The crew met at 9 a.m. in the Conference Room. David revealed what had been found to all of them, and apologized for the need for secrecy. There was laughter and applause around the room. He went on to explain how they would now start cutting into the U-boat to see if it contained what they were looking for. He displayed a 3-dimensional diagram of a U-boat on the largest widescreen on the wall. He rotated the view of each room as they came to it, and used a green laser pointer to identify the sections they would explore.

"This U-boat was designed to carry 48 men, though it often carried more. There were less than 30 bunks available, so the men had to share them. While you were on duty, there would be someone else in your bed. The boat was incredibly crowded. When it started on a trip, over twelve tons of canned and fresh food were stored in crates in every conceivable nook and cranny, and we can expect to see the remains of some of that, especially in the forward and aft torpedo sections. The section that's exposed, and that we've looked into, is the Aft Crew and Torpedo Room, here."

He tapped on the rear section of the diagram. "This contained some of the bunks, plus torpedoes and two torpedo tubes. If our U-boat wasn't involved in any combat action before she sank, she'll have 14 torpedoes on board, along with 26 mines and 220 rounds for the 88mm deck gun. So be really careful what you step on or cut into. All those munitions could still be live, and if they go off, it'll be one hell of a bang. I'll be the first to enter any compartment, so I can look for anything explosive and identify it, hopefully."

"The next compartment we'll enter, after some cutting, is the Electric Motor Room. While underwater, the boat was run by two large Siemens electric motors, and they, plus some of the batteries, are located here. We'll have to check this room for residual battery acid."

"The next compartment forward is the Diesel Engine Room," David said as he pointed at the diagram, and to a black and white photo that was taken in such a room. "This contains two massive MAN diesel engines, over 20 feet long and 5 feet tall. Normally the boat ran on one diesel while on the surface, while the other was used to recharge the batteries. While the boat was running, this room was a real hell-hole, with high-speed turbochargers making an ungodly racket that led to eventual hearing loss, and temperatures over 100 degrees Fahrenheit."

"The next compartment is the Control Room. This is roughly the center of the submarine, and includes the periscope and map tables. Here you see a ladder that led up into the conning tower and to the surface. All these tubes and controls on the walls controlled the air and water for the boat, including the compressed air that made it rise up again."

"In front of the Control Room are the Captain's and Officer's Quarters. The Captain and his four officers were the only crew members that had their own bunks. This is probably the area where we'll find the safe we're looking for, since the Captain would want to keep a sharp eye on this cargo. Right in front of their cabins is the Radio Room."

"Next we have the Galley, where meals were prepared around the clock. After the Galley come the quarters of the Petty Officers and Chiefs. This consists of 12 bunks and some storage lockers. If the safe isn't in the Captain's cabin, it may be here. Note that there's another watertight circular door at the front of this section. Each opening had grab bars above it so that while running from one section to the other you would grab the bar, lift yourself up over the high metal doorsill, stick your feet through the opening and push yourself through, all in a split second."

"Finally, we have the Forward Crew Quarters and the business end of a U-boat, the Torpedo Room. The whole purpose of moving quietly and underwater was to get within firing range of an enemy ship, so you could fire one or more torpedoes from the four tubes at the front of this room, ejecting them with compressed air. You should be able to recognize the torpedoes if you find them. Each one is about 23 feet long, and weighs 3,500 pounds. They were lifted by this winch up here in the overhead area. Most of the crew slept in hammocks suspended from the walls."

He let them soak it all in before saying, "That's what we'll be working on, gentlemen, in teams of three. One will work the torch, a second will assist him, and a third will be safety backup. And now I'll turn the meeting over to our chief technogeek, Shawn."

Shawn smiled at the introduction and displayed a diagram of the tunnels on a side screen. "I'll be in charge of the teams that are laying lights, cameras and sensors in the tunnel complex. The schedules for all the teams are on this screen, which you can copy to your iPads. Besides the lights for the torch team in the sub, we'll set up lights and cameras in the tunnels. The right tunnel seems to go too deep to explore very far, so we'll concentrate on the tunnel running to the left, in a westerly direction. We hope to explore that tunnel to find a way around to the front of the submarine. If we run out of lights, we'll have to wait until the rest of the shipment arrives, in about a week."

David closed the meeting by addressing Larry and the paleontologists. "Larry, you take the small boat and support Erika and Moshe. Take them wherever they need to go, and keep an eye on them. I'll be in the cave much of the time, so send somebody to get me if you need me. The chart with suggested dive times for everybody will be out on deck and has been downloaded to your iPads or whatever else you've got. Team leaders are responsible for planning and checking actual times, to make sure nobody stays at depth longer than is safe." He looked around at them. "Gentlemen—and princess—it's time to start your engines. Let's find us some treasure!"

The meeting broke up with a scraping of chairs as the excited crowd rushed to the equipment racks.

Chapter 24

The initial excitement about working on the sub turned into repetitive drudgery for the next weeks, as section after section was cut from the U-boat and removed. It was methodical, exacting work, conducted in very cramped quarters, and extremely limited by the amount of time each diver could spend in the water. Periodically, work had to be halted because the oxyacetylene cutting caused so much dirt and clutter to be kicked up that the water became beclouded, and it was impossible to see anything.

The exploration of the left tunnel halted after the team ran out of lights, almost three miles from the sub. They had placed one every two hundred feet. Each light had a proximity sensor attached, to turn the light on when it sensed an object moving nearby and start an attached video camera. The resulting video could be seen on monitors on the ship or on the waterproof handheld displays that the crew members carried.

Although some wanted to explore farther into the cave system, David forbade it until additional lighting could be installed. He explained his decision to Erika and Moshe one evening, when they were on the stern of the ship. Moshe had joined David and Erika in their usual evening routine. They were in deck chairs with their feet up on the railing. David was smoking an Earth Supernatural cigar, while Erika puffed on an ACID Blonde. Moshe had been persuaded to try a cigar, but he smoked it in little puffs, and looked at it suspiciously. It was clearly not in his comfort zone.

"Caves are inherently dangerous," David noted. "And underwater caves are even worse, because you're limited with air and visibility, and it's possible to get jammed and stuck in a tight space with all the equipment on your back. I went spelunking–cave exploring–a few times with friends when I was in college." He added, "I discovered that I really despised it. I hated the dark, when you don't know what's behind you, and discovered that I have a touch of claustrophobia. I totally froze a couple of times."

"Anyway," he blew out a smoke ring and turned to Erika, "how's your dig going?"

"It's brilliant," she beamed. "We've made real progress on the excavation, even with just the two of us. Larry is helping us out some, especially when we can use a small suction pump to get rid of loosened sand around the fossil. We'll make a lot more progress when our team comes down in two weeks."

"Great," smiled David. "Good on ya, as you'd say. Now I have something to show you." He reached around his neck and undid the gold necklace he always wore, with a gold coin suspended from it. He tapped on the coin and handed it around. "Do you know what this is?"

Moshe held it up in the moonlight and watched it sparkle.

"Looks like an American double eagle," he said. "Weighs slightly over an ounce, contains exactly an ounce of pure gold. This one is in very good condition, almost uncirculated, year 1898, Denver mint." He smiled shyly. "I used to collect coins when I was a kid."

Erika took the coin from him, hefted its considerable weight in her hand, and looked at it closely. "It says it's an American $20 coin," she said. "It's beautiful. I assume that's Lady Liberty on one side, and the American eagle on the other, with 13 stars representing the 13 original colonies. Why do they call it a double eagle? I see just the one."

"There was already a $10 gold coin called an 'eagle' in 1849," Moshe replied. "So when they started minting this, which was worth twice as much, people called it the double eagle. The U.S. Mint created this coin during the California gold rush, when gold was pouring in from the mines, and they wanted to put it into general use as currency. At the time there was a lot of paper money in circulation—some of the States and even private companies were printing their own. The double eagle changed all that— because it was literally worth its weight in gold, it became the standard currency everybody wanted. It stayed in circulation until 1933, when Franklin Delano Roosevelt took the country off the gold standard, and ordered all gold coins to be melted down. Since then, the double eagle has been sought after by collectors all over the world."

David gave Moshe the thumbs-up sign and laughed. "Very good, professor!"

"Does this have something to do with the U-boat?" asked Erika.

"Yes, it does," David answered. "The boat we've been looking for—that we've finally found—at one time had 5,000 of these coins on board. It had gotten them in payment from a Japanese submarine that it met in these waters. The money was supposed to pay off the head of a spy network the Nazis had for their operations against Allied shipping in the Caribbean and along the Atlantic coast." He looked down and knocked the ash off his Earth cigar before continuing. "The gold was supposed to pay the head spymaster, but was never delivered."

"What did the Germans sell the Japanese? And why take payment in American gold?" Erika asked.

"They sold them advanced technology such as radar that the Japanese needed, as well as strategic materials, including mercury. In wartime, mercury, also known as quicksilver, could be worth more than its weight in gold, because it was used in making switches and relays and electronics."

"As for why they demanded payment, by the middle of 1942 the Germans were not feeling very generous toward their Japanese allies, who had helped get them into a war with the U.S., but had not helped them in their war against the Russians. What killed the Germans' chances of taking Moscow—and eventually cost them the war in the East—was the release of over 20 Russian divisions that had been stationed on the border between Siberia and the Japanese. When the Russians found out that the Japanese had decided not to attack them, they sent those divisions West on the trans-Siberian railroad, from whence they arrived just in the nick of time to beat back the German panzers, which were already in the suburbs of Moscow."

"After that, the Germans asked for cash on the barrel head, and in gold and silver, not in the paper notes the Japanese were printing by the bucketful. The Caribbean superspy obviously couldn't use German Reich marks, so he asked for hard currency that couldn't be counterfeited, specifically US gold coins. The Japanese found an old stash of gold coins, which had been sitting around since they'd gotten them from the U.S. around the time of the Gold Rush, and sent them over to pay for their goodies. Japanese records show that the gold was transferred to the U-boat."

"So there's at least $100,000 on the sub," Erika noted.

"A lot more than that," Moshe chimed in. "Gold during the Gold Rush was worth $20 an ounce, but it's now over $1,500. And you've got 5,000 ounces. But it's still more than that."

He grasped David's coin and held it in the air. "You paid close to three thousand dollars for this?"

"That's about right," David said.

"That's because the collector's value added a thousand bucks," noted Moshe. "That's for a double eagle in decent shape. If this were in mint condition, it could be worth over ten grand. But this is relatively recent. Do you think the coins you're looking for may be older than this?"

"I know they are," nodded David. "I found a telegram from Japan in the German Naval records. It said the coins were all from before 1860. They wanted to know whether they were still good. The Japanese emperors had a habit of canceling out currency from previous rulers. The Germans cabled back that the coins were acceptable."

"So these coins are from the California Gold Rush era," Moshe continued. "Uncirculated coins from that era are almost unheard of. $10,000 would be a bargain for such a coin. But that's still not all." He looked at David. "May I?"

David smiled. "Go for it. You're doing great."

Moshe continued. "Because these coins have provenance–proof of where they came from, and a story associated with them–they could be worth several times the normal collector's value. Depending on how they were sold, each coin could easily bring tens of thousands of dollars."

Erika let out a low whistle. "That means the gold is worth...at least a hundred million dollars!"

David nodded. "Now you know why we're all working so hard."

Moshe looked at the remains of his cigar, which was burned down to a stub, and tossed it overboard. "Well, us poor working stiffs have to be up early tomorrow, so I guess I'll turn in," he said. He petted the ever-present Bucky, who sat nearby on a deck chair, and bade his goodbyes.

David looked seriously at Erika, and leaned in close, sinking his voice to a whisper. "Actually, I'm glad I've got you alone."

Erika took the cigar out of her mouth and pretended to look at it thoughtfully. "Well, I'm flattered, but this is awfully sudden, and I..."

"No, no," David replied impatiently. "I no longer think of you that way. I know that you belong...that you're involved with someone else. So we're just buddies."

He looked out at the ocean, and did not see Erika's hooded expression. "What I wanted to say was, the German government had only one request when they gave me the rights to salvage anything I wanted from the boat. That was to return the bodies of any of the U-boat's crew that I found."

"And so?" she asked.

"There should have been at least a dozen bodies in the back sections that we opened up. But here's the strange thing. We haven't found a single one. Not only that, but I'm not sure the coral did all the damage to the sub. In places it looks like something bent parts of the hull. And there are long, wide scratches on the sides, like tooth or claw marks."

"What are you trying to tell me?" she asked.

"I'm worried there may be some major predators down there, like large man-eating sharks. I wanted you to know that my fear of the dark and closed-in spaces isn't the only reason I'm not letting anyone else explore deeper in the caves right now. And I'm worried about you. I'll continue sending a crew member to watch your backs, but please be careful." He gave her a wry smile. "I'd miss you, buddy, if anything happened to you."

He turned to go, and called, "Hey, Bucky!" The cat responded by jumping off its chair and following him, close on his heels.

Erika looked down at Bucky, and called after them, "You know, that's not really a cat. That's a dog in cat's clothing!"

He turned and smiled. "I'd never had a pet before, so I just assumed cats could do all that stuff—come, follow me, stay, jump up. He can do all of those."

He leaned down to scratch the cat's head fondly, then rose up to smile warmly at her. With a final, "Good night," he turned and departed.

Erika re-lit her cigar, and gazed out at the moonlight's jagged reflections on the water.

"Buddy, eh?" she said softly to herself, and stared across the broad expanse of water with an enigmatic smile.

Chapter 25

The next morning started with dirty gray skies and choppy seas. Reluctantly, David green-lighted the day's underwater operations. He knew time was running out. Any day could be the start of the storm season, and he knew he could not re-assemble the team after that, as he had done once already. This time there was simply not enough money left.

Fortunately, although the sea itself was turbulent and visibility was very low, the water in the caves was relatively undisturbed. Because the currents near the ship could be treacherous, each man going to or from the tunnel was required to attach to a safety line. Since Erika and Moshe could not work on their dig under these sea conditions, they joined David as he took a tour of the tunnels that had been explored and set up with lights.

They steered their aquasleds along the main left tunnel—it was called "Route One," while branches from it had subordinate names like Route 1.1, 1.2, 1.3 and so on. The tunnels team had not ventured very far into any of the side branches, preferring to stay on the main route.

As they proceeded, they triggered the light/camera systems that had been mounted along the walls. David watched a display on the instrument panel of his aquasled. As they activated a particular light they received the video feed from its camera. At that moment David was looking at an image of the three of them, with data listed along the top of the screen:

CAM 112   Rte 1   NrInt 1.3   Status: Green

This part of the display gave him the camera ID number and location, the nearest tunnel intersection, and the equipment condition and battery status. On the right hand side of the display was listed:

CAM
55
56
112
134

This indicated which cameras were currently active. David was puzzled. "That's strange," he told Erika and Moshe. "I know we're triggering camera 112, and cameras 55 and 56 are in the sub, but there shouldn't be anyone ahead of us right now."

He thumbed the joystick to position it over the "134" and clicked on it, and the video picture changed to the camera at that location.

David looked at the small display closely. "It looks like some kind of animal is coming toward us. I can't really see what it is yet. Its outline is fuzzy, but it seems pretty big. Maybe a shark—"

Just then his earphones crackled. "David, this is Larry. We just broke through to the Control Room. Do you want to check it out?"

"You bet," David replied eagerly, and turned his sled around immediately. "Come on, you guys, I'll show you how far we've gotten, and what the inside of a U-boat Control Room looks like," he told his companions. "Let's go – full speed ahead!"

They all sped toward the sub, forgetting the dim picture they had just seen in their excitement to check out a newly opened compartment, with its promise of mystery and treasure.

On the Global Explorer, the displays in the Electronics Room were much larger and clearer than on the small screen that David had looked at. One of the 60-inch flat screens on one wall displayed multiple frames, showing all the cameras that were currently on. Two frames alternated between successive vidcams as they showed David and his two companions jetting back to the sub.

The screen also showed, clearly, a young Mosasaur passing by one camera after another, with the numbers on the bottom of each frame counting down: 134, 133, 132. Remarkably, the front part of the Mosasaur changed color as it approached each light, changing from gray to silver-white. As it went by the light, it was almost silver in color, becoming difficult to see against the white light reflected from the walls of the tunnel around it. Finally, as it left a lighted area, the silver color started getting progressively darker.

The ominous sight of the Mosasaur swimming lazily along, flinching every time a light came on, did not have an audience–the Electronics Room was totally empty, as Shawn had abandoned it to be in on the find. Although there was a digital video recorder with RAID redundancy to record the video feeds, no one had remembered to turn it on, and it was not recording anything, redundantly or otherwise.

Finally, the Mosasaur turned left into the tunnel named 1.12, and disappeared. The remaining frames being displayed automatically increased in size to fill the entire screen. There were now four cameras active, one outside the sub and one for each of the three compartments that had team members in it.

There were six people crowded into the sub when David, Erika and Moshe arrived. David gave a quick description. "This is the Rear Torpedo Room. We had to cut out all the bunks and remove lots of cans of food and supplies. This is the Electric Engine Room, where we had to remove panels and some engine parts. Here's another hatch. Watch your head as you go through, since there's some sharp corners. We had to cut through these doors, since none of them would open any more. Here's the Diesel Engine Room. These engines were too big to cut out, so it's a tight squeeze to get through. Which brings us to the Control Room. It looks like the hatch has been removed, so I'm ready to go in. Can somebody give me a flashlight?"

David cautiously entered the room after removing his flippers. He moved very slowly, so as not to stir up debris. He shone his light from left to right, chilled by the eerie feeling that he was the first live human to enter this space in over eight decades.

On the port side he could make out a number of control wheels, which looked similar to the steering wheels of cars, as well as rows of gauges and dozens of valves. At the far end was a map table and the compass station. Straight ahead, he could see the periscope well and the speaking tubes. As he squeezed by the periscope on the starboard side, he was able to make out the fore and aft planesman controls. He knew the planes themselves were located on that part of the sub on the outside, to the left and right, and this is where the pitch of the boat had been controlled. He shone his light to the end of the compartment and saw a closed hatch. He tried twisting the opening wheel, but it was frozen shut.

"It looks like the hatch to the Officers' Quarters is locked tight," he spoke into his microphone. He carefully swept the sides and floor of the compartment with his flashlight. "It doesn't look like there are any munitions in here. And there appears to be no room for any kind of safe."

He moved back toward the others in the compartment to the rear. "Go ahead and enter," he said. "Bring in the lights and a video camera pod, and start cutting on the forward hatch."

As an afterthought he turned to Larry. "Listen, when you go in, you'll see a ladder to the right of the periscope well. It leads up to the conning tower. Have somebody go up there and open up that hatch, too. It leads to the outside."

"Okay," replied Larry. "But why? We can be pretty sure there's no treasure up there."

"I know," David agreed. "But I just remembered something from my Quarters in the Marine Corps. I had a little garden, where I fought ongoing battles with gophers. I remember each nest always had at least three ways out. Let's give ourselves a little insurance, just in case." He turned to Erika with a wry smile. "See? You can learn a lot by living poor as trailer park trash."

Chapter 26

The next day opened with clear blue skies and a mild westerly breeze, and the crew breathed a collective sigh of relief. By late afternoon, the next hatch had been breached, and David entered into the Senior Officers' Quarters.

The cutting team reported that after they cut through the hatch, water rushed into the compartment, implying that it had stayed watertight until then. As David entered the compartment, he saw that the inrush of water had thrown up a lot of debris, which now floated everywhere, and he could barely see a foot in front of his face mask.

He pushed past the Captain's Cabin to the open compartment that held the other four officers, and moved his flashlight forward to illuminate the turbid gloom.

"I can hardly see my own hand in front of my eyes, there's so much crap in the water," he reported to the rapt audience gathered behind the hatch in back of him. "The light's reflecting off all of this debris, so it's like being in the middle of one of those snow globes you see in souvenir shops."

He made out the metal railing of a bunk, and used it to pull himself closer. He pulled back the remains of a curtain and then shrank back in shock as his light reflected from a grinning skull, lying on the remains of a pillow. He let out an involuntary, "Whoa!" as he grabbed harder onto the side of the bunk to steady himself, and slowly brought his jagged breathing back into control.

"What?" "What's the matter?" "What's wrong?" chattered a chorus of voices behind him.

Larry asked, "Do you want me to come in?"

David stared at what had frightened him. "No, no, it's OK. What scared me, er, what I'm looking at right now is one of the ship's officers." David used his light to peer at the remains. "There's no real body left, just a skeleton and...shrunken body. The uniform's still in good condition. It looks like he was an *Oberleutnant*, a first lieutenant."

He pulled himself up to the upper bunk, again using the railings. "There's another one in this bunk," he reported. He turned and pushed himself across the aisle, pulling aside the remains of another curtain in front of a bunk, which had once afforded some measure of privacy for its occupant. With quick motions he checked both bunks on that side, and reported, "Yup. There's two on the starboard side. It looks like they're all present and accounted for."

He moved forward, feeling his way almost blindly, guided by his memory of the pictures posted in the Equipment Room on the ship. He had been in an actual U-boat of this type, the *U-505*, which had been captured and moved to the Museum of Science and Industry in Chicago after the war. But that sub had been cleaned up so tourists could go through it, he thought to himself. This one was far more cluttered, and hard to move around in with the dive tanks on his back.

His flashlight illuminated a round doorway in front of him. He had reached the forward end of the compartment. "The forward hatch is closed," he announced. He tugged on the handle, but it did not move. He moved back in the compartment toward the Captain's Cabin, but stopped next to one of the other officer's bunks for a minute, suspended in the water halfway between the deck and the ceiling. The only sound he could hear was his own heavy breathing, which sounded like Darth Vader in *Star Wars*.

He imagined for a moment what it must have been like for these men in the last moments of their lives, as the air ran out and the lights flickered one last time and gave way to total darkness. A wave of claustrophobia came over him, and he could not breathe for a moment.

To take his mind off of his fear he spoke to the others, and described what he was seeing. "From their uniforms, it looks like there's one lieutenant and three ensigns." He paused.

"They're all dressed in full formal uniforms, which is unusual. Because of the heat in a U-boat, the crew usually ran around in rough pants and shirts, or even undershirts. These four guys must all have gotten fully dressed when they knew the end was near. One of them must have been a Catholic. He's holding a rosary in what's left of his hand."

He looked around under the bunks, and quickly searched the area. "Doesn't look like there's a safe here, just some personal storage lockers. I'm now going forward, past the Radio and Sonar Rooms on the starboard side. They appear to be full of...radio and sonar gear. No room to hide anything there. I'm now at the Captain's Cabin. The wood door is still functioning."

David took a deep breath. He had put off this moment as long as he could after entering the compartment. He knew that his best chances of finding a safe were in the Captain's Cabin, and he dreaded the risk of failure, of coming up empty.

He steeled himself and continued. "I opened the door. It's still in one piece, but really thin and flimsy. I can almost...yes, I can see him lying in his bunk. Funny, he's not in his uniform—his jacket is on a chair next to his bunk. The shoulder epaulets show he is, or was, a *Kapitaenleutnant*, what would be the rank of Commander in the US Navy."

David frantically shone his light around the small cabin. He realized he was getting light-headed, the first step to rapture of the deep. He knew he should be heading back to the boat ASAP, but he could not tear himself away. There! He saw the familiar outline of a safe, and, not trusting his eyes, felt along the front of it, feeling through his neoprene gloves the rectangular metal outline and the protruding round wheel of a combination dial. He tried to keep his voice steady.

"To the right of the bunk, next to his sink and wash basin–is a safe, about three feet by four."

He had to stop for a moment to let the hubbub of voices in his earphones die down. "I suggest we get working on it right away. When it's near the ship, let me know, so we can hoist it up with the winch."

He recognized Erika's voice in his headphones. "Congratulations, David. Listen, Moshe and I are about out of air. We're heading back right now."

"Good. See you on the ship," he replied. He knew that he should go with them, but he wanted to stay just a few minutes longer, to leave instructions for the team. He talked with the crew members, and went through the list of what he wanted done. He noticed his throat had gone bone dry. He pointed at the bottom of the safe. "It looks like it's bolted to the floor. Call for help. It's likely to be heavy!"

With an effort, he pushed himself out of the cabin and passed through the hatch to the others, who patted him on the shoulders in gestures of congratulations. He turned toward the crew, and said with a voice that was hoarse, almost a croak, "Make sure someone brings body bags down here, so we can remove the bodies and send them home. Handle them carefully."

He grabbed one of the crew as he swam by. He wasn't even sure of who it was, as his vision was getting blurry. "Come back to the ship with me," he told him.

He knew he was doing more than just following the safety rules, which required that no one ever swam alone underwater, but was always accompanied by a diving buddy. Deep down in his bones, he was totally and utterly exhausted, and could not trust himself to follow the proper decompression procedures. Now that he had found the safe, all he wanted to do was sleep. The crew member turned out to be Ben, who carefully looked at his watch and depth gauge as they returned to the surface in the prescribed stages.

Chapter 27

Early the next morning, David was so dead to the world that he did not hear the light knocking on his door, or the creak of the door opening and someone entering his cabin.

Erika stood next to his bed and looked down at him. She smiled and shook her head slowly, not wanting to disturb the tableaux in front of her. David was sleeping on his left side, his left arm flung out over the bed. Bucky lay next to him, his chin resting on his master's elbow. Both were making soft snoring noises. Erika had stood there for a full three minutes when the cat, sensing something, awoke and raised his head, eyelids blinking sleepily.

"G'day, you two," Erika addressed them, and sat down on the bed to shake David awake. He finally came to, and sat up, yawning. He looked at her in confusion, and asked, "What's going on?"

"They just called in to say the safe will be on deck in about an hour," Erika told him. "You told Larry you wanted to be awakened when the safe came in." She touched Bucky's nose lightly with a finger, which he licked.

"Oh," David said uncertainly. He looked down and noticed he was lying on the bed in his underwear, which showed a bulge from an early-morning erection. "Sorry I'm not dressed to receive company," he told her wryly.

She looked down with a smile and wolf-whistled. "Not bad. Not bad at all." She rose to leave, and said, "I'll see you on deck shortly."

David looked at Bucky, who looked perturbed that his sleep had been interrupted.

"Do you think she's flirting with me?" he asked him. "Why would she do that? She's already got Reginald."

He thought a minute. "Maybe she just wants me on the back burner as backup, in case something doesn't work out. Or maybe she just wants to rub my nose in it, show me what I'm missing."

"Gurk meek," was the reply.

"You don't think so, huh? Well, you should talk. I thought we both agreed to keep our distance, and here you go kissing her. Traitor!"

David was on deck 10 minutes later. The omnipresent Bucky marched behind him, tail up and swinging left and right. One of the crew members came up to David, an urgent look on his face. "Captain?"

"What's up, Collins?" David asked. He realized he did not like this young man, who always had a smile pasted on his face.

"I need to make a call to shore," Collins replied, "and the Radio Room is locked. Larry, he say nobody can use the radiophone until we get back to port. But this is real urgent."

"What's so urgent?" asked David.

Collins's eyes flick back and forth, quickly, before he answered, "It's my fiancé. She supposed to have her baby today, maybe right now. I gotta make sure she all right."

"Well, if she's in the hospital, I'm sure she's being taken care of. I'm sorry, Collins, we're keeping radio silence. My rule stands: anyone caught using a radio is off the crew. I don't want any reporters or anybody else listening in and joining us out here."

"But, Captain..."

"Sorry, that's it. This was part of the agreement when you signed on."

"But this is special..."

David felt himself growing angry, "What part of 'No' don't you understand?"

Collins stomped off, visibly angry.

David pointed over to Larry, who was in the vicinity, and waved him over.

"What's up?" Larry asked.

"Collins. How did we get him on board, again?"

"He claimed to be a ship's mechanic," Larry said. "I think he's somebody's cousin."

"Un-enlist him the next time we dock, please. I don't have a good feeling about him."

"Sure, David, will do," Larry replied, and turned back to getting the winch ready to haul up the safe.

Chapter 28

The safe was hoisted on board a half hour later. Almost the entire crew was on deck, watching, including Bucky, who ran to and fro, caught up in the excitement. The solitary crew member below deck was Bob, who was running a quick check on his diesels, now being used to power the hoist bringing up the safe. Satisfied with his engines' status, he hurried upstairs. He heard a voice speaking urgently. Curious as to who would have a reason not to watch the safe coming in, he followed the sound of the voice and found Collins on a remote corner of the deck, hidden by one of the lifeboats. He was speaking on a satellite phone. He jumped up when Bob yelled, "What are you doing?"

"Nothing, nothing," he replied. "I just needed to make sure my fiancé is all right. She's in hospital today."

"Hand me the phone. Now!" Bob replied. Collins thought of arguing, until he saw Bob's eyes, which seemed to drill into his brain.

"You got no reason to..." he started.

Bob seized the phone and grabbed him by the neck. "Let's go see David! Right now!" he growled. He pushed Collins ahead of him, and they walked rapidly toward the group near the bow.

Bucky circled back and forth on deck. In the midst of one of his frequent switchbacks, he got in the way of the incoming Collins, who stumbled over him. Collins caught himself, straightened and aimed an angry kick at the cat, connecting with a thump. Bucky skidded under the railing, and fell into the water over 20 feet below.

"Hey!" Bob yelled, and David turned and asked, "What? What happened?"

"Bucky went overboard right there," Bob told him, pointing to the section of railing that Bucky had been kicked through. Without saying another word, David jumped onto the railing and dove into the water.

Bob stalked over to Collins, grabbed him by the collar, and growled, "You son of a bitch!"

"It wasn't my fault," Collins whined, "I didn't see the stupid thing."

Bob took a deep breath. "Ben," he yelled. "Come over here!"

While still holding Collins by the collar, he told Ben, "Put this piece of shit in the spare Zodiac."

To Collins, he said, "You go, right now! Take the boat to Paradise Island Resort, and tell the harbor people to hold it and call us. Once we get the Zodiac back, we'll send your gear and your last paycheck to Anguilla. If you stay here any longer, David will be back, and he'll kill you." As Collins started to open his mouth, Bob growled, "And if he doesn't, I will!"

Ten minutes later, David sat on the deck and ministered to his feline friend. Bucky had coughed up some water, and was soaked and bedraggled-looking, but appeared all right otherwise.

Erika brought a couple of large towels, and David dried most of the seawater off the sorry-looking cat and then cradled him on his left arm. He looked down at the still-dripping Bucky, who burrowed his nose under David's shoulder, seeking his favorite refuge.

"It's OK, boy, you're safe now. I'll take care of you," David crooned to him, his voice starting to crack. "Come on. Who's my big strong monster?"

Erika put her hand gently on his shoulder, and said, "Well, Krikey, aren't you the pair!" as she put a towel around David. "Are you going to live?"

She got a weak smile in return, as he rose off the deck with, "Maybe."

Bob came up and explained what had happened, and laid a restraining hand on David's arm as he started to move away. "It's OK, he's gone. I took care of it," he told him.

Erika petted the part of Bucky that wasn't sticking under David's shoulder. "I'm glad Bucky's OK, but you're ruining your whole image," she accosted David, her eyebrows arched.

"Huh?" asked David, puzzled. "What do you mean?"

"You kept telling me all you care about is this treasure, and there it is, sitting on the deck, and you're not even looking at it, you're so wrapped up in one small cat."

"He's not small!" David retorted. "He's..." He stopped. "You're fucking with me," he told her. He smiled. "OK. I'll pull out of it."

He walked briskly over to the safe, and tipped it from side to side.

"OK," he told Larry. "Get this thing inside and figure out how to open it. And keep working on the forward hatch of the Officers' Quarters, full speed."

"How come?" Larry asked, puzzled. "Don't we have the safe now?"

"We don't have a safe with 5,000 one-ounce coins in it," David replied. "This thing weighs 100 pounds total, at most."

He turned to the crew. "Okay, you guys, I'll tell you later what we find in this safe. It's not the treasure—that's still waiting for us. Punch through the hatch to the Petty Officers Quarters, and get a hold of me as soon as you do."

He looked at the sky, which was overcast, with black clouds gathering on the horizon. "Go as fast as you can. If a storm catches us, we're screwed!"

He turned away from the men and went below, unaware of the strange sight he had presented, barking commands while cradling a wet cat on one arm. As soon as he got to his cabin, he dried off Bucky, who still looked bedraggled, but appreciated the attention. David unlocked a compartment in his desk. He took out a satellite telephone, scooped Bucky up on one arm, and walked to a private part of the deck to call AJ and tell him the news.

Below the ship, two Mosasaurs, a mother and her female offspring, circled in frustration. The young female had been alerted when the cat fell into the water, and had started to rise up to investigate. She stopped when a second, larger body hit the water. She started to move in again, but stopped when a third object suddenly splashed the surface.

She approached once more, but hesitated when the first two objects disappeared. The third object, however, seemed to still be a candidate, and she turned toward that, observed by her mother, 100 feet further below.

Up above, Collins pushed the electric starter, and the small outboard motor sprang to life. He headed for Paradise Resort. "Damn it!" he swore to himself. "But at least I got the message off that the safe was coming on board. DuBois oughta be happy with that." About a half mile from the ship, he took out his satellite phone to make another call. He felt a bump on the port side of the boat, causing him to lose his grip on the motor control handle.

"What the hell was that?" he said aloud. He let the engine idle in neutral and looked over the side, but saw nothing. Shrugging his shoulders, he turned and put his hand on the motor, but drew it back sharply as he felt a sharp shock. It felt as if a hundred hot needles had suddenly been shoved into his hand.

"Ow!" he yelled, sucking at his fingers to try to stop the stinging. The engine stalled out suddenly. "Damn!" he muttered in frustration. "Now what?"

The young female approached from below, positioned herself under the right side of the boat, and flipped it over with her snout. Collins went into the water, losing his cellphone, which passed by the adult female watching from the depths. He tried to scramble

up onto the turned-over Zodiac, which was surprisingly difficult. He positioned both arms and one leg on top of the slippery gray boat bottom, and desperately tried to find a handhold to pull himself up the rest of the way. The young female made a twisting turn underneath the boat and started her approach, jaws starting to open, when her mother stopped her with a series of clicks. She swung smoothly out of the way as the larger animal rose toward the boat.

Collins could feel that something was going on underneath him, and increased his desperate scramble to get his whole body on top of the Zodiac. He heard a splashing behind him and looked on in horror as a massive head with a mouth of nightmarish proportions appeared on the surface, gazing at him calmly. He froze.

The creature opened its jaws only a little and enveloped his lower leg, which was dangling in the water. There was a sickening crunch as she neatly and surgically took his leg off just below the knee. She remained on the surface another moment, looking at him with his Adidas-clad foot dangling out of the front of her mouth, looking as if she wanted to show him what she had done. Then she sank out of sight. Below the boat she let out a series of clicks for her offspring. Both of them continued to look up as they sank downwards into the Stygian depths, their pale white skins fading out like ghosts backing into a haunted mansion. The adult Mosasaur had one more lesson to teach.

That lesson was not long in coming. The enormity of what had just happened finally hit Collins, who started swinging his injured leg up and down, violently splashing the water. Blood started to pump out of the leg. It formed an expanding mist under the surface, as pink as a cumulus cloud hanging over a sunset.

The first shark, a large dark blue hammerhead with an off-white belly, appeared in less than five minutes. He circled the boat, lifting his eyes slightly above the water to see what was going on. He took a cautious bite out of the boat, but noted that it was not good to eat. The area that he punctured started leaking air, and slowly spun the turned-over boat in a circle. Had the shark been human, the scene might have reminded him of a large Lazy Susan on a table in a Chinese restaurant.

Collins finally hauled himself totally on top of the boat, but carelessly stuck out his right arm to the side. The shark approached and bit the hand and forearm off with razor-sharp teeth. Collins stared dully at the spot where his forearm and hand used to be, now empty space except for two spurting streams of bright crimson arterial blood.

He screamed as he saw two other fins approaching. He recognized they were makos, and remembered that these were among the most dangerous man eaters. They gazed at him with flat black eyes that seemed to suck out his soul. He looked first toward Paradise Resort and then toward the ship and yelled for help, but realized it was hopeless.

The second mako bumped its nose against the boat, causing its passenger to slide further into the water. At the last moment, Collins managed to find a handhold on the slippery rubber surface. At first he felt only a bump as the mako sliced off his other leg just above the knee. Then the pain hit him, and he started to shriek, a high keening tone that might have curdled the blood of any humans unfortunate enough to hear it, but which did not faze the three hungry diners. He heard the boat hissing as another air bladder was bitten by one of the sharks, and then felt himself sliding slowly, inexorably, into the water. His vision blurred and grew cloudy as one shark after the other ripped additional chunks out of him.

Hundreds of feet below, the monster lay in wait. She had formed a picture of what was happening above, and sent an alerting series of clicks to her daughter. They emerged slowly from the darkness, like pale angels of death. They saw that the three large sharks had been joined by several smaller ones. All of the sharks were oblivious to the trap, totally focused on their gory meal, which was still moving feebly and holding on with one hand.

The adult female went for the hammerhead, seizing it and snapping it in two with one ratcheting motion of her lower jaw. Turning quickly, she did the same to one of the large makos, and whirled again to bite the other one in half.

She had affirmed her reputation as the world's most efficient killing machine, killing three of the ocean's most formidable predators before they were even aware of the danger.

Her daughter seized a five-foot leopard shark and concentrated on that, biting large chunks out of it and sending them down her gullet. She looked around and noted that the remaining sharks had fled. She filed away what her mother had wanted her to learn: patience can turn one kill into several. She started on one of the sections of the hammerhead, gorging herself on bloody chunks. Mother and daughter continued their gruesome meal with relish, until their bellies were full. They had finished off the sharks when they heard a splash. Collins's hand had finally released its grip, and what was left of his upper body now slid into the water. The adult snapped her head to the right and swallowed it in one gulp, almost as an afterthought.

Chapter 29

An hour later David was in the Equipment Room, surrounded by a handful of people, including Erika and Larry. He announced that AJ had been notified about the safe. He would arrive in a couple of hours.

"Let's see what we've got," he said, as the safe door was swung open. "There's no water coming out, which is great– it means the safe was watertight, and the documents should be dry. That'll make AJ really happy."

He pulled packages out of the safe. He ticked them off as he looked at them. "Here's a Bill of Lading, the ship's log, what looks like the Captain's diary, a set of sealed orders marked *Streng Geheim*—that means Top Secret, and a lot of file folders that seem to contain codes and other documents. Let's take a look at the Bill of Lading. That's a list of what freight the sub is carrying."

He produced a photocopied document, and explained. "This is a copy of the Lading Bill I got from the German Museum of Naval History." He looked closely at both lists. The first page was identical in both, but on the second page of the U-boat copy there were several items crossed out with the notation "Wgf. an I-249." He looked at the others. "It notes that various items were transferred to the Japanese sub, including two 500 kilogram containers of mercury."

His heartbeat quickened as he saw a notation written in ink in a precise hand, "Ang. 1 Satz 5.000 Goldmünzen, Am., USD20, in 4 Säcke."

It was the gold coins! They had been taken onto the sub, all 5,000 of them, in four bags! But where were they? His eyes flew to the rightmost column on the page, where he saw the annotation "Pz. Schrank 2"– safe number two! He examined the other items on the page, including one that read, "Krone, Englisch, 18. Jahrhundert," and in the right hand column, "Pz. Schrank 1." With relief he saw that Nana's coronet, the 18th Century crown he had been looking for, was apparently in this safe. He saw a large sack in the back, but decided to look at that later. He turned to his small audience.

"It says here..." he drew out the moment a few seconds longer, "...that there are four bags of coins in a second safe on the submarine." He joined the others in their whoops of joy and high-fiving all around. He put the Bill of Lading and the rest of the articles back into the safe, and picked up the Captain's Diary, and said, "Let's see if we can figure out what happened to these guys."

He sat down and opened up the diary, aware that these pages had been written well over a half-century ago.

"The Captain's name was Werner Schlenther," he announced, "He was a *Kapitaenleutnant*, a Commander, and he was born July 4, 1910. So he was about 32 when he wrote this."

He looked at the rapt faces in front of him. "You'll have to be patient with me. My German is really rusty. And this is old-style handwriting, which is a little cryptic."

"Let's see, it says here that they sailed from St. Nazaire, France, on June 14, with provisions for up to 100 days. He had just... found out that his younger brother had died, on the Eastern front, near some place called Smolensk."

He started flipping through the pages. "Here he meets up with the Japanese sub, at night, and drinks sake and cognac with a Captain Mikasashi while the stuff is being transferred. He then heads for Anguilla. Ah, here we are. The last few pages."

He took a deep breath. "On July 4, 0230, proceeding 161 degrees South. The seas are still rough, but the storm is dying down. Several times during the night we have seen strange lights on the horizon, which we feared to be American or British destroyers. There have also been irregularities in our compass readings, and I have asked Petty Officer Eisenhauer to check it out. There is a rumor that the Allies have some new kind of radar, which can detect us from far away. Perhaps it can also interfere with our instruments."

"I was on the bridge with Lt. Weissmann when a bright light suddenly flashed in front of us, off the port bow, approaching us directly at high speed. I ordered an immediate dive, and we traveled underwater at 50 meters depth at maximum speed. Our sonar indicated something behind us that matched our speed, though the enemy did not use active sonar on us. Because our maps showed a group of islands to the South that had extensive coral reefs all around them, I ordered a change in course."

"Petty Officer Eisenhauer reported that all our electronic gauges were behaving strangely, giving wild readings. Since we were now navigating totally in the blind, I gave the order to surface, to try to fight it out with whatever was pursuing us. We were starting to rise when suddenly there was a loud collision, and everything and everyone went crashing toward the bow. The inside of the boat was bedlam, with lights flickering on and off and water coming in from everywhere. There was no word from either the bow or stern torpedo compartments, but I received reports that these had been breached, and that the other compartments were being sealed."

David glanced around. "This is the final page."

"As I sit writing this, I am aware that we are in an impossible situation. Almost the entire crew is dead, and the only two compartments still intact are the Officers' and Petty Officers' Quarters. We seem to have crashed into something. I presume it is a coral bank or an underwater mountain, although our maps show there should be none in this area. Perhaps the malfunctioning compass caused us to crash into what we were trying to avoid. It looks like our boat is one more of the many victims of the curse of the Bermuda Triangle.'"

"'I have spoken privately with Weissmann, my old and trusted friend. I told him how I felt about this mission, that I resented having to deliver freight like a delivery boy, but even worse, that I had to pay off spies, men who are traitors to their country.'"

David read the next two sentences only to himself. "I am also aware that the spy demanded the crown we are carrying for him, and that this was obtained by the Gestapo from some man named Weinstock. I do not imagine they used any gentle means to get it away from him."

He continued reading out loud. "I had a last discussion with the survivors, four officers and six Petty Officers. I told them that we had radioed for help, and such help could well be on the way, since U-boat headquarters was aware of our position. I praised them for their bold and courageous service that was so vital for our Fatherland. I told them whatever lies I could dream up to make them feel better. But we all saw the truth in each other's eyes. After the others went to their own compartment, we closed the hatch, and we officers broke out the last of our cigars and brandy, and enjoyed them at leisure, as if we were at a party."

"When the air started getting heavy and hard to breathe, we retired to our bunks. I am now sitting here in the near darkness with my little pocket lamp, feeling the small room and the heaviness of the sea all around pressing in on me. My last thoughts are of deep shame, of bringing these fine men down here to a miserable end. And of talking my brother into joining the Party and the Army, all of which ended up in his death somewhere in the vast depths of Russia, fighting people he did not know and that he had nothing against."

"I have a feeling I am going to hell for what I have done, or helped to be done. And, right on time, I can hear loud tearing and ripping sounds at both ends of the boat, as if angels of darkness are coming to get me. Now I hear a strange screeching sound, as if giant teeth were raking along the hull. Perhaps it is the devil. The devil, indeed."

Chapter 30

Later, alone in his cabin, David looked at the papers and other objects he'd removed from the safe, which were arranged on his desk in stacks. He'd found a large bag that held a wood-and-glass box, in which he could see the gold coronet he'd been searching for. Before he stopped to examine it, he quickly ran the documents from the U-Boat through a scanner. On a whim, he also copied the Captain's diary. "I want to finish reading it," he told Bucky.

A few minutes later, his mobile phone buzzed. It was Ben, who said, "AJ and somebody else will arrive in half an hour."

David finished copying the scanned files onto a memory chip, and inserted the original papers into his desk.

He carefully opened the wooden box and took out the coronet. It was a thin gold headband beset with two rows of jewels that sparkled like fire. He examined one of the stones with a 20x loupe he kept in his desk, and shook his head. "This is a really big royal blue sapphire, Bucky," he said. "It's probably pretty valuable."

A second stone drew a low whistle from him. "Now, this is really interesting. It's a ruby, about 30 carats in size. But I can't find any inclusions in the thing." He explained, "Rubies normally have impurities or striations called 'feathers.' If they don't, they're either man-made or were 'augmented' by heating them or injecting plastic to fill up cracks or holes. But this ruby has been underwater for over 70 years. They didn't have that technology back then." He let Bucky sniff the stone, and noted, "I'm assuming Nana believes the crown is worth a lot more than half a million, and that's why she was willing to invest in finding it."

As he polished the brilliant, skilfully carved facets of the diamonds and colored stones in the coronet, he thought back to the moment when he first discussed this with Emma Weinstock, his great-aunt in New York. She treated him as if he were her own grandson, and he had called her "Nana" since he was six years old. Emma had offered financial help to his mother, but she was too proud to take it, and instead worked double shifts as a waitress to support them.

After his life collapsed around his ears, Emma had called him and invited him to ice cream sundaes in Central Park, one of their favorite pastimes when he was young. "What are you going to do next, David?" she had asked. She knew the situation with his ex-wife. His shoulders slumped as he admitted, "I don't know. I've wasted my life. I made a lot of money, but I've never done anything that makes a difference. I'm a complete and utter failure."

Emma looked at him silently.

He asked her. "If you could have anything in the world you wanted, Nana, what would it be?"

"Why, the crown, of course," she had replied immediately.

"The crown?"

"Yes, dear. Long ago, when I was very young, when we lived in Rome, my father bought a crown at auction in London. It belonged to some English nobleman that had hit on hard times, with gambling and drinking, I think."

"What happened to it?"

"One day in 1942, the Gestapo came to the house early in the morning. I heard them and my father arguing in the other room. They arrested him and took the crown away. I never saw either one again."

"Later, I was sent to New York to live with relatives. I inquired about the crown after the war–it was a coronet, really, much smaller than a crown–at the Survivors Art Center, which traces paintings and other art that the Nazis looted. They discovered it was sent to German Navy Headquarters, but could trace it no further."

"German Navy Headquarters?"

"Yes," Emma replied. "I can't imagine why their military wanted it."

David had asked. "Nana, what if I found it for you?"

Emma had started to laugh, but instead went to a bureau and wrote out a check. She said, "You'll need money, and a lot of help. Let me know how much more you need. I'll go as high as half a million."

David had taken the check and said, "This is just a loan."

She had rejoiced with him in each step of his progress–finding the crown listed in old military documents in Kiel, Germany, and then finding it had been shipped out on a U-Boat that was sunk in the Atlantic. Finding the U-Boat seemed like a long shot to her, but she had gladly invested in David's expedition. Unfortunately, the money covered expenses only for the first year, and he had faced defeat, until AJ jumped in and bought him more time.

And here he was with the crown in his hands! David heard a light knocking on his door, and AJ's voice, "Hey, David!" He quickly put the crown back into its box, and placed it into his closet.

"Come on in, AJ," he said as he unlocked and opened the door to his cabin, admitting AJ—who clasped his hand and gave him a quick hug—and a tall, stiff man wearing a bland tie and a dark suit that was out of place in the tropics.

AJ introduced his companion with, "This is Leonard Bedrosian, my boss." David shook his hand briefly, noting that it was ice cold. He studied the new man for a moment, noting that he had a prominent, aquiline nose, dark blue circles under his eyes, and a comb-over that tented a patch of open scalp.

"Have a seat," David invited, pointing to the two chairs in his cabin. AJ sat on the bed, reaching over to scratch Bucky behind the ears.

"Where are the documents?" Bedrosian snapped. His eyes darted around the room, and rested on the safe. He crossed over to it and opened the door, exposing an empty interior. "Where are they?"

David bristled. "May I remind you that you're guests on my ship? If you keep talking to me like I'm your fucking butler, I'll throw you off of it!"

Bedrosian's pale cheeks actually registered some color as he opened his mouth to reply, but AJ restrained him with a, "Whoa! I know we're all anxious to get to this. Leonard, why don't you sit down and let's find out what David has to say. If he has good news for us, like he said on the phone, we don't want to steal the man's thunder."

Bedrosian's scowl turned into an oily smile. "Of course. Just a little anxious, Mister Kilmer. I'm sure you understand." He settled into a chair, his smile still pasted onto his face, its sincerity undermined by rapidly shifting, reptilian eyes.

David gave a quick summary of their discovery of the U-Boat and the extraction of the safe. "The great thing is that the cabin the safe was in was still watertight, so the papers survived in pristine shape," he noted. "And here they are!"

He opened a large drawer in his desk and extracted the various sets of papers he had found after opening the safe. He deliberately handed each packet to AJ first, to the obvious annoyance of Bedrosian. "Here are the Captain's Log, the Bills of Lading, the communications encryption codes, different sets of maps and the Technical Manuals for this submarine."

"These have been opened and looked at," Bedrosian scowled. "Our agreement was that no one else would look at these papers."

David looked at him sternly. "No one else has, other than me. These papers describe what's on the sub, Bedrosian, including locations of dangerous munitions I needed to know about to keep from blowing up my crew."

Bedrosian sputtered, "Our agreement..." He looked at AJ, "What we paid for..."

AJ laid a restraining arm on him. "Chill, Leonard. Let's see what else he's got." He knew David well enough to realize the best was yet to come.

"Finally," David continued, pulling open another drawer and extracting a slender metal case from it, "there was this."

They looked at the thin rectangular metal box, which had a lock and unbroken seal on it, and an official form fastened to the front with *Streng Geheim—Kommandosache* stamped on it in bright red ink.

"If the mission of this sub in this region was to contact a spy network, it looks like the codes and IDs for doing so are all in this folder."

Bedrosian reached out to seize the metal case from David, who forestalled this by swiftly handing it to AJ. Frustrated, Bedrosian sputtered, "Yeah. And maybe it's nothing at all."

"I'll spell it out for you," David shot back. "That attached cover letter says 'Top Secret' and refers to—and I quote—'Communications Codes and Identities of Contacts for the Anguilla/Caribbean Sector,' and is personally signed by Admiral Raeder, head of U-Boat Forces. It references 'Fall Elektrisch Blau,' or 'Operation Electric Blue.' Perhaps you'd like me to open it up and make really sure?"

Bedrosian grabbed the metal container and examined it from all sides. "It's unopened?" he asked.

"Yes," replied David. "Not even the U-Boat Captain had opened it yet. He was apparently waiting until he got closer to Anguilla, or received some type of signal, to break the seal."

Bedrosian looked at the form attached to the box, peering closely at the signatures and official stamps. "And it refers to 'Electric Blue'? You're sure that's what it says?" he asked.

"Yes, I am," replied David. "And now I have something else for you." He pulled a typed form from the top of his desk. "I want you and AJ to sign this. It says that you received what you paid for, and acknowledge receipt thereof."

Bedrosian looked at the typed receipt as if it could bite him. "I'll take this back and get it signed for you," he said. "I'm not in a position to..."

David interrupted him in mid-sentence. "If you're not a qualified representative of your company, you shouldn't be picking this up. This material is not leaving my custody without a signed receipt."

Bedrosian scowled, but reached for a pen and signed the bottom of the form, as did AJ, over a line that said "Witness." David handed him an extra copy of the form, and said, "That's it, then. I hope you're happy with your investment."

AJ stood up and pumped David's hand vigorously. "We're beyond happy, David," he enthused. "This is a huge win for all of us. Nobody believed me when I said you could pull it off. This is fantastic."

He nodded toward Bedrosian. "Leonard is actually overjoyed. He just doesn't show it too well."

Bedrosian stood, holding tightly onto the metal case. "Yes, actually, good work, Mr. Kilmer." He looked at his watch. "I've got to get this back to Wash–, er, back to my management right away." He looked at AJ. "We've got to go."

AJ nodded. "Go ahead. I'll be with you in a minute." Bedrosian shook hands stiffly with David once more and hastily exited the cabin.

AJ came toward David, visibly more relaxed with the departure of his boss. "Sorry about that, David," he said ruefully. "He's kind of an asshole. But..." and his face brightened, and he grasped David by the shoulder, "...you did it, man. Congrats." He looked questioningly at David. "What about *your* treasure?"

David shrugged. "I haven't found it yet, but it feels like we're close. If we find the coins, you'll get something out of it. You deserve it."

AJ shook his head. "No thanks, man. You don't owe me anything. I just hope you make it out of here in one piece. I'm picking up some funny vibes in town. Something's up. I'm worried about you."

David looked at him anxiously. "I'd like to ask you a favor." He opened his closet and picked up the wooden box with the coronet in it, and stuffed it into a nylon athletic bag. "Could you get this to someplace safe for me, please?" he asked. He scribbled Emma Weinstock's New York address on a sheet of paper and put it into the bag. "If anything should happen to me, here's the address to send this to. Make sure it gets there at all costs. It's real important, OK? But no one else can know about this. No one!"

AJ looked directly into David's eyes. "All right, my friend. I swear I'll keep it safe, and forward it if anything happens. I can probably get it in the diplomatic mail pouch at the Embassy on St. Maarten."

"That would be great," David said. "Get it away from here as soon as you can. The person getting this means a lot to me—she's family."

AJ nodded. "Your family is my family, my brother. Consider it done."

The two men shook hands warmly, and AJ left the cabin. David picked up a walkie-talkie and called the Bridge. "Come and wake me when they break through to the Petty Officers Quarters," he said when Bob answered, and threw himself on the bed for a nap, exhausted.

Chapter 31

AJ looked at the darkening skies around his speedboat and turned to Bedrosian. "Leonard, what's in that folder? You know you can trust me."

Bedrosian scowled. "No way."

AJ pleaded with him. "I get the feeling that whatever's in that folder is going to get my friends on the ship killed."

Bedrosian shrugged his shoulders mockingly. "Your so-called friends on the ship are not my concern, and they shouldn't be yours, either. You've earned a commendation and maybe a promotion with this operation. I suggest you leave it alone!"

AJ shook his head. "I can't just let them get hurt!"

Bedrosian looked at him sternly. "Your first obligation is to national security. The rest is secondary. You know you have to let people go in this service. If you don't, you'd better learn it quick. Case closed. Just get me to the St. Maarten airport as fast as you can."

AJ steered the boat at full speed, considering his options. His chance finally came as they were less than 30 minutes from St. Maarten's Harbor. Bedrosian started looking anxious, and finally told AJ, "I've got to go to the head."

He started to pick up the briefcase that he had inserted the metal folder and the Captain's Log into, but changed his mind when he discovered he could not make his way in the bouncing speedboat without having both hands available. He laid the briefcase onto a table and lurched urgently toward the head in the back of the boat.

AJ did not hesitate a moment. After locking the speedboat's control wheel on autopilot, he quickly opened the briefcase. "For once, I can finally use my operations training," he thought to himself. He quickly pried the wax seal off the German folder with a thin blade, and scanned the contents.

He let out a low whistle. "God damn it, that's what I was afraid of," he said under his breath. He glanced toward the back of the boat, where he could hear flushing noises. He quickly ran a cigar lighter under the wax long enough to partly melt it, and pressed it back into place. He inserted the folder back into the briefcase, shut it and returned it to the desk. He had just returned to the wheel and resumed actively steering the boat when Bedrosian reappeared, and glanced immediately toward his briefcase.

As AJ approached the pier he addressed Bedrosian, keeping his voice matter-of-fact. "By the way, just out of curiosity, Leonard. If that folder had information that affected some of the officials in the Caribbean today, what would you do with it? Just hypothetically speaking, mind you."

Bedrosian smiled coldly. "Just hypothetically speaking, that would be wonderful. It could mean that we would have some key people in this area under our control? Which would be worth a lot to our government. Just like the rest of the, er, material you provide."

AJ continued. "Again, just hypothetically, if whoever was affected by it threatened to kill David and his group or do them real harm, would you use the material to save them?"

Bedrosian stared at him. "Are you insane? And throw away valuable political capital? I don't give a shit about any of those treasure hunters. They've served their purpose. And if I hear of you doing anything more with them, you may need to start thinking about another job!"

As the boat docked, Bedrosian leaped off with his briefcase. A dark limousine waited for him nearby. He turned to AJ. "I'm headed to the airport to take a flight to D.C. If I were you, I'd start setting my priorities in order. So long!"

AJ muttered under his breath, "I suspect you're right, at that." He looked at the gym bag that held the package with the crown, and got out his satellite phone to call the American Embassy. A secretary picked up the phone. "Paul Sparks, please," he requested. She forwarded him, and he smiled as his friend answered.

"Hey, Paul, this is AJ. Listen, I need a favor. Can I drop something off with you to go to Washington in the diplomatic pouch? It's really important. No, it's unclassified, but it needs to stay locked up in a container. Thanks. I'll be there in 15 minutes." He hailed a cab and gave the driver directions to the Embassy.

Chapter 32

A few hours later, David was awakened by Werner, who was shaking him by the shoulder. "Come on, wake up!"

"What?" David started to ask, and Werner told him, jubilantly, "They're about to open the hatch on the Petty Officers' Quarters. They've been working in shifts through the night. With a little luck, the big safe might be in there, like you said."

"OK, I'm up," David groaned as he slowly swung his legs over the edge of the bed. He looked at his watch. "My God, I slept for over 5 hours. Werner, why am I so tired all the time?"

Werner sighed. "Because you're spending too much time on the bottom," he chided. "Your body hasn't had a chance to recover. Are you sure you want to go down again?"

"You bet," David answered. "Ask Mark to join me."

Half an hour later, David and Mark Zinni were in the dark water in their dive gear, checking the controls on their diving sleds as they slowly motored below the surface of the water. David glanced around. The sky above him was heavily overcast, with clouds racing across the horizon, revealing silver slices of moon every now and then. Sunrise was still over an hour away. He could make out Dragon/Paradise Island, a few miles distant on the horizon. The depths of the ocean below were hidden in an eerie pitch black.

As he submerged deeper, he could feel the presence of a great many creatures in the ocean around him, all of them invisible. He had never liked night diving; the small cone of light cast by the aquasled in front of him illuminated almost nothing, and the sense of something sneaking up behind him in the darkness caused the hair to stand up on his neck.

To snap himself out of it he talked with Mark. "Everything OK with you, partner?"

"A-OK," Mark replied. Let's get going."

They cranked up the sleds and headed for the cave entrance, following a cable with small lights strung along it that ran from the ship to a post near the cave entrance. Because the cable was slack, it tended to drop precipitously toward the bottom at the beginning, and they descended slowly, watching the depth gauges and getting adjusted to the pressure. As the cable started to even out and the way to the cave entrance in the mountainside was approaching directly in front of them, David was about to twist the accelerator grip when he was stopped by an exclamation from Mark. "Whoa, what is that?"

"What is what?" David replied, rather irritably. He wanted to get this dive over with.

"To our right, where the bottom drops off real fast," Mark replied.

David stared in that direction, but could not make out anything in the darkness. "Beats me," he said. "I don't have your eagle eyesight."

"Turn off your lights," Mark suggested, and switched off his headlight and instrument panel. David hesitated a moment and then did likewise, plunging them into total darkness. He let his eyes adjust, and then he saw it too–a faint glow of faint sources of light somewhere to the right and far below. They were near the shelf, where the bottom abruptly plunged from about 200 feet down to 3,000.

"How far away do you think it is?" he asked Mark.

"Hard to tell without knowing how big it is," Mark replied. "It looks like either four or five lights. Some in a group, and one a little farther behind. They seem to be heading for the same mountain that we are."

"There are lots of large critters living deep in the ocean that are bioluminescent," Dave ventured, "But I don't know if any of them move in herds or groups, except some types of jellyfish. But they're moving too fast for jellyfish." A thought struck him. "I remember seeing something like this in Texas. See the way they're moving back and forth a little? It reminds me of cowboys herding cattle. But what kinds of ocean creatures can herd other fish?"

"Actually, that's not uncommon," Mark, who had a degree in oceanography, replied. "Dolphins can herd whole schools of fish, using bubbles to frighten and concentrate the prey tighter and tighter together. They gather as a group below the school of fish and drive them up toward the surface with these so-called "bubble nets," and then chomp into them when they're all bunched together like a ball. That way they can eat fish they could never catch in the open ocean."

"But what kind of creature can do the same thing horizontally?" David asked. "Do you think these could be humans?"

"I don't know, but we might as well head into the cave. The rest of the team is waiting," Mark replied, and turned the power on his sled back on. As soon as he did, he gasped. "Shit!"

"What's the matter?" David asked.

"Look at my instrument panel," Mark replied. "It looks like a Christmas tree!" David looked over, and was speechless at what he saw. The instruments and lights on Mark's sled were flickering at random, and his headlight had only a feeble glow.

"Let me try mine," David yelled, and activated the starter button. A couple of clicks told him a story he did not want to hear. "Mine won't start at all! What the hell do we do now?"

"Probably the same thing you do when Microsoft Windows crashes," Mark replied dryly. "Turn it off, wait a few minutes, and then reboot."

They switched off their machines and waited in the darkness, which David could feel pressing down on him. A few minutes later, he said, "Go!" and they both pressed their starters. Both sleds sprang to life, and a moment later the headlights blazed a path in front of them.

"It looks like whatever was wrong went away," David said, puzzled.

"Yes, it did," Mark replied. "By the way, those lights we saw have disappeared."

Chapter 33

The six adult Mosasaurs discharged their electric organs at regular intervals as they approached the wide cave entrance near the bottom of the submerged mountain, hundreds of feet below the surface. The power arcs from each of the two males stretched out from the head in wide curves to the end of the tail, over 60 feet to the rear. The females were even larger than the males, over 70 feet long and weighing over 20 tons. The Mosasaurs were not activating the high voltage they used for killing prey. Rather, they were using low voltage discharges that let them drive their prey along. Occasional rapid click-click-click signals from the lead male gave them directions on which way to turn, or how fast to proceed.

The electric organs of the two youngsters, who were approaching 20 feet in length, were still relatively undeveloped. The mother Mosasaur noticed that quite a few fish were managing to slip out of their trap. It did not matter. There were hundreds of fish being pushed into the yawning mouth of the cavern, which was over a hundred feet across. The herd of refugees included many large fish, including grouper and a few sharks. Once in the labyrinthine underwater cave system, all of these could be hunted down at leisure and devoured.

Although the adults preferred to hunt giant squid to maintain their bulk, the youngsters were not yet able to penetrate to the necessary depths to take the deep-diving squid, and did not have the power to take on such large prey.

The electric organs of these Mosasaurs were similar to those of electric eels, but on a larger scale. They consisted of hundreds of differently charged cellular groups, similar to the cells of a battery, which could be set off simultaneously. The killing effect was limited to a few hundred feet, but the electrical force could reach out beyond a thousand feet, and could disrupt electronic instruments even beyond that. To find food at even longer ranges, Mosasaurs had developed an incredible sense of hearing and the ability to sense pressure waves via small ducts that ran along the jaw line. They also had an acute sense of smell that could sense prey over a mile away.

A large grouper tried to escape the trap. It turned around within the funnel shaped opening to the cavern, and swam for its life. The Alpha male of the group sensed its movement in the darkness, and wagged its long flat tail, not unlike the motion of a crocodile, to build up speed. As the grouper tried to dart by on his left side, the Mosasaur extended its two left flippers, fan-shaped appendages with incredible strength that allowed the animal to turn on a dime. It struck the 500-pound fish and impaled it securely in long rows of backwards-curving 9-inch teeth. The ancient land-borne ancestors of the Mosasaur would have had to open their jaws at this point, to get the prey to move back into the mouth, using gravity to make it move in that direction, but this male had no need of gravity. His lower jaw ratcheted back and forth, moving a 300-pound chunk of fish to the rear, where the teeth in the roof of his mouth held it fast. Another movement of the lower jaw and the grouper disappeared as if it had never existed. The behemoth continued forward, sensing the rest of its dinner struggling along through the caverns ahead.

Chapter 34

David and Mark entered the cavern, guided by the lights that had been placed along the walls, and parked their aquasleds next to the U-Boat. David removed a package that had been strapped to his sled, and within minutes they were inside the submarine, listening to the reports of the team on site.

"We've removed the door to the Petty Officers Quarters," one of the crew members informed them, "and we're ready to rock if there's a safe in there!"

David smiled, and gave him a thumbs-up. "Way to go." He turned to the entryway, and then, as an afterthought, asked the man in front of him, "By the way, Larry, did you guys manage to open the hatch in the conning tower?"

Larry shook his head from side to side, the motion causing the hair behind his mask to wave to and fro. "Not really. We concentrated on this first."

"That's fine," David said, "But make sure it gets done before you leave here. Call in another team if you have to." He handed Larry the bag he had brought from the aquasled. "And put this right next to the hatch in that compartment."

"Sure," said Larry. "By the way, what's in the bags? I saw you placed one in each compartment."

"They're insurance," David replied. "Each one has an emergency kit, with a couple of flashlights, an emergency air tank with mouthpiece, a first aid kit with tourniquet and pressurized bandages, some beef broth in a crushproof container, and a small spear gun. Call me paranoid, but I wanted something handy in case one of us got trapped in one of these compartments, or encountered some dangerous beastie, at least until help arrived."

"I like that kind of thinking," Larry replied. "And now, I'm gonna bust a gut if you don't check out this next compartment soon. I've only got about ten more minutes of bottom time left before I have to go back!"

"Coming right up!" David replied as he swam through the portal into the next compartment of the U-Boat. He explored carefully, not wanting to stir up debris that would impair his vision. He found what he was looking for almost right away. It was almost anticlimactic. On the port side of the compartment, under the Chief Master Petty Officer's bunk, was another safe, and this one looked large enough for the size of the cargo that David and his fellow treasure seekers were interested in.

David carefully checked the area for munitions or other dangers. Finding the area to be safe, he called back, "OK, Larry, looks good, come on in, very slowly."

When Larry drew abreast of him, he pointed toward the safe, and said, "There it is! Rock and roll!"

Larry's eyes shone brightly. "You think this is it?"

"We won't know until we get it up on top," David replied. "It's not over till the fat lady sings. But if she's not singing yet, at least she's humming."

David exited the compartment and worked his way to the rear of the sub, automatically checking equipment items they had installed in the last week, including the emergency kits, video camera stations, and power profile indicators for the lights.

Satisfied with the progress, he returned to the ship with Mark, left word to wake him when the second safe came on board, and collapsed on his bunk once more, almost landing on top of the snoozing Bucky, who moved out of the way just in time, loudly protesting his disturbed slumber.

Chapter 35

DuBois turned to his assistant, Lieutenant Charlebois. "A boat went out to the Global Explorer and came back, and you're just telling me this now?"

Charlebois almost stuttered his reply. It was well known what could happen to people that displeased DuBois. "Yeah. There were two guys on board, AJ and some white guy from the States."

DuBois's nostrils flared, a sure sign of agitation. "We know they found the submarine and brought the safe on board. We found out that much from Collins. Unfortunately, he had to blow his cover to tell us. By the way, whatever happened to him?"

The Lieutenant shrugged his shoulders. "Don't know. His last transmission after telling us the safe was coming on board was, 'Oh shit, here comes Bob.'"

DuBois thought for a minute. "If a boat went out to the Global Explorer after that, they may have offloaded the gold. If they're on Anguilla, I want you to get those fuckers, and grab anything they may have on them. And I mean NOW!"

The Lieutenant shook his head. "They didn't come back to Anguilla. They went to St. Maarten. Our people saw the white guy going straight to the airport with an escort. We couldn't touch him."

"Was he carrying a lot of luggage, like hundreds of pounds of gold coins?" DuBois asked anxiously.

"No, all he had was a briefcase."

"At least he didn't get the treasure," DuBois said, relieved. "Where is AJ right now?"

"We don't know. He disappeared in St. Maarten with a light gym bag. Somebody said he took a business trip to Martinique. He usually goes there for just a day or two."

"Put a guard on his boat," DuBois snarled. "And find out where he is. Right now!"

"Aunt Marie might know," his subordinate said.

"Send a couple of cars out to her house and question her," DuBois told him sternly. "And don't do it too gently. It's about time we got rid of that old bitch."

He called in Major Monrey, his second in command, and told him, "Two men left the ship, but they had nothing on them, so the safe must still be on board. Our group should be ready by now. Get cracking!"

He got into his police car with Monrey, and told the driver to put on the lights and siren. They went to the harbor at full speed, screeching to a stop near the largest of three police boats tied up at the docks.

He jumped on board, and briefly reviewed the constabulary standing there. There were several regular policemen and eight members of a Jamaica street gang that he had brought in and deputized the previous week. "Let's go!" he shouted, and the crew quickly cast off. The boat surged through the water, carving twin foaming waterfalls with its bow as it headed out to sea.

Chapter 36

Aunt Marie was taking a nap when her security alarm went off. She went to the window and drew back the lace curtains to look out at the yard, but could not see anything in the gaining twilight. Suddenly the door crashed in, and several tough-looking men in camouflage clothing with green armbands bearing the legend "Police" burst in, guns drawn.

Two of them forced Aunt Marie to sit in one of her chairs and handcuffed her to it, while the others searched the house. One of the men, with the twin silver bars of a Captain on his collar, turned off the lights in the room, leaving only one lamp burning, which he turned into Marie's face, so that she could barely see anything beyond the light. He spoke with a thick Jamaican accent.

"We need some answers. If we get them, you might live through the night," a voice from the other side of the bright light told her. "Where is AJ?"

She heard other cars come to a screeching halt in front of her house. More policemen poured into the house. They all wore camouflage uniforms, and several had evil-looking automatic weapons slung across their chests.

She shook her head. "Why would I know where anyone is? I just live here alone. That AJ, he's always on a business trip. Why don't you check the airport if you want to find him?"

The man with the Captain's bars on his shoulders snapped at her. "We asking the questions around here, not you!"

"Who cares what you doing?" Marie shot back at him. "I'm a citizen of this country, and a long-time resident of this island. You are foreigners. You have no rights here."

The Captain slapped her sharply across the face. "That is not for you to say. We are members of a special squadron of police looking for terrorists on this island."

She tried to look at the Captain, but was dazzled by the bright light. "The only terrorists I see here are you gangsters. You the ones come busting in here. You the ones attacking God-fearing folk."

The Captain pulled up a chair, turned it around and rested his forearms on its back. He turned toward one of the men, an angry-looking thug with a crisscross of scars on his face. "Corporal, let's see what you learned in your gang in Kingston. Let's go!"

Chapter 37

David was awakened by Erika, who was gently shaking him. He awoke slowly as her face swam into focus. "Hmmm," he said dreamily, "I was just..."

He sat up on the bed abruptly. "Hi. You've wiped me out. You can put the money on the nightstand. Leave a generous tip."

She smiled at him, fatigue showing in her eyes. "Yeh. In your dreams!" She reached down to pet Bucky, who was completing a wide yawn. "I was doing some research and heard a commotion on deck. The second safe is coming in. Larry asked me to come get you. It'll be on here in about 20 minutes."

David looked at his watch. "You're up late. It's past 3 a.m. Let's go get coffee."

As he filled two cups for them in the galley, he nodded to Bob and Ben, who were nursing steaming cups at a table. They sat down with them. David turned to Erika. "What's keeping you up?"

Erika sighed, shaking her head. "We've been going over the Big Mo fossil in the hillside. We hoped to find evidence that the remains were in early Quaternary layers, about 20 to 30 million years old."

"Can't you just do carbon dating on the fossils?" Ben asked.

"No, unfortunately not," Erika replied. "For one thing, we don't have the actual remains of the animal."

Seeing Ben's eyebrows shoot up quizzically, she explained. "The way carbon dating works is this. Animals breathe in fresh air, which has a known quantity of radioactive versions of materials such as carbon and cesium. After they die, the radioactive material decays over time. Since we know the half-life of carbon—the time it takes for half the radioactive form to die off—we can measure how much radioactive carbon is left, and calculate how long the animal has not been breathing. But fossils are not the bones themselves; they're sand and minerals that have replaced where the bones used to be."

She continued, "In any case, carbon dating is accurate only around 60,000 years. So we look for other organisms that we can recognize in a layer, so we can get an estimate of how old that layer of sediment is."

"So what's the problem?" Ben inquired. Haven't you been able to find other dinosaurs in that layer?"

Erika smiled gently. "They're reptiles, Ben, not dinosaurs. Similar, but different."

"Oh," Ben said. "I wondered."

"Anyway," Erika continued, sitting on a chair and watching as David warmed his hands with the hot coffee cup, "we found a couple of other animal fossils in the same layer as the Big Mo. The trouble is, they look like modern animals—we found a modern-looking turtle femur and something that looks like the jaw of a dolphin—a dolphin, for God's sake!"

She shook her head again. "I don't know how the remains of modern animals—from the last million years—could have gotten mixed up with those of a Mosasaur. Maybe there was a major underwater upheaval and the sedimentary layers overlapped each other. But it's frustrating. If I dared suggest that the Mosasaur lived at the same time as these other animals, my esteemed colleagues would laugh me out of the room!"

"So what do you do next?" David asked her, as he stood and got ready to leave.

"Keep going as we are, and wait for the rest of the team to show up in two weeks," Erika replied glumly. "We need major excavation into the hillside to find out what's going on. And we might not be able to finish before the storm season comes in. It's a pity. I was so hoping we might have found a new species of Mosasaur. That's my dream. But without serious evidence for the date of the layer it was found in, it'll be much harder to prove our case."

"Well, if this safe is what I think it is, I may be able to assign some of my guys to help you," David said. "Let's go and take a look."

A couple of hours later, the large safe was in the Equipment Room, with rivulets of water gushing from it. Nobody minded this, since the Equipment Room was used for wet diving gear, and was equipped with water drains and runoffs.   Larry, Erika and David sat down in chairs, watching with barely controlled excitement as Bob worked on opening the safe. Finally, after extensive manipulation and drilling, there was a loud click, and the door started to open. Water gushed from the inside. As they impatiently waited for the flood to subside, they heard the approach of a motorboat outside.

"That must be AJ returning," David said to Larry. "Could you go get him, please, and bring him in here?"

After Larry had left, Bob opened the door fully, and David shone a flashlight into the interior. "Looks like piles of soggy documents and some large bags," he remarked laconically.

With trembling hands, David reached in and gingerly pulled out one of the bags, which appeared to be constructed of hessian burlap. As it emerged from its shelf in the safe it slowly came apart and then split open. A bright waterfall of gold coins cascaded to the floor, clinking loudly and brilliantly reflecting the bright overhead lights of the room.

The four people in the room bent down in unison to pick up handfuls of the coins. There was dead silence in the room for a full minute as they felt the magic spell that gold has had since time immemorial. They turned the coins over in their hands, marveling at the fine definition of details on Lady Liberty on the obverse, and of the American eagle with its laurel wreath and lightning bolts on the reverse.

"Man, oh man, they're perfect! Uncirculated, without a scratch. Just as we'd hoped," breathed David. He turned to Erika. "Where's Moshe? He'll be really excited to see this. These mint marks are all from the 1850's, and some are from 1849." He rubbed one of the coins with his fingers. "No wear, not a scratch. They must have gone directly to Japan from the mint in San Francisco."

He looked at Bob. "And we'll be rich, really rich. All of us." He handed a fistful of coins to Erika. "Here you go!"

"Really?" she asked, her eyes full of wonder.

"Why not?" David chuckled. "There are 5,000 of them."

"And it was so kind of you to get them for us," said a voice behind him.

Chapter 38

David whirled around to stare at Colonel Nicholas DuBois, who had entered the room with two uniformed policemen behind him, one of whom was holding a pistol pressed tightly into the right side of Larry's neck. DuBois wore a navy blue trench coat that dripped water onto the floor; apparently it had started raining outside. His hands were shoved tightly into the coat's pockets.

"What the hell is going on?" David shouted.

Larry was in obvious agony in the background. He kept clenching and unclenching his hands, helpless to do anything, a purple vein standing out on his neck in stark relief. He started to explain, "I'm sorry, they were already on board when I got there."

DuBois held up his hand. "We are here in the name of the Government of Anguilla to appropriate..." he chose his words carefully, "...certain valuable property found within the territorial waters of Anguilla."

"The government was going to get its share," David snarled.

"We, er, had information otherwise," DuBois retorted coolly. "Just to be on the safe side, we are also appropriating this ship and confining your crew."

A Resort Guard with sergeant's stripes on his camouflage uniform walked in and whispered in DuBois's ear. He smiled at the man, and told him, "Thank you, Sergeant Pelloy."

He turned back to David. "It appears that your crew has been secured and locked up safely. We will now return to Harbor City and bring that safe to Government House. If it turns out that there is anything of value in it, you will be paid your share in due time by the Department of the Treasury."

"What the hell do you mean, *if* there is anything of value in it?" David demanded. "You can see that there are gold coins spilling out of it!" He stopped. "Oh! I get it! This safe is going to be empty when it reaches Government House, isn't it?"

"I won't dignify that with an answer, Mr. Kilmer," DuBois replied. He turned to the two policemen. "Be so kind as to place these people in handcuffs." He smiled bleakly at his captives. "You are now in protective custody."

Noticing that his guard's attention was distracted, Larry made his move. He shifted his weight slightly and shot his hand up to grab the guard's wrist, turning the pistol away from his neck. With his other hand he twisted the pistol out of the guard's hand, slamming so hard into the man's chest that the guard stumbled across the floor and fell. Larry was about to bring the pistol up in his right hand when three shots rang out. Everyone froze for a moment. Larry looked down at his chest to see two exit wounds. He touched the wounds, and looked surprised to see his fingers turning bright red. He slowly sank to the floor. His last sight was of Colonel DuBois, who held a smoking .357 Magnum Smith & Wesson.

David rushed forward and knelt on the floor to hold Larry's head up. "Larry!" he called out urgently, but he could see he was unable to answer, and moments later the body sagged in his arms.

"You bloody murderer!" Erika screamed at DuBois, who leveled the pistol at her and David.

Hearing footsteps running down the hall, DuBois shouted at the Resort Guard on the floor, "Harkness! Get your bloody arse off the floor and shut that door!" He waved the pistol in his hand at Erika and David. "You two. Get back over there and sit down, now!"

When David remained standing, DuBois pulled back the hammer on the gun. "Or die. I don't care."

David walked over to a chair next to Erika and sank down into it, his breathing coming in ragged gasps.

DuBois snapped at the policemen. "Hurry up with those handcuffs? Cuff their legs to the chairs as well."

When the handcuffs were in place, and David and Erika were helpless in their gray metal chairs, DuBois went over to where Larry lay on the floor, eyes staring up sightlessly. He placed two fingers on the man's neck and slowly shook his head.

"He's gone. Oh well, a suspect shot while resisting arrest. No problem. Or maybe he can just go missing on the way back. The crew is all shut up in the Conference Room, so there'll be no witnesses to say otherwise."

"No one will believe that David and I were shot while resisting arrest," Erika shouted at him.

"I suppose you're right," DuBois agreed amicably. "But we had special plans for you two, anyway. You see, you are going for one more dive on your submarine." He checked his watch. "As soon as we've placed the explosives on board."

"You're blowing up the submarine?" Erika asked.

"Yes, my dear. I understand there are some papers of interest to us in this safe, but we want to be absolutely sure there is no, er, other incriminating evidence ever found on board the sub. 500 pounds of Semtex should take care of that."

"500 pounds?" David asked, incredulous. "You'll blast half the mountain away."

DuBois smiled thinly. "We happened to have friends at the Resort who were able to supply us with a goodly amount of the stuff, and we want to be really, really sure that there was no way anyone could get near that site again, from any direction, to look for safes or anything else."

He checked his watch once more. "You two can wait until we're ready. When the explosives are in place, you will return to the sub with several of my officers." He looked at Larry's body on the floor, and had an inspiration.

"In fact, I think he can go with you." He turned to the sergeant. "You'll turn off the video cameras before our men start placing the explosives, right?" The man nodded.

"Good. Put these three into their diving equipment. After they're all on the sub and you've set the fuses, turn on the video long enough to show they're in there, then kill the lights on the sub and leave."

He turned to Erika. "It'll appear on the videotape that the three of you went into the sub, the lights in the compartment went out, and then you apparently bumped into a torpedo or something in the darkness and caused an explosion. How unfortunate."

Erika responded by spitting at him.

DuBois's face lit up with anger. He took two strides forward and slapped her across the face with the flat of his hand, right-left and then left-right. After controlling his rapid breathing, he addressed the sergeant once more.

"Put everything back in the safe and close it. Get two men and a cart to help you get it to the boat. Tell no one what is inside."

He pointed to Erika and David. "Be so kind as to put duct tape across their mouths, and blindfold them. Put a double guard at this door, and let no one in. I'm leaving after the safe is loaded, but I'll radio for another Police boat to come here. After you've recorded the video of the three in the sub, get on that boat and back to Harbor Town as quickly as possible."

As he walked out the door, he added as an aside, "Remember, we know exactly how much is in that safe. If a single coin is missing, it will come out of your hide!"

As David heard the Police boat leaving, he wondered how DuBois knew exactly how many coins were supposed to be in the safe, as well as the existence of incriminating documents.

"The only good news, "he thought to himself, "is that he doesn't know about the first safe. He's somehow heard we found a safe, and thinks this is it. I just hope the contents of that safe, especially the crown, are somewhere safe in AJ's hands."

Chapter 39

It was dawn by the time David and Erika were finally fastened to two of the four aquasleds. The tape was removed from their faces so that their masks and breathing apparatus could fit properly. Larry's body was fastened onto the back of another one of the sleds, and the procession started off slowly into water that was turning a brilliant blue as the sun climbed higher.

"Nice sunrise," David remarked for the benefit of Erika, hoping to cheer her up a little.

"No talking," Sergeant Pelloy told them harshly. Within 20 minutes they were at the submarine. One of the policemen remained at the mouth of the tunnel so he could maintain communications with the ship, while three others went on with David and Erika, holding spear guns on them. David was saddled with the grisly task of pulling Larry's body into the sub and arranging it in front of one of the video cameras, a task made more difficult by the handcuffs he was wearing.

Finally, all three of them were arranged in a group, and Sergeant Pelloy relayed the message to the ship to start the video recording. "OK, kids, smile and wave to the camera," Pelloy told Erika and David, who each had one hand free for this purpose; the other hand was manacled to bolts on the wall behind them.

"Go fuck yourself," Erika told him.

In response, Pelloy jabbed her with his spear gun, eliciting an "Ow!"

"The next time I draw blood, and after that I get rough," Pelloy threatened, and Erika went through the motion of waving for a few minutes, until Pelloy, who was staying to the side, out of sight of the camera, told them, "Goodnight, kids, don't stay up too late."

He disconnected the light, and the interior was plunged into darkness, the only light the tiny red spot below the video camera. "Woops, no light anymore. They'll keep the camera running another few minutes, then pull the cord like the transmission was broken."

"When does this thing go boom?" David asked Pelloy as he started to leave, finding his way back along the nylon guide rope that had been installed along the length of the U-boat.

Pelloy laughed harshly, a rasping sound in the loudspeakers built into their masks. "About five hours, enough time for us to get back and for our Police boat to be far away from here. But I wouldn't worry about that. Your air will run out much sooner!" He laughed again as he left the U-boat, and Erika and David heard only a faint crackling of the departing men talking with each other.

"Well, this is a shit sandwich," Erika exclaimed sourly.

David sank despondently onto the floor, slowly overcome by the indescribable horror of being trapped within the cramped space in the darkness. His memory replayed the journal of the dead U-boat Captain, the feeling of loneliness, of the creeping cold, of the horror of claustrophobia, knowing that the walls of the sub would feel like they were closing in on him, and that there would be no way out.

He knew the darkness would make the fear even more acute, since everything would feel like it was only inches away in the ink-black surroundings. And then it would start getting harder to breathe, the pressure on his chest would increase unbearably, and he would choke and wheeze for an extended length of time. After that, the final horror would come, as death closed in and he drowned.

Chapter 40

Erika put a hand on his knee. "Hey, mate, any good thoughts to cheer a girl up?" she asked. He did not reply. She could feel him growing more and more tense and starting to hyperventilate. She moved her hand up his leg, until it would go no further.

"Hey, mate! Hey!" she shouted. Finally, even though she was not touching skin-to-skin, but only through a layer of thick neoprene, the stimulation was enough to jolt him back to life.

"Are you doing what I think you're doing?" he asked with a weak smile.

"I'm just trying to pump some life back into you," she said. "Come on. You think you're so smart. Get us out of here!"

"Let me think just a minute," he said. He thought back desperately, his mind reeling. He turned to face her, although he knew she could not see him in the pitch black.

"Can you turn around and reach toward the top of the bunk above you?" he asked her. There's a mesh sack up there with a strap on it. If you can reach the strap, you can pull the bag down."

"I'll give it a try," she responded. He felt her moving next to him, and heard her banging against the petty officer's bunk behind them in her efforts to reach the top bunk.

"I can't make it," she panted. "It's just a couple of inches out of reach."

"Do you have anything on you that's a couple of inches long?" David asked, while feeling around on his suit for anything he might have that could be used as a tool. "Wait a minute," he cried. "Let me get my flipper off!"

He removed his footwear painfully, slowly, his breathing sounding ragged and unnaturally loud in his ears. Finally, he was able to hand it to her.

"OK, push the skinny part of the flipper under the railing of the top bunk, push it in as far as you can, and then use it to leverage out the bag." He waited in the dark, wishing he could see what she was doing so he could help.

He heard her grunt, "Wait a minute," and then, "Here comes something," and then, "I got it!"

She handed him the bag in the darkness. "OK, here you are. What is it?"

"It's a little survival kit I left there. It has some small air tanks and food and water and a flashlight with extra batteries, in case someone got caught and had to wait until help arrived."

"Bloody great. We'll survive a little longer, and the light will be nice. But no one's coming to save us, are they?" She hesitated a moment. "I'm sorry. I guess this is a good time to be grateful for small favors, eh?"

He pulled out the flashlight and almost turned it on before he remembered the video camera was still running. "Listen, keep an eye on the vidcam and tell me when the red light goes out," he asked her.

"All right," she said. Then, a few minutes later, "It's out."

He turned on his flashlight and set it on the floor. There was a repetitive clicking noise, and then a sharp light flared in the darkness. "What's that?" she asked.

"It's a small oxyacetylene torch," he replied. "Did I forget to mention that?"

He applied himself ardently to the task of cutting one of the links of his cufflinks, and was rewarded when it eventually snapped as he yanked back on it sharply.

"Good on ya, mate!" she exulted. "Now can you do me?"

"I would if I could, but there's no fuel left in this thing," David replied. He paused. Then, sensing her desperation and feeling guilty that he was teasing her, he said, "Did I mention that I left one of these bags in each compartment? Give me a minute and I'll get another torch."

He picked up the flashlight, took off his remaining flipper, and headed toward the Captain's cabin. He heard her voice clearly in his headphones.

"If—when—we get out of this, I'm going to bite one of your ears off."

He chuckled as he found the bag on the bunk where he had left it. Before returning to Erika's side, he checked the door aft from the Officers' Quarters. He tried to open it, but it was jammed shut. He shone his flashlight all around the perimeter of the door, but could see no opening he might get a crowbar into. The policemen had somehow closed the door and secured it from the other side.

"So that's what all that extra chatter was about," he thought to himself. "They weren't taking any chances of us getting out and trying to go back. Damn. That also means I can't reach the Semtex in the back compartment and dismantle the bomb!"

He had seen the plastic explosive when they had entered, stacked in packages in the aft torpedo room, on top of the torpedoes stored there. They were obviously expecting that these would also go off and cause a secondary explosion.

He sighed heavily and swam back to Erika, who was elated when he managed to cut through a link of her handcuff with the torch from the second bag, setting her free. With infinite regret he told her that the door leading to the back of the submarine–and the cave to the open ocean–was closed to them.

"Any chance of cutting the door with these torches?" she asked, and he shook his head.

"No, they're too little. They wouldn't even be able to warm it up."

"Well, I have faith in you," she said, patting his arm. "What are your next plans, Captain?"

"We're going up a ladder," he told her, putting his flippers back on.

"And why would we do that?" she asked.

"To see if a very tired crew chief still remembered to do what I asked of him at the end of his shift," David replied.

Five minutes later, he was at the top of the ladder leading up to the conning tower. David had gathered all the emergency bags he could reach and consolidated their contents in two of the net bags, one for him and one for Erika. He was now looking up at the hatch that once led to the upper deck. It looked like it was still in place!

He took a deep breath, and gingerly pressed upward on the hatch. It gave way! With a quick sideways shove he was able to move it aside. He noticed the jagged perimeter of the opening, where his crew had cut the hatch off, and then propped it back in place.

"I'm going to go up first," he told Erika. "Be very careful you don't cut yourself on one of these sharp metal edges."

He floated up through the hatch and shone the flashlight around him.

"What do you see? Don't keep me in suspense!" Erika pleaded from below.

"It looks like the roof of the cave is a few feet above me," David replied slowly. "And in back of me is the conning tower, and it's a total mess, a metal nightmare that's blocking the way toward the back of the cave. And in front of me is... God knows what. It looks like the cave goes that way for quite a stretch." He helped Erika out of the hatchway, and she looked around quickly.

"Then it looks like we go on in the God-knows-what direction," she said cheerfully.

"And we do it as fast as our flippers can push us," David added. "We've got to get as far away as we can before the bomb goes off.

Are you ready?" He shone the flashlight at her face, careful not to blind her, and saw that she was nodding.

"I'll take the lead right now, then we'll alternate, so we use up only one flashlight at a time. Let's rock!"

They swam slowly forward through the narrow space between the top of the submarine and the roof of the cave. After they passed over the bow of the U-boat the cave offered them more room, and was relatively straight. The flashlight could not discern any ending ahead.

They swam hard and fast, their legs burning and their lungs on fire, while David continually checked the time and his air level. He made Erika check hers also, during infrequent rest stops, and then they double-checked each other's readings. He didn't bother looking at the depth gauge. It didn't matter how deep they had to proceed, there was only one way to go, and that was ahead. He knew that if the cave ended or became so narrow that they could not go any further it would be all over for them, but he refrained from sharing this thought with Erika, no matter how often it came up in his mind.

They had swum for what seemed like forever when he heard Erika's voice in his head, "David! I think I'm out!"

He stopped, and noticed that he was feeling breathless and light-headed. "Turn on your flashlight!" he told Erika, and they stopped swimming, hanging in the middle of the cave with only slight paddling motions of their fins, while he looked at the readings on their air tanks.

"They're empty," he said gloomily, then caught himself, and said cheerily, "OK, next!"

He pulled out one of the small emergency tanks from his net bag and handed it to Erika, then took out a second one for himself.

He took off his BCD vest and removed the now useless tank. He connected the reserve tank, and turned the valve to release air. He exhaled to clear some water that had gotten into his face mask, and then took a tentative suck.

"Ah, air, blessed fresh air! It's fine, of course," he told Erika confidently. He put his vest back on and then connected the small tank to hers. "Should be good for around 15 minutes, each."

"The good news is, we are now rid of these double tanks that have been dragging on us," he said cheerfully. "Let's go, I'll take the lead," he called with a lot more confidence than he felt.

They had traveled for about ten minutes on the small tanks when David, who was still in front, noticed that the tunnel was moving upwards. This continued for a few dozen feet until his head broke the surface.

"Erika, there's an air cave up here," he shouted. In a moment, her head popped up next to his.

"Would the air be safe enough to breathe?" she asked.

"Let's get out of the water, and we'll see," he replied. They swam another two hundred feet, and exclaimed with delight as an island rose up on their right. They climbed out of the water, slipping backward several times on the mossy and slippery rocks. They finally found a rock flat enough to sit on, and looked at each other, panting heavily into their masks.

Chapter 41

"OK, this is it. Let me try first. If I turn green and fall over, you'll know it's not safe to breathe," David said, mustering as much of a smile as he could. He carefully removed his mask, leaving it near his mouth just in case, and took a few cautious gulps of air.

He was silent for a moment.

"Well? Krikey, don't leave me here, waiting!" Erika complained at his side.

"It stinks, and it's humid and hot, but I don't feel bad. I think it's OK," he ventured.

Erika took her facemask off and gulped in the cave's air. "I'm beyond complaining right now. This'll do," she said, gasping. They both leaned against a rock outcropping for a few minutes, as their labored breathing gradually returned to normal.

"Wow," David said, looking around. "I don't believe it. I really don't believe it."

"What, that we found a place with air?" Erika asked.

"No, I can't believe that you're beyond complaining," David said.

"Wanker!" she exclaimed, and whacked him on the shoulder.

"We might as well take off our flippers," said David, bending down to undo his straps. "We can't climb around here with them on."

"Might as well take off our outer diving suits, too," she added, unzipping her neoprene top. "It's hot as hell in here."

David held the light as Erika stripped down, and looked on with guilty pleasure as the lower half of her inner bathing suit rucked dangerously far down as she pulled down her diving pants.

She looked down and let out a *whoops*. "Sorry, didn't mean to show off my landing strip!"

"Your what?"

"My landing strip. That's what the blokes down under call the patch of pubic hair that's not bikini waxed. I've heard it called a Mohawk in the U.S. You didn't notice?"

David chuckled. "Since I probably won't survive past today, it's useless to lie. Yes, I did notice. And a very good looking landing strip it is, too."

Erika smiled wryly. "Anything I can do to amuse you." With an effort, she got to her feet. "Shall we?"

"We shall," affirmed David, who held onto a handhold in the rock as he got up, afraid of losing his balance on the slippery rock flooring.

Both of them put their discarded equipment into the net bags, which they slung over their shoulders. David shone the flashlight around, exploring their surroundings.

"We're in a large cave that's partly submerged. It looks like the ceiling is over a hundred feet up, and this rocky outcropping we're on goes around the perimeter of the cavern. Let's hope it'll lead us to some way out." He took a few cautious steps. "Slippery as hell. Let me start off in front, with only the one flashlight on. I'll keep it low so we can watch this floor. It's so humid in here the water is practically pouring over these rocks."

"David, hold on a minute," Erika said.

He turned to look at her. "What's up?"

"Turn off your light a moment."

David did as she asked. It took a minute for his eyes to adjust and recover from the bright glare of the flashlight he'd been holding.

"It...it's light in here," he said in amazement. He saw he was surrounded by a green-blue glow.

"Yeh," she replied. She scraped at the wall of the cavern with the knife from her bag, and held a sheet of lichen-like material in her hand. It gave off a dull neon-colored glow.

"What is it?" David asked, wide-eyed.

"It's some kind of bioluminescent plant. It's clinging to the sides and ceiling of this cave." She pointed at the top of the cave. "Look up there. It's thicker in some places than others. It almost looks like a starry sky above us. It's beautiful."

"That's good news," he replied drily. "It means we can save the flashlights."

They had been moving along for about 25 minutes when the cave suddenly opened up and the path rose steeply. Their ledge now became a regular hillside, with the water level over two hundred feet below them on their left.

A dark shape fluttered overhead, and they both ducked. It brushed past Erika's hair, and she turned to push it away, losing her footing in the process. She screamed as she started to plunge toward the sharp rocks far below. Her fall was suddenly arrested, and she dangled in space.

She looked up and saw that David had one hand on the shoulder strap of her net bag and one hand in a fissure in the rock. She shrieked again as the rock came away in his hand, and he slid toward the edge, his right arm frantically scrabbling for support.

The flashlight he had been holding careened over the edge, and they could hear it rebounding from parts of the cliff and then the rocks below before landing in the water with a faint splash.

David managed to wrap his arm around a rock that held firm, and they stopped sliding.

Erika started hyperventilating. "Oh my God. Oh my God. Oh my God," she breathed as she clung to the straps of her equipment bag.

"Don't move! Don't move!" David cautioned her. "Or I'll lose my grip. Let me find a foothold." He brushed his leg over the rock he was lying on until his right foot found a depression.

"O.K.," he reassured Erika, who was trying to remain calm while dangling in space above certain death. "I've got a foothold, and I think I can grip it with the tread on my bootie." David mentally congratulated himself for having worn Rock Spyders, with their extra thick tread, inside his diving fins.

Slowly, agonizingly, he pulled Erika up and directed her to use her hands and feet to help him. Within minutes they were both back on firm ground, panting heavily.

Erika grabbed him in a hug and kissed him on the mouth. "Thanks, mate!" she said, breathing heavily. "You almost lost it there yourself, coming after me."

"No problem," David replied. He paused. "Let's keep going until we come to someplace we can sit down."

"What was that damned thing?" she asked angrily, as they kept climbing.

"Who? What?" David wagged his head slightly, momentarily confused.

"That black flying thing that almost knocked me off this ledge!"

As answer, David took a spare flashlight out of her bag and shone it straight up. On the ceiling, about 50 feet above them, they saw a large black lump that appeared to be breathing, inhaling in and out. He moved the light slightly, and they saw other black lumps, hundreds, perhaps thousands of them.

"That, dear Rika, is another piece of good news," he finally said. "It looks like a bat, something like a Mexican fruit bat, but larger."

"And this is good news because..."

"It means there's a way out of here," David replied, his eyes shining. They had reached a flat spot on the rocks, and he threw down his bag, and looked around.

"Bats need fresh air to breathe, and they need terrestrial prey like insects to eat. I don't see any of those in here, so there's got to be a passageway to get to the outside."

She caught on to his mood. She dropped her bag and grasped his hand, looking into his eyes and smiling, and for a moment they were as happy as teenagers out on a first date. "So we've got a shot at escaping?" she breathed, almost afraid to voice the thought.

"Yeah, unfortunately," he said with a lopsided grin.

"Unfortunately?"

"Well, in here, since I'm literally the last man in the world, I thought I might have a chance with you. Outside, I'll be back to fighting the competition again."

She punched him playfully on the arm, once, twice. "Idiot!"

She turned serious, concerned, and gently laid her hand on his right cheek. "No one's ever done anything like that for me," she said almost plaintively. "You risked your life to save me."

He smiled as he said, "Yeah. Like a St Bernard. In fact..." He reached into the bag and brought out a little airline bottle of cognac, and stuck it into the top of his thin inner diving suit. "Can I offer you some brandy from around my neck?"

She laughed quietly as she took the bottle and started pulling the zipper down the front of his nylon top. "Aren't you hot in that thing?" she asked, her eyes narrowing.

"Yeah. I'm dying in here," he said, his mouth suddenly dry. He started pulling down the zipper on the front of her suit. He sat on a rock and pulled off the rest of his inner suit, leaving only a pair of yellow bathing trunks. He again looked on with guilty pleasure as the lower half of her bikini slid dangerously far down as she pulled off her nylon pants. He cleared his throat. "To be totally honest about the landing strip, I stared as hard as I possibly could."

She put her right arm around his neck and sat on his lap. "I'm glad you're interested." Her face drew closer to his.

"You were just saying how grateful you were," he said, almost whispering the words.

"Yes," she breathed back at him, drawing still closer. She pulled back a moment.

"Wait," she said. She made the T-for-time-out motion with her hands.

He misunderstood the gesture. "Of course, you don't have to..." he started to say.

"The defensive shields are down, Mr. Sulu," she said, smiling softly.

"Oh," he replied.

"Too much talking," she said, licking her lips and then covering his gently, but with increasing urgency.

They started slowly. She ran her tongue over the outside of his lips, and then bit his lower lip. They started kissing with increasing urgency. He kissed her neck, then followed with a series of small nibbles. They kissed deeply. They were breathing heavily. He pulled down her bathing suit top to reveal small but well-formed breasts, and focused his attention on those. Her nipples immediately became hard and long and pointy, and she emitted a small whimper.

She pushed her hands against David's shoulders to stand up. She reached down to pull off her bathing suit bottom, tossing it to one side with her left foot. He stood to pull off his swimsuit pants, hopping on one foot for a minute. He guided her to his seat on the rock, and bent in front of her to kiss her, starting with her lips and then running a zigzag pattern down her body, giving extra attention to certain parts. He was lost in the task when he heard a slow moaning and felt her body go rigid with sudden urgency. She pushed off from the rock and made him regain his seat. She knelt down and reached out and ran her tongue over him. She smiled as she kissed him very deliberately, looking up at him as he inhaled sharply. He thought about saying something, but wisely decided not to.

She lifted one leg and sat down on his thighs, straddling his lap. She ran her hands lightly over his chest. She reached one hand down to guide him, and then wrapped both arms around his neck as she kissed him deeply.

He hooked his arms around her shoulders, pulling her down, gulping as he felt her sudden intense heat. Her whole body tensed immediately. She bit her lips and let out a series of shrill *Ooh-Aah-Aah* gasps. She stared at him, wild-eyed and unfocused, and then closed her eyes and grasped his arms tightly, nostrils flaring and lips parted. Intense moments later, her eyes flew open and she sucked in air with a sharp whooshing inhalation and then made a strangled *Ummm* sound. She held still for a minute, and then lowered her head slowly to his chest and held up one finger in a "give-me-a-minute" gesture, as her shoulders heaved with the effort of catching her breath.

Minutes passed. He enjoyed the closeness, even with the sweat and humidity, and gently stroked her hair. She suddenly raised her head and looked in his eyes purposefully. She rose to a sitting position and rotated her hips in a series of figure-8's. She then tilted her pelvis slightly to slide down and fully envelop him. He grasped her back and buttocks tightly to pull her closer, a task made difficult as sweat made her increasingly slippery from the exertion and humidity.

Erika stopped all movement for a moment, and kissed him lightly and whispered, "This is really nice, David," into his ear. She continued, "I know I should be saying something...intimate...right now, but I'm all out of practice. Give me some time, OK?"

He held her with a desperate intensity, kissed her neck, and softly whispered back, "You take all the time you need."

Tears streaked down her cheeks as she started moving against him once more. She dug her fingernails into his back and bit into his shoulder again and again, drawing bright ruby-red droplets of blood, but he ignored the pain. The deliberate rhythm of their bodies seemed to go on forever, until she suddenly picked up speed. He grasped her shoulders with all his strength as she became a blur of motion, until they both suddenly gasped and cried out. They subsided, and seemed to melt into each other, and then sank slowly down on the rock next to each other. He held her with one arm and smiled at her as they tried to catch their breath.

"Whoa!" she gasped. She gently stroked his cheek. "Thanks. I really needed that. It's been, er, way too long since I've done that." She kissed him on the nose. "Or even really wanted to."

David raised his head up, and looked surprised. "Really? I thought that, er, you were getting it on with Fowler this whole time."

"No, I never did 'get it on' with him." She gave him a calculating look as she continued stroking his cheek. "It's true that I thought about it. And we did swap some spit. But that was it. Not that it's any of your business."

There was a moment of silence, and then his eyebrows shot up. "Really? And why, er, did we not get it on with his quasi-lordship?"

She gave him a rueful smile. "You wouldn't understand. It was something about a scene in the moonlight." She curved her eyebrows down into a frown. "But I'm sure you haven't had any days off from your lady friends."

He looked embarrassed. "My lady friends have been pretty much on the Pause Button since the day I met you. I honestly haven't a clue as to why."

She smiled gently and put a finger on his lower lip, stroking it gently. "How about a little more catching up, then, eh?"

He glanced at the luminous hands on his diving watch. "I figure it'll be a couple more hours before that explosive goes off. We need to be alert for that. There'll probably be a tidal wave of water coming through here."

She bent down and bit his lower lip. "We'd better hurry, then."

"Sounds good," he replied. "But how about we find a more comfortable place? My butt is killing me."

"All right," she said, as she slowly got up and put her bikini back on. "But hurry. Don't keep a girl waiting."

Chapter 42

They picked up their net bags and kept on climbing over the rocks. Eventually they reached a plateau, and could see the cave widening out in front of them. It was hard to see the furthest reaches in the dim light, but it seemed to go on for hundreds of yards. In front of them the path descended down to a flat, sandy beach, with mounds of rocks emitting vents of steam.

"There's a nice beach to make out on," she said. "It'll be like university days."

David laughed as they started the descent. "I'll take your word for it. I went to university in Pittsburgh, far from any warm beaches."

They stopped behind one of the rock piles and looked at the steam coming out of the top.

"No wonder it's so bloody hot in here," she said. "Steam vents going far down into the earth."

"This is like a corner of hell," he noted.

She pouted. "Being with me is like a corner of hell?"

He smiled and lifted up her chin. "Not at all. Though it was a little tricky on that hard, pointy rock back there."

He took a thermal blanket out of the gear bag and spread it out.

She bent down and ran her hand over the ground. "Unusual. Finely ground volcanic rock. But enough chit-chat. Where were we?" She slid down onto the blanket and held out her arms.

He looked at her somewhat suspiciously. "We're still on Time Out, right?"

"Yes, yes," she said impatiently. "I'm still all lovey and non-sarcastic. Now will you hurry the fuck up?"

David put his right arm behind her back and stroked her face with his left, kissing her deeply as he started to slowly lower himself down.

His head started swimming as he lost himself in the kiss.

"Ooh, I love the way you moan," she said, mumbling the words while still kissing him. "It's so deep."

"What?" he asked, raising his head.

"Like you were doing just now. Boy, if you start moaning like that while we're just kissing, you're going to go off the charts when we..."

"I wasn't moaning," David said.

They both looked at each other, startled. This time he heard it, too, a low moan that grew in volume until it echoed off the walls of the cave.

They both rose cautiously, and looked over the top of the mound of rocks they had been lying behind. For a moment, the vent of steam obscured their vision. As they peered intently into the semi-gloom ahead the steam abated, and a picture of the terrain started to emerge.

They were about 20 feet from the water's edge. Beyond the water was another shoreline, perhaps 200 feet away. They saw sand and rocks had been piled up into a shape resembling a huge nest. In the front of the nest were what at first looked like two large crocodiles. They appeared to be fighting over something.

"What are crocodiles doing in a cave?" David started to say, then dropped his voice to an urgent whisper. "Wait. Those aren't crocodiles. They seem to have flippers instead of legs." He turned his head to Erika, who was staring straight ahead, her mouth wide open.

"Rika?" he whispered anxiously.

"Oh—my—God!" she exhaled slowly.

"Do you think they could be some kind of ancient animal, maybe even related to..." he whispered, but saw that she was not listening to him.

She appeared to be in such deep shock that he turned and looked again, squinting his eyes to make out the scene. Then he saw it. One of the two squabbling animals bit the other one, which elicited a yelp of protest. The moan started up again and turned into a rumble with a deep clicking sound, a warning from a colossal head that lifted up from the sand and fixed stern eyes onto the offending offspring, which released its victimized sibling and backed off.

The other animal started to drag off the prize, then thought the better of it and backed off as well. The rumbling finally stopped as the huge head swung first to one side, then the other, and finally settled down again.

David followed the line of the body back from the head. He bent down to her ear, and kept his voice very low. "That thing has to be 50 or 60 feet long!" he said. "I couldn't see it at first because it's the same green gray color as the background. But, look!" he nudged Erika, "There are some bands of color, sort of a coral red, flashing down the side. Now they're fading out. Maybe she's calming down 'cause her youngsters are behaving."

He paused. "What is it?"

He paused again. "It couldn't be..."

"Yes," Erika replied dreamily, dropping her voice to a low whisper as David put a warning finger to her lips. "It is. It's a mother Mosasaur and her two babies." David absently noticed she pronounced it "bye-bees." "And they're... alive!"

She started to rise involuntarily to get a better look. David grabbed her shoulder and pulled her back down.

"No, no, no," he hissed urgently. "Whatever they are, I don't think they're vegetarians. Look at those long teeth! And did you see what the 'bye-bees' are playing with? I think there's a shoe on the end of it!"

They heard roar from further down the cave on the right, far enough away so they couldn't see the source of it.

"God, there's more," she marveled. "We're in the midst of a whole pod of them!"

"Oh, joy of joys," David muttered sarcastically. "We've got to get out of here, and fast."

"Why?" Erika replied evenly, still in her trance state. "I need some time to study them, to observe their behavior. This is the dream of a lifetime!"

"In maybe an hour or so that bomb will go off, and we'll have a tsunami of water in here washing us all up together, and then you'll be able to study them really, really close. Unfortunately, they'll also be studying you."

Since she wasn't responding, he added, "Besides, you can come back later and observe them whenever you want." This seemed to bring her back to reality.

"Oh, OK. What're you proposing?" she asked.

"We've heard roaring to our right, which appears to be North. So we know there's more of them there. To our left is South. Somewhere down there is the lagoon, and at least one of these tunnels leads into it. Mark found that out as he mapped the caves. If we can get that far we might be able to get out."

He looked around at the walls. "Trying to climb up the walls to find where the bats get in and out is no longer an option. The Mo's would see us or hear us."

"Can I look at them a little while longer? This is...so beautiful," she said softly.

David's face softened. "You know I can't refuse you anything when you use that little-girl voice on me," he answered. "Besides, our best hope is that if we wait, they snooze out and sleep deeply."

Erika crept around the side of the rock mound on all fours, oblivious that her bikini-clad butt was waving to and fro in front of

David's nose. She watched the nest, enthralled, as the mother Mosasaur settled down. The flushes of color disappeared from her side, and she turned a uniform green gray, similar to the light that the wall plants were giving to the entire cave. The youngsters soon seemed to lose interest in their leg and also settled down. Within minutes they stopped moving, and began breathing rhythmically.

Erika whispered. "Do you believe this? Isn't this incredible?"

David tapped her on the shoulder. "Get dressed. Time to boogie."

"They can change colors, like chameleons," she whispered excitedly.

"Great, that's wonderful," he whispered back. "Now get into your gear and move on out!"

They slipped into their dive gear. David took flashlights and batteries from their gear bags. "Take only what you absolutely need," he spoke very quietly into her ear. "We can't take the bags with us, they'd drag us down." They took a moment to strap on the last of the small reserve air tanks.

"Walk low and slow. Bring your flippers. We'll put them on in the water," he cautioned.

They made their way to the left and eased partway into the water before putting on their fins. Erika accidentally splashed one, and it sounded like a rocket shot. David held up a hand, and they both froze and looked across at the nest, which was harder to see from water level. But they heard no sign of motion, so they started to swim, slowly at first and then more rapidly, toward the mouth of a tunnel they could see to the left.

They continued along the surface, glancing anxiously back over their shoulders toward the Mosasaur nest every few minutes. They looked anxiously up as they entered the tunnel, but the ceiling did not come down to the water's surface, and they were not forced to swim underwater and start on their precious last air tanks.

They swam for about 20 minutes, and emerged into another cave, also glowing with the greenish light of lichens on the walls and ceiling. There appeared to be no nests in the area. A beach emerged on their left, and David motioned them over to it. They sat on the sand, breathing hard.

"So far so good, knock on wood," David said, knocking on his own head in an attempt to make a feeble joke. "You OK?"

"Yeh," she said, "No worries."

David looked around. "We seem to be safe here. I think we can speak, but very quietly." He laid one hand on her shoulder. "Are we still in time-out mode?" he asked.

She smiled. "Why would you ask that?"

"Because I want to say something, and I don't want you to rip my head off or get all sarcastic on me," he answered.

She bit her lip. "Was I really that bad?" she asked.

"Much worse," he replied with a crooked smile. "But I wanted to say that back there with you—except for those monsters waiting to devour us, and the air smelling like a graveyard, and the fact we're trapped under the earth and will probably die soon—except for that, I was having the time of my life."

"I hope we both survive," she said. "Promise me that you'll stay my friend, and stick around. It was hard enough breaking you in. I don't think I have the energy to break in another one."

"I'd like to give you something," David said softly. He unsnapped the gold chain with the Double Eagle coin from around his neck and gently lowered it over her head, brushing her hair aside. "I want you to have this. In case I get munched by Big Mo, this will be...something to remember me by."

"David, you shouldn't. You said you were never going to give that up," she argued, but he put a finger on her lips.

"I want you to have it. Besides," he grinned as he looked down at himself, "It's all I got."

She kissed him, fully and gently, on the mouth. "Thank you. But you're not going to get eaten by a Big Mo," she said, "and I'm going to tell you why." She moved her hands up to her neck and removed the necklace with the silver talisman that Aunt Marie had given her.

She put it around David's neck and closed the fastener. "I'm convinced that Aunt Marie gave this thing powerful magic. It'll keep you safe if one of those big mean animals starts nibbling on your toes."

He looked down at it, sliding one finger across the marks on the silver. "Thank you," he said. He smiled his lopsided smile. "We've given each other everything we've got," he stated slowly, "Like the O'Henry book."

She nodded. "*The Gift of the Magi.*" She bit her lip. "This all feels so...nice." She touched his cheek, and let a finger remain on his dimple a moment. "Am I dreaming this?"

"Let's discuss it over dinner after we get out of here," he said with more confidence than he felt.

He saw her looking at the water, wide-eyed. "Ready?"

She looked panicked. "I just saw something in there. With a big fin. There's other things in the water besides Mosasaurs. I...I don't want to go in!"

He put his arm around her shoulders. "Tell me the truth. Which frightens you more—getting into the water with a bunch of flesh-eating monsters, or being kind and loving with me?"

"Oh, you, definitely," she said without hesitation.

He jerked a thumb at the water. "So you really have nothing to worry about."

She chuckled. "Well, when you put it that way..."

She noticed he was suddenly not paying attention to her, and asked him, "What?"

He was looking past her left shoulder, squinting his eyes to see. "Is that what I think it is? Maybe I'm hallucinating."

Chapter 43

Erika turned her head in the direction he was looking at. In the faint light she saw what appeared to be a bright yellow-and-blue aquasled at the far end of the sandy beach. They took off their flippers and walked toward it. Their excitement rose as they got closer. He reached out a hand to touch it. It was real.

"My God, it's a sled!" David said in wonder.

She walked around it and saw its twin, in light blue. "And look, there's another one behind it!" She shook her head. "Bloody hell!" she exclaimed. "These look just like the ones from the ship."

"Yes, but they're not. All ours have the ship's logo right here," he said, indicating a spot on the side of the sled. He flipped the seat back, and mused, "Let's see if...Yes! There's a SCUBA tank in the storage compartment. Now if we had a key...Sweet Jesus, the key is still in it! The owner must have been planning to come back soon."

He flipped the seat of the second sled to look at the compartment underneath. "Here's another. We've each got a full sized air tank!" he exclaimed.

Erika looked around. "I wonder where the original owners are," she said.

"Probably wound up as Mosasaur chow," David remarked. "Let's hope they start." He turned the key in the first sled and grinned with excitement when he saw the lights on the instrument panel start to glow. "Looking good. It's barely in the green, but it should be enough to make the lagoon or whatever we wind up in when we get out of here. How about you?"

"Looking good here, too," Erika reported. "Help me on with this tank. And then could you please help me push the sled into the water?"

David helped her put it on. "This is a whole new you. Being nice, no sarcasm, and asking for help. Where's the Erika I knew, and what did you do with her?"

She punched him on the arm. "You keep that up and..."

A thunderclap almost lifted them off the ground. "Oh, oh," David whispered. "Get these sleds into the water. Hurry!"

They frantically pushed first one, then the other sled into the water, as the air seemed to grow alive with rocks and dust falling from the ceiling. "Turn on your mask radio mike," he shouted as they got aboard their sleds. "Let's keep heading to the left."

"Visibility is shot with all this dust in the air," she said as they headed toward the left exit tunnel. Suddenly a draconian shape appeared in the water before them. A giant mouth opened up to display rows of teeth.

"Oh, my God," she screamed. "Go back, go back."

David turned as he heard a roar behind them. "Too late, here it comes!" he shouted. "Hang on!"

They clamped their legs onto the sleds as hard as they could as the wave caught them and swept them right by the startled Mosasaur. They shot through the tunnel out of control, twirling around and occasionally bouncing off the sides. "Turn on your lights," he shouted into his dive mask microphone.

The double lights carved out bright twin cones in front of them as the wave started to slow down. They emerged into another cavern, with beaches along both sides.

"Get out of the water onto the left beach. The wave will suck us backward!" he yelled.

"I can't get out. I'm getting pulled back!" she screamed.

"Find some rocks to jam your sled into!" he shouted back. He found a group of stalagmites in the water and wedged his sled in between them. "Come to me," he yelled.

She turned her throttle all the way up to full power, but was slowly being pulled back. He found a rope on his sled and threw it to her.

"Wrap this around the handlebars!" he cried, and she frantically did so. He wrapped the rope around his back and started to pull, taking the strain in his legs after propping them horizontally against the stalagmite columns. Slowly, her sled came toward him. The veins stood out on his neck as he continued pulling. Her sled threatened to go on the back side of the columns, toward the receding wave, and she had to push off again and again with her right leg. Finally, the sled moved far enough to the side that David was able to pull it in. He quickly wrapped the rope around a narrow section of one of the stalagmites and grabbed her hand.

"Are you OK?" he asked, anxiety plain in his voice.

"Yeh," she said, looking herself over. "A little banged up, but I'm good."

"And parts of you are excellent," he said with a wan smile. She leaned over from her sled and they held each other for a while.

A few minutes later, an afterwave came back, going the other way, forcing them to cling onto their perch. They turned off their lights to conserve power as they watched waves undulate back and forth from the force of the explosion. After another 5 minutes the waves settled down, and the water appeared to return to its normal level. They could hear splashing noises in the distance, indicating large bodies of rock still falling into the water.

"Time to go," David said, looking down at his instruments. "If that explosion blocked the other exits, those Big Mo's are going to be coming this way any minute. Mask on?"

"All systems go," Erika responded as she gave the motorcycle-style grip a quick twist, and saw the sled respond by nudging forward.

He pointed to the leftmost tunnel. "Turn on your lights and let's head down there. If we..."

He stopped as he saw Erika looking over his shoulder, her eyes growing ever larger. "What?" he said, turning his head.

"Ohmygod!" she screamed. "It's coming this way!"

"Follow me," David yelled. "Go-go-go-go!"

He cranked the handle on the sled, and it leapt forward. Within 50 feet or so the rock ceiling dipped, and they directed the sleds under water.

"From the compass reading, the lagoon should be on our left," David spoke slowly into his mike, focusing his energy onto the twists and turns of the tunnel in front of him. "Are you following me OK?"

"I'm on you like stink on shit!" she returned.

"That's no way to talk about your fearless leader," he whispered in mock seriousness. He forced the sled to follow a left bend in the tunnel.

They came out into another cavern, several hundred yards long and 50 yards wide. They shot to the surface. "Let's stay up when we can, so we go faster with less drag," he gasped.

"Two tunnels up ahead," Erika cried sharply.

"Bear left," David said after a glance at the compass. He looked back and saw a luminous shape starting to emerge from the tunnel into the cavern. "Hurry," he shouted needlessly.

They shot into the leftmost tunnel exit. The roof quickly lowered until the rock was only a foot above their heads. "Dive, dive," David shouted, twisting the controls for the forward vanes on his sled downwards. They quickly came to a fork. "Left, left," David screamed, and then almost choked as his headlights reflected off rows of gigantic, bright white teeth coming at him. "Right, right, right," he yelled, twisting his controls desperately to the right. Both sleds pulled hard right into the other branch, and then twisted to and fro from the turbulence of the animal that passed behind them.

"I don't think it made the turn," David said. "It might take it a while to turn that big body around."

"Let's hope they all crash into each other," she whispered.

They entered another, smaller cavern, with rows of whitish crystals embedded in the sides. There were three tunnels at the end.

"Go left," David whispered urgently. "This looks familiar."

They leaned into the turn, shooting into the leftmost tunnel. It was spacious, over 30 yards wide, an almost perfect tube with smooth rock walls. As they went in they were briefly blinded by a string of lights that turned on, illuminating their way

"I thought so," said David. "We brought lights as far as that last cavern. They should help a lot."

"Oh, God," moaned Erika, as she looked behind her and saw two Mosasaurs pursuing them, less than a hundred yards back, swimming with sinuous snake-like motions side by side in the tunnel.

"Turn left here," David spoke quickly, as they came to a fork in the tunnel. Look for a green arrow to go to..." He broke off as the snout of a juvenile Mosasaur appeared from the tunnel of choice.

"Right turn," he yelled, and they both managed to swing right and enter that tunnel, but not before David's sled bashed hard into the side of the tunnel while making the turn.

They no longer had the advantage of wall lights, and had to depend on their sled headlights. Both cranked their sleds to maximum speed, but David noticed immediately that something was wrong with his.

"Uh, oh," he said, plainly worried. He could hear a clanking behind him as the left propeller struck its badly bent protective metal shroud. He fought the controls desperately as his sled started wildly yawing to the left.

"What is it?" Erika yelled.

"My sled's busted. I don't have time to try to fix it," David groaned.

Erika slowed her sled until they were side by side. He looked directly into her eyes. "You go on. Hurry! Get your butt out of here! Now!"

Erika scooted forward on her sled. "Come on. Jump on up!"

He shook his head. "No good! The sled will be too heavy with both of us, we'll just both get killed. Go! I can at least slow them down!"

Erika narrowed her eyes. "Get on the back of this sled. I'm not leaving without you. If you don't, I'll turn off the key and throw it away!"

David growled. "You stubborn, mule-headed..."

He stopped when he saw her reach for the key. "All right, all right, I'm getting on." He clumsily pushed away from his sled and clambered up behind her as she started to accelerate. "OK. Gun it."

The sled shot ahead. David looked over his shoulder a moment later, and saw that the two adults and the juvenile had reached his sled and one of them was biting into it. The sled slowed them down for a vital minute, and then he saw them coming onwards again. He hunched down, hanging on to the passenger grips on the sled and trying to keep as low a profile as possible.

The largest of the animals was now in the lead of the group behind them. David glanced back, and his blood chilled—it was less than 10 yards away. He looked over Erika's shoulder to the digital position display. "We should reach the lagoon soon," he said. "Keep cranking, and don't look back."

He looked around for something, anything, to throw at their pursuers. He realized all he had was his SCUBA equipment. He remembered a scene from *Jaws*, where Roy Scheider threw a compressed air tank into the Great White Shark's mouth.

"I've got nothing to lose," he thought, as he took several quick breaths and then uncoupled his face mask from his SCUBA jacket. Behind him, he could see the Mosasaur opening and closing its jaws, its rows of teeth visible even in the dim light as it repeatedly just barely missed the back end of the sled. He struggled to slip out of the jacket, fighting the resistance of the water from the sled's movement as it buffeting him from side to side. He wrapped his foot through a foothold in front of his seat, twisted around and lunged backwards, pushing the whole SCUBA jacket, with its tank and attached paraphernalia toward the wide open maw of the pursuing predator.

The outfit entered the Mosasaur's mouth, and it clamped down, thinking it had gotten its target. It bit down hard, but noticed that this was not the prey it wanted, and tried to spit out the whole assemblage. Unfortunately, the straps snagged in its mouth, which was designed to keep prey from escaping. Confused, the animal stopped the chase, and frantically turned its head from side to side and then started rolling, trying to dislodge the annoying SCUBA outfit from its throat. The other two animals stopped behind it, blocked by the desperate actions of the huge male.

David looked back and noticed they were pulling ahead, and were not being pursued for the moment. "This would be great," he thought, "if I had air." He leaned over Erika's back and felt along the side of her diving jacket to find the spare air hose and mouthpiece called an "octopus" by divers. She slowed down and reached back to help him, and he inserted the mouthpiece and gratefully took several deep breaths. They both looked up as they saw daylight ahead.

The walls of the lava tube dropped away suddenly, and they emerged into the clear water of the lagoon, at a depth of about 90 feet. Erika instinctively headed for the surface, but David grabbed the back of her arm tightly and signaled her to ascend slowly to avoid the bends. He glanced anxiously over his shoulder, but saw no evidence of Mosasaurs following them. Since he lacked his mask with its mike, he had to wait until they surfaced to speak.

"I don't see them behind us," he said. "I had to signal you to go up more slowly, else...you know."

"I know, I know," she shot back. "Stop being a back seat driver." She saw the resort's docks on their left, and steered the aquasled in that direction. David kept looking back over his shoulder. "I think they gave up on us," he said.

"They'll be back," she replied. "And they'll be pissed because their nesting grounds are now probably screwed up. I don't want to be in the water when they start pouring out of those caves."

"Maybe they just weren't that hungry."

Erika turned to face him. "They don't have to be hungry," she said.

He looked puzzled. "Normally, animals only kill to eat, right?"

She grasped his shoulder for emphasis. "Normally yes. But these are different. We've found many animals that had been bitten right through by them, but not eaten. So keep a lookout."

It took him a moment to grasp what she said. "They killed because they liked it?"

She nodded. "Correct. This is a killing machine. It kills for the sheer joy of killing."

Chapter 44

As they sped along the surface of the lagoon, a Zodiac motorboat intercepted them, and a uniformed guard shouted, "Pull over and stop."

"We can't," Erika shouted back. "We'll explain at the dock."

"We'll see about that," said the voice. "Follow us!"

The faster Zodiac pulled up to the marina docking area head of them. Two guards kept automatic weapons at the ready, while the third threw them a rope.

"Tie that onto your Aquasled," he said, and Erika complied, then swung herself over onto a stairway and climbed up. David followed behind her.

"I'm Dr. Erika Bettelman," she said to the senior guard, a Sergeant. "I've been here before. Lt. Governor Fowler knows me well. Is he in residence?"

The Sergeant looked skeptical, but put away his weapon. "OK. I think I see you before. Follow us." He led the way, speaking into a hand-held radio.

David and Erika arrived at the main building with their police escort. As they entered the lobby, they were thunderstruck to be met by Colonel DuBois and several of his officers.

"DuBois! What the hell are you doing here?" David yelled.

DuBois scowled. "I could say the same thing. How did you get out of that submarine?"

Erika shouted, "We want to see the Lt. Governor, and we want to see him now! You're not getting away with this!"

"You're not giving the orders around here," DuBois replied, scowling. He pulled out a pistol and kept it aimed at the two. "Put them in handcuffs," he ordered guards. "Take him to the gym and her to the boardroom."

Erika and David struggled in vain as they were handcuffed and led away.

David sat in the gym, with his hands and legs cuffed to an upright aluminum chair. The floor of the room was clear glass, and looked down into the lagoon. It gave him a strange sensation of falling. He watched a small manta ray pass by below, flapping its wings in slow motion, lit by banks of underwater lights. He looked up and noticed one wall was also made of glass, with a panoramic view of the lagoon.

DuBois came in with one of his men, a giant whose uniform barely fit. His name tag said, "SGT Morton." DuBois pulled up a chair. "We have the treasure, thank you very much. That belongs to the people of Anguilla," he said smugly.

"You mean it belongs to you, to finance your so-called revolution," David said bitterly.

"How did you hear about that?" DuBois asked, surprised. "That is not for outsiders to know. But yes, with that money and some other, ah, investments, we should be able to liberate this country from its imperial oppressors, and be free at last."

"Free to do what? Let drug smugglers use this island as a safe haven, out of reach of any law enforcement?"

DuBois smiled grimly. "Call it what you like. The country of Anguilla will belong to its people again, not some far-off colonial power."

"What do you want from me?" David asked. "Why didn't you kill me right away, since I'm a witness to your stealing the gold?"

"Good question. There's one more thing we want, that we did not find after you had, er, left for the submarine. We found a second safe, but there's an item that's missing. We'd like to know where it is."

"I have no idea of what you're talking about," David said angrily. "You stole everything I had."

DuBois slapped him hard across the face, left-right. David tasted the metallic tang of blood.

"You know that is not true," DuBois said quietly. "You will save yourself a lot of pain if you tell us now, instead of later." He leaned over David. "And you can take that American-supremacy sneer off your face." He slapped David quickly, right-left across the face, crack-crack, then punched him straight in the face, hard enough to knock both David and the chair backwards. DuBois nodded to Morton to pick the chair back up.

David bled copiously from his nose, making it hard to breathe.

"These are only love taps compared to what is coming," said DuBois menacingly. "I will enjoy making you scream. Believe me, you will. I will then put duct tape across your mouth. I'm thinking of taking a video, so I can enjoy it again and again."

David spat blood at him. "Just wait until Fowler hears about this. Killing your visitors will end the tourist industry."

DuBois laughed hollowly. "I don't care about the tourist industry. Fat Americans and Europeans coming here, snooping into everything. We will have a different kind of tourist, distinguished visitors who support our agenda, and who are willing to pay for the freedom they find here. But, you're wasting my time. Sergeant, see whether you can find out what he's done with what I'm looking for. I'll be back in an hour or so."

DuBois left, closing the door firmly behind him. Morton moved in front of David and smiled down at him while putting on a pair of gloves. He was still smiling as he started punching David, quick jabs to the head and then body blows, the marks of a professional boxer, and David's vision filled with blood and pinpoints of light, until he fell into unconsciousness.

When he awoke, the room was empty, except for one solitary guard, half asleep in the chair. It was dark outside, but the lagoon under the glass floor remained lit, and David could see the myriad life forms below. David saw the guard's name tag said "Embry," and managed a stage whisper. "Hey, pssst! Embry!"

The guard woke up and looked at him, his face turning surly. "What?"

"Come over here a second. I have something for you."

The guard approached. "You think I let you go, you crazy," he said.

"No, no. I just need to reach Mr. Fowler. He has to be on this island somewhere," David replied. "Please just get a hold of him, and tell him I'm here. He will want to know that."

The guard looked at him suspiciously. "And why I want to do that?"

David twisted his head to the side. "You can have my watch. It's really expensive, a Rolex Mariner diving watch. The girls love it, you'll see. You can have it, if you just tell him his friend David is here."

The guard went behind the chair and untied David's watch. He tried it on, looking at it appraisingly. "OK. As soon as the next guard comes in, I'll call Mr. Fowler."

"That may not be for hours. Can you talk to him now, on your radio? Else, I'll tell DuBois about the watch, and he'll take it away from you."

The guard thought it over, and said, "Sure, why not?" He went to a corner of the room and spoke into his radio microphone. "OK, I let him know," he said when he returned.

David smiled through his pain. "Thank you so much."

Twenty minutes passed before there was activity and the sound of people entering the room. All the lights came on again. One of the people entering was the Lt. Governor.

"Reggie!" David blurted out. "Thank God, I'm so glad to see you."

"I say! David, what's happened to you? You look awful! What's going on?"

David told him, "DuBois arrested me when I came to this island. He tried to kill me after seizing the gold on my ship. He's trying to take over the country and become its dictator."

Fowler looked behind him into the hall. "Oh, he is, is he? He hasn't told me about that."

Colonel DuBois appeared next to Fowler. For once, he looked embarrassed. "As assistant to you, of course. When we take over, you will be president, with me as Director of National Security."

"Yes," said Fowler skeptically, "Try to remember that!"

David shook his head, confused. "What? What did you say?"

Fowler looked at DuBois impatiently. "I don't have time for all this chitchat! What about the container with the crown? Has he got it?"

David felt like the bottom fell out of his stomach. "The crown?" he asked feebly.

"Yes, the crown," Fowler replied with rising irritation. "The one that belonged to my family. The one we were supposed to get back from the Germans. That crown."

"How could you know about the crown?" David asked with mounting despair. It suddenly hit him. "Wait a minute. The crown and the gold—it was someone in your family it was going to. That someone was getting paid by Operation Electric Blue."

"Yes, quite," Fowler replied casually. "My grandfather. He was also Lt. Governor of Anguilla. *Lieutenant*"—he sneered at the word—"Governor. While his highness Lord Blythe-Simpson played the high and mighty. My grandfather did all the work, while someone with a title got to run things and play the muckety-muck. Just like me. That crown belonged to my family. The Jew Weinstock stole it from us. I want it back."

"Weinstock?" David gasped.

"Yes, I believe you know someone with that name," Fowler replied with a grim smirk.

"I don't know any Weinstocks," David said quickly, recovering. "And I don't have any crown."

"Actually, he may be telling the truth," Fowler told DuBois. "Erika confirmed that a boat came up to the ship after they opened the first safe. That was probably AJ, taking the crown away."

"Erika?" asked David. "What have you done to her?"

Fowler beamed. "Done *to* her? Nothing. Done *with* her, well... She and I are very close, the best of—oh, how to say this—bosom buddies."

"I don't believe you!" David spat the words out.

"*Really*?" Fowler asked him, drawing out the word into comic proportions.

"Never. She never got close to you. She told me so!" David was vehement.

"I'll be right back," Fowler said over his shoulder, as he left the room. "I have something to show you."

He was back within minutes, and inserted a disc into a DVD player under a 60 inch screen on the wall in front of them. He turned to the others in the room. "You can go. Come back in 15 minutes."

After the door closed, Fowler hit the Play button. "This is what Miss Bettelman and I have been doing tonight and every other night she's been here—after she finished telling me about what you were doing on the ship."

His voice climbed higher and his upper class English accent got more pronounced as he warmed to his subject. "Women like men of power, men like *me*! And she saw that I was soon going to become even more powerful. No more *Lieutenant* Governor. I'll have control of this country, and an island resort that will make me a millionaire many times over. How could she refuse? Do you think she'd choose *you* over *me*?" He laughed shrilly.

The screen showed Erika walking around a bedroom in her underwear. With a sickening realization, David realized she was wearing the panties with the blue hearts that he had glimpsed the night they had dinner on shore. She smiled as she put on the electric blue skirt that David had bought her, and then put on the rest of the outfit, twirling from side to side and smiling flirtatiously.

The video switched to a different room. Fowler sat on an upholstered white couch, naked. The camera showed her from behind, as she unzipped the skirt and dropped it on the floor before she went down on her knees in front of him. Fowler started moaning and making appreciative noises that sounded like, "Good girl. Good girl!" in time with the rhythm in his lap.

David felt as if he had been punched hard in the gut. All the air went out of him. He could not breathe, and the room seemed to swim in front of his eyes. He looked down, and the floor appeared to be falling away from him into the Abyss. He started heaving, and tasted the bitter bile of vomit in his throat.

Fowler stepped behind him, grabbed him by the hair and pulled his head back and upward. "No you don't, you're going to watch. You're going to watch the whole thing!" His voice became shrill. "She chose *me*!"

He let go of David's hair, and muttered. "Ah, what do I care what you see or not."

The screen now showed a picture of Fowler's back as he was copulating on the couch, with moans and screams from both occupants. The camera switched to a close-up of Erika's face looking upwards and uttering a laughing, "Bloody great!" In the back of his mind, David wondered why she would choose that expression. The scene changed to a bed, showing Fowler from the rear, naked and very pale white, focusing his frantic attention onto the naked butt on the bed in front of him. He moaned, "Oh, Lord! Oh, Lord!" Erika's voice kept time with "Yeh! Yeh! Yeh!"

Fowler hit the Eject button on the DVD player and removed the disc. He inserted it into its case as Colonel DuBois and the others returned.

"I want to find out where the crown went to, and whom it got sent to," he said to DuBois. He looked menacingly back at David. "Try not to kill him before you find out."

DuBois nodded to his assistant, who put on heavy leather gloves that had flecks of dried blood on them.

"Do you want to tell me now?" the man sneered. "You know that you will eventually. Please don't tell me right away. I need the practice."

He started punching David, who did not even look at him. David's eyes were focused somewhere in the distance, beyond feeling and pain, and remained there until blessed darkness overcame him.

Chapter 45

AJ was agitated. He had just arrived back in St. Maarten from a short business trip, and was having a drink at the house of his friend Paul from the Embassy. He was speaking with Leah, who had been working for the past three days as a reservations clerk in the Paradise Island Resort. She had slipped outside in order to report to AJ, who could hardly believe what he was hearing from the other end of the satphone.

"Are you sure?" he asked. "David and Erika have been captured? And David's being tortured?"

After Leah answered in the affirmative, he asked, "What about the ship? What have they done with that? Did they take the gold?"

"I don't know," Leah answered. "I don't think there's anyone else from the ship here besides David and Erika. I'm not sure how they even got here. But one of DuBois's thugs is beating on David right now, trying to find out where something from the boat went to, a crown or something."

"Oh, my God," breathed AJ. "How could they know about that? I put it into the diplomatic pouch here, myself."

"The situation here is getting more and more dicey," Leah noted. "There's more so-called policemen coming in, and they brought in electronics specialists to put in some kind of radar. They're also mounting video cameras around the entire lagoon. This place is getting fortified like Ft. Knox."

"Radar," AJ said to himself.

"Yes, long-range radar, big antennas on high points of the island, much more than you need for just a small airport. And a lot of yachts have come in. Looks like some kind of high rollers from Central or South America. One of them looks like Munez, that cartel leader from Columbia. A couple of yachts have names that sound like they're from the Middle East. Most of these guys are walking around with heavily armed bodyguards. They've been holding meetings during the day and partying at night, in a closed-off area I can't get to."

AJ said. "It may be time for you to get out of there. This is..." He stopped as he heard other voices on the line.

"As I suspected. We have a spy amongst us," a voice that sounded like DuBois said, from a position that sounded like it was within a few feet of Leah.

"What are you talking about?" Leah replied heatedly. "I'm just calling a friend. I'm on a meal break from my duties at the front desk."

Another voice laughed harshly. "Listen to the bitch try to deny it! She's talking on a satellite phone, so we can't listen in. Just owning such a thing on this island means you're a spy! And we have photos of you with AJ and Kilmer!"

There were sounds of a struggle, and then a voice that AJ did not recognize came on the line.

"Who is this? Who is this she's talking to?"

There was a pause while AJ held his breath, trying to think of what to do next.

"It doesn't matter," the voice continued. "We'll know who you are and what this is all about within a few hours, or within a day or so. We have time. And we have her. We'll get around to you soon enough."

The connection was broken abruptly.

AJ cursed furiously. He quickly dialed Bedrosian and filled him in on the situation.

"We've got to get the three of them out of there. Who can you send me? How soon can we go in?" His concern was palpable.

At the other end of the line, Bedrosian laughed harshly. "Are you shitting me? Send in an armed team right now? And bust up a joint agency initiative that's got visibility at the highest levels? Under no circumstances. Don't even think about it. We'll go in when we're good and ready. Keep me informed." He disconnected.

AJ started to dial Aunt Marie on the satellite phone when he noticed that the battery light was red. He remembered he had two chargers, one on his boat and one at Aunt Marie's. He tried calling Marie on his friend's land line, but got only a voice message. He asked his friend for a ride to his boat, and took off full-speed for Anguilla as soon as he fired up the engines.

As he approached the harbor, he had a sense of foreboding. Repeated calls to Marie had gone unanswered. Instead of heading to his usual slip, he weighed anchor out in the harbor and used his Zodiac to take him to land, away from the main traffic area. As he made his way to his car, he noticed several police patrols. Each officer had a submachine gun around his neck, something that was unknown in the Anguilla of a year ago. They seemed to be patrolling near the empty spot where his boat should be. He reached his car, and slowly exited from the back entrance of the parking lot. He headed for Marie's house, carefully watching the traffic in his rear mirror.

His sense of foreboding grew as he pulled up in front of her house. The front door stood open, but there was no sign of Marie.

He pulled a Glock Model 23 .40 caliber from a locked compartment in his Jeep, and carefully walked around the house. He could not see inside because the shades were drawn, which was also unlike Marie. He used his key to enter by the back door.

He did not see a sign of anyone. "Aunt Marie?" he called out. He went into a second room, and called out again. "Aunt Marie? Are you here?"

He stopped as his nose picked up the telltale scent of propane. He moved into the kitchen, and saw that the gas vents on the stove had been left open. He turned off the vents with his left hand, carefully keeping his gun at the ready with his right.

There was a muffled cry in an adjoining room, and he went in there, his gun now held in both hands in front of him. It was difficult to see because of the drawn shades. He moved to a window, raised the shade and then opened it up, gasping for fresh air. He did the same with the other windows in the room. He was afraid to turn on a light switch, since any electrical arc could set off the propane.

With the windows open and the shades up he could finally see around the room. Marie was in a corner, tied to a chair with duct tape. More of the tape covered her mouth and the lower half of her face. He quickly glanced behind him down the hallway and then approached her. As he gently removed the tape from her mouth, he saw that her face was bruised and battered.

"Aunt Marie!" he cried, horrified. "What did they do to you?"

Marie labored for breath. He removed the rest of the tape quickly and helped her to one of the open windows. She breathed the fresh air for a few minutes before she could answer. "Bomb," she gasped.

"What?" AJ asked, puzzled.

"Bomb," she replied. "They put a firebomb in here. I saw them put it under that table in the corner. It's supposed to go off and burn me down."

AJ quickly moved to the table and pulled out a device with a digital timer attached to it. The display said, "00:23:11."

He racked his brain for the explosive ordnance training he had gone through. He looked at the wiring. It seemed to be a simple mechanism, a timer with prongs into a cake of C4, with no booby traps that would go off if the circuit was disabled. He pulled the igniter out of the C4, and then quickly returned to Marie. He helped her out of the house into the fresh air outside. He half carried her, with one arm around her while holding his weapon with the other. He sat her down on an outdoor bench.

"What happened?" he asked. "Who did this?"

She explained that a group of men in military-style uniforms had slipped into the house, seized her, tied her up in the chair, and then beat her during questioning. "They asked me if I knew where a crown was, something that David had. And they asked where you were. After I wouldn't talk, they set that bomb and left after turning the gas on in the kitchen. I guess they thought that the house would burn down totally, and me along with it."

"God, Auntie, if they'd killed you because of something related to me, I would never have forgiven myself," he said as he hugged her fiercely.

She looked him straight in the eyes. "I appreciate that, AJ, but I believe these goons want to get rid of me sooner or later. I'm convinced they're ready to take over this island." She thought a moment. "One of them mentioned that DuBois was on Dragon Island. And that he'd seized David's ship."

AJ told her about his conversation with Leah. "And now they've captured her, and David and Erika. I've got to get them out of there before they kill them! Bedrosian won't lift a finger. In fact, he gave me strict orders to stay away from the island. He's prepared to let all of them die!" He shook his head. "Auntie, what am I going to do?"

She took his hand in hers. "What do you think?"

He looked at the ground. "I should get whatever help I can and go rescue them. But if I disobey orders, it's dereliction of duty, and I'll be betraying my oath."

Marie smiled. "I know you hold duty to your country close to your heart. You have to decide...are you being loyal to your flag, or to the people hiding behind it?"

AJ took a deep breath. When he looked up again, all doubt was gone from his face. "You're right. Loyalty should be a two-way street." He thought a minute. "Now I just have figure out a way to get onto that island and help them."

She patted his hand. "One of the members of my congregation is on the island, working as a maid. I had asked her to see if there's another way in or out besides the lagoon entrance or the airport. She told me she found a path to a small beach. It's rocky and hard to see, but it looked to her like there was a way for a boat to get close if someone guided it in."

AJ brightened. "That's great, Marie. I'll get a team together. I've got a few friends in American and British Special Forces that might disobey orders for me. And if David's crew on the ship is still alive, some of them might volunteer. I think I can get some weapons and other gear in St. Maarten."

He looked at her. "Will your friend help us? Can she meet us with a flashlight, if we go in at night?"

"Yes, she will," Marie replied. "She will do it, but only for me."

"What do you mean?" AJ asked.

"I'm going with you," Marie stated firmly.

AJ shook his head. "Aunt Marie, be reasonable. You're all banged up. You need to go to hospital, not out on an insanely dangerous mission!"

Marie looked him in the eye, her face set. "Either I go with you, or my girl Katharina does not help. You decide."

AJ's shoulders slumped. "This isn't fair, and you know it. Why do you want to go to that island so bad?"

Marie smiled faintly. "I've been reading the signs. Something is going to happen on that island that will change everything. And I have to be there."

She got up from the bench. "I got to put on some different clothes. I can't go climbing around in this dress. Help me in the house. I'd better get my cane to steady me up." They entered the house, with AJ helping Marie up the steps. As she rummaged around her closet, AJ told her he had to recharge the battery of his satellite phone. Marie went to a drawer and pulled out a spare battery pack. "Go ahead and use this until yours is full up again," she told him.

AJ did as she said, and started dialing numbers and speaking rapidly.

As AJ drove away from Aunt Marie's house with her in the passenger seat, he suddenly saw a police car behind them, its lights flashing. He thought about running for it, but Anguilla is a small island—there was really no chance of getting away. He pulled over and got out of his Cherokee. An officer with sergeant's stripes approached him, gun drawn.

"Hey, John," he greeted him cheerily. "What's with the gun?"

The officer looked down at the pistol, embarrassed. "I've got orders from headquarters to take you in, AJ. They say you're a dangerous criminal."

AJ looked at him sternly as he pushed the pistol to the side. "Would that be the same dangerous criminal you served with in the Marine Corps, Gunnery Sergeant Baisley?"

"I'm sorry, AJ," the policeman said. "But you've got to come with me."

"John, I need your help. Have you called this stop in yet?"

"No," Sgt. Baisley replied. "What are you getting at?"

"Something funny's going on. I've just found out that Dave Kilmer and my assistant Leah have been kidnapped and are on Dragon Island, being tortured by DuBois. I've got to get them out of there!"

Sgt. Baisley looked hesitant. "You know what you're asking me to do?" Seeing a movement in the car, he whirled toward it, pulling his gun up again. "Who else is with you?"

AJ laid a hand on his shoulder. "It's Aunt Marie. Yes, the two of us are a real pair of hardened criminals. Like Bonnie and Clyde!"

Baisley looked exasperated. "What is this Kilmer to you, anyway? Why do you have to go help him?"

AJ looked him straight in the eyes. "I met him in the Marine Corps, after I met you. He was a lawyer with JAG, kept me out of the brig. He stuck his neck out for me. He's family."

Sgt. Baisley shuffled his feet. "He was Corps, huh?" He paused. "You can't ask this of me, AJ. I got a family to take care of. If DuBois finds out about this, I'm finished."

AJ pointed at a "Semper Fi" sticker on the back of his Cherokee, and at a tattoo with the same motto on Baisley's forearm. "Remember that?"

The policeman hesitantly touched the word "Fi" on the Cherokee's bumper sticker. "Fidelis, huh?"

AJ tapped the other word on the sticker. "I've found out that the Fi is easy. It's the Semper that's hard." He added, "Besides, you know and I know that sooner or later DuBois is going down. He's wanted for murder and extortion in Haiti, and this stuff he's pulling at the Resort is going to get the US and Britain on top of him. Do you want to around him when that happens?"

Sgt. Baisley sighed. "All right. You had me at Semper Fi. What do you need?"

"I need to get to the docks, so I can get to my boat. DuBois has taken over David's ship. I'm going to see if the crew is still on it. Once I find them, they and some friends of mine are going to sneak into the Resort."

The policeman pointed at the Cherokee. "Get your car out of sight behind those bushes. Then get in my car, both of you, in the back, and hide below the seat."

AJ and Marie quickly complied. Sgt. Baisley pressed down the pedal, and heard an *Umph* from the back seat as he sprayed gravel making a U-turn. He slowed as another police car came from the opposite direction and waved him over to a stop.

"What's up, John?" the other called to him. "You see any sign of him?"

"Naw," Sgt. Baisley replied. "Haven't seen the son of a bitch. You keep an eye on this road, I'm gonna go down to the docks, see if he's trying to steal a boat."

"Good idea," the other replied. "Later."

Ten minutes later, the car came to a stop. "There's a policeman watching the docks," Sgt. Baisley whispered. "He's one of those new guys out of Haiti. I don't know him."

"I'll take care of him," AJ replied. "Let me borrow your gun."

"You're not going to..."

"No, just a little love tap," AJ said, smiling. The sergeant reluctantly handed him his Colt M1911.

AJ was back in ten minutes, and was about to hand Sgt. Baisley's gun back to him, when he noticed that he was talking on a cell phone. "What's up?" he asked.

"I just told my wife to take our daughter and have a friend get them off this island right away. They can stay with friends in St. Martin."

He tapped the tattoo on his arm. "I'm coming with you. You'll need someone to stay with the boat when you go on Dragon Island."

AJ grinned. "Semper Fi, bro. Let's get going. We're going to take the Zodiac out to my boat."

Twenty minutes later, they were on the open ocean in AJ's boat, the twin turbo-diesels roaring, moving in the direction of the Global Explorer at dangerous speeds. They had to hang on tightly as the boat fought the waves, banging into them repeatedly.

As they approached the ship, there was a beeping from one of the instrument panels in the cockpit. AJ gave the helm to Baisley and went over to look at the display.

"What is it?" Marie asked.

"It's a type of military radar, from the direction of the Resort. And it's just about to acquire us." AJ used a rollerball control attached to the panel to issue commands. "There. That should settle it."

Seeing the puzzled look on Sergeant Baisley's face, he said. "We're sending out spoofing signals. They're still getting a radar return, but they think the ship is passing far to the East of here."

They approached the Global Explorer slowly and cautiously. There appeared to be no one moving about on deck. After pulling up alongside, Baisley kept the boat under control while AJ hoisted himself on deck. He made a quick tour of the deck, keeping one hand on his pistol. On the back deck he found a Resort Guard on a deck chair, sound asleep. He pointed the pistol at his head while nudging him with one toe to wake him. The man's eyes grew wide as he saw the weapon. "Tell me the truth and you get to live," AJ said tersely. "Where's the crew, and how many guards are on board?"

"They're in the Conference Room. And there's just me," the man replied sullenly.

"Move!" AJ said, waving his gun. "If you call out, it'll be the last thing you do."

When they reached the Conference Room, he knocked on it and asked, "Hello?"

"In here!" came a muffled reply. AJ motioned with his gun, and the Guard produced a key and unlocked the door. Inside, AJ saw the entire ship's crew, minus David, Larry, and Collins.

"Werner!" AJ called out. As he came forward he handed him the pistol and said, "Keep him covered. I want to make sure there are no others."

He returned a few minutes later, and saw the Guard had been fastened to one of the chairs with his own handcuffs. Several crew members shook AJ's hand and pounded him on the back.

"What happened to you guys?" he asked.

"We got grabbed by DuBois's men," answered Werner heatedly. "The bastards came up, swarmed on deck with guns, told us we were all under arrest, and herded us in here. We've been here ever since."

"Are you OK?" AJ asked.

Werner looked around. "Yeah. We ran out of water a while ago, so we're pretty thirsty. But other than that, we're fine. I guess they parked us here while deciding what to do with us."

"Do you know what happened to David and Erika and Larry?" Bob asked.

AJ looked grim. "I don't know what happened to Larry. But David and Erika are at the Resort on Dragon Island right now, and David is being tortured by DuBois. I think they may have stolen the gold."

"There's an easy way to check that," said Bob. "The big safe with the gold was in the Equipment Room."

They quickly made their way there, and looked around. Other than the neat rows of diving equipment on the wall, it was empty.

"Both the safes are gone," noted Werner, pressing his lips together tightly in anger.

The group gathered around the room. Bob showed up with an armful of Fiji liter-sized water bottles that he tossed to the crew members, who caught them and started to slurp them down noisily.

"What will they do to David and Erika?" asked Moshe.

"I believe they'll torture them until they have whatever they want, and then they'll kill them," said AJ.

"What can we do?" asked Mark.

"I'm getting a team together to go to the island and rescue them. There's a secret way in, and a friend is going to help us find it. I have some Special Forces colleagues who are going to meet me in St. Maarten, and they're getting weapons and ammo." He hesitated a moment. "Do any of you want to join us?"

There was unanimous assent.

AJ hesitated. "I need to tell you there'll only be around a dozen of us, and there may be over 50 Resort Guards and private goons on the island. It could be a suicide mission."

Werner asked the only question. "What caliber should I bring?"

AJ grinned at him. "Do you have anything long range, with a really good scope?"

Werner nodded. "A 7mm magnum Sauer hunting rifle with a Zeiss 12X zoom scope. I have shot elk with it at over 500 meters. I was planning on going hunting on the way back home."

AJ's smile turned grim. "You'll get to hunt with it soon. But I think it'll be very different from elk."

He turned to the group. "Anybody with military experience?"

Moshe said, "Israeli Army. Artillery." Mark added, "German Army, tank commander." Shawn said, "US Navy. Communications officer."

AJ asked, "Anyone with weapons experience?" Shawn was the only one who did not put up his hand.

"Good. Bring along any weapons on this ship. We're going to get on my boat and head to St. Maarten as fast as we can. Get your gear from your cabins and let's meet on deck in 10 minutes."

Ben pointed at the Guard. "What should we do with him?"

AJ scowled. "Do what he did with you. Just leave him there and lock the door."

Within 15 minutes they were on AJ's boat, greeting Sgt. Baisley and Marie. Within minutes they were on their way, still jamming the radar signals coming from the Paradise Resort.

Chapter 46

They were able to make out the island to the Northeast, ominous and black against the brooding sky. The moon was almost completely obscured by thick and oily clouds. The wind started to pick up, and the waves grew fierce, cutting down their speed. Raindrops spattered the windows of the pilot's cabin, which contained AJ, Baisley and Werner, with the Sergeant at the wheel. AJ studied the radar receiver screen intently. "I think we've been able to spoof them so far," he said. "I don't think they know we're coming."

Werner looked at the equipment. "Whom do you really work for, AJ?" he asked. "I don't think you need this kind of equipment for selling wine to night clubs in the Caribbean."

AJ smiled. "I work for CIA. Unfortunately, they're not going to help us. That's why it's just us, and my four friends from Special Forces that joined us in St. Maarten."

Werner laid the map of the island on the small table in the cabin, and said, "It certainly looks frightening. Like a skull with a wide open mouth. The top here is the mountain range, and the mouth is the lagoon, surrounded by high and steep cliffs. Is this a caldera?"

AJ nodded. "Yup. The lagoon is really deep. It's the hollow part of a volcano. The island rose from the sea, like the Hawaiian Islands did." He pointed at a spot marked with an "X" on the bottom of the island, slightly to the right of the entrance to the lagoon. "And here's where we get off."

The rain grew heavier, cutting visibility further, and thunder rumbled ominously in the distance. The boat approached to within a few hundred yards of the Southeast part of the island. A brief sliver of moonlight lit the foreboding black backbone of cliffs in front of them. The island looked like a dark castle straight out of a Harry Potter movie.

"It looks like there's no place to land," Mark said, scanning the tall and jagged cliffs with his binoculars.

AJ looked at the GPS coordinates that had been given them by Marie's friend Katharina. "We're at the right point, within maybe 100 yards. We should see a light."

He cut down the engine to reduce its rumble, keeping it at a bare minimum so he could avoid the deadly rocks in front of him.

They saw a light coming down the cliff along a zigzag path. It stopped at the waterline. They could now see it was a flashlight held by a young woman, who pointed it down and then left and right. They saw a tiny stretch of sand, perhaps 30 feet across. "Somebody get up front," AJ said, and Mark quickly volunteered.

Gingerly, the boat approached the tiny landing site, straying dangerously close to the sharp rocks on either side. Finally, they heard a *Sssss*, as the prow of the boat knifed into the sand.

AJ looked at the team, and said, "All ashore that's going ashore!" Turning to Sergeant Baisley, he said, "Take the helm, John, and back it out really carefully." He stopped. "What is it?"

Sgt. Baisley furrowed his brow in concentration. "I've been thinking. I've got this police uniform on, and I may know some of the guys there. That could buy you some time. I should go with you. Shawn can drive the boat."

AJ looked at John, and then at Shawn. The computer geek was obviously out of shape, and not much use for a mission involving climbing and then combat. He turned back to Sgt. Baisley. "Are you sure? If they recognize you and report it, it could go bad for you."

John smiled grimly. "I used your satellite phone to check on my wife Mary. She and our daughter Sarah are safe with family in St. Martin. I'm all in, as they say in poker."

AJ squeezed Sgt. Baisley's shoulder affectionately, and turned to Shawn. "We need somebody who's really good at communications to man the boat. Take it out after we leave, and stay someplace far offshore, and listen for my call on the satellite phone. See if you can pick up any radio traffic here on the island, and if you overhear something important, warn us on our satphones."

He continued, "Shawn, by tomorrow we'll either have rescued the three of them and brought them to this beach, or you'll be picking up survivors. Assuming there are any." He paused. "You figured out how to use the radar jamming and spoofing system, right?"

Shawn grinned. "You bet. I want one of those for my car."

AJ shook hands. "Good luck. Hope to see you tomorrow."

Mark was the first of the team to jump down on the beach. He looked at the person behind the light, and called, "Katharina?"

"It's me," she said. "Where is Auntie?" She looked at the group assembling in front of her. When Aunt Marie was helped down onto the sand, she ran to embrace her. "I'm so glad to see you. But it's really dangerous here. Let's get farther up the trail, so a passing boat can't see us."

They walked behind her in single file up an increasingly steep and treacherous trail. Occasionally there was a sheer drop-off to the ocean below. At one point, Werner stepped too far from the cliff face, and felt the path start to crumble under his right foot. He clung to the cliff and looked down to see a cascade of small rocks fall straight down for over 200 feet into the crashing waves.

A short time later, the path turned inland, and they came to a small clearing. They huddled together, with Katharina in the middle. AJ introduced the team to her, including his Special Forces friends, Jim Morrison, Steve Roth, Tony Cervo, and Alex Lighter. "Tell me what's been going on," he asked her.

"There've been a lot of yachts coming and going, and some airplanes and helicopters," she replied. "They had a big meeting a few days ago, and partied through the night." She hesitated. "I heard a rumor that they captured a couple of spies and were holding them." She pulled out a map of the island, and did a quick review. "The lagoon is kind of circular, with an opening to the ocean at the Southern end, and the Resort built along the Northern shore. The airport is here, to the left of the Resort buildings. Behind the Resort buildings are mountains. They go on to the Northern tip of the island."

The team members resumed the trek, and finally reached the crest of the trail. They stopped for a moment, and looked at the lagoon spread out in front of them. It was outlined by a concrete road along its periphery that was lined with street lights. Many of the trees had twinkle lights that ran up the trunks and into the branches.

AJ scanned the lagoon road. He whispered to Katharina. "Is that a guard shack on the far side of the lagoon entrance?" he asked.

She nodded. "Yes. There's another one on this side that you can't see. In between them is a double fence, with a catwalk on top. It reaches from the bottom to about ten feet above water level. They call it a shark net, but it's really to keep out any boats they don't want to enter."

She motioned along the concrete roadway. "There are also patrols that drive up and down the pathway." She pointed at the resort. "Most of the buildings have glass walls with views of the lagoon, so people inside can see you when you get close. The Guard headquarters are over there to the left."

She waved at the mountain range in back of the lagoon. "And there's an unmanned outpost up there, on top of the highest mountain, with a whole bunch of antennas. I hear they have this whole part of the Caribbean on radar."

They started down the trail, and ended near the lagoon roadway. AJ held up his right hand as he heard voices coming from the road, and the group stopped. He slid along the ground on his belly until he came to a spot with a view of the roadway. He saw a Jeep with blue lights on top. Four policemen stood around it, smoking cigarettes and joking with each other. He made his way back to the group, stooping over as he moved. He motioned to Katharina to come over to him. "There's a patrol with a Jeep right in front of us on the road," he whispered. "Is there any way to get around them?"

She shook her head. "No. From here on up, it's only the lagoon road."

"Damn," he hissed. "How are we going to get past these guys? If we shoot them, the rest of them will hear us, and we'll have lost the element of surprise."

He turned back to Katharina. "Where's the building where they're holding David, Erika and Leah?"

She pointed to the Resort complex. "You mean the spies? Two of them are in the building on the right, with the blue neon running along the top. I don't know about a third spy."

AJ bit his lip. "That's about a mile. We could make it in maybe 20 minutes or so, if we could get past the patrol."

He turned to the team. "I'm the only one with a silenced weapon." He tapped the Skorpion submachine gun hanging by a strap around his neck. "I'll go ahead and try to take them out. Unfortunately, they're spread out, so I don't think I can surprise them all. If it doesn't work, shoot them with your weapons and keep going. Grab their Jeep if you can."

He noticed that Marie seemed to be distracted.

"Marie? Are you OK?" he asked. "Do you need anything?"

"No, I'm fine," she said absently. She looked off into the lagoon.

Werner looked in that direction. "What do you see?"

"Mkele Mbembe is here. I can sense him."

AJ looked grim. "I wish he were. We need some kind of distraction, desperately." He turned to the group. "Any suggestions?"

Marie touched AJ's arm. "I think I can help you. Give me a few minutes."

She moved a few feet away from them, and closed her eyes. She clasped the silver talisman fastened around her throat and started chanting softly, rocking back and forth on her heels.

They could hear rustling in the nearby palm trees as the wind started to pick up. A light rain started to come down, and they could hear the boom of distant thunder.

Werner looked impatiently at AJ. "We don't have a lot of time," he said.

AJ held up his hand. "Give her a few minutes. I've learned over the years never to question Aunt Marie. Just hold on."

A few more minutes passed as they crouched in the darkness and gusting rain. Suddenly, they heard shouting from across the water, followed by several shots. One of radiophones in the jeep rang, and a guard answered it and spoke a few tense words, punctuated with a lot of loud "what's" and "where's." He turned it off and spoke to the others.

"Something's up. Let's go," he said.

They threw away the cigarettes they had been smoking and jumped into the Jeep, which then drove up the road toward the top of the lagoon.

AJ looked at Marie. "Thanks," he said.

"No problem," she replied, smiling.

AJ led the group as it emerged onto the road. He turned back to Katharina. "You said there were two guard shacks down here," he said. She pointed to the entrance to the lagoon. "They're on both sides of the entrance."

AJ looked at the guard stations, each about 15 feet square. "After we take out the one on this side, can we go across that catwalk to get to the other one?"

"It shouldn't be a problem," said Katharina. "The catwalk has handrails. If Sergeant Baisley goes in front, they probably won't get suspicious."

"Cool," AJ replied. He handed a package to Sgt. Baisley. "Remember our cover story. We've been sent here by DuBois to do drug testing, because he heard some of the guards were getting high while on duty. It's supposed to be a surprise visit." He grasped John by the shoulder. "I'm so glad you came with us. Your uniform will make this a whole lot easier."

Baisley nodded. He pointed to Werner. "Since you're the doctor, and we're injecting these guys to knock them out, how about you come with me," he said.

Werner chuckled. "Am I going on this mission because I'm the best qualified, or because I'm the most expendable?"

Baisley grinned. "However you want it. Let's go. If this works, we should be back in about 20 minutes or so." They started to jog in the direction of the guard shack.

Looking through infrared binoculars, AJ could see them speaking with one of the guards, and then being admitted into the small building. After about 10 minutes, he saw both men walking gingerly across the catwalk and then entering the guard shack on the far side. A short time later, they emerged and started back onto the catwalk.

While they waited, AJ reviewed the Resort with Katharina. "How many people did you say are there, total?"

She ticked them off on her fingers.

"First, there are the leaders of the Resort Guards. There's DuBois, he's the most dangerous, and two majors and a Captain at the Guard Headquarters, with about five men for support."

"Second, there are boat and vehicle patrols. Two boats, one Jeep, and five electric All-Terrain Vehicles. There are a few patrolmen on Segways, those electric things you stand on with bicycle handles and two big wheels. In total, probably a dozen guys on patrol per shift."

"Third, the two guard shacks at the lagoon entrance have two men each, there's one more shack to the left of the buildings at the top of the lagoon, and one more at the airport, plus around 20 guys resting at headquarters. So, around 60 Guards total."

"Fourth, there are about thirty guests. They've brought some women, maybe a dozen, but they don't look like they're a threat. The men are a bad bunch, and many carry pistols. They each have at least one bodyguard. A bunch of those guys have automatic weapons, those things you carry on straps over your shoulder. So, thugs and bodyguards, maybe 70."

"Fifth, there are workers that have been brought in from the Yucatan, and a few from Anguilla, like me. There are gardeners, maids, cooks, cleaning help, workers like that. They don't have any weapons. They live in mobile homes near the airport, and are not usually out at night." She thought a minute. "So, of dangerous bad guys, I would guess, maybe 130 total."

AJ smiled grimly. "Is that all? Well, we have our work cut out for us." He turned to the group. "We've gone over the Rules of Engagement. Shoot first and ask questions later. Immediately shoot anyone with a weapon. Try to avoid unarmed native workers."

He paused. "You each have a set of handcuffs. If you can capture anybody, cuff them and ask them where the three hostages are.

Especially Leah—we're really not sure where they're holding her. Everybody got it?"

After he saw all the heads nod, he looked toward the top of the lagoon as he heard the sound of shots. "What's going on? Are some of the guests shooting at each other?"

"I wouldn't put it past them," Katharina replied. "They get pretty crazy. They've been told this is like an adult Disneyland, and that they can do anything they want."

The radio crackled to life, and Baisley's voice came on. "Hey, can a couple of you guys come down here? We need help carrying stuff." AJ nodded at Jim Morrison and Ben, who trotted off in the direction of the guard shack.

A few minutes later, all four of them returned, dragging heavy sacks.

"What's that?" AJ asked.

Morrison replied with a smile. "They found toys." His smile grew wider. "Special Forces guys love toys." He opened the bags. "They have enough stuff to start a small war. An M240 light machine gun. Two M209 40mm grenade launchers. Four fully automatic M16s. Lots of grenades and ammo."

"That's great news," AJ replied. "Now we've got some decent weapons. Go ahead and pass them out."

"They had two heavy machine guns and a 30mm cannon mounted there, but those were too heavy to lift," Morrison said. "Looks like they were ready for all comers—even the US Coast Guard."

"How did it go with the guards?" AJ asked.

"Worked like a charm," Baisley replied. "We told all four of them that we were doing drug tests, and had to take a blood sample. That made them nervous, but we assured them the test was going to come out all right. Then Werner made them look the other way as he injected them. They're out like babies right now. How long does that stuff last?"

"I put quite a good dose into each syringe," Werner replied. "They should be awake in 24 hours, if they're lucky."

"Then let's get going. No time to waste," AJ said. "Marie, you stay here with one of the satellite phones. See if you can go back up the trail and find a high place that overlooks everything, and let us know if anyone starts sneaking up on us. The rest of us are going to go up the roadway single file, keeping to the right in the darkness as much as we can. Katharina said there's another guard shack just before the main buildings. We'll try our ruse one more time."

He pointed down the row, starting with Sergeant Baisley. "John, you have the first group. Try to bluff your way in with your uniform. If that doesn't work, go in with all guns blazing. Jim, you're leading the second group, to rescue our friends. Katharina, you stay in back with me. Werner will look for a good sniper position and give you cover. Everybody remember their hand signals? Let's see them."

Baisley and Morrison got in front of their groups and quickly reviewed the hand signals for stop, advance, get down, cover your flanks, and move-forward-while-keeping-low.

Satisfied, AJ continued. "Each group has a satellite phone. Make sure you use the earpieces, so the enemy can't hear them. Stay in touch." He looked at them proudly. "There's 11 of us. You all know what to do."

"Hey, don't forget about Auntie. She's a fighter!" Katharina complained.

"Sorry. There's 12 of us. A dirty dozen."

"I'm not sure we'll be talking on our satphones a lot," Tony said. "I've tried using mine, and I'm getting lots of crackling background noise."

"Some kind of strange electrical interference around here," AJ said. "Use hand signals if you have to. Let's move out."

The men jogged down the road toward the buildings. They heard more gunshots and shouts coming from that direction.

Chapter 47

The male Mosasaur led the family unit emerging from the tunnel that opened into the lagoon. At almost 70 feet long, he was the length of two school buses, and weighed over 20 tons. He and the female and their two offspring had been separated from the rest of their pod by the massive explosion, which had sealed off most of the key tunnels connecting the nests. They had tried in vain to rejoin the others, attempting one tunnel after the other, but could not get through the piles of fallen rock.

The male was both frustrated and angry. His brain sensed that another powerful predator had somehow attacked him, and he wanted to retaliate with all his strength. He emerged into the lagoon in a rush, and immediately sensed traces of the hated human smell that he associated with danger.

He heard a patrol boat nearby, and surfaced part of his head to take a look. It was a Zodiac Rigid Inflatable Boat with two men in it, one in front standing behind a steering wheel and windshield, the other one sitting on a bench in the back. They were cruising slowly with an electric motor, an expediency that had been demanded by the guests, who had complained about police patrols with noisy outboard motors ruining their sleep at night.

The Mosasaur waved its tail to and fro to pick up speed, overtaking the boat in less than a minute. He leaned over the stern of the boat and grasped the back patrolman and pulled him into the water in one smooth motion.

The front patrolman continued an ongoing conversation about his mother-in-law in Kingston, and what plans he had to get even with her. He stopped for a minute, to ask, "Hey, Rod. You got a cousin who sells weapons without serial numbers, right? Can you set me up with him? Rod?" He turned around to look at the back, which was dark, lit only by the two blue police lights from the light bar above his head. "Rod? Did you pass out, man?"

He cut the motor and looked more closely, totally baffled as to where his partner might have gone to. He started to step carefully toward the back, then gasped as the whole boat rose in the water and he was thrown overboard. The impact knocked the air out of his lungs as he went under the surface. He saw what appeared to be a pale white shimmering and wondered in the back of his mind when they had started installing underwater lights in this part of the lagoon. That was the last thought he ever had.

Two guests passed by in an electric golf cart, one of the dozens available in the Resort. Each held a tall drink in his hand, and the cart slalomed along the path, almost pitching into the water several times. The driver looked at the lagoon and slammed on the brakes, causing both of them to spill part of their drinks. He jabbed his semi-comatose companion in the ribs. "Hey, look at that!"

He picked up a phone from the dashboard and dialed security. "Hello? Hello? This is one of the guests, Mr. Bernardo. Do you know you have a boat out here with no one on it?" He nodded. "Yes. A police boat. On the Northwest side of the lagoon, near lamp post..." he squinted his eyes to read in the near-darkness, "...near lamp post 121. Say, when are you going to get all these things lit up, eh?"

The voice on the speakerphone replied, "Sorry, sir, don't know what could have happened. Another patrol boat will be there within minutes to check it out."

Patrolman Manzy on Patrol Boat One picked up the call, and alerted his partner as they headed at maximum speed in the direction of lamp post 121. "Strange," Manzy commented. "They don't usually both get drunk at the same time. Wonder what's going..."

He never got a chance to complete his sentence. His eyes flew open with incredulous horror at the apparition on his port bow. A dragon-like head had appeared there, cocked at a slight angle, and an immense eye stared at them. The patrolman looked behind the head to see an undulating body that seemed to go on forever, easily keeping pace with their boat. He jabbed an elbow into the side of his partner, who was looking at the other shore. "Hey! Am I...?"

The Mosasaur raised his head out of the water, and brought it down at an angle, behind and on top of the two patrolmen. It seized both of them in its jaws, and plucked them neatly from the boat.

Patrol Boat One continued on without its crew, eventually beaching itself about ten yards from the golf cart. Mr. Bernardo looked into the boat in amazement, and then stared at his companion. He waved at the empty boat, whose electric motor was still running.

"What the hell? Are they running these damn boats by remote control now? Is this supposed to be some freaking cost-cutting measure?"

They could hear a barrage of shots across the lagoon, but it was too dark to see what was going on. The radio in the stranded police boat crackled to life. "This is dispatch. All units report in. Automatic weapons fire near Dock 5. Repeat, automatic weapons fire."

Bernardo waved his drink, a potent Tropical Itch with a Bendy Straw and a slice of pineapple decorating its rim, at his partner, and slurred, "Hear that? It's not just the boats. They've even got their guns on automatic. Goddamn bean counters!"

Chapter 48

AJ and the group moved up the lagoon pathway, avoiding the lighted areas as much as possible. They came upon the Jeep they had seen previously. Its four Resort Guards were milling around it, asking questions on their radios while looking intently out into the lagoon. One of the men started firing his automatic weapon in a wild burst into the lagoon. He approached the very edge of the water, craning his neck and putting his hands over his eyes to shield them from the rain.

"What you shooting at?" one of the others yelled at him, straining to make his voice heard over the sound of the rain.

"I thought I saw something white in the water," the shooter answered. "Do we have any submarines in the lagoon?"

"You smoking mojo again," another man commented, standing next to him. "Nothin' out there."

Sgt. Baisley, serving as point man, crouched about 20 yards away, hidden by darkness. He turned to AJ to ask, "Should we shoot them? They're lined up pretty much in a row right now."

"Sounds good to me," AJ replied. He looked at his four Special Forces friends. Two had shotguns, and two had M4 versions of the Colt M16 assault rifle. He motioned the two with the assault rifles to him, and whispered, "OK, Tony, you take out 1 and 2. Jim, take out 3 and 4. On my signal."

He was about to start counting down when he saw both men lowering their rifles, their mouths dropping open. He turned toward the lagoon and saw a terrifying vision. A monstrous head with open jaws emerged about 20 yards from shore, and bore in rapidly. It pushed a 5-foot bow wave in front of it, which crashed into the shore and its parallel pathway, soaking the guards.

The mouth turned slightly sideways, and then opened so wide that the men thought they were looking into the pit of hell. The monster seized the two men standing at the water line and closed its jaws on them, resting its head and forward flippers on the shore. The only visible parts of the guards were two sets of hands and feet protruding through rows of teeth.

The other two guards did not move for a moment, rigid with shock. The closer of the two swiveled his submachine gun on its shoulder strap in the general direction of the Mosasaur and pulled the trigger. Nothing happened. He looked dumbly at his weapon for a moment before realizing that he had left the safety switch on. His companion was somewhat more prepared, and managed to get off a short burst of 9mm, of which two rounds hit. In response, the Mosasaur swung its tail section around until it rested on land. There was a loud *ZZZT*, and blue flames enveloped the two guards.

Both leaped into the air and started a bizarre dance. Their limbs jerked as if they were marionettes and their strings were being pulled by a puppeteer on amphetamines. They flung their arms out wildly, and their weapons went sailing far away, one into the lagoon and the other into the darkness beyond the pathway.

Lightning crackled in the distance, making AJ and his men jump. They glanced for a second in the direction of the lightning, as the sound of thunder rolled over them. Their heads swiveled back to the bizarre scene before them. The Mosasaur had not moved. The hands and feet sticking out of its maw wiggled, as if trying to signal for help. The blue light around the two guards had disappeared, and they had lost their motion and were drooping, as if their marionette strings had been cut.

The blue light started dancing again, with a *ZZZT* that stretched the guards to their full height, all limbs extended. One fell down, and started writhing on the ground, moving up and down as if hitting speed bumps. The other one remained standing, and started to look as if he were on a barbecue. His left eye expanded and then popped out of his head. His face peeled back like an overcooked baked potato. As the swollen skin curled back on itself, it revealed his jaw line, giving him an obscene grin as his teeth were exposed. Then the whole skull emerged, as chunks of skin and hair started raining on the ground below. The man slowly descended upon the other guard, and their twitching subsided.

The Mosasaur made a bowing motion with its head and pushed off with its front flippers. Within seconds it had disappeared into the lagoon.

For a full fifteen seconds, no one in the group moved. Then almost everyone formed the same word: "What...?"

AJ got on the satellite phone to Marie. "Aunt Marie, are you up in a high place where you can see the lagoon?"

Her voice crackled in his ear. "Yes, I am, AJ. I can overlook parts of the lagoon really well."

"What was that... *thing* that we just saw?"

"That was Mokele-Mbembe, of course. Who else would it be?" she said, with an "I told you so!" tone in her voice.

"Mokele-Mbembe..." AJ repeated, his mind not registering for a moment.

"What Erika calls a Mosasaur."

"A Mosasaur. And it's alive!"

"Of course. Like I said."

"Are there more than one of them?"

"I think I saw a second one. It wouldn't surprise me. When God sends a messenger, he often sends more than one."

"Um...thank you, Auntie. What was that thing he did with the blue light, that seemed to fry the two guards?"

"I told you that Mokele-Mbembe is the Angel of Lightning. He killed those two hoodlums with it. I think Erika called it 'discharge of electric organs.'"

"So Erika was right. This thing is not just big and dangerous, but can shoot out electricity. Thank you, Auntie."

He turned to the rest of the group. "That was a Mosasaur. There is at least one more somewhere in the lagoon. They have electric charges, like a huge electric eel. If you see one and are standing in water, get out immediately and get on top of wood or something that's an insulator."

He stood and waved his arm. "At least it took care of these four guys for us. Let's go!" He started toward the structures at the top of the lagoon again, breaking into a light trot.

"I can hardly wait to see what you come up with next," Werner commented as he joined the line of men.

Within minutes, they approached the guard shack. There were four men inside, all of them shouting on walkie-talkies. While the rest of the group crouched behind decorative bushes, some thirty yards away, Sgt. Baisley walked toward the guards, closely followed by AJ and Morrison.

Baisley shouted, "Good evening!" and waved his hand in greeting. One of the men yelled at him, agitation evident in his voice. "Who the fuck are you?"

Baisley replied calmly. "I'm Sergeant Baisley of the Anguilla police. I work for DuBois. These men with me are animal trainers. There are some big crocodiles here that escaped from a zoo. We'll help you catch them."

The man was confused and suspicious, and pulled out his submachine gun, but kept his index finger outside the trigger guard. "Crocodiles? Are you responsible for these things that are jumping out of the water all over the place?"

"Not really," AJ answered as he sprang out from behind Baisley. "Now!" he yelled, and pulled the trigger on his MP5, spraying the two men outside the booth. Morrison quickly danced toward the door, and shot the two men inside.

They waited a minute. The only sounds were of a few cartridges bouncing on the concrete with a metallic *tink-tink-tink*. One of the men groaned briefly, and Morrison placed one more shot into his temple.

"Grab those walkie-talkies," AJ told them. "Then we can listen in to what the guards are saying, and maybe find out where DuBois is."

Morrison and Baisley picked up the four walkie-talkies and the weapons the guards had dropped, distributing them to the other men that had come up behind them. AJ looked at the captured weapons. "Good. Search the bodies and the shack, and get any extra ammo you can carry. Let's go."

They continued up the pathway, getting closer to the yacht harbor and the first buildings. Each building stood on pilings that had been driven into the lagoon, and had a full glass wall facing the water. Small bridges connected the buildings with each other and the concrete pathway that ran behind them.

Katharina pointed to the third building in the row. "That's the gym. That's where I think they're holding David." She pointed to the far left of the row of buildings. "And way down there is Police Headquarters. That may be where they're holding Leah."

AJ bit his lower lip. "Unless we get a boat and go around, we'll have to fight our way past each of these buildings to get to her."

Werner had been looking around the beginning of the Resort area that they had now entered. He saw a giant piece of outdoor art, well over 20 feet tall, with a flat surface on top. He poked his son Mark in the ribs. "Look at that!"

Mark made a sour face. "I don't think this is the time to be looking at art objects," he commented.

"No," Werner retorted. "It's a shooting stand. Help me up, quick!" He jogged to the base of the art work and set down his hunting rifle. Mark cupped his hands, and Werner gained footing midway up the statue. Mark reached up the Mauser rifle, and Werner climbed to the top of the work, situated himself, laid out his ammunition, and started looking for targets. "It's just like my hunting platform in Austria," he thought to himself. "Except that these deer only have only two legs instead of four. And can shoot back."

The rest of the group moved forward again, with Baisley, Morrison and AJ in front, followed at a distance by the others. The three in front stopped suddenly when a four-seat All-Terrain Vehicle with three guards in it appeared. Sgt. Baisley moved out in front of the group. He held a walkie-talkie to his head in an attempt to look like one of the Resort Guards.

The leader of the oncoming guards looked like a defensive football player. His bald head appeared to merge into mountainous shoulders without benefit of a neck. He had small, piggish eyes that were bloodshot, set into a pushed-back face that seemed formed into a permanent angry scowl.

He climbed out of the ATV, which shook from side to side as his weight offloaded, and walked belligerently toward Baisley. "Put your hands up in the air," he growled. "All three of you."

Baisley slowly raised his hands, but the smile never left his face. "Hold on, hold on. There's no need for that. I'm Sergeant Baisley, from the Anguilla Police. I work for DuBois just like you do. Let's not do anything foolish that gets somebody hurt."

The guard was unmoved. "I don't care who you say you are. If you make one move, I shoot you where you stand."

He turned to the two men that had moved next to him. "Jonason, you cover them from the side. DuPont, you put cuffs on them. Make them lie down while you do it."

Baisley looked at the man's name tag, and tried one more time. "I'm telling you, Corporal DuPont, we all work for DuBois. These men are animal trainers. They're trying to help."

The massive bull of a man brought his submachine gun up higher. "Go ahead. Say one more word and I pull the trigger."

DuPont motioned for AJ to get on the ground. "Put your hands on top of your head. I'm telling you just once."

AJ started to kneel. Baisley looked at the giant in front of him, and considered what options he had, if any.

Werner had gotten relatively comfortable on his perch. The irregular features of the work of art concealed him well, but still afforded clear fields of fire. He had a laser rangefinder, and had dialed in the distance to the confrontation between the guards and his team mates. Fortunately, the rain had slowed, and the group stood clearly outlined in the halogen light under a lamp post. He had just wiped the raindrops off the optics, and now quickly brought the rifle into firing position, pressing the rubber-tipped stock between his shoulder and right cheek. His finger flipped off the safety while he centered the crosshairs of the Zeiss optics on the chest of the guard. He took slow, controlled breaths as he released the first stage trigger, then moved to the second stage. The crosshairs slid up the chest, and then came to rest on the guard's eye. The trigger finger started its slow, even squeeze on the second trigger. The hollow-point 7mm magnum round spiraled down the barrel and bored its way through the intervening air on the way to the target.

Down at ground level, Sgt. Baisley had been focused on the bloodshot left eye of the guard. Suddenly, it seemed to change magically, turning from reddish to black, and mushrooming in size as the hollow-tipped bullet collapsed on impact, blowing the eye and most of the guard's brains out of a wide, jagged hole in the back of his head. The impact snapped his head back, jerking the arm holding his weapon away from Sgt. Baisley.

The guard named Jonason whirled his head around toward the sound of the shot. He started to move, but it was too late. A lead-tipped bullet shattered his jaw and throat, and he staggered away from Morrison before collapsing on the ground. Morrison reacted quickly. He swiveled his weapon toward the third guard and squeezed off a burst of three shots, one of which put a hole into the middle of his forehead.

AJ got off the ground, and looked in the direction of the invisible Werner, giving him a thumbs-up sign. Morrison poked the big guard's body with his rifle. "I thought Werner was just showing off, but it's a good thing he hit him in the head. Look, they're wearing Level 3 armor vests."

AJ nodded. "Grab the vests and guns and give them to our team. We're up-arming pretty well, here."

He looked up as the rest of the team came up and looked down at the three bodies. He looked at Katharina, and said, "We're really grateful for your help. I think we can take it from here. Can you make it back to Aunt Marie? Take one of the radios, so you can contact her."

She nodded. He gave her a quick hug, and watched as she made her way back along the path, hugging the buildings on the left.

He turned to the others. "OK, you guys. Fifteen down, about 110 to go. John, Jim, Steve, go ahead and use this ATV. You other guys look for more of them. Let's go!"

Chapter 49

Fowler entered the Recreation Room and approached the unconscious David. "Throw some water on him," he ordered one of the guards, who happened to be drinking a large cup of Cola. The man looked around, and then glanced down at his cup and threw its contents into David's face.

David slowly came back to consciousness. He looked down at his lap, puzzled to see ice cubes lying there. He looked up to see Fowler scowling down at him.

"Something's going on in my resort," Fowler growled.

"*Your* resort?" David countered, speaking slowly and slurring his words. "You told me it was controlled by a mystery partner."

Fowler hooted. "Of course, you idiot. *I'm* the mystery partner!"

"You're deliberately creating a pirate's haven here?" David queried.

Fowler snorted, lifting his nose into the air in a *hauteur* gesture. "Why not? They're willing to pay. Anything. Just so they're not bothered by outside police or the US Coast Guard. I'll make a fortune."

He placed a forefinger on David's forehead. "And I deserve one, after all the years spent slaving along on salary while attending rich people's parties." He paused. "Do you know how many multimillionaire mansions there are in Anguilla and St. Martin? Do you know what it feels like to visit them like some poor relative, being handed food and drink like a charity case?"

David thought to himself that he knew exactly what that felt like, but decided that Fowler did not want that input right now.

"By the way, thank you for the gold. I know you worked hard for it. Over two years, was it, you spent looking?" Fowler snickered. "It'll take a while to sell it all. In the meantime, I'll take in a few million from this resort. I promise you that I'll enjoy all of it!" Fowler suddenly turned stern. "You still haven't told me where that old bitch with the crown is. You're not planning to, are you?"

David stared at the floor.

Fowler shrugged. "Doesn't matter. I think I know her last name, from the Jew that stole it from my great-grandfather. And I have a record of some calls you made to New York from Anguilla." He looked down at David's shocked expression. "Yes, I've had the telephone exchange on Anguilla monitored for months."

Fowler's walkie-talkie buzzed. He yanked it out of his belt and put it up to his ear. "What?" he asked irritably. He listened for a minute, his irritation rising.

"What do you mean, two patrol boats have disappeared? How can they disappear? And another patrol is shooting at somebody? What the hell is going on?"

He listened for a minute. Obviously not satisfied with the answer, he screamed into the handheld, "Well, then go out there and find out!"

He glowered at David. "You wouldn't know anything about this, would you?" David shook his head.

Fowler dialed another number. "Ferrer? Get your ass to the helicopter right now. Have that thing ready to go in 10 minutes. Yes, the one with pontoons at Dock 2. Move!"

He turned to a Lieutenant behind him. "You know where those sacks are. Get three or four guys to help you and put them into the helicopter. Now!" The officer fled out the door.

Fowler turned to the last person in the room, an overweight sergeant named Avila. He started to say something, but stopped at the sound of assault rifles shooting in the distance. He shouted into his handheld. "DuBois! Where are you?" At that moment, the Colonel burst into the room.

"What the hell is going on?" Fowler screamed at him.

DuBois scowled. "Somebody has invaded the resort. I don't know how many. It may be several dozen. I don't know how they got in. We saw nothing on the radar."

"I'm leaving," Fowler cut him off. "I'll go to my place in Martinique with the gold, to keep it safe. Call me there after you've got this taken care of." He nodded in the direction of David. "Oh, and tie up any loose ends. That means both him and Bettelman and that other bitch. I'll talk to you soon." He stalked quickly out of the room, slamming the door behind him.

DuBois walked to the helpless David and looked into his face from a distance of a few inches. He smiled, an evil grimace.

"Yes, I will give Miss Bettelman my personal attention. Something she will never forget." He turned to Sergeant Avila. "Take care of him, and dump his body into the lagoon. Then go up to dispatch and see where they need you most." He started issuing commands on his radio as he left the room.

David and Avila looked at each other. David was still groggy, and could taste blood in his mouth, but decided he had nothing to lose. He tried bluffing.

"Listen, Sergeant Avila, you don't have to do this. That's a major group of US and British Special Forces and the DEA coming in here. DuBois is history. If you kill me it'll be murder. If you let me go, I'll make sure you get set free. There'll be a reward, too. A hundred thousand, US."

Avila cocked his head, considering this. He was about to answer when his radio crackled. It was DuBois. "Avila! Are you finished yet? Help these guys load the helicopter!" Avila snapped back to attention as he clicked his handset on, said, "Yes, sir! I'll be right there," and clicked it off. He drew his revolver, a worn Beretta 92F, and pointed it toward David. "Sorry. I gotta finish. And then I gotta go."

David struggled against his bonds. "Just tell him you killed me, and go ahead."

Avila shook his head. "No. Say good-bye. What you lookin' at?"

David stared in disbelief through at the doorway. Someone in a camouflage uniform had an M4 up to his shoulder, aimed in the direction of David and Avila.

David spoke quickly. "You know, it's no big deal to shoot me from two feet away. A five-year old could do that. I bet you couldn't hit me in the head if you backed up to the wall and made a shot from 20 feet. You'd miss by a mile."

Avila laughed. He said, "I'm going to punch a Smiley Face in your forehead." He backed up toward the glass wall.

David could see that the newcomer's rifle was following the Sergeant.

Avila said, "Here comes..." His head exploded as three shots hit it in rapid succession. He fell to the floor as his pistol slid into a corner.

The man approached David, and peered at him intently. "You look like the pictures of David we've seen," he said. "Are you him?"

David nodded. "Who are you guys?"

The man introduced himself and someone behind him. "I'm Alex Lighter, and this is Tony Cervo. We're part of the rescue team that AJ brought in." The man used his knife to cut the duct tape. David rubbed his aching wrists and quickly shook hands with both of them.

"Where's the lady, Bettelman?" Lighter asked. He pulled out a map of the complex and held it in front of David, who looked over the names of the rooms and stabbed his finger down on one of them. "Here! They mentioned they had her in Fowler's Conference Room."

Lighter looked at the bruises and caked blood on David's face. "Can you come with us? Can you..." Just then, his radio sprang to life. He pressed his headset close to his ear. "What? Where? OK, we're on our way." He turned to David and Cervo. "That was Morrison. They're pinned down, and need help ASAP."

He took a closer look at David, who was spitting blood on the floor. "You'd better rest. We'll come back when we can."

They started walking away when David yelled, "Wait! How can I recognize the team? I don't want to shoot somebody by mistake."

Cervo nodded at him. "It's your ship's crew, plus four Special Forces guys who are all wearing camouflage like we have on. And there's an Anguillan policeman named Baisley. That's it."

David stared at him. There's only around a dozen of you?"

Cervo smiled grimly. "Actually, 13, counting Aunt Marie up on a hill." He and Lighter disappeared out the door.

David shook his head, trying to clear the fog. Avila's radio, which lay nearby on the floor, crackled. "Avila, this is DuBois. Where are you? Move your fat ass over here. We're in the Rec. Room, moving the bags to the helicopter at Dock 2. Avila?"

David looked at the map that had been left with him. He saw that the Recreation Room was to his left, in the direction opposite to that of the Conference Room. He picked up Avila's weapon and dropped the slide to check the ammunition. It had eight rounds, plus one in the chamber. He headed out the door and turned left.

Almost immediately, he ran into one of the guards, carrying a box of supplies. The guard glared at him, and then recognition dawned. "You're the guy they were keeping..."

David shot him once in the forehead. The man's head snapped back, and he dropped his package and stumbled backwards. David snapped two more shots into his chest. He walked over and took a close look. The man was dead. He had been carrying an Uzi on a sling. David slipped it off, and took two spare magazines from the guard's belt. "OK, now I've got some firepower," he said to himself. "Thank God I fired one of these at that shooting range in Las Vegas!"

He looked down at the rubber diving suit he still wore. "This might be a little obvious," he muttered. He looked down. "He's about my size." He quickly put on the man's jacket and pants.

He ran toward the Recreation Room, passing down a long gallery with a glass wall facing the lagoon. As he ran along the tiled walkway, there was an explosion in front of him, and he flailed his arms and frantically pushed back with his feet, trying to stop.

A Mosasaur burst through the glass wall. Pieces of glass flew everywhere, reflecting the interior lights like thousands of diamonds, and a wave of water splashed the tile floor for dozens of feet in each direction. David slipped on the wet tiles and fell. The Uzi flew out of his hands and skidded along the drenched flooring. He was suspended on his hands and knees, holding his shoulders slightly off the ground as he stared at the behemoth before him.

The Mosasaur had wedged the front of its body into the gallery. Its 10-foot head swerved in first one direction and then the other, scanning the area. It held still after it turned to its right, and stared at David.

He tried desperately to remain motionless. He remembered a scene from the film *Jurassic Park*, where people managed to remain invisible to dinosaurs by not moving. He stared as the jaws slowly opened. The rows of pale white teeth reminded him of the cavern, with its stalactites and stalagmites. Drool hung over the tops of the lower row, connecting them like webbing. He noticed that the drool had a reddish tinge, and there appeared to be pieces of flesh stuck in it. An eye the size of a serving plate stared at him as the head continued slight side-to-side motions. The jaws opened wider, and an obscene-looking dark-red forked tongue bulged out.

David glanced around, moving his eyes but not his head. The floor was full of shards of broken glass. One of the pieces was under his right hand, cutting into it with excruciating pain. He noticed a rivulet of bright red blood moving from his injured hand toward the monster. He remembered that Mosasaurs were supposed to have an incredible sense of smell. He wondered if the animal would go into a frenzy the instant it tasted his blood.

"Oh, well," he thought. "I've got nothing to lose." He started baby-talking to the apparition in front of him. "Hi, there. You don't really want to eat me, do you? There are lots of nice plump guards outside. You'll like them better."

The head stopped moving, the tip of the darting tongue now only a few feet away. The stream of blood from his hand moved inexorably forward toward it. The eye blinked. He tried a different tack, still speaking in the slow, calm tones one might use with a child.

"Aunt Marie said you were angels. Angel means messenger. Are you a messenger?" He thought a minute. "What kind of angel could you be other than a devil, and what message could you bring, besides death?" To himself, he thought, "God, I'm hallucinating!"

The beast started a low rumble. He thought it sounded angry, and hastily revised his approach. "That's what some people might think, but not me. If Aunt Marie says you're an angel, you're an angel." The rumble stopped.

David's arms were aching from holding his chest and head off the ground, but he was afraid to move. He whispered to himself, "I gotta say, this does help focus your mind on what's important."

His eyes were irresistibly drawn to the little trail of blood that continue to move from his cut hand toward the Mosasaur, like a small, thin snake, inch by inch, crawling ever closer toward the quivering tongue and nostrils.

"One thing I realize is how precious life is. If I live, I'm going to treasure every minute."

He felt something moving, and glanced downward, toward his chest. The silver amulet was sliding down, from deep inside his t-shirt toward the shirt's open neck. He could not stop it without moving his hand. He watched in horror as it hit the floor with what seemed like a resounding *thunk*. The amulet lay on the tile, facing its giant namesake. The Mosasaur's eyes blinked.

David wondered whether he should just crawl backwards on his hands and knees and make a break for it. To his surprise, the Mosasaur's eyes blinked once more, and then it quickly closed its jaws. It moved its head back to the left and pulled backwards, exiting the hallway.

David remained where he was for a moment, looking first at the silver talisman on the floor, then at the wide hole the behemoth had made in the glass wall to his left. He thought he could hear a faraway shrill, keening cry.

He got up slowly. He pulled the piece of sharp glass out of his right hand, and wiped the blood off on the pants of his borrowed uniform. A glance at the wall showed a whole section of it had shattered. There was no sign of the hulking beast outside. He looked toward the far end of the gallery, and saw a large door leading to another hallway, with arrows labeled "Dock Area A" pointing left and "Conference Room" pointing right. Through the glass wall he could see several men struggling with heavy sacks, heading toward a helicopter sitting on pontoons at the dock.

He picked up his Uzi and turned left when he reached the hallway. He stopped to catch his breath, and grasped the silver charm to put it back inside his t-shirt. He remembered the moment when Erika had given it to him, and then the moment when she stopped her sled and refused to move unless he came with her. He shook his head to clear it.

"What am I doing?" he asked himself. He glanced at the gleaming charm another moment before he slipped it back inside his T-shirt. Then he turned around and ran in the opposite direction.

The Mosasaur moved toward the shrill cry. Within two minutes she located her female offspring. It had leaped onto a dock in pursuit of a guest named Garcia, who was heading for his yacht with his two bodyguards. One of the bodyguards had backed up and fallen off the dock. He was splashing in the water. The second bodyguard wound up securely held in the young Mosasaur's jaws.

The drug kingpin had drawn a .357 magnum with a mother-of-pearl handle out of an intricately carved leather holster and had emptied it in the direction of the animal. Two of the shots had hit their mark, one in the Mosasaur's left flipper, and one in its tail. The wound in its flipper was causing considerable pain. It let out another long, keening howl, and dropped the bodyguard onto the dock. He lay there, writhing, his head moving from side to side as pink foam bubbled out of his mouth.

The man backed up slowly as he emptied the spent cartridges out of his gun. He had inserted six fresh cartridges when heard the sound of running feet, and turned to see three more of his men rushing to his aid. They looked at the creature in front of them, which was still emitting its shrill cry, moving its head from side to side.

"What is it?" one of the newcomers asked in wonder. "An alligator?"

"That's a really big alligator," the other commented. "But it's gonna be a dead alligator in a minute!" He unslung the belt holding his suspended Uzi, and pulled back on the bolt, letting it slam home a round into the chamber.

Garcia held up his hand. "Wait just a minute. Let me shoot it again. I want you to take a picture of me with it when it's dead." He cocked back the hammer on his silver-plated Smith & Wesson.

"What's it doing?" one of the guys behind him said. "It sounds like it's crying."

Garcia turned to him and laughed. "I'll give it something to cry about!" He expected the man to laugh, but instead he gasped loudly.

He had barely started to say "What?" when the question answered itself. A vision from hell rose next to them. The head of the female Mosasaur rose over ten feet above the dock. She opened her jaws and roared, the sound shoving them backwards as if they had been struck by a giant fist.

She lowered her head and seized the nearest of the guards. The movement of her body caused a wall of water to roll across the dock. The gusher of seawater lifted the young female Mosasaur back into the water. She took the wounded guard with her, munching him as she backed away into the lagoon.

The three men stood as if in freeze-frame for a full five seconds. The sight of their companion squirting blood in the leviathan's jaws them back to life. One swung his Uzi in her direction and pulled the trigger. He cursed as he discovered he had forgotten to pull the bolt back. He was in the process of doing so when the predator started an electric discharge. His fingers froze into position, and then his hands were consumed in a blue flame that blackened his skin and burned the clothes off his body. He caught a brief glimpse of his fellow bodyguard, whose skin peeled away from his face, the edges looking like pieces of pork rind. Then his eyes exploded like eggs in a microwave oven.

The drug king's body started an irregular jerking motion. The hand holding his fancy pistol came up to his head, and the trigger finger contracted, blowing the side of his face away.

A silver-blue arc jumped between the men, making a *whop-whop* sound like a Van de Graaff generator. Various types and colors of bodily fluids rushed out of the men through whatever exits they could find. All three of them sank spasmodically to the ground, their roasted bodies continuing to twitch.

The Mosasaur, satisfied that its offspring was safe, gulped down the man she had seized in two mouthfuls, and then slowly sank back into the lagoon.

Chapter 50

Erika heard the door to the Conference Room open, and looked up to see Fowler entering with a guard. "Reggie," she exclaimed. "Thank God, it's you!"

Fowler rushed over and leaned to hug her. He looked aghast at the handcuffs that anchored her wrist to one of the anchored legs of the stainless steel conference table. "Sergeant Malloy!" he shouted. "Go find a set of handcuff keys and remove these from Doctor Bettelman at once!" The guard hurried off to comply.

Fowler grasped both of her hands in his. "What's going on?" he asked. "I just arrived. I know DuBois went out of control. I'll have him arrested, but his men are running around with weapons. We are in great danger."

"We found the treasure, Reggie," she told him. "And then DuBois came and stole it and tried to kill David and me. We escaped and came here, and he had us arrested. I don't know where David is."

"I just heard over the radio that DuBois's men are holding him," Fowler replied, anxiety in his eyes. "They've threatened to kill him unless they get what they want."

"What?" she cried out in frustration. "What do they want?"

"The crown," Fowler replied. "The crown he found on the sub. It wasn't on the ship, so he gave it to somebody." He grasped both of her shoulders. "What happened to it?"

"I don't know anything about a crown!" she exclaimed in anguish.

He grasped her shoulders harder. "Think! Think!"

She stopped suddenly and looked at him suspiciously. "Wait a minute. How did you know this thing wasn't on board the ship? Only DuBois could have told you that!"

Fowler sighed. Turning toward the door, he said loudly, "You might as well come in." The door opened and DuBois appeared with another guard. Both of them drew their weapons and pointed them directly at Erika.

"Reggie, what's going on?" she said sharply.

Straightening his tie, he replied, "What's going on is that you are no longer useful. It doesn't matter. I think I know where the crown went to."

She lunged at him, but the two guards grasped both of her arms and held her back. They handcuffed both of her hands to the metal table leg and forced her down into a chair.

"You shitheel!" she screamed at him. "You liar!"

His only reply was a *tsk-tsking* sound.

"It was you all along running this place!"

Fowler nodded. "I see you've learned that things often aren't what they seem." He turned to DuBois. "I've got to go and bring the gold to safety. Take care of her, and call me later."

He gave her one last look. "Good-bye, my dear. I'm sure the Colonel has a few surprises for you. I wish I had the time to join the party." He turned and walked out the door.

DuBois motioned to the two guards. "Go help the Lt. Governor. I won't need your help. Close the door behind you."

As the door closed behind the departing guards with a firm click, DuBois approached Erika, a sneer on his face. He pulled her chair out from under her and she crashed to the floor, struggling against the restraining handcuffs.

He pulled a syringe out of his jacket pocket and held it up to the light. It contained several cubic milliliters of a yellowish liquid. "Look at what I have for you," he purred. "I have some left over from working on the spy they sent here."

She kicked at him desperately with both legs, but he pushed them to one side and injected her in the shoulder. He stepped back. "This should only take a minute. You'll start getting relaxed, but you'll still be awake enough to enjoy everything I am going to do to you." He leered at her. "We can talk about our first meeting, for a start. And then we'll play some games. I only wish I had a whole week for this."

He bent down to look at her more closely. She was still wearing the rubber diving suit that she had arrived in. "Oh. A skin-tight suit. That looks naughty," he noted. "And how convenient. There's a zipper that goes the whole length." He slowly, deliberately, unzipped the top of the suit. Erika tried to struggle against him, but could barely move.

"And now we come to your bra," he continued. "Flowers around the edges, very nice." He pulled out a folding knife and unsnapped it. Slowly, deliberately, he inserted the blade under the front of the bathing suit top, turned its blade up, and cut the connecting band, exposing her breasts.

"And now, let's play," he said, bending over her and touching her chest lightly with the knife.

He was interrupted by an urgent knocking on the door.

"What is it?" he shouted irritably.

The door opened a crack and a guard's face peeked in. "Colonel," he said urgently. "Guard Headquarters is telling us they're being attacked. They need help!"

DuBois looked down at his victim. "Duty calls. Don't worry. I'll be back!" He walked through the door to the adjoining Board Room. Six resort guests sat at a large light-colored maple table with intricately inlaid exotic woods.

One of them rose from his chair and started to complain. "What kind of luxury resort is this?" he screamed. "You promised us total security. I just heard two of my assistants were attacked!"

"Sit down, sit down," DuBois told him roughly. "Let me get on the radio and find out what the situation is. I'll be right back." He motioned to his guard. "He'll stay to make sure you're safe."

He marched out the door, swearing loudly.

Chapter 51

David looked down at his map. He could see that the only entrance to the Conference Room that held Erika was from the Board Room. He crouched low and peered around the corner. He saw that the room was encased by glass walls, and had seven men inside, all of them tough-looking. He looked at the Uzi that he had captured, and then at his two spare magazines.

"I'll never talk my way past that bunch," he said to himself. "So, I'll have to Rambo my way through. That'll probably take at least two magazines. I'd better bind them together, so I don't drop one." He turned back and went into one of the offices along the hallway. In a desk he found several large rubber bands. He also found two Band-Aids for the cut in his right hand, which was still bleeding.

He turned one of the clips upside down and then wrapped the bands around both clips to fasten them together. He took a deep breath, and noticed he could feel the rapid beating of his heart. He returned to his place near the Board Room, and crouched to peer once more around the corner. The men in the room seemed to be busy in animated conversation. He took a deep breath, and rose. He hoped that the uniform he was wearing would help him achieve surprise.

He entered the room, gently opening the door. Several of the men looked up at him. One of them reached for a shoulder holster. David grasped the Uzi firmly and fired in bursts, sweeping from left to right. The scene in front of him seemed to happen in slow motion. Holes puffed up like mini-volcanoes on the shirts and jackets of the men before him, and they were firmly shoved backwards as the bullets slapped into their flesh. The clip ran out just as he reached the last man to the right.

David ejected the clip with his thumb while grasping it and twisting it around with the other hand, and slapped the fresh magazine up into the weapon. He chambered the first round of the new clip, and swept the room from right to left until that clip was exhausted as well.

Without pausing, he pulled the third magazine out of his pocket, inserted it, and walked around the table, stepping carefully over the bouncing and rolling empty cartridge cases while dispatching several men who were still moving. Satisfied, he moved quickly to the door at the end of the room and looked beyond it. "Erika?" he called. "Erika?" He couldn't see anyone.

He heard a faint noise from the far end of the room. He approached it carefully, and glanced down to see Erika sitting on the floor, her wrists handcuffed to the table. He knelt and touched her cheek with his hand. "Erika? Are you all right?" he asked anxiously. He saw her eyes were unfocused.

"David?" she asked, her voice dry.

"Who else?" he replied, running one thumb over her pale cheek. "Hang on, let me get you out of these handcuffs," He turned and ran into the other room. He found a set of keys on the dead guard, and quickly returned and unlocked her. He zipped up the top of her wet suit and pulled her to her feet. This proved difficult, because she was woozy from the effects of the drug.

She stood swaying on her feet until he wheeled a chair up behind her and set her in it. He reached for a bottle of water on a sideboard, twisted off the cap and splashed the water in her face. Her eyes started to focus. "What's wrong?" he asked her, his face tense

"He shot me up with some sort of drug." She added, smiling weakly, "You look like hell."

David was about to answer when he heard a noise in the next room, and reached for his Uzi on the table. DuBois burst through the door and held a pistol pointed directly at him.

"Move an inch and you're dead," DuBois snarled, and David froze.

"How did you get loose? Why are you wearing a Resort Guard's uniform? And who are those men that are attacking my resort?"

David put up his hands and approached him slowly along the side of the table that was opposite to Erika. He remembered a lesson from his Krav Maga class on grabbing a gun from someone holding it on you, but DuBois was still too far away to try it.

"That's a lot of questions," he said pleasantly. "Which one would you like to have answered first?"

"First tell me who those people are, and how many of them are here," DuBois said. "And you can stop right there!"

David was now about six feet from him. It was still too far. He needed a distraction. "Those people are the ship's crew and a whole Company of British and US Special Forces. They came to help Erika. That's right, to help Erika. Help!"

He hoped she was getting the message.

DuBois furrowed his brow in annoyance as he said, sharply, "What are you talking about?"

Erika suddenly crooned, "Hey, Colonel, look at what I have for you!" and unzipped her jacket. She pulled it wide open, exposing her breasts while wiggling her body suggestively.

DuBois looked at her for only a moment, his eyes widening. He quickly swung his gaze back, but David was already in motion. The gun discharged as David knocked it aside and then grasped it with both hands, twisting the pistol's grip around till he heard the snap of DuBois's trigger finger breaking. He yanked the weapon out of his hand.

David heard a *thunk* behind him and his eyes darted in Erika's direction. DuBois leaped at him, and the gun wedged in between their bodies. David pulled the trigger twice, but the shots went wild as his right hand was shoved aside.

He let go of the weapon, flinging it into a corner, and shoved the Colonel away from him. As DuBois started for the pistol, David whirled and grasped his Uzi from the table. He crouched down to aim, and fired just as DuBois turned with the Smith & Wesson.

Two of his shots found their mark, striking DuBois in the chest and making him tumble backwards and slam against the wall.

David slowly advanced around the corner of the table and approached DuBois, whose back painted a bright crimson trail on the wall as he slid to the floor.

DuBois slowly reached for the S&W he had dropped. David fired one more shot, his last. A red rose blossomed in the middle of the Colonel's forehead. His upper body slowly slumped to the right.

David returned to Erika and was horrified to see her lying prone on the floor, a pool of bright red blood forming below her. He examined her quickly. She was unconscious. A gash ran along the side of her head, weeping copious quantities of bright arterial blood. He moved his hand along the wound, and saw with relief that it had not penetrated the skull. He could also feel a bump on the back of her head. He knelt on the floor and laid her head in his lap. She was unconscious.

He looked at the side of the table, and saw it had traces of blood on it. "She must have hit her head right on the edge," he told himself. He tore the sleeve off his borrowed uniform and bound it tightly around her head to stem the bleeding. The flow slowed to a trickle. He touched her face, his voice strained. "Don't you die on me! Don't you dare die on me!"

He heard steps approaching. He started to rise when two men entered the room with guns drawn. With relief he saw that it was Ben and Mark from his crew.

Ben approached and laid his left arm on David's shoulder. "Wow, that was close," he said. "I almost pulled the trigger when I saw that uniform. The torn-off sleeve made me stop for a second." He looked at Erika. "Is she OK?"

"I don't know," David replied. "A bullet grazed her scalp, and she slipped and hit her head, hard. She probably has a concussion." He looked at Mark. "You're in medical school, right?"

Mark nodded as he pulled off his backpack and unzipped it to remove his First Aid kit. "I can clean and bind the wound, but I can't do anything about the concussion. We need to get her out of here to a hospital," he said.

David looked down as Erika's head was being bandaged. "She could barely move, but she flashed her tits at DuBois to distract him so I could get him." He gave a proud half-smile. "She was magnificent!"

He stood up to retrieve his weapon. "Mark, stay here with her until you hear from us," he said. "Shoot any of their guys that you see. Ben, let's go find the others, and get to one of the helicopters to get her out of here."

They went through the bodies in the Board Room, gathering 9mm ammo to reload their weapons. David turned over one of the men on the floor and saw he wore a gold pendant with a Double Eagle coin in it. He unclipped it and put it on. As Ben looked at him, he said, "Hey, at least I got one gold coin out of this!"

When they were outside, he asked Ben, "Have you found Leah, yet?"

Ben shook his head. "We think she's in the Resort Guards Headquarters. That's at the other end of this complex."

David bit his lip. "We'd better hurry. If whoever's in charge over there realizes why they're being invaded, he may kill her immediately."

Chapter 52

The group of rescuers moved carefully along the path. AJ and two of the men drove in the ATV, followed by the others on foot. The rain came in bursts, drenching them and cutting down visibility. Dawn was still over two hours away.

"This is taking way too much time," Morrison complained to AJ. "Isn't there some way we can bypass these buildings and go directly to the Police Station?"

They were almost up to the first dock. There were three power boats and a sailboat tied up to it.

"We could steal one of the yachts, and either hot-wire it or hope it has keys," AJ replied. They approached the dock at a crouch, looking for Resort guards or armed guests. They stopped when they heard one of the yachts start up. Diesel fumes rose from the back, along with the *blub-blub-blub* of coolant water.

Someone screamed, "Let's go! Let's go!" from the flying bridge. A crew member hastily threw off the ropes holding the yacht to the dock, and then hung on to the railing as the vessel plowed through the water toward the entrance of the lagoon.

AJ was about to move toward the dock again, when Morrison grasped his upper arm tightly and motioned toward the yacht. "Look!"

The boat had stopped its forward momentum and was going around in circles. The top of its bridge was torn off. As they watched, a Mosasaur rose out of the water, grasped two of the crewmen in its jaws, and disappeared again. Bubbles boiled around the side of the boat, which was suddenly partly lifted out of the water and tipped over on its side. Its twin screws rotated vainly in the air. The boat started to sink.

"So much for that idea," Morrison remarked sourly. As they turned away from the docks, they heard a helicopter starting up. A moment later, it emerged from behind a yacht that had blocked their view. It moved forward in the water on pontoons for a few dozen feet and then rose quickly into the air.

"I think that's Fowler in the cockpit," yelled AJ. He raised his submachine gun to his shoulder and squeezed off a full magazine, joined by Morrison and several others of the team. Within minutes the helicopter was hundreds of feet in the air and heading away from them.

"It's too far away now," Morrison noted. "But I think we hit it a couple of times."

"Let's move out," AJ ordered. "Morrison, take your guys and hit that outdoor Dance Floor area. Katharina says a lot of them hang out there. You can hear the music from here. The rest of us will bypass it and go on."

"Roger," Morrison replied. His men moved out with practiced silence and swiftness. Within minutes, they approached the Recreation Area. The party was still going on, the music so loud that the attendees had not heard the shooting around the Resort area.

Morrison and his team held up a few minutes while Werner repositioned himself on the roof of a nearby building. By this time, each team member had an MP5 submachine gun with extra clips, souvenirs from the guards they had neutralized along the way. The four men carefully entered the area and gazed at the scene in front of them. For a few minutes, the orgy and dancing continued unabated, augmented by the deafening music. Then one of the bodyguards, who had remained sober, noticed the intruders and shouted a warning.

The team quickly fanned out and deployed for the best fields of fire. From a low crouch, they started shooting in aimed and controlled bursts of three. In contrast, most of the bodyguards stood straight up and shot as fast as they could, with the result that most of their rounds poured into empty sky. Their gangster clients slowly woke up to what was going on and dove for the floor, looking for their clothing and weapons. Almost on cue, the team members ejected their spent magazines and slapped in full ones, emptied them in turn, and then repeated the procedure.

Morrison called, "Cease fire," and they waited for the smoke to clear. He walked over to a control for the sound system and flicked the power switch, and it became suddenly still. The only sounds were the clatter of empty cartridges and the wailing of the women, who had not been hit, and the groaning of the men, who had.

Morrison waved his gun at the women who were still there, standing or sitting, frozen in total shock, and yelled, "Get out! Now!" One of the women reached for her clothing, but he waved the gun threateningly. "No! We have to be sure you're not hiding weapons! Leave your clothes here and run!" The women did so, most of them barefooted.

Tony Cervo looked at Morrison and said wryly, "Great line. 'You have to stay naked so we can check for weapons.' I'll have to remember that one!"

Morrison grinned. They checked the bodies of the men, and made sure they were dead, with grim efficiency.

Five minutes later, Morrison looked up from checking one of the bodies. The once transparent glass floor was now scored with blood stains, so the ocean reef below was hardly visible. "I count 14 in here. I think we're whittling them down. Now, if we can just..." He broke off as several bullets flew past his ear and smashed into the suspended mirror ball, scattering thousands of light reflections throughout the dance area. They crouched and whirled in the direction of the shots. They saw two bodyguards with Kalashnikovs standing on the roof of an adjacent two-story building, shooting at them. There was a *Crack* and one of them flew backwards, tossing his assault gun into the air. A second crack and the head of his companion exploded like a dropped watermelon. He leaned forward, slowly let his rifle drop to the ground below, and then followed it in freefall.

Morrison rose carefully, looked around and pumped his fist, giving a thumbs-up sign and a, "Thank you, Werner!"

"No problem," a faint voice answered from the distance.

Chapter 53

AJ and Baisley drove in the ATV up the concrete path toward the next building, with other team members following behind them on foot. The rain became more intense, hampering visibility. AJ's radio crackled. "Somebody's coming at our 6 o'clock." The transmission was poor, so he could not tell who had said it, but he stopped the ATV and signaled his team to get into defensive position. They knelt next to the vehicle with weapons drawn, looking at the trail behind them. Two All-Terrain Vehicles approached, their headlights stabbing through the darkness and rain.

Baisley attempted to continue the ruse, and yelled, "Halt! This is the Police! Identify yourself!"

David yelled back from the nearer of the two ATVs, "That's too bad. We hate those guys!"

AJ and the others rose and rushed to greet him. AJ put a hand on his shoulder and examined him closely. "Jesus! Did you lose an argument with a meat grinder?"

David smiled grimly. "Yeah. But you should have seen the other guys. And that includes that asshole DuBois, who's getting a bunk assignment from the Devil right now!"

The news of DuBois' demise cheered the group, and they pounded David on the back. AJ introduced David to the team members he did not know.

"I left Mark with Erika," David said. "She'll make it, I think. But she needs to get airlifted to a hospital, fast. And we'd better hurry up and get to Leah. I heard DuBois give an order to 'clean up any loose ends,' and I think that includes her. Ben and I brought you two ATVs to speed things up."

AJ looked them over. They were similar to his vehicle, an ATV based on a motorcycle engine, driving on wide knobby tires meant for cross-country driving. Each had six wheels, two seats side-by-side, a steering wheel, and a cargo area in back that could also hold one or two people. A roof and a windshield helped keep off some of the rain.

AJ turned to the rest of the group. "You heard the man. Let's all get on the ATVs and move out. David, ride up front in this one with me."

As he piloted the first ATV forward, AJ turned slightly toward David, and asked him, "Do you know your Mosasaurs are tearing up the place? And they're freaking gigantic? And they can do that thing Erika mentioned, shoot electricity out over long distances?"

David nodded. "Yeah. And they can change colors like a chameleon. And they breathe air, and are quite happy out of the water. Watch for them on the path ahead."

Chapter 54

At the airport, several of the most prominent guests were piling into the largest of the helicopters, a twin-engine Sikorsky. There was considerable pushing and shoving to get on. Several of the guests were yelling into their cell phones for their own pilots to come to their private aircraft, but got no reply. Over a dozen guests and bodyguards had crowded in when the owner of the craft decided it was full enough. Several of the women from the party were still trying to get on, but were roughly shoved down the stairs with cries of "Andale!" and "Puta!"

The large chopper took off, its heavy load slowing its ascent. It headed out over the lagoon, its red and white lights reflecting off the waves directly below.

A hundred feet below the surface, the male Mosasaur could hear the dull thumping of air beaten down by the chopper's airfoils onto the water. He stopped. An ancient memory floated to the surface of his brain, from a time eons ago, when his kind ruled the planet's waters, and lay in wait for the giant pterosaurs that flew overhead, beating their wings and skimming the waves while looking for fish. He twisted his body into a tight upward spiraling turn and moved his broad, massive tail powerfully to build up speed. He could hear that whatever was making the noise was almost overhead as he launched himself bodily out of the water. He grasped the front end of the air vehicle with his jaws. The Plexiglas windows burst out of the pilot's cabin in a bright spray of shards.

The helicopter pilot tried to regain control, but the aircraft was clearly overmatched. The huge animal suspended below it hung on grimly. The Mosasaur, angry that its prey was not falling back into the water as it should, let loose a massive discharge of electric power. Bright blue and white arcs danced along the outer skin and crackled throughout the Sikorsky. It tilted left, crossing over the shoreline and headed straight toward the Resort's Power Station. The pilot stared with horror as the walls of the station rushed up at him. The last thing he saw was the rows of 55 gallon fuel drums stacked carelessly around the walls.

The helicopter and its gargantuan extra passenger hit the station with incredible force. The fuel tanks on board burst and sprayed out their contents, which were immediately ignited by the white sparks from the monster's electric discharges. Avgas streamed like molten lava onto the fuel drums below, which joined in the conflagration.

The resulting explosion sent a shock wave throughout the resort. It knocked people and the walls of buildings over, and sent a deadly shower of metal, concrete and wood chunks in all directions. The pyrotechnics were awe-inspiring. A fountain of flame shot up, bursting into yellow and red and orange pinwheels and exploding white stars. Burning helicopter parts rained from the sky. They landed on the Tahitian-style thatched roofs of the guest villas, and set them ablaze. The Resort started burning in spite of the light rain. More eruptions occurred as flames found propane tanks and other flammables. Bright cinders shot into the night sky like mad fireflies dancing a frantic waltz.

Chapter 55

David held up his hand, and AJ stopped the vehicle when they heard the explosions far ahead. The Northern part of the Resort looked like a Fourth of July celebration on steroids. They saw flames shooting up, and heard the crump of explosions. They listened intently to one of the radios they had captured.

AJ turned to the group. "It sounds like a helicopter crashed into the power plant. It's setting off secondary explosions from rows of fuel drums. They said to watch out, there's a lot of burning stuff flying around."

David asked, "Can you fill me in on what's ahead?"

"Sure," AJ replied, and drew a rough map in the condensation on the windshield of the ATV. "The lagoon is roughly circular, with an opening to the ocean at 6 o'clock on the bottom. There's a path carved out of the hillside all around the lagoon. We're right here, at about the 1 o'clock position. The path opens up in front of us, with buildings for the guests on the lagoon side. Storage buildings and shops are on the right side of the road, butted up right against the rock of the hillside. The road is the only way through, unless you go through the buildings. Leah is at the Guard Headquarters, here at the 10 o'clock position. The power plant is near there, and there's a road that leads inland to the airport and tennis courts and other stuff. We're trying to get to Leah ASAP."

David looked up to see Jim Morrison appear with a fourth ATV. The men distributed their heavy loads of weapons, ammunition and equipment among the vehicles. David looked up the road with a feeling of deep apprehension. He conferred with AJ. "I don't like driving straight down the road. We've lost the element of surprise. We could be running straight into an ambush."

"What do you suggest?" AJ asked.

"How about we create a diversion? Put a couple of dead bodies in the front of an ATV, and have that go ahead of us to draw fire. And turn off the headlights of the other vehicles, so they don't stand out in the darkness."

"Let's do it," AJ replied. Within minutes, Jim Morrison's vehicle had the bodies of two dead bodyguards duct-taped upright on the front seats, looking almost comical in their brightly colored Hawaiian shirts. Morrison crouched under a tarp behind the front seats, next to Ben. He had to strain to reach the steering wheel with one hand while using the other to push the accelerator pedal with the butt of an M16 assault rifle.

The little caravan started up the road through the hellish landscape, swerving to avoid incoming flaming helicopter parts or building sections. Most of the lights of the resort had flickered out when the power station blew up, but a few came back on as backup generators kicked in.

Within a couple of hundred feet, Jim yelled into the radio, "We're hit! We're taking fire!" David and AJ looked up, and saw bright muzzle flashes from two windows in the top story of a brick two-story building to the right.

The voice of Tony Cervo crackled in the headphones. "Back up! I'll lay down cover. Steve, go get 'em when I give the signal." Cervo fired the M-249 5.56mm Squad Automatic Weapon at the windows, causing long rows of powdered brick puffs to crawl along the wall of the upper story. As the two attackers ducked, he yelled. "Steve! Go!"

Roth moved forward to use the foremost ATV as cover. They could hear the *thunk* of the first 40mm grenade from his M79 hand-held launcher, followed almost immediately by a second one. They saw the grenades fly like super-fast tennis balls through the two window openings. The third was still in the air when the first two went off, blowing the two attackers out of the windows, along with large chunks of wall.

They waited until the brick and cement pieces stopped raining down, and then looked for further signs of the enemy.

Roth checked the two bodies quickly, and yelled "Clear!" They resumed their forward progress.

Morrison looked ahead intently, doing his best to steer his ATV from behind the two bodies, when he saw something strange in his headlights. "AJ, there's a building that seems to be moving into the street!" he spoke into his headset. AJ and David, in the front seats of the following ATV, strained to see what was going on. "Stop!" David yelled. "That's not a building! Back up!"

"Whoa!" Morrison exclaimed, as what had looked like the wall of a building moved into the center of the roadway. A flash of lightning revealed the bright white rows of teeth of a Mosasaur.

"My God! That thing's over 20 feet long!" Morrison said as he frantically jammed his ATV into reverse gear.

"I can get it with my SAW!" Cervo shouted over the radio.

"No! No!" David cried. "Don't shoot it!"

"Why the hell not?" Cervo asked.

"That's a baby. If you hit it, you'll really piss off its mother!"

"You've got to be shitting me!" Morrison said as he slid to a stop next to the group.

"If only!" David muttered. "Everybody—hold your fire. AJ, there's an entrance to the building on the left. Let's go through that, and get back on the road on the other side."

"Roger, that!" AJ yelled. "Everybody into the building on the left! Now!"

The group of vehicles made a sharp turn and headed for the entrance. They hit the brakes suddenly as a Resort Guard appeared before them. He pointed a submachine gun directly at their heads.

"Stop!" he yelled. "Put up your hands and step away from those vehicles!" He walked into the middle of the roadway so that he could cover all four ATVs.

AJ looked behind the man. The Mosasaur was approaching, slithering its body and accelerating its movement with its strong flippers. "One of those things is behind you," he said. "You'd better get out of here, now!"

"Yeah, sure," the guard sneered. "I said..." He stopped when he heard a crackling behind him, as if giant peanut brittle were being broken into pieces. He turned and his eyes flew wide open. The Mosasaur had turned partly sideways. Long tendrils of electricity emanated from its side, neon blue with scorching-white centers. One of the ropes of electric charge reached out over the wet roadway toward the guard, and zipped up the front of his body.

David's guts clenched as he heard a popping and sizzling sound, and then he watched in horror as the head and entire body split down the middle, and body parts slowly sank onto the street. It reminded him of a dissected animal from biology class, except that all the parts were pale pink and red, and liquids gushed everywhere.

Without hesitation, AJ cranked up his ATV and swung left, yelling, "Go, go, go!" and then, "Eyes closed!" seconds before his vehicle crashed through the glass doors.

David glanced back to see the Mosasaur stopped next to the body. It was licking it with an obscenely long tongue. "My God! It's tasting it like oysters on the half shell!" he muttered.

They headed along the building corridor at breakneck speed. The battery-driven ceiling lights showed rows of offices with glass walls flash by, all of them dark. The four ATVs were in low gear because of their heavy loads, and the shrieking din they made in the enclosed space was deafening.

A frightened-looking young woman stuck her head out of one office to see what was going on. Her jaw dropped as she saw the strange-looking vehicle caravan approaching, led by an ATV with two men in Aloha shirts in the front seats that waved their arms in front of them while staring like robots. She quickly pulled her head back.

A uniformed man came out of another office, and jumped back as the group bore down on him. Ben yelled, "I got it," and tossed a grenade after him as they went by. They could hear the *BLAM* of the explosion behind them, and then a deluge of glass shards hitting the Spanish tile floor.

AJ yelled, "Eyes closed!" again as they exited through another glass door at the far end of the corridor, tires squealing and skidding as they made a hard right, then a hard left back onto the roadway. Pieces of burning debris continued to fall from the sky and litter the ground. All four ATVs had to swerve around them, like skiing in a slalom race.

David screamed, "Jim! Look out! Above you!"

Morrison glanced up to see a gigantic head swooping down at him from the top of a two-story building on his left. He pulled his arms back just in time as monstrously long jaws seized the bodies in the front seats. The behemoth shook the vehicle, and he barely managed to hang on. "Cut the tape! Cut the tape!" David screamed, as the vehicle became airborne.

Morrison tried to reach his knife, to cut the duct tape fastening his passengers to the vehicle, but found he could not do that and hang on. He pushed himself away from the ATV, and landed heavily on the roadway. He limped toward the nearest vehicle, and willing hands pulled him aboard.

He looked up to see the monster shaking its head. Sharp teeth cut through the restraining tape, and the two bodies disappeared into the mammoth jaws as the ATV went sailing into the air, to crash onto the road and break into pieces.

The drivers of the remaining three vehicles steered them to the far right of the pathway, keeping as much distance from the nightmare on the roof as they could. David looked behind him as the vehicles accelerated away. The monster had jumped onto the next rooftop, which was outlined by a continuous line of garish pink and green neon lights. He could see it battling with several guests. One man tried to elude it by jumping off the roof. The Mosasaur's long neck swiveled quickly and caught him in mid-air. It bit him in half. David could hear a sound like chicken bones crunching. It then let his now divorced body parts drop to the ground, showing no further interest in him.

"They're killing machines," David said to himself, his stomach churning. "They like it!"

"What?" AJ shouted. He was trying to regain control of the ATV as it bounced through the midst of a deep puddle.

David looked back to see a Resort Guard riding a Segway 2-wheel personal transport. He stopped in the middle of the roadway and lifted up an RPG launcher. He aimed it at the Mosasaur, and pulled the trigger. The rocket-propelled grenade was just starting to accelerate when the beast seized it, and with a mighty wrench of its neck spat it back at its originator. The guard stood transfixed as the warhead hit him and blew him airborne with a mighty lava-colored fireball.

David saw the leviathan on the roof rear back to let out an ear-shattering roar. It looked and sounded like an ancient dragon guarding a castle. The creature then leaned its head far over the front of the roof and swung it from side to side, searching for its next victim. Long blue electric arcs shot out from its sides, brighter than the neon lights along the roofline.

Its head froze, and anthracite eyes the size of pizza platters fixated on a man who bolted out of a door underneath and ran up the street. He slipped, and got back up and started to run again, pumping his arms in all-out desperation. A nearby burning vehicle illuminated the terror on his face, and showed him stop suddenly as a blue-white bolt hit him. He arched his back, and then rose up on the tips of his toes, as if he was trying a ballet move. His face started to melt like hot candle wax. He clapped his hands to the sides of his head, trying to keep it together. The holes of his mouth and eyes grew ever darker and wider, and he started to resemble Edvard Munch's painting, *The Scream*. He melted into a bony pile on the roadway.

The vehicles whined under full load as they sped away along the roadside. "OK!" David yelled at AJ. "I think we're far enough away from that thing!" AJ jerked the wheel to the left to avoid an unlit street lamp that had jumped out of the darkness, over-steered into a skid, and then corrected, getting back onto the main roadway. The second ATV followed, but the third turned over.

"We're OK. Keep going," came Ben's voice from the third vehicle. "We'll catch up with you."

Two Resort Guards appeared from the darkness. AJ accelerated, forcing them to jump to either side. David shot the left one twice, and then twice again. Sgt. Baisley put three rounds into the other.

"Aim for the head," David yelled. "Two to the chest had no effect. They're wearing armored vests."

"Roger. Extra points for head shots," Roth replied laconically.

They entered a section of road that was illuminated by lights from two buildings on the left. They immediately started taking incoming rounds. "To the right, get under cover!" AJ shouted, and they screeched to a halt behind a brick wall next to a parking area.

Morrison crept up to AJ and David, who crouched directly behind the wall.

AJ turned to Morrison. "It looks like there's maybe ten or so in a prepared position taking us under fire. Any ideas?"

Morrison spoke into his headset. "Steve? Can you shoot some grenades at them?"

"We're all out of 40 mike-mike," Roth replied. "All we have left are hand grenades, and we'll have to get closer to use those. It looks like they have vehicles parked around them for cover. Might be tough to put one in the middle."

AJ spoke into his headset. "Aunt Marie? Can you see where we are? What's up ahead?"

After a few moments, Marie's voice came in. "Katharina says they're in front of a jewelry shop. There's an alley after that, with a big white propane tank in it, and then a clothing shop."

"A propane tank. Interesting," David said. "Werner, are you up high somewhere where you can see this area?"

"I am," came Werner's voice on the radio. "I can see the propane tank, but I do not have a line of sight to the guards. They are hidden behind their vehicles."

"If you can shoot the tank and it starts leaking propane, a couple of grenades in the general area should set it off," AJ said. "We won't have to be accurate."

"I'll go with the grenades," Morrison said, but David shook his head.

"No. You've done enough. And you're limping badly. I have a pretty good throwing arm. My turn."

He collected three hand grenades, and said, "I'll creep forward on the right as far as I can, and see if I can reach that doorway for cover. If I make it, Werner, I'll give you a shout. OK?"

"It's what I live for," Werner answered drily.

Roth, AJ and Morrison lay down covering fire as they told David, "Go!" He burst from cover and rolled over to the side of the building on his right. He rose and ran as fast as he could, staying low and ducking as shots whistled by his ear. His cheeks and neck were cut by flying pieces of concrete. He made it to the doorway and took cover, breathing hard. He stuck his head out quickly to get his bearings on the enemy position, and pulled it back as a furious fusillade of shots raked the wall and doorway, throwing up a cloud of debris.

"OK, Werner. Up to you. Put a couple into the propane tank," he spoke into his headset.

"Here we go," Werner replied. Several shots rang out. "Damn. I don't know whether they penetrated. They have concrete or something protecting the tank," he said.

"How about the inlet valve?" David asked. "Where they refill it?"

"Sure," was the reply. "Why not?"

Another shot rang out, and then another. It was hard to hear the rifle shots against the background of the fire coming from the enemy in front. Werner suddenly said, "OK, I think I blew off that part of the tank. There's a whitish spray coming out."

"Wait a few minutes for the propane to spread, Steve, and then give me covering fire," David said.

"Roger, wilco."

David took the grenades out of his pockets. He had to wipe his hands to hold them, because he was sweating so hard. He breathed deeply. His mouth was bone dry, and he could hear the pounding of his heart, which sounded deafening.

A hail of fire erupted from the team behind him. He heard the rounds hitting the vehicles concealing the enemy. He ducked out of the doorway and ran forward with short, quick steps. He hit the ground and pulled the pin on the grenade, and then reached back with his arm before throwing it in a high arc. He got off the second and third, and started crawling back. He could see one of the guards had spotted him, and was looking directly at him while bringing up his weapon.

He was about to turn and try to run for it when the first grenade went off. The sharp explosion was followed immediately by a massive blast that shook the ground and blew vehicles and guards into the air. It lifted him off his feet and he hit the ground hard, knocking the breath out of him.

David's hearing was suddenly gone, replaced with silence tinged with a low thrumming and ringing. His vision blurred, and he became disoriented. He stood up and leaned against the building for support. Everything around him seemed to move in slow motion, in absolute silence. He looked to his right, and saw an enormous orange-yellow fireball rise up, resembling a nuclear explosion. One of the team's ATVs came up to him, and he could see someone open and close his mouth, perhaps yelling at him. He stared dully, trying to figure out what he wanted. Another team member grabbed him and pulled him into the back of the ATV, and they moved forward again. They swerved hard left to avoid one of the vehicles the guards had used for cover. It lay on its side, its canvas cover on fire and its wheels spinning wildly. Several pieces of charred canvas floated in the air toward an oily, shining pool of diesel fuel spreading across the road.

They entered a dark section of roadway. Their only light now was from the blazing buildings in the distance, and they drove slowly. AJ saw dark forms, and spoke into his radio. "I'm going to turn on my lights for just a moment. There's something weird in front of us."

He turned on the lights and blinked his eyes, temporarily blinded by the bright illumination after the darkness. He shuddered as the forms turned into three bodyguards coming from the right side of the roadway. They were staggering along, seemingly aimless, like zombies. The one on the far left had an arm missing, and was pressing a cloth to the socket in a vain attempt to slow the gush of blood. The one in the middle had his hair and most of his clothing burned off; the skin of his legs looked like beef jerky. The one on the right appeared to be desperately fighting with pale snakes. As he came closer, they could see he was trying to stuff his intestines back into a gaping hole in his abdomen.

David looked to the right, and could see a wide, milky-blue shape emerging from the alley between two buildings. He tried to shout a warning, but his mouth was so dry that he could only manage a croak. Fortunately, AJ saw it at the same time, and shouted, "Hard left! Hard left!" He swung the ATV to the other side of the road. He jammed down on the accelerator as the following vehicle struggled to keep up.

David looked back to see a 20-foot Mosasaur leisurely start to devour the three men. It knocked one of them off his feet with a sweep of its head, and then closed its jaws on him. The main body of the man disappeared, and only his head and four limbs stuck out. The animal made a chewing motion, and all five appendages plopped onto the roadway, rolling in different directions. He could see the mouths of the other two men opening wide, and their limbs flailing, but could not hear them screaming in his silent world.

They passed another vehicle turned over in the road. As they passed it, two Resort Guards rose up and raised their weapons.

One fired at Morrison's ATV at point-blank range. Alex Lighter in the rear ATV raised his M4 and put two 3-round bursts into the man's head. Roth fired his M4 at the second guard, and the man went down. He quickly went over to him and picked up his weapon. "Why didn't he shoot?" he wondered. He examined the weapon, a 12-gauge shotgun. "Wow. He forgot to take off the safety."

"Good thing," Morrison said. "The other one got me with a couple of rounds. I think the vest stopped them, but my ribs hurt like a motherf—"

"Let's move!" AJ shouted, and both vehicles revved up and moved forward again.

David's hearing slowly returned. It felt like emerging from the bottom of a swimming pool out into a busy train station. He wondered for a moment at the wall of sound that hit him—the roaring of the ATVs, the crash of the wheels as they hit items in the road, occasional explosions in the distance, and the whistling of burning objects as they came down to crash on impact. He found a liter bottle of water, and drank it down without pausing.

Ben arrived driving the third remaining ATV, and the team members moved forward several hundred feet without event, until pinging and clanking sounds off their vehicles notified them they were taking incoming rounds again. They hit the brakes and raced behind a small construction bulldozer to the right of the road.

AJ rang up Marie. "Auntie, we're taking fire from up ahead on the left. It looks like there's a brick wall they're using for cover."

Marie's voice came on in a moment. "Katharina says there's a wall like that in front of the gift shop parking area.

"Any propane tanks or other things that could help us?"

"Afraid not."

David said, "That building is on the lagoon side. Ask if it's made out of glass."

AJ relayed the question, and replied a minute later, "Yes. It's a luxurious shopping area with glass-brick walls so you can see from the inside into any direction." He turned to David. "What are you thinking of?"

Baisley answered for him. "He's thinking that we can't get close enough to throw grenades, since they have a perfect field of fire. If we lay down a lot of covering fire onto the building behind them, the shower of glass shards may force them to duck while one of us makes it through. Is that about right?"

David nodded. "AJ, you and Baisley make a run for it in this ATV. I'll stay behind, to lighten the load. We'll hit them with everything we've got. Steve, we got any flares?"

Roth nodded. "Good," David said. "Anyone looking should get blinded for a while."

AJ thought a moment longer, and said. "OK. That's probably our only chance. Good luck, you guys."

David reached under his jacket and said, "Oh, one more thing." He handed AJ his armored vest. "Put this around you for added protection, and stay low."

AJ grinned at him. "You da bomb, man."

As one, the rest of the team handed over their vests. Roth arranged them to up-armor the ATV. He placed a vest to cover each of the wheels on the left side, so the rubber would not get shredded.

AJ nodded to the team with a grim smile. David clapped him on the shoulder, and said, "Go get Leah. We'll see you soon!"

Jim Morrison gave the signal. "Now!"

A massive amount of firepower was let loose suddenly. Al Martin fired tracer from the SAW machine gun, and every sixth bullet left a bright burning trail. It looked like a river of fire reaching out for the target area. Roth shot 40mm flares as fast as he could load them. The rest fired their assault rifles, slapping fresh magazines in one after the other.

The front of the building across from them seemed to explode. A tsunami of light-green glass shards rained down on the enemy group hidden at its base. AJ revved up the ATV and raced along the far right side of the road, his head and body hidden behind a stack of armored vests.

Taken by surprise, only a couple of the guards rose up to fire at the fleeing ATV. One looked up, and saw a shower of glass shards rain down. A 6-inch piece of glass jammed into his left eye. It squirted white and red liquids onto his assault rifle, which he quickly dropped while his hands flew to his ruined face.

"Cease firing!" Morrison yelled, and the shooting next to him quickly died down. "AJ, you make it?" he spoke into his headset.

"Yeah, we're good. A little banged up, but we got lucky," AJ replied.

"Good to hear! Good hunting," Morrison said. He looked at the two ATVs. Both of them had flat tires, and no spares. He turned to David. "So, we're pinned down. Our ATVs are shot to shit. And we're now really low on ammo. You got any other bright ideas?"

He saw his friend was leaning against the bulldozer with his eyes closed, and shook him by the shoulder. "David?"

"Oh! Sure!" David replied, as he shook off his exhaustion. "Let me borrow your satphone." After he put on the headset, he called Marie. "Aunt Marie, do you have a flashlight?" he asked.

"Sure, a really big one with LED lights," she replied.

"Shine it down this way in about three or four minutes," he said.

He pulled out a white handkerchief and waved it in the air as he slowly stood up. "Hey, you guys!" he yelled. "Anyone left over there? Talk to me!"

One Resort Guard with a bleeding face rose from behind the wall. "Yeah. What you want?"

"We're willing to let you surrender, if you come out right now. If not, we'll start shooting grenades and calling in artillery fire."

"You're full of shit! You got no artillery."

"Not with us. It's up on the hillside. Can you see it?" They all looked up to see a bright light from the hillside above the lagoon.

"That's the laser rangefinder. They're setting the distance now, and will blow you away with 82mm mortar fire in about five minutes," he said. "I'll give you two minutes to come out, hands up."

"Hold on, hold on!" the man yelled anxiously. "We coming out right now!" He and three others emerged from behind the wall with arms raised, supporting two more men who appeared badly injured.

David smiled as he looked at the team. "Anyone got handcuffs?" he asked. The ever-resourceful Roth opened a bag and waved three pairs of them in the air.

Jim Morrison looked at David. "Did I hear you're a lawyer?" he asked.

David nodded. "Yeah. I have a law degree."

Morrison shook his head and gave him a lopsided grin. "No wonder you're so good with bullshit."

David grinned back. "It's only bullshit if they don't believe you," he said.

Chapter 56

AJ and Sgt. Baisley approached the Guards Headquarters Building in their ATV. AJ tried to contact the rest of the team, but got only static.

They could see a Resort Guard with a submachine gun slung around his chest guarding the front door. AJ slid out of the ATV before the man could see him, and Baisley drove it the rest of the way to the building. He walked boldly up to the man front, while AJ skirted the sides of the building, staying away from brightly lit areas.

Unfortunately, the Guard was highly suspicious. Before Sgt. Baisley could get close enough to distract him, the man pointed his weapon at him.

"One more step and you dead," he snarled. Baisley could see that the Guard's finger was starting to tighten around the trigger of the submachine gun in his hand.

"Easy! Easy," Baisley said loudly, smiling for all he was worth, with his hands up in the air. "I'm Sergeant Baisley of the Anguilla Police. I was just coming with some information. I am on the same side as you. I have my identification in my wallet."

"I hear there are some guys attacking us wearing police uniforms. Move one mo' step, an' I blow you away," the guard snarled. He moved closer to Baisley. "Who are you, and what you doing here?"

Sgt. Baisley could see a shadow dancing behind the man. A minute later, AJ materialized behind him, grasped his forehead with one hand and quickly drew a razor-sharp knife across his exposed throat with the other. The man's eyes flew wide open in surprise, as bright blood spurted from a cut that looked like a wide smile. AJ pulled him to the ground before he could emit an alarm, and deftly plucked the Heckler & Koch MP5SD out of the dead guard's grasp.

"I've always wanted one of these, with a built-in silencer!" he said, appraising the precision machinery.

"OK. Happy birthday!" Sgt. Baisley replied, shaking his head.

They entered the Headquarters building, Baisley in front. There was another Sergeant behind a tall wooden reception desk, yelling into a phone. He looked up as Baisley approached and calmly asked, "I've got to get to the prisoner, Leah-something. Where is she?"

"Interrogation Area 2," the desk Sergeant replied, and then squinted his eyes in suspicion. He quickly reached for his belt holster. Baisley shot him in the forehead, causing it to snap back, followed by another shot that caused the man to crash backwards, along with the high swivel chair he had been sitting on.

Baisley watched for other Resort Guards as AJ approached, searching for a building diagram on the wall next to the front desk. He found what he was looking for, and ripped it off the wall. "Here's a walkway with three cells on either side," he pointed out on the map. And then Interrogation Areas 1 and 2. I hope we're in time. Let's go!"

They moved briskly along, peering into each room as they passed it. A passageway crossed in front of them as they approached the Interrogation Areas, and AJ had just darted across it when shots rang out. "You go ahead," Baisley told him. "Save Leah. I'll keep these bastards off your back."

AJ nodded at his friend. Almost in unison, they said, "Semper Fi," and then AJ disappeared down the hallway. He could hear occasional shots behind him.

He approached a metal door marked "Interrogation Area 2," and looked through its small window. The lights inside showed a horrifying sight. Leah was shackled to one wall by her wrists. Her clothing hung in tatters, and her head drooped oh her chest. A Resort Guard lieutenant stood in front of her.

AJ quietly opened the door and let himself in. The lieutenant slapped her across the face.

"Last chance. Tell me the name of your control and what other CIA agents are working here or you die. I've been told to clear up loose ends. You're a loose end." He held a Beretta 92F in his right hand, the black metal gleaming evilly under the bright ceiling lights. The sound of its slide being drawn back cracked through the silence of the room.

AJ sank to one knee and sighted along his newly acquired weapon. He had checked to make sure it was loaded with a full clip of 20 rounds of 9mm. He squeezed off the first round.

The guard said, *Oof!* in surprise, and slowly turned around. AJ hit him with three more shots in the center of his chest. AJ had decided not to try a head shot, since Leah was directly behind the man.

He was startled to hear two quick shots from his left, and felt a searing pain in his left shoulder. He whirled quickly and instinctively pulled off two shots at the figure standing there, hidden by the darkness.

Another series of shots rang out, and he could feel the bullets whizzing by his left ear. He fired two more shots at the muzzle flashes, and the figure behind them crashed into a table against the wall. A weapon skidded along the floor.

AJ turned back to the man near Leah. He had sunk to one knee, and was struggling to raise his weapon. AJ put three more shots in his chest for good measure, which finally caused the man to drop his Beretta and crumple to the floor. AJ checked him for signs of life and kicked away his weapon. He checked the other man, a uniformed guard, as well. Both of them were dead.

AJ rushed to Leah and raised her head, looking for signs of consciousness. Her face was battered and bleeding. He whispered to her, dread evident in his voice. "Leah?" He saw a faint flicker, and then her eyelids flew open as she recognized him.

"AJ! You came!" She barely managed to speak the words through her cracked and swollen lips.

AJ turned to look for the keys to the shackles that were holding her. He could find no keys, but discovered various instruments designed for either torture or surgery on a wooden side table stained with blood. He laid down his weapon and picked up two scalpels, which he used to cut the leather restraints around her wrists. He caught her as she sank to the floor.

"You came," was all she managed to say. "You came!"

"I'm here," he replied, a tear starting a path down his face. "I..." He whirled abruptly as he heard footsteps behind him in the hallway.

The door was hit with such force that it almost came off its hinges. A dark-haired man with a moustache stood in the doorway. He was not in uniform, but AJ could recognize a trained killer. He drew a knife out of a leg sheath and charged at AJ like an attack dog. AJ moved one of the two scalpels he still held to his right hand and held it out as he met the attacker. He did his best to keep the blade in his left hand hidden.

The man came swiftly and struck at AJ, the blade passing within inches of his gut. AJ danced out of the way, heading in the direction of the door. The man was not tall, but very strong and quick, and moved with the grace of a bullfighter. He faked with his left hand and slashed with his right. AJ backed out of the door and down the hallway, trying to get him away from Leah. He backed out a back doorway and stumbled down a set of stairs onto the sand. He could see the water of the lagoon less than 20 feet behind him.

The man jumped down the stairs and came right for him, descending with the knife blade as a toreador might give a death stroke to a bull. The razor-sharp knife sliced through AJ's Kevlar jacket and raked his ribs. AJ felt red hot pain explode along his right side, and a sticky flow of blood soaked his shirt. He whirled his right hand in the air, distracting the man, and then lashed out with the hidden blade in his left hand, gashing the man's forearm down to the bone. The man backed off a second, a look of surprise on his face, followed by a sudden shock of pain.

The man lunged forward with his right arm, aiming for AJ's heart. AJ got inside the motion and blocked the move with his left arm, aiming for the man's throat with the weapon in his right. He missed his target by less than an inch. The man crashed his elbow across AJ's face, forcing him backwards. He slipped in the sand, losing the scalpel from his right hand in the process.

He regained his footing and lunged at the man with his remaining weapon. The man bobbed and weaved, easily eluding AJ's thrusts. The man danced with his blade, looking like Muhammad Ali in the ring. He quickly scooped up some sand and threw it at AJ, seeking to blind him.

AJ managed to avoid the sand by dancing backwards and turning his head aside. He took quick stock of himself. His right side ached terribly, and leaked blood. His left shoulder had a bullet wound, and his arm felt numb. He was also exhausted, and running on his last stores of adrenaline.

The man in front of him was good, and he knew it. He almost swaggered as he moved around AJ, seeking a weak point for an opening.

He threw a quick series of jabs, with his knife leading the way.

AJ moved in on him and grabbed the wrist behind the knife with his left hand—his weak hand. His left shoulder sent out searing pain signals with every move. He rammed his right elbow at the man's head and tried a series of inside kicks at his groin.

The man grabbed AJ's left wrist. With both knife hands held fast by each other, they moved closer together, fighting with elbows and knees, and trying head butts and kicks. The man battered AJ back into the lagoon, and they slipped and fell into a few feet of water, coming up with water and sand dripping down their bodies. The man made a feint and a quick swipe with his knife, and AJ was too slow to avoid it. The knife gashed his left shoulder, leaving a bright red trail.

AJ grabbed the man's knife wrist again, and gave him right-fisted blows deep into his gut and lungs. It was enough that the man stumbled backward onto the sand. AJ went down with him and did not stop, but punched him over and over again, each blow almost as painful to him as to his target.

They rolled around in the sand. AJ managed to smash his forehead into the man's nose, breaking it. Both of them had lost their weapons by now. The man wrapped a powerful forearm around AJ's head, using the hand of his other arm in a claw hold to try to dig his eyes out.

AJ grabbed sand with his good hand and smeared it into the man's face. The man broke off and rolled away. They both rose to their feet and rushed at each other. AJ was tired. His lungs burned, and every part of his body seared with pain. He knew, and the other man knew, that he was on the edge of collapse.

They traded punches, and the other man looked at him, expecting him to back off. Instead, AJ rushed at him full force, holding him with his weakened left arm as he punched at him with his good right hand. They stumbled back into the water and both of them fell. They rose slowly.

The man saw a nearby rock with jagged edges, and lifted it over his head to smash it into AJ. With the last of his strength, AJ whirled to plant a roundhouse kick straight into his enemy's solar plexus. The man dropped the rock and staggered back, plopping down into a sitting position.

AJ grabbed the rock and staggered to the man as he was trying to get up. He knew he would never have the time or strength to raise the rock above his head and bring it crashing down, so he thrust its jagged edge at the man's head with all of the strength he could muster. He heard a solid *thunk*, and pulled the rock back and beat it against his opponent's head, again, and again.

The man slowly sank back on his knees, and then settled down on his back. He stopped moving, and stared straight up. AJ knelt next to him, and hit him with the rock yet again, until he saw that it was totally red. The weight and jagged edges had done their work.

He felt for a pulse in the man's throat, but found none. He found he could not get up, so he crawled slowly forward on his elbows and knees. He held his bruised and bloodied hands in front of him. They seemed to swim before his eyes.

He pulled himself along the sand toward the stairs. He looked up, dazed, unsure whether he had the strength to pull himself up the steps. Miraculously, Leah appeared, limping badly. She sat on the bottom stair and tugged at his shoulders to pull his head onto her lap. Hot tears splashed onto his face.

"I was afraid I'd never see you again," she said, stroking his cheeks. "But you came for me."

"Of course...I came." He faded in and out of consciousness. "And I want to tell you..."

"What?" she asked. "What do you want to tell me?"

"...how I feel, 'bout you. But..."

She put her ear next to his mouth to catch his faint whisper. "But what?"

"...but ...have to borrow... cat." He faded into unconsciousness.

She leaned over and kissed his forehead as she whispered, "Poor dear. He's hallucinating."

Chapter 57

Fire continued to consume much of the Resort. Two guards came running out of an adjacent building, clothing and hair on fire, trying to outrun their pain. One of them ran at Leah and AJ, who was regaining consciousness. They both looked around for something to use as a weapon. Three shots rang out in a burst, then another three. A look of utter surprise crossed the man's face as he sank to his knees and then toppled over in slow motion.

David appeared in back of him and nudged him once with a toe. The man grunted. David fired another burst of three shots into him. "That was for Rika," he muttered angrily.

He saw AJ and Leah, nodded to them, and sank onto one of the stairs. AJ looked at him. "Keeping it to 3-round bursts," he said approvingly. "Good going."

Ben arrived a few minutes later. He grunted a brief greeting, sat down on a step, and started to reload an empty ammunition clip, but stopped, totally exhausted, and just stared at his weapon.

An ATV drew up. It had so many dark bullet holes in its white paintwork that it looked like a Dalmatian. Three of the team members got out and slowly sank to the ground. They all wore bandages, smudged with dirt and blood. A second ATV drew up, and Morrison got out. He told AJ, "Everyone's accounted for. Some are really banged up, but no one got killed. We found spare tires for the ATVs." Several more members of the team arrived and also sank to the ground. They nodded mutely at each other as they arrived. They were too tired to speak.

David got up with a groan and staggered to his ATV. He rummaged in a bag, and extracted a bottle of Jack Daniels he had grabbed off the table in the Conference Center. He offered it to AJ with, "Here. For those cuts."

AJ said, "Thanks," and sloshed a little on the cuts over his ribs and shoulder. He then took three long gulps from the bottle and handed it to Leah. She tilted her head back for a drink and returned the bottle to David, who tossed it to Ben. The bottle made the rounds from man to man. The last participant, Roth, polished off all but one last sip, and tossed the bottle back to David.

David looked out over the Resort. Fire lit up most of the buildings, with flocks of bright-white embers flying through the air. A gasoline tank exploded in the distance. A muscular man in a white guayabera shirt came staggering up the road. He stopped and looked down, desperately holding onto his stomach as fluids leaked out between his fingers. He staggered sideways to his right, twirled twice, then stopped and toppled over. He did not move again.

Several almost naked women ran by, screaming, in the direction of the airport.

A large sign hanging over the road that had proclaimed "Paradise Island Resort, Grand Opening" was ringed by fire. It separated in the middle, and both parts slowly descended onto the roadway. The flames consumed the sign until only the word "Paradise" remained.

A Jeep down the road exploded, and one of its seats flew through the air, bounced several times, and came to rest 30 feet away, burning with acrid black smoke. A tire rolled through the middle of the group, came to a stop, and fell over. No one even looked up. The exhaustion was total.

David looked out at the inferno. He swallowed the last ounce of whisky and turned to AJ. He gestured at the scene in front of them with the empty bottle, and said, "Well. It looks like our work here is done!"

Chapter 58

The group gathered together a few hours later. Dawn illuminated the structures of the Resort, although the light from the burning buildings was still far brighter.

David took stock of the situation. None of the team had been killed, but the toll was nevertheless serious. Erika was still unconscious. He had radioed the hospital in Anguilla to prepare an emergency medical team for her arrival. A similar team was preparing to receive Leah, who was badly bruised and cut, and was suffering from dehydration and loss of blood. Two of the four Special Forces members had fractured bones, and several other team members had cracked ribs and deep bruises and cuts. They would likewise go directly to the hospital. Mark Zinni, who had a pilot's license, had gotten one of the planes in the airport gassed up, and was ready to go.

Sgt. Baisley was uninjured, but exhausted, and would be dropped off on St. Martin, near the house where his wife Mary and daughter Sarah had taken refuge. He had agreed to come back the following day, to take any prisoners into custody and put the island under police control.

The rest of the team had superficial wounds that had been treated with First Aid. David had asked them to stay and help gather up computers, legal documents and other materials for AJ, as well as video footage from the Resort cameras.

The injured members of the team prepared to depart for the airport, accompanied by Werner as attending physician. Mark was already warming up the engines. They all shook hands and hugged—some of them very gingerly, because of wounds and bruises. David and Leah gave all the rescuers their profuse thanks.

David and AJ decided to take an ATV to head down to the mouth of the lagoon and pick up Aunt Marie and Katharina.

Chapter 59

The adult female Mosasaur sensed her mate was gone forever, and turned all of her attention to her two offspring. At over 20 feet long, each would have counted as a giant in almost any other species, but they were dwarfed by their colossal mother, who extending almost a third of a football field and weighed well over 20 tons.

They followed her up to the double shark net at the mouth of the lagoon, as she checked the barrier's entire stretch for any holes that promised escape. There were none. She came to the surface and looked at the fence above the surface, which extended about 10 feet above the choppy battleship gray water, topped by the catwalk with handrails. Lights punctuated it along its entire length, still turned on although dawn had broken over an hour ago. The rising sun remained hidden behind battleship-gray clouds. She backed up, turned her massive body rapidly with her flippers and rushed at the barrier, emitting a series of clicks. As she backed up, both youngsters followed her.

The young female went first, diving deep and then straining to gather speed. She cleared the top with inches to spare, the end of her tail slapping against the railing of the fence.

The young male tried next, but crashed into the catwalk on top of the net and bounced back, splashing into the water and sending a wall of spray in every direction. On his next try, the mother stayed right behind him, and as he approached the surface, she came up under him and used her giant head to help lift him bodily out of the water and over the barrier.

Both youngsters waited on the open ocean side of the fence, their heads above the waterline, whining anxiously. She replied with a short burst of grunts, and then turned her head and swam back to the middle of the lagoon. Although she was capable of doing well over 30 knots, she eschewed speed to move majestically and inexorably along the top of the water, showing the entire length of her body, preceded by a giant V-shaped bow wave, to the watchers gathered on the shore.

All activity stopped around the lagoon, and every face turned to watch the spectacle. AJ and David had arrived in their ATV, and were standing with Aunt Marie and Katharina near the fence at the bottom of the lagoon.

Marie held both hands to her chest, clutching the silver totem of Mokele-Mbembe around her neck, a miniature of the titanic presence before them. Tears poured from her eyes, and she spoke words that AJ could not understand, punctuated by many *thank you's*.

AJ looked around at the surreal scene, lit by the rising sun pushing through the clouds. A dozen Mayan gardeners from the Yucatan peninsula had reported for their duties, clad in identical white shirts and pants. All of them were on their knees, facing the lagoon with bowed heads. They recited ancient prayers while holding their broad white straw hats reverently in front of them. Several made the sign of the cross, over and over, mixing pre-Columbian and Christian traditions. He heard muttering that sounded like *serpiente arco iris enarbolen*. AJ smiled. "The rainbow serpent," he said, and corrected himself. "The flying rainbow serpent."

The Mosasaur reached the center of the lagoon, arched her back and dove deep, the line of her back seemingly taking forever to fully submerge. She then burst majestically out of the water, and the ten-foot head hung in space, surrounded by an electric-blue plasma cloud of sparks and water droplets. The jaws opened to reveal rows of teeth that looked like ivory daggers.

A roar exploded from that throat, a raw primeval thunderclap of defiance like nothing anyone there had ever heard before. It rolled across the lagoon, across the destroyed and burning boats, docks, buildings, and vehicles, and the dozens of bodies that looked like they had been slammed by a giant's hammer.

The roar hung in the air. Then, incredibly, the monster emitted an even louder bellow, a shockingly loud jet engine blast that seemed to go on forever, and reverberated from the buildings and the mountainsides beyond. It was so intense that several of the survivors on the shore clapped their hands over their ears and closed their eyes tightly.

Having finished her defiant warning to anyone foolish enough to think of following, the female rotated her head to take one last look around the lagoon, flashes of red and coral running the length of her upper body. She slowly lowered herself into the water and started her run. She seemed to flow rather than swim the distance to the fence, her color changing from lighter and lighter gray to blue as the dawn lit up the water. Then, abruptly, she disappeared.

David looked down at Aunt Marie, who was down on one knee, repeating her incantations. The tears streaming from her eyes were suddenly lit up like bright crystals from the rays of bright light breaking through the morning cloud cover. He swung his head back to the lagoon as the same rays illuminated the creature rising from the sea before them.

The colossal head broke out of the water, followed by what seemed like a train-length of body, the front flippers spread out like giant wings. The head rose up and the great eyes flew wide open as the entire animal rose from the water toward the sky, waves of spray bounding off, rows of bright colors marching across its skin, a cape of spindrift trailing behind. Raw colors blazed out, radiating in spirals, the brilliant intensity shockingly painful to the eye.

The watchers lining the shore shared the same experience. As the Mosasaur reached the top of its arc, its entire body out of the water, time seemed to freeze for a moment, and the creature appeared to flout gravity. Thousands of fat water drops radiated out from the leviathan and seemed to hang in the air like necklaces of bright white-blue diamonds. The only movement was from long ropes of blue-green electric charges roiling up and down the colossal beast's sides, like arteries of blazing fire trailing from the head back to the surface of the water, crackling and snapping on the way. The immense eyes seemed to bore laser-like directly through anyone gazing up at the apparition.

The freeze-frame moment dissolved slowly as the Mosasaur continued its path through the air, bending its body as it started to descend. Time speeded up as the cavernous mouth opened and closed, revealing and then hiding rows of curved white fangs.

It cleared the fence by many feet, as if the barrier's existence were irrelevant. The pointed snout entered the water on the ocean side of the barrier, and the body took forever to follow, until it had disappeared. A tall wave crashed against the fence, tossing its massive floats up and down like children's toys.

The unbroken silence continued for several more minutes. Sounds returned suddenly. People started speaking again, birds started chattering, an ATV's starter made cranking noises. The onlookers around the lagoon looked at each other in a daze. Some wiped tears out of their eyes as they tried to describe what they had just experienced. Others slumped to the ground, exhausted.

David and AJ both kissed Marie, and the three of them held onto each other tightly.

Chapter 60

David saw AJ as he came down the hall of the hospital. They shook hands and embraced.

"Careful," AJ said, "It's been three days since the fight, but I don't think I have a spot on me that's not banged up."

David grinned. "I know the feeling. How's everybody else?"

"Tony and Alex are out of the hospital already," AJ replied. "The others should be out within a week. We were really lucky that no one from our side got killed." He added wryly, "Except, maybe, that one Mosasaur."

David grinned weakly. "Yeah, you could say that. And Erika's finally out of danger. I've been watching over her the last three days. They gave her a sedative, so she'll sleep a while longer, but she'll be fine. No permanent damage."

AJ suddenly looked serious. "We're not out of the woods yet. I got a report that Fowler's helicopter crashed, but he escaped in a life raft. And some of his guys on Anguilla got away, after they heard about what happened at the resort. He's somewhere out there, with over a dozen trained killers. And I've gotten reports they're coming after you."

"Me?" David asked. "Why me?"

"Why was DuBois torturing you?"

"To find out where the coronet was. The one I gave you. The one I'm taking to my Nana, whom it belonged to."

"Does that thing mean something special to Fowler?"

"Yeah, he says it was stolen from his great-grandfather."

"Right now it's in my apartment in Northern Virginia. I suggest you join me up there, really quick. And watch your back."

David nodded in reply. AJ noticed his friend appeared distracted, and looked at him closely. "What's wrong?"

David explained what Fowler had told him and shown him on the island. He made AJ swear that he would not tell anyone else.

AJ shook his head. "I'm surprised. I would have thought different of her. And I thought she really liked you. But you can't argue with a video."

David nodded. "The sex scenes were bad enough. But what really put me over the top is when she put on the blue outfit I got her and modeled it for him."

"My God! How did you feel?"

"I threw up. A lot. I was puking for distance."

"Is it over between you two?" AJ asked. "That would be too bad, after all you've been through."

"I don't know," David replied. "Maybe not. I know everybody lies sometime. I could live with that. I just need some time to process this. I feel...all raw inside." He looked at his friend. "And I don't have my normal therapist to talk it out with. Have you heard anything about Bucky? I keep asking, but no one seems to know."

He hesitated as one of the nurses came up to them, her eyes cast down. "What's the matter, Molly?" he asked.

"They've...brought Bucky in," she replied. "He's in the OR." She looked away. "I'm so sorry," she said, and started to cry.

David whirled, and ran toward the Operating Room. He entered the white, sterile, brightly lit room to see his companion lying on a stainless steel table, surrounded by a doctor and two nurses. They were wiping blood off. A small mound of red-stained bandages and cotton swabs was growing nearby.

"What's going on?" David blurted. He looked down, and was horrified by what he saw. The oversized cat he knew seemed to have shrunk by half. His fur was matted and covered with blood.

"He was brought in a few minutes ago by one of your crew," said the doctor. "It looks like he was shot, once or maybe twice. He may have attacked someone—he has blood on his fangs. There's no bullet lodged in him, but he's lost too much blood, and there's no way we can replace it."

He shook his head. "I don't know why he's still alive—but he's fading fast." He looked sadly at David. "I'm so sorry. There's nothing more we can do." He turned to the nurses and motioned them out of the room.

David picked up his friend very gently. Bucky's eyes opened slightly, and he made a tiny sound, something like "Meep." His front paws started moving feebly. David placed him on left his arm, and with a mighty effort the cat pulled himself along until his face was buried under David's shoulder.

"I know why he's still alive," David said, his vision starting to blur. "He wanted to go to his safe place...and tell me..." He couldn't bring himself to say the word. His continued stroking the cat and talking to him. The doctor let himself out of the room, and closed the door behind him.

Doctor Chopra met AJ out in the hall. He shook his head in answer to the unspoken question.

"Damn!" AJ said, angry and sad. He went into Marie's hospital room and told her the news.

"Oh, no! That's awful. That cat was like God's little angel to him," she said. She looked at AJ. "There's something else. What is it? Tell me!"

AJ looked at the floor. "It looks like Erika lied to David. He found out that she'd been...intimate with Fowler the whole time, and then denied it. And it looks like Fowler or one of his men shot Bucky."

"So he loses his best friend, and the guy who shot him was sleeping with Erika," Marie said. "He must feel like the world has totally caved in. Can you go bring him here? I'm still a little too woozy to get up."

AJ went out in the corridor and asked the nearest nurse if she'd seen David.

"He's left already," she replied. "He left an envelope for you at the front desk."

AJ walked to the front desk and saw an envelope with his name on it. He opened it to read the note.

> Dear AJ,
> Thanks again, bro, for everything. Bucky's gone, and—I'm totally numb. I'll catch up with you in Washington to pick up that package.
> David
> P.S. If, for any reason, something happens to me, could you please deliver it to Mrs. Emma Weinstock.

A New York City address was written on the back.

AJ asked the girl behind the desk, "Was he carrying anything when he left here?"

The girl nodded. "Yes. He had an Adidas sports bag. He was holding it real gently, like it had eggs in it or something."

AJ nodded. "I think I know where he's going." He took out his cell phone and started dialing.

Chapter 61

David arrived at the little pale-white country church on top of the hill. The Jeep cast long shadows to the sides of the road in the fading twilight.

He gently picked up the blue Adidas gym bag that held his friend, grabbed a small shovel out of the back seat, and walked across the deserted graveyard next to the church, past the flat miniature houses that served as grave markers, and stopped under the tree at the edge of the cliff. He looked down the steep slope in front of him, out over the salt flats far below and to the ocean off in the distance, where the sun was sinking in a pool of copper-tinted liquid gold.

He unzipped the bag and laid Bucky's body down gently on the ground. He busied himself digging a hole under the tree, for once oblivious to the beauty of the scene spread out in front of him. The sun turned blood-red and then pink and then yielded to the silvery moon, which laid a bright glittering path across the salt ponds below. When the hole was deep enough, he carefully arranged the cat's body in the grave, speaking baby talk and fussing over small details to keep his mind off the finality of the moment.

"OK, Bucky, here's your stuffed mousie. Put your paw on it so it doesn't get away. And your favorite blue blankie...I'll tuck it around you, so you don't get cold."

He stopped, his heart lead-heavy, and covered his eyes with a hand, wiping away tears. His voice choked as he said, "Now that I've lost you, who's going to wake me in the morning? And whom will I talk to?"

He smiled sadly as he said, "You know, Bucky, every day we were together, I complained about you wiping your snotty nose off on my arm. And now...I'd give anything I own just to have you do it one more time."

He picked up his ukulele and sat next to the little grave, leaned his back against the tree, and said, "Remember all the nights we sat here talking and singing?" He started to play.

> *Someday, somehow*
> *Gonna make it...*

He ran his fingers over the beautifully inlaid Koa wood of the instrument and slowly lowered it into the grave. His face became a mask of pain.

"It's no use," he whispered to the silent form. "Someday will never come. I lost the treasure. I lost Erika. I lost you. Everything's...gone."

He rose. He leaned against the tree with his left hand. His knees were wobbling. He walked the few steps to the edge of the steep cliff, and gazed, unfocused, at the salt ponds beneath.

A dark cloud slithered across the moon, and the night turned pitch black. His vision grew foggy. He felt a vast and bottomless emptiness building in front of him, sucking everything down into itself. He was vaguely aware that his right foot had loosened small rocks from the edge of the cliff, and that they were falling and crashing far below.

He teetered forward as a sudden gust of wind urged him ahead.

Chapter 62

David felt a strong hand grasp his right shoulder, and a deep voice rumbled in his ear.

"Hey, mon, is dis a private party or can friends and family join in, now?"

"What the..." he said, startled, and jerked back from the edge. He turned his head to see AJ holding onto his shoulder. Behind him he recognized other faces, members of the ship's crew.

"We heard you were burying Bucky tonight," said AJ, pulling him back gently, "so we wanted to join you in the send-up. Is that okay with you?"

David relaxed visibly. "Sure. I..." He looked on in increasing astonishment as he heard cars coming up the road, the sound of car doors slamming, and saw dark shapes filtering into the graveyard. He recognized waitresses from Johnno's, and nurses from the hospital, and shopkeepers, and hotel workers, and many others he knew on the island. Several people brought in lanterns, and set up folding chairs.

Jake Jamison, the woodcarver, brought a small, intricately carved rosewood coffin and laid it on the ground near Bucky.

David looked down at coffin and then at the gathering crowd.

"Listen, I've gotta tell you. I'm broke. I can't pay for any of this."

Words floated out of the semi-darkness. "Dat's okay." "We're here for you."

He shook his head. "No. The treasure's gone. I have nothing..."

Molly, the nurse from the hospital, took both of his hands in hers, and looked at him solemnly.

"Listen, David. Maybe you thought you only had friends here as long as you had sacks of gold waiting for you, but that's not so." She looked at the nodding crowd behind her, then back at him.

"The way it is on this island, we all have times when we can work, and then times with nothing. We survive by helping each other out. You helped us out when you were up, now we help you. You need a drink at the bar, you run a tab. You need a place to stay, we'll find you one. You're family now."

Heads around her bobbed in agreement.

"You and Bucky are part of this island. We all know about the nights you and him visited the hospital, and read books, and told stories. You made children laugh, and old people less lonely. And you and your friends saved our island from DuBois and his gangsters."

Sergeant Baisley came up, smiling. "I have something for you," he said. He handed David an official-looking envelope, which contained a Certificate of Residency. "You're an official resident. You don't need a visa any more. This is your home."

David was speechless. He hugged Baisley as the crowd broke into applause.

He looked down at the coffin. "Is that for Bucky?" he asked.

"You bet," said Jamison. "Jus' happen to have one his size. Let's put him in it. We'll take care a' dis'. You jus' take it easy."

Someone handed David a bottle of Pyrat, the local rum, and led him over to a folding chair that had materialized. "Sit down. Take some."

David took a few quick gulps of the Pyrat while he watched his friend being taken out of his earthen grave and upgraded to the coffin.

Molly told David, "We have an empty gravesite we can put him in for tonight. We'll finish it later. We'll put up a marker, and make it a place you want come back to."

"Oh, look," someone said. "Here comes de preacher."

David looked up to see the Reverend McClyde tottering through the graveyard.

"Let's take Bucky in back of the church to finish this," suggested Molly, as she lifted the coffin and headed that way. She looked around at the others and whispered loudly, "Remember, don't let on Bucky's a cat. We told the Reverend it was a little boy."

Reverend McClyde came up, breathless, and stared at David with rheumy, myopic eyes.

"You're having a burial here, tonight? This is highly irregular."

"We doin' it just de one time, preacher," said Jamison. "It came up sudden, like. We jus' wanna say a few words, sing a coupla songs. We'll pay you the burial fee tomorrow."

"I guess it's all right, then," said the Reverend, mollified. "What was the dearly beloved's name?"

"His name was Bucky," David said softly. "Buckminster, er, Kilmer."

"Buckminster. Yes. How old was the dearly beloved?"

"About five."

"Ah. So sad when a child is taken by the Lord at such an early age."

"It wasn't the Lord that took him, it was those ass...it was Fowler and DuBois that killed him," said David, with some heat.

"Oh, dear. I'm so sorry. Well, let's get started."

Willing hands set up a little podium from the church on a concrete slab. Someone held a flashlight to read by. Somebody said, "Here comes the coffin," and every head turned toward the church. There had been an active competition for who would have the honor of being a pallbearer, and four large bouncers from various island bars had won out. In front was Ray-Ray, a huge Samoan who could barely fit three of his fingers through the carrying handle of the little coffin, which now resembled a football being carried by four defensive linemen.

They appeared around the corner of the church, and solemnly shuffled into the graveyard and up to the grave. Several men held bottles of rum in that area, and they drew themselves up stiffly, holding the bottles straight in front of them, like an honor guard of soldiers at "present arms." The casket was lowered into the shallow grave. The pallbearers straightened up from their burden, and were all solemnly handed rum bottles by the honor guard. All eyes turned to the podium.

The minister took out a book, and started reciting from Psalms. The crowd murmured key passages along with him, standing respectfully and with bowed heads, although every now and then there was the slosh of Pyrat starting its journey down a thirsty throat. To speed things up, AJ suggested that Molly sing a song, and the preacher was gently led from the stage to a chair and handed a half-full bottle, which, after due consideration, he accepted.

Molly sang in a clear bright voice, and the hauntingly beautiful strains of *Amazing Grace* filled the air.

In Johnno's bar on the beach far below, the atmosphere was somber. The place was almost empty, as all the customers had taken their drinks and joined the crowd on the hilltop, and the usual non-stop jukebox had been turned off.

The only patrons were a family of tourists, the Katzenbergs. The father had ordered a Cuba Libre for himself, and a glass of white wine for his wife. Although Melanie, the daughter, begged for a drink, the mother told Jessica, the barmaid, "Nein. She is only 17. Give her a Cola, not too much ice."

The daughter howled her frustration. "Why must you treat me as a child? I hate this vacation. I wish I had stayed home." The mother tried to put her arm around her, but the daughter recoiled from it.

"Why are they singing on top of the hill?" the father asked Jessica. "Is it a party?"

Jessica wiped away a tear. "It's a funeral. One of our island residents named Bucky," she said. "In fact, take your drinks with you. I'm going to close the bar and go up there, too."

"Who was this Bucky?" Katzenberg asked. "What did he do to have such a funeral?"

"He was a good friend. He was a cat," she replied, brushing away another tear.

"A cat?"

"Yes. A cat."

The man turned to his wife, waving his rum drink in a circle in front of his tropical shirt. "Sie singen fuer eine Katze," he told her.

"Eine Katze?" she asked him.

"Ja." He shook his head. "I will never understand these people."

Jessica closed down the bar. She put several bottles of Pyrat into a sack and locked the door.

"Can I get a ride with you?" she asked Katzenberg. "Someone else has my car."

He shrugged his shoulders. "Why not?"

They drove up the winding road and parked the car at the end of a long string of vehicles stretched out along both sides of the roadway.

As they joined the crowd, they saw David step up to the podium. Katzenberg nudged his wife and whispered, "Look. It's Herr Doctor Kilmer."

Chapter 63

David took a deep breath and gazed out at the crowd.

"This is both the saddest and the happiest day of my life," he said. "It's the happiest day because I suddenly see I have a home much bigger than my little cabin on the ship. It's..." he waved his arm in a wide circle, "...huge. And I have more family than I ever dreamed of. That includes all of the crew. When they were invited to come rescue me, on what looked like a suicide mission..."

He turned to smile at Werner, who grinned back. "...the only question one of them asked was, 'What caliber should I bring?'"

He grasped the podium firmly. "I looked everywhere for a home, and a home found me...here!"

He continued, "And it's the saddest day because I lost my good friend. I'll never find a better one."

He smiled sadly. "To me he wasn't just flesh and blood, but a symbol of hope, like an angel sent down to tell me that I had another chance. I often wanted to give up, but he never let me. Each morning, he'd wake at daybreak, and walk on my face until I surrendered and got up with him to greet the dawn."

"What a strange young man," murmured the preacher.

David bit his lip. He drew out a small sheet of paper, and said, "I have a little prayer I'd like to say." The heads of the crowd bowed as one, as he wiped his eyes and started.

Dear Lord, if you could spare the time
To send an angel to the gate to meet Bucky
When he arrives, all lost and forlorn.
If you could pat him now and then, I'd be really glad
For he's never been alone until today.
And, even in Heaven, I know he'll be sad
Without my voice to chase his fears away.
You see, we were inseparable, and now
He won't understand being dead.
I don't understand it well, myself.
Please, dear God, give him a nice place to wait
Through the long, long years,
Until the day I meet him at your gate.

The very earth seemed to voice a collective sigh of, "Amen!"

David looked toward the coffin. "Bucky, I'll say, 'See ya.' But I can't bring myself to say the 'G' word."

The singers started up again. And they did say the "G" word, singing songs of good-bye—of good-bye to ancestral homelands, good-bye to go work far away, good-bye to mothers and fathers, good-bye to little upturned faces suddenly wrenched away, good-bye to warm homes and memories, good-bye to love and life.

But they also sang songs of hope and faith, of sunrise bringing another day, of love awakening, of babies born, of finally returning home again, of girls named Maryann playing in the sand, of the end of a day working banana boats, of friendships and deep faith that carried through.

As they sang, they held hands and joined with each other and with the music, which became a living, amorphous form embracing a multitude of faces. Men with deep, basso profondo voices immersed the crowd in a deep rumble, and posed counterpoint to the clear, high sopranos of the women. The melodies and voices intertwined sinuously, and fused into a living essence.

The music flowed like molten honey down the steep hillside, across the silvery lane cut by the moon over the salt ponds, and over the rows of little clapboard houses by the road. An old couple turned their faces up to the source, and their eyes sparkled, and arthritic hands sought each other like fluttering moths in the moonlight, and grasped tightly, as if for the last time. It spilled over Johnno's Bar and the Sandy Beach, empty except for black-and-white seagulls huddled together. It finally merged with the boiling waves of the sparkling ocean, which joined in, and pushed its waves forward to descend as crashing cymbals.

Time flowed as swiftly as tears and laughter and streams of golden rum. Those streams had not bypassed the Katzenbergs, holding hands with their new friends, and swaying in time to the songs. A bottle of Appleton Gold reached Mr. Katzenberg, who took two gulps and passed it to his wife, who took a long drink and passed it without thinking to her daughter Melanie, who tasted it with such enthusiasm that the bottle was empty when it resumed its journey.

At the podium, audience members were sharing memories of Bucky. A beautician named Janice told of meeting him in the hospital after having a miscarriage two years ago. "I was...shattered," she said. "I was frozen. I was ashamed, I couldn't talk with another human being, even my husband Maurice," she said, pointing at Ray-Ray the Samoan bouncer. "And then Bucky came and lay right next to me, and started to purr, and suddenly everything was all right. God was telling me there was a second chance. And I brought my second chance with me tonight, my daughter Minnie." The Samoan held up a baby girl, tiny in his massive hands, to the roar of the crowd.

Mrs. Katzenberg turned to Melanie, weeping openly. "I also lost a baby," she said. "I never told you. I am so...sorry. I was afraid I would lose you, also." The daughter held her mother tightly as they wept, pausing only to grab a bottle of rum as it passed by.

Up by the podium, the music was halted as someone asked David, "What was Bucky's favorite song?"

He smiled. "Bucky loved holidays. I'd find a present in the morning at the foot of the bed, like a dead lizard or mouse. Last Christmas, I woke up to find two dead rats at the foot of my bed. Two of them!" The crowd murmured its appreciation.

"What?" asked the hard-of-hearing preacher. "What did he give him for Christmas?"

"Two dead rats," Molly told him cheerfully.

"Dead rats?" said the preacher. He shook his head. "I will never understand these people."

David continued, "He loved Christmas music, especially *The Little Drummer Boy*. He'd listen, and keep time with his tail. It's about this little boy who didn't have any gifts, so he gave all he could..."

Melanie Katzenberg yelled out. "I know this song. The David Bowie cover version."

Eager hands pulled her up on stage, where she joined hands with the others as they sang.

> *Come, they told me, pa rum pum pum pum,*
> *A new-born King to see, pa rum pum pum pum.*

In a crystal-clear voice that squeezed the hearts of the listeners, Melanie sang the counterpart.

> *Peace on Earth, can it be*
> *Years from now, perhaps we'll see*

Papa Katzenberg's heart almost burst with pride as he looked up at his daughter. He hugged his wife tightly with both arms.

A pyramid of flowers and small toys grew steadily in front of Bucky's gravesite. Many people wrote personal messages, and slipped them under a rock that anchored them against the wind. David left a simple note, which would later be engraved on the gravesite. It said:

He was a good bear!

Melanie left one under the same rock. The night wind fluttered the edges of both papers. Hers read:

And so it came to pass, that in a land far, far from home, the Katzenberg family enjoyed their best vacation ever, while singing Christmas carols in the middle of August, in the center of a graveyard, holding hands and laughing and weeping with intimate strangers, in honor of a cat. A cat they had never known, but whose bright spirit sparkled like starlight in the eyes of everyone he touched.

Chapter 64

Erika awoke slowly in her hospital bed. The room seemed to be spinning, but began to slow down. Her mouth tasted like the bottom of a bird cage. She became aware of tubes and wires attached to her arms. Ponderously, she opened her eyes fully.

Bright sunlight streamed in through the windows, almost blinding her. Slowly the vague shapes around her resolved themselves into faces she recognized. AJ and Moshe were looking anxiously down at her. The first words she heard were Moshe's.

"Hey! She's coming awake!"

AJ leaned over her and took one of her hands in his own, gently, so as not to disturb the attached apparatus. "Welcome back to the land of the living," he said as he smiled down at her.

"Where am I? What happened?" Erika looked around and saw she was in a two-bed hospital room. A bank of monitors and displays ran squiggly lines and Christmas lights behind her head. The other bed was empty.

AJ answered her first question, "You're in the hospital in Anguilla," he said. "You've been out for quite a while. Three days, in fact. You had a concussion, and loss of blood, from a bullet wound and when you hit your head on the edge of a table. You got off lucky, with no permanent damage. You started to come around last night, but faded in and out, so the doctor gave you a sedative so you could rest. He said you'd be waking up at around this time."

A doctor came in and looked at Erika, the monitors, and then her visitors. He started tut-tutting. "What are you people doing in here? This patient is still in intensive care. Nurse! Nurse!"

A plus-sized nurse appeared outside the door, ready to charge into the room. AJ firmly closed the door in her face, and turned to the doctor. "Doctor, could you give us a few minutes, please?"

The doctor started to open his mouth to protest, and AJ repeated, this time more firmly, "Please! Now!"

The doctor sighed theatrically, and headed for the door. He turned around and said, the edges of his lips turned down in a pout, "Five minutes. No more!" and marched out.

Erika turned to AJ and Moshe. "What happened? I remember explosions, and gunfire, and fighting, and...oh my God—Fowler! That rat bastard! And Mosasaurs, real Mosasaurs, chasing us through caves into the lagoon and...then I was dragged somewhere and handcuffed. And DuBois holding a knife at my throat, and a lot of noise, and David coming in to rescue me, and...everything going black."

AJ continued holding her hand, gripping it tightly. "DuBois and Fowler were in it together. The mysterious head of the directors of the Resort was Fowler. DuBois brought him the safe with the gold coins that he stole from the ship. They got the gold, but there were also documents and another valuable object that Fowler wanted that I'd already gotten out of the country."

He paused. "They also roughed up Auntie. I just managed to keep them from burning down her house, with her inside."

Erika's alarm was evident in her voice. "Aunt Marie! Is she all right?"

AJ nodded. "She's in this hospital right now. You'll see her soon."

Moshe picked up the tale. "Fowler turned out to be quite the vindictive one. After torturing David to find out where the missing part of the treasure was, he intended to kill both of you. He took off when he saw the Mosasaurs tear up his precious resort. I saw one of the Mo's gulp down a guard like he was a Chicken McNugget."

He added, proudly, "You know, I had the computer modeling on them down pretty good. They were even bigger than we thought, and we didn't know about their ability to change color. But my animation of their movements was right on, though I didn't think they could move around on land as much as they did, and..."

AJ laid a restraining hand on Moshe's shoulder. "To finish briefly, we came in with the ship's crew and some friends of mine. Two of our guys helped David escape, and he rescued you. Fowler saw the jig was up, grabbed the gold, and escaped in a helicopter. We got off some shots at the chopper, and it apparently crashed in the ocean. The governor's on his way back right now, and there's a joint task force of British and American Special Operations guys on Dragon Island, gathering evidence. The Mosasaurs killed a lot of the bad guys. There were four of them, two adults and two youngsters. One was killed, but the other three got away."

Erika looked around the room again, still bewildered. "Where's David?"

AJ hesitated. "He's gone. He said he had to go away for a while."

Erika's eyebrows shot up. "He's gone? Gone? He didn't even say good-bye?"

Moshe shuffled his feet. "I think he wrote a note, but he threw it in the trash."

Erika had difficulty taking it all in. "Where is it? Let me read it!"

Moshe picked through the trash can to produce a crumpled-up piece of paper. "Here it is!"

Erika snatched it from him, and read it out loud:

Rika,

After what's happened, I've got to go, and get away from everything that reminds me of Fowler. There's a Chinese poem that says:

Goodbye, my friend,
It's time for us to part.
The long road ahead rises up to meet my feet.
The sunset lingers
Like the sorrow in my heart.

In spite of everything, I believe that deep down you felt about me as I did about you. If this isn't the day for us to be together, maybe in some other year, or in another lifetime. Bucky and I will always be your greatest fans.
Love,
David

Erika turned to AJ and Moshe. Tears welled up in her eyes. "What does he mean, in spite of everything? And why would I remind him of Fowler?"

AJ looked at the ceiling. "Fowler told David, as he was torturing him, that you spied for him, and that you two were, er, together. As lovers."

Erika's face went from pale to red in a heartbeat. "What? Me and Fowler? Why would David believe I lied to him?"

AJ gazed at his feet. "Well, Fowler said so, and..."

Erika said, "Stop. It doesn't matter." She waved the paper in her hand. "This says it all. He dumped me. He's gone!"

She squeezed her eyes tight in agony. "Damn, damn, damn! I should have known better. If you get really close with a friend, they go away! Will I never learn?"

AJ reached a hand out to her. "Erika, please try to..."

She waved him off. "No, no more trying. It's over!" She waved at the door. "Please leave me alone. I'm going back to sleep." She turned in her bed toward the wall, ignoring them.

AJ looked at Moshe, and both of them shrugged their shoulders helplessly. "OK, get some sleep, and we'll talk later," AJ mumbled.

"Yes, get some sleep," said Moshe, though he noticed that she didn't look like she was falling asleep. Her shoulders were heaving and shaking uncontrollably.

They both left, and closed the door quietly behind them.

Chapter 65

Erika twisted the accelerator grip of the aquasled as hard as she could, but the Mosasaur was gaining on them. She looked back to see David slipping out of his seat. He was holding his throat, as if he couldn't breathe. She tried to reach out to him, but his fingers slipped through hers, and he slid off the back of the saddle into the open maw of the monster. She saw him sliding down its throat, looking at her desperately, trying in vain to form words. She screamed.

From somewhere far away, she heard a voice calling her. She sat up in bed, confused, trying to focus on the tubes and wires growing out of her arms. She looked up into the anxious face of Aunt Marie, who was calling to her from the next bed. AJ and Moshe were standing between the two beds, looking down at her with worried faces.

She smiled weakly. "Aunt Marie? What are you doing here? What happened?"

Marie answered with a wicked grin that created new wrinkles on top of the existing ones in her weathered brown face. "The same guys that tried to kill you also beat me up. That's how I wound up in hospital."

"Kill? Beat?" Erika looked around, still in a daze. She sat up suddenly, eyes wide, and looked at AJ. "I remember what you told me." She turned back to Marie. "Are you going to be OK?"

Aunt Marie smiled bleakly. "I'm too tough to die that easily. AJ saved me and the house from burning down. I'll be fine as soon as I get outa here. Get some real medicine. Use my own potions. These doctors here don't know nothing. Quacks!"

Erika managed a faint smile. "I'm happy you made it through."

Marie rose up on one elbow, animation surging in her voice. "And best of all, I finally got to see Mokele-Mbembe. When he came out of the lagoon, he jumped right over the retaining sea fence, right into the air near where I was. And the sunshine reflected off him in every color of the rainbow, and he turned to me, and..." The old woman choked with emotion, and tears sprang into her eyes, "And he greeted me! He looked right at me, right into my heart!"

She grabbed a tissue and blew her nose. "Now do you finally believe what I been telling you 'bout him? That Aunt Marie's not just imagining things?"

Erika nodded her head as vigorously as she could manage. "Oh, yeh! Too right! I'll never doubt you again, Auntie. By the way, your charm worked wonders! That may have been the only thing besides luck that kept David and me from being Mo' food in the caves."

She looked at Marie, and bit her lower lip. "I know David left me. I read his goodbye letter." She held up both hands as Marie started to answer. "No need to say anything. I thought that...we connected in the caves, and...that it might turn out otherwise, for once. But it's OK, I've accepted it. It's past history."

She took a deep breath, and asked, "What about Bucky? Is he safe?"

AJ lowered his eyes. "Bucky's dead, Rika. That crazy cat actually attacked Fowler on the ship, trying to protect David's cabin, and got shot. One of our guys found him on the boat and brought him to this hospital last night, but he'd lost too much blood. David saw him in his last moments, and then left to bury him. The poor guy looked like a walking ghost."

"Oh, no," Erika said, a tear glistening in one eye. "Not Bucky! He loved that cat! It was his buddy. So, how is he?"

"He's OK. He got banged up a lot, like most of us did, but he's healing, and it looks like no permanent physical damage. He left this morning, to take care of insurance, get the ship returned, and finish up a bunch of paperwork." AJ added, "I'll meet him in Washington."

Erika attempted a small smile. "Tell him I'm sorry to hear about Bucky, and that I wish him well."

Auntie sat up again, grimacing at the pain of doing so. "Goddamn men, never tell you anything important! Listen, child, that man was in here for three days while you was unconscious, from morning till night, worried out of his mind while you were trying to decide between life and death. He stayed in here, and slept in his clothes on this bed when he got tired. He was on the phone getting you the best specialists, begging, threatening, whatever he had to do. He got a Dr. Schmalzried all the way from Los Angeles. He was a sight, just lookin' at you, dead quiet. Last night you started comin' awake a few times, and the doctors said you would be OK."

Marie stopped to wipe a tear out of her eye. "And then they brought Bucky in. An' AJ say he looked like...he say it make you hurt, just lookin' at him. He buried Bucky late last night, and then came in this morning and asked me to move in here from my room, keep an eye on you."

Erika took a deep breath. "I appreciate his help. But in the end, he made up some bullshit excuse to leave and get away from me."

Aunt Marie raised herself up on her elbow a little more, and looked directly at Erika. "What bullshit excuse are you talkin' about?"

Erika bit her lip. "He told AJ that I'd been fucking Fowler and lied about it. Since I never did, he had to make that up just to get away from me."

She wiped a tear from her left eye with a hand that had a catheter inserted into it. "It's OK. I knew it would happen sooner or later."

Marie furrowed her brows. "Something's not right here!" She looked at AJ. "You know something you're not telling."

AJ looked defensive. "I can't. He made me swear not to tell."

Marie sat up and started to swing her legs out of the bed. "If you don't tell everything you know right now, AJ, I'm going to get my cane and beat you like a rag doll. See if I don't."

AJ looked with alarm at Marie, and then held up both hands. "OK. OK." He turned to Erika.

"David told me—and made me promise not to tell anyone else—that Fowler showed him a videotape of you and him in his suite, doing the humpty-hump."

Erika's eyes flew wide open. "What?"

Moshe whispered quietly to himself, "Oh, no!"

AJ continued. "The video was very detailed about you getting it on with Fowler. It also showed you running around in your underwear. And even putting on and showing off that blue outfit that David bought you."

Erika was livid. "That's impossible! I gave Fowler a few good-night pecks on the cheek—all right, I kissed him and let him paw me a little, I shudder to think of it now—but I never, ever..."

Moshe piped up. "I have a confession to make."

The others turned to him. There was an urgent knocking on the door, and it started to open. AJ leaped to the door and slammed it shut. "Later!" he shouted, then turned back to Moshe. "So?"

Moshe was studying the floor very intently, and looked sheepish as he said, "Fowler asked me to do a little computer-controlled video editing for him. He had a video clip of another woman, and asked me to show him how to insert Erika's face where hers was. Then he gave me some clips of Erika—you were laughing and screaming, playing tennis or something—and had me show him how to composite it together with other scenes. I left the editing software with him. He told me it was just for a joke, for a party he was throwing for you. But the shots I saw had no nudity, I swear!"

Erika lay back on her pillows and looked at the ceiling. "He took a video of him and some other woman, and inserted my face and voice."

It was AJ's turn to look at his feet. "David said most of the footage was from the back, with you—I mean the other woman—doing a strip tease, and then approaching Fowler on a couch and going down on, er, getting intimate with him, and then shots of both of you—both of them—from behind, doing, er, things. And then there were close-ups of your face, in front of him, looking really happy."

He added. "I think I can figure out the rest. When we went through the suites in the Resort, we found a control room with monitors. There were video cameras everywhere, in all the bedrooms. He must have taken footage of you in your room."

Erika shook her head as if to clear it. "But why? Why would Fowler make a video like that? And why show it to David?"

AJ pulled up a chair and sat down. "Well, we now know he was one sick puppy. I guess if he didn't get to have you, he wanted at least a fantasy video of it."

He continued, "And as for showing it to David, he knew David cared about you. And he was vindictive to the point of insanity. That seems to have run in the family. His great-grandfather felt so slighted that his family lost their claim to nobility that he spied... that he did some really nasty things."

Erika stared into AJ's eyes. "AJ, whom do you really work for?"

AJ hesitated, but Aunt Marie looked at him sternly. "You tell that girl de' truth or I'll tell her for you!"

AJ sighed. "I work for the Central Intelligence Agency. It had an interest in finding out who headed the spy network that told the German Navy where to send their U-Boats, which is why it funded David. The U-Boat had documents showing that Emmett Fowler, Reggie's great-grandfather, was the spy."

He continued, "The sub was bringing the spy what he wanted for his services, which was gold coins and a crown that had belonged to his family at one time."

Erika's brows furrowed. "If Fowler convinced David that I had betrayed him, why did he risk his life to save me?"

Marie's eyes brightened. "Long time ago, he asked me about you. Said he was afraid to trust anyone again. An' I told him, you gotta trust somebody! Las' thing he told me afore he left, he said, 'Auntie, I believe she has a good heart, even if she's afraid to show it. But if I look at her right now, I'll see her with Fowler, and think of him killing Bucky. I need time away.'"

Erika beat her blanket with her fist in frustration, making blips on the monitor behind her jump up and down. "But that doesn't change anything! He walked out on me!"

Marie eyes narrowed as they focused on Erika. AJ slowly slid off his chair and backed a few feet away. The temperature in the room seemed to drop 10 degrees.

"Let me review this for you, young lady. See it from his point of view, if you can get out of your own head."

She ticked off on her fingers.

"First, he sees the video of you freakin' the ears off his worst enemy, the one who killed his best friend. Now, I know it's easy to doctor up photographs, but video is usually straight-on evidence—unless you have a professional messin' with it." She scowled at Moshe, who returned to his intense study of the floor.

"Second, he had the chance to go after the guys dragging the treasure off, shooting them and getting it back. Instead, he turns away from them, to save you."

"Oh, my God," Erika breathed. "He gave up on the gold for me?"

Marie continued, unstoppable. "Yes, he comes and rescues you, the one he thinks betrayed him, and almost gets killed doing it."

"Third, he brings you here to the hospital and watches over you like a mother hen until he's sure you're OK."

Marie looked her straight in the eye. "Would *you* do that for somebody you think lied to you?" Her gaze bored directly into Erika. "Child, what do you want from a man?"

Tears sprang out of Erika's eyes. "I'm...I don't know what to do."

"What do you really want, child?" Marie's voice was suddenly gentle. "Do you want to be right—or do you want to be happy?"

Erika shook her head. "I can't even think straight. I remember DuBois, and heard something about monsters attacking. Was that the Mosasaurs?"

AJ nodded. "Four of them. They really tore up the place."

She addressed Moshe. "Moshe, the only way I'm going to let you stay alive, mate, is if you got some good footage of my Mosasaurs."

Moshe looked crestfallen. "I didn't have a camera with me. But...I have something for you!"

He went to a closet in the corner of the room and pulled a briefcase out of it. He placed it on Erika's bed and opened it to reveal a laptop, which he promptly turned on.

"What's this?" she asked.

"There's a note," he said, pointing to an envelope taped to the laptop.

Erika ripped it open. Inside it said, in David's handwriting:

Rika,

Here's some content for your next presentation.
Go get 'em!
--Your fan club

AJ leaned over to click on one of the folders on the screen, and a video clip of a Mosasaur surging over the barrier to the lagoon started to play.

"This is something David pulled off, with some help from me. As far as I know, this laptop has every photograph taken of the Mosasaurs in the lagoon, every bit of video footage, every record from the surveillance cameras. He didn't allow anyone off that island with a single picture of your critters. The public has not seen one iota of any of this. It's all here!" He smiled at her proudly.

Erika was open-mouthed. Her eyes threatened to bulge out of her head. Slowly she formed the words. "No one else...has seen this?"

AJ continued. "And the hospital is holding parts of the Mosasaur that got killed. David said it was muscle tissue from the animal that crashed into the power plant."

Erika was trying to absorb the enormity of this. "I have tissue from an animal that's supposed to have been extinct for 65 million years. Is there enough for me to put a couple of slices under a microscope?"

AJ nodded. "Yeah, there should be enough for your microscope. David put ten pounds of it with your name on it in a freezer. Plus nearly 15 pounds of bones."

Erika looked at him, her mind reeling. "There's ten kilos of live Mosasaur. In the freezer."

AJ nodded. "Well, not quite live, but frozen, in great shape. David said it was mostly from the tail section."

Erika looked around at all of them. "And no one else knows any of this?"

Moshe nodded his head. "Nobody. AJ and a couple of his friends threatened a bunch of reporters with automatic weapons at the doors to the hospital. That seemed to discourage the rest of them."

Erika said slowly to herself, "Oh...my...God!"

Chapter 66

An hour later, AJ walked down the hall with Marie, who moved slowly, with the help of a cane.

She sighed. "Too bad she got sidetracked into the photos before she decided what to do about David. Now she's gonna be totally focused on that, believing it's what will make her life all happy, and a big success."

AJ looked at her suspiciously. "Did David really say that he still cared for her, no matter what?"

Marie chuckled. "Not exactly. The poor boy was in shock. But I know it's what he would have said."

She walked a few more steps. "How did you know?"

AJ winked at her, "If he'd really said it, he would have started with, 'Bucky thinks that...'"

Marie laughed sadly. "Bucky sure was an angel, a messenger. Guess the messages were going both ways."

"Poor guy," AJ said. "I think he'd rather have that cat back than the 100 million dollars."

Marie looked at him. "Son, you just gave me an idea."

Chapter 67

David took the elevator to the fourth floor and rang the bell of Apartment 423. The door was opened by Leah, who squealed as she gave him an enormous smile and hugged him tightly. She released him, and he was then almost bowled over by AJ, who grasped his right hand and slammed his chest into him.

"It is so good to see you," AJ grinned. Leah nodded behind him.

"Same here," David replied, moving into the apartment and looking around. "Hey, not too bad." He looked out of a glass door onto a balcony. "You have a river view here?"

"Yeah, my dad bought this long ago, while he was stationed here, and then gave it to me. I kept it even while I was living in the Caribbean," AJ replied.

They all stood on the balcony, watching the majestic sojourn of the Potomac River coursing by and savoring the moment. Leah put an arm around David. "I'm so sorry about Bucky," she said.

David nodded. "Thank you."

She smiled sadly. "At least he had a beautiful funeral."

"Yes, he did," David said, but then turned to ask her. "How would you know? You were still in the hospital."

"Oh, I missed the first one," Leah replied brightly. "But everybody had such a good time, they had another one a week later, and invited the half of the island that wasn't there before. They're thinking of making it an annual event."

David shook his head, chuckling. He turned to AJ and said, "I've got something for you." He unzipped a compartment in his wheeled suitcase. "You've been wanting to do something to make your father proud, and get a medal even he would look up to, right?"

AJ started to protest, but David held up a hand. "Let's be honest, here."

AJ hung his head. "Yeah. I suppose so."

David pulled a manila envelope from his suitcase, and told AJ, "What you did at the Resort was insanely courageous, and probably saved Anguilla many lives and much suffering. That should make your dad proud a dozen times over. This award might help, too."

He stepped back and handed AJ the envelope. "Let me be the first to congratulate you. You have been awarded the Anguillan Medal of Honor."

AJ opened the envelope. It bore the seal of Government House, and contained a letter from the Governor, asking him to come to

Anguilla to receive an award from a grateful island, to be presented in the name of the government of Anguilla and the British Crown.

AJ looked puzzled. "I've never heard of this award."

David nodded. "It's brand new. Just as the Victoria Cross was created for actions during the Crimean War, and the American Medal of Honor for the Civil War, this was created by Anguilla for what you did."

AJ looked at David. "I'm not accepting this unless you and the team get one, too."

David grinned. "I figured you'd say that. The rest of us are getting the award in silver."

AJ looked stunned. David continued, "Your medal is huge, an ounce of solid gold, on a ribbon with the flags of Anguilla and Great Britain on it. No medal your father has can even come close to it."

Leah told AJ, "Time to celebrate. Could you get some champagne and glasses, please, AJ? Let me talk with David a moment."

AJ went off to the kitchen as Leah led David onto the balcony. Her eyes were moist. "Thank you for doing that."

"Nothing more than he deserved."

She looked at his throat. "What happened to that big gold coin you always wear around your neck?"

David unconsciously touched his neck, and then smiled. "I guess it found a better home."

She kissed him on the cheek. "You're a good friend."

He looked at her. "What's your situation? Are you two, er, together?"

She looked out at the water. "Not yet. I'm staying at a hotel here, and officially, I still work for him. We're scheduled to meet with his boss. I'm worried about what'll happen with that back-stabber."

David took her hands in his. "I have an idea for a win-win situation for both of you. Will you back my play, even if it's risky?"

She replied without a trace of doubt. "Whatever will help AJ. No matter what."

David sighed. "Someday, maybe, I'll have someone like you watching my back."

He moved into the living room. AJ was pouring champagne into glasses.

He spoke firmly. "AJ, it's time for you to retire from the Agency."

AJ looked uneasy. "I'm probably getting fired from it. Bedrosian's scheduled a meeting on Friday, at Langley."

"Fuck him. You're going to act first. Call a meeting for tomorrow. Not in Langley, where they're in control, but at the office in Rosslyn. Get the Director out there, and tell him to bring Bedrosian. And then make your demands."

"You think I can get the Director to come? Are you crazy?"

"No, I'm not crazy. I'm your attorney. Let's drink this bubbly and then go for a walk, and go over the details."

Leah waited anxiously. An hour later, they reappeared. She was relieved to see they were both laughing.

"As your attorney, I believe that's your best strategy," David concluded as they walked into the condominium.

Leah laughed. "You sound like the lawyer character in *Fear and Loathing in Las Vegas.*"

AJ looked at her. "David advised me on what to do next. It means quitting the Agency. Do you..."

Leah nodded. "The answer is yes. Do it!"

David grinned and turned to AJ. "I almost forgot. You should be able to get another medal out of this. The Director can give you this one, no sweat." He wrote on a piece of paper, and handed it to his friend.

AJ looked at the paper. "But how will I get him to come out here? I can't just call him."

David shook his head. "Talk with his secretary, and explain what we talked about. She controls his schedule, and can make up a story. Convince her."

AJ nodded. "All right, I'll call right now. She and I are tight. She'll do it for me."

He grabbed David by the arm. "I almost forgot to tell you in all the excitement. You're in real danger."

"What?" David asked.

"Fowler and several of his goons came into Miami yesterday. We found out about it too late to grab them. They may come after you, or Mrs. Weinstock, or both of you." He walked to a safe behind a desk and opened it. "Here's the package you asked me to take care of."

David took the bag and glanced inside at the wood box with its precious cargo. "I'd better fly up right after the meeting."

"Hold on," AJ said. He returned to the safe. "While you were busy, I did a little homework as well."

He handed David a black container, which opened to reveal a Glock .40 caliber automatic with shoulder holster.

"I pulled a few favors at the US Marshall's office. They work closely with the Agency." He added, sourly, "As opposed to the FBI, which hates us."

He handed David a badge with some paperwork, and put a hand on his shoulder. "You are now a deputy US Marshall, with a permit to carry that weapon anywhere you want, concealed."

David hugged him. "Thanks. That helps a lot." He took out his phone. "Right now, I need to call an old friend, a Marine Corps general, to ask a favor."

"By the way," AJ added. "Our radar stations may have picked up where that helicopter went down. Don't get your hopes up, but we have a shot at it. I'll let you know."

Leah pulled David aside again, and whispered into his ear, "You know, you're more than a friend, you're family. When you get to your Nana's, you'll have a surprise waiting for you." She smiled mysteriously.

He whispered into her ear. "I've got one for you, too. After he gives his little speech tomorrow, he'll ask you to go to Anguilla with him, to live together. If he starts stuttering or fumbling for words, just say yes. But promise you'll act real surprised."

Leah broke into a huge grin, and whispered, "Oh, I promise, all right!"

David pulled out his cell phone and started dialing.

Chapter 68

The three friends exited the Metro station in Rosslyn and walked up to street level. It was a typical Summer Washington day, already hot and humid at 10 in the morning. All of them wore suits and carried briefcases.

"So you two are not going to tell me why we're meeting with our boss and the director?" Leah asked.

"Nope. I want you to look as if this is news to you, so they can't hold you responsible, in case things go wrong. And David's here because he's an outsider, so they can't pull rank on him," AJ replied. He turned to David. "Can you give us a minute?"

David nodded and walked ahead. AJ took a deep breath as she looked directly into his eyes, waiting.

"When I caught up with you at the Resort, and we held each other, and started, er, kissing." He gulped. "Did you really mean it, that is, if we weren't working together, we could, er, be together?"

A slow smile spread over her face. "Yes, I really meant it."

"Would you be willing to quit your job? At one time, it was the most important thing in your life, for you and your family."

"Absolutely. After you saved me, I realized what was really important in my life."''

"Last question. Do you trust me?"

"You saved my life and risked yours, like a crazy man. You don't even have to ask."

"Really?"

"Yes!"

"Then it's time to meet with the Director."

They came to a tall office building. It had no CIA markings on the outside. It seemed to belong to a bank, or one of the many other businesses in the area. David met them in the lobby, and they showed their ID's to a guard, who looked at a list and then made a phone call. Nodding at them, he offered a sign-in sheet.

"One thing I've got to ask," Leah said as they headed to the elevators. "Why are we meeting both the Director and Bedrosian here, instead of at headquarters?"

"They're on their home ground at Langley," David replied. "They can call in resources. Such as guards. And they have huge offices that are meant to intimidate you. Here, we're more on even ground."

They entered the elevator, and AJ swiped a card. When the doors opened, another guard looked at their IDs and entered their names on a list. AJ swiped his card to get through a door, then led them toward a conference room with glass walls and windows looking out over the Potomac River.

They saw both John Whelan, the Director of the CIA, and Ed Bedrosian seated at the head of a long conference table. Both men wore scowls on their faces. They were clearly unhappy. Bedrosian stared at David. "Who the hell are you?"

David handed his card to Whelan. "I'm of counsel to AJ. You can call General McCracken at Southern Command to find out who I am. Sandy knows me, and can vouch for me."

Whelan nodded. "Yes, I know Sandy. Let's get started."

Bedrosian snarled at AJ, "Are you out of your fucking mind? I just found out that you requested this meeting. You know it's against Agency regulations to bypass the chain of command. Your ass is on the line."

"I know that," AJ replied, coolly. "Fortunately, I have a few friends who impressed on the Director how important this meeting is."

"If I'd known about this ahead of time, I would have fired your asses on the spot," Bedrosian growled. "What is this all about?"

"You'll find out soon enough," AJ replied coolly. "Just pay attention."

Bedrosian took out his cell phone and started speed dialing a call. David reached him in a few quick steps, and snatched the cell phone out of his hand. As Bedrosian looked on slack-jawed, David tossed it to AJ, who slammed the phone down on the table, breaking it. He then flung it into the opposite corner of the room. He beamed at Leah. "I've always wanted to do that!"

Bedrosian was furious. He stood, staring down at the Director. "Did you see what he just did?"

David spoke calmly to Whelan. "Are you going to tell your manic attack dog to shut up now, so we can talk?"

Bedrosian turned to him with growing disbelief in his eyes. "*What* did you just say?"

"I'm trying to save the Director's career and reputation," David replied.

"Did you just call me a dog?" Bedrosian sputtered, leaning over the table.

Whelan, a canny veteran of Washington politics, had sensed an undertone. He turned to Bedrosian, and said, "Sit down and be quiet!"

"What?" Bedrosian stammered.

The Director said nothing. He merely raised one eyebrow. Bedrosian sat down quickly. The Director turned back to David. He looked at his watch.

David smiled. He said nothing for all of two minutes, pulling folders out of his briefcase and making the others wait. He also looked at his watch.

Bedrosian opened his mouth to speak. The Director raised both eyebrows this time. Bedrosian closed his mouth quickly.

"I have three Agenda items," David intoned. "First, I wanted to give you the chance to commend these two brave agents. Agents AJ and Leah pulled off a successful raid of a drug cartel, one that was on the point of taking over a Caribbean island. The raid resulted in the death or capture of six major drug kingpins and three suspected leaders of terrorist organizations, as well as dozens of their associates. It also managed to seize a number of laptops and documents that they did not have time to destroy."

"I am well aware of Operation Night Train," the Director said, nodding at Bedrosian. "The ADO Caribbean has already briefed me on this very successful operation."

David gave the Assistant Director of Operations for the Caribbean a moment to beam and soak in the Director's praise before he said, "Did he also mention that it was done without his leadership or permission? That he had absolutely forbidden it? In fact, it should be called Operation Bullshit, because it had no name, it was AJ and a group of his friends who went in—against the specific and absolute orders of the ADO Caribbean!"

The Director's forehead started growing wrinkles. He looked sternly at Bedrosian. "No, I wasn't aware of that. It seems a few details got left out."

"I had planned this operation, but at a later time," Bedrosian whined. "I told the agent to wait, until we could catch even more of both the drug cartel and the El Mahoud leaders. He endangered the whole situation by acting too soon. I didn't put this in the report because—"

He stopped as the Director held up a hand. "I want to hear more from them," he said.

"They had captured agent Thomson, and were torturing her to death to get information," David continued, looking briefly at Leah, who nodded in assent. "This means they could have gotten information out of her, and then bolted, taking all of their computers and documents with them."

David pulled a sheet of paper from a file and glanced at it. "Which reminds me. What kind of information did you get from Operation Night Train, Director?"

Bedrosian sputtered, "That's classified. It's..."

David interrupted him. "I didn't ask you. Director, why would you classify...nothing of any value?"

Whelan turned to Bedrosian, who turned pale as he responded, "We're still decrypting and analyzing that. It's taking time."

David looked up and said, "Actually, John...may I call you John?"

Whelan nodded. A corner of his mouth started to twitch.

David continued, "Please call me David. John, it'll take a lot of time, like, forever. In fact, you'll never get the data from the Resort."

Whelan started to smile as his ADO sputtered next to him. "And why would that be, David?"

"Because I have all of it, John." David pushed a sheet of paper across.

"And what is this?" Whelan scanned the paper.

"It's authorization from the local government authority for me to appropriate all relevant documentation and data. Signed by a Captain John Baisley." David chuckled. "I felt I had to leave something behind for Bedrosian's flatfooted minions, several days later. So I left the restaurant's computers. You may want to tell your decryption team to let up. Those "menus" they're trying to crack really are just menus."

Bedrosian looked at the door as David noted, "Your ADO was trying to call in the guards to arrest me. I don't think the rent-a-cops downstairs will do that great a job, do you, John?"

Bedrosian stared at David's briefcase. "If you have that data with you, I demand that..."

David interrupted, "You can't demand shit!"

The ADO slammed a fist on the table. "This is a matter of national security. If you don't hand over the documents, you will be..."

Whelan snarled at him, "I told you to shut up!" He turned back. "David, would you be so kind as to give me the documents?"

David smiled. "You, personally, I'll give a copy to, gladly. But not to any of the assholes you have working for you. I do have three, er, requests in return." He glanced at AJ and Leah, who leaned forward from their red leather chairs, wide-eyed.

Whelan waved his arm magnanimously. "Pray continue."

David read from a sheet of paper. "I took the trouble of typing them up, so we can sign them. The first is that you sign this Memorandum of Understanding between you and Southern Command, agreeing this was a joint operation with Sandy. If you do so, *he* will send you a copy of the data."

Whelan glanced at the paper. "He already has a copy of this?"

David chuckled. "Yes. I'm a big believer in insurance." He glanced up. "Got betrayed by an ex. You know how it is."

Whelan nodded. "Oh, yeah. We've all been there."

David continued, "Second. I understand you're planning to promote Ed there and hand him an award. Something about pulling off a multi-service, multi-national operation, the first one in the Caribbean with this level of success. You have reconsidered, and are going to demote him and post him somewhere as far from the Caribbean as possible. I think Somalia or somewhere with lots of desert would be appropriate."

Bedrosian sputtered as he rose from his seat. "You're not going to let this, this, this..."

The Director held up his hand again, and Bedrosian fell back into his seat. "You said you had three points to make," Whelan said. "What was the third one?"

"You are going to give Leah and AJ both promotions. You are going to insert full credit for—what was it, Operation Night Watch—into their records, and erase anything negative your ADO has inserted. You'll commend these brave agents for outstanding work, and award them the Intelligence Star and the Exceptional Service Medal. You are then going to give them honorable discharges from the service, with two years of pay, free of taxes."

Bedrosian stopped sputtering for a moment. He stared at them with pure disbelief in his eyes.

The Director had the ghost of a smile cross his face. "Those are three, er, interesting points. I guess I have no choice on the first point. But why should I agree to items two and three?" he asked. "Even though I'm grateful to you, do you have any idea of what you're asking?"

"Oh, yes, we do," David replied cheerfully. "It's quid pro quo, because we're doing you a huge favor!"

"I refuse to hear any more of this..." Bedrosian shouted, rising up once more.

The Director turned on him and snarled. "If you don't shut up, I will personally kick your ass down the hall!" He turned back to David. "A favor?" He asked. He drummed his fingers on the table.

"Yes, a favor," David replied. "AJ, take it away."

AJ rose, and spoke heatedly. "We're granting you a favor, because I'm not going to do what I'd really like to do. What I should do." He started to smile again, this time bitterly.

"Which is?" the Director prompted. He did not glance at his watch this time.

"Which is to expose Bedrosian, and you, as his boss, to the media in both the Caribbean and the US. Let me count the ways." He raised his left hand, and started ticking off the points on his fingers.

"One. Bedrosian lied about who started this operation, and how it went down. That dishonors the brave men that risked their lives—on their own initiative—to pull it off."

"Two. When I told Bedrosian that Leah—agent Thomson—was in direct threat of being tortured and killed, and other, er, helpers of the Agency were, as well, I was told that those were 'acceptable losses.' That would not sit well with members of the Agency."

He turned to Leah. "I was ordered to abandon you. I was also directed not to tell you that, under any circumstances. I want you to know that I never even considered following that directive, not for one moment."

Leah's eyes softened, but then her face turned hard as she swung it in Bedrosian's direction.

Bedrosian started to open his mouth. This time the Director slammed his fist on the table and glared at him. He closed it quickly.

David smiled grimly. "Mr. Bedrosian was probably about to say, 'So what?'" He got up and paced around the table. "So what if we lied? So what if we deceived our allied agencies and countries? So what if we hung an agent out to dry, to suffer horribly, and then die? It's all been done before."

He whirled, and faced the Director. "Which is why we come to the final point. Are you aware of the nature of the intelligence AJ's been gathering in the Caribbean?"

The Director nodded. "Of course, I get regular reports on it. We get HUMINT from him and other agents throughout the region, including photos and covertly recorded interviews. It's all quite normal, other than that those countries are not, er, formally aware that we are spy–, ah, that we are collecting intelligence within them. What's your point?"

"What about the X-rated videos, and the, ah, special personnel you've hired?" asked AJ.

"The X-rated videos?" the Director asked. Bedrosian's color suddenly turned ashen.

"Yes, the videos," AJ said. "Part of my job was to get videos of prominent political and business leaders in the Caribbean, especially visitors from the US and other countries, as they were, ah, conducting themselves in compromising positions in houses of ill repute or similar locations." He paused a moment, then continued.

"When such Persons of Interest did not commit such acts on their own volition, we hired certain women, and a few men, to take the action to their hotel rooms, and ply them with potent substances. We learned all these tricks from our friends in Russia and East Germany. With the video footage from our vidcams, we had great material for blackmail, either right away or in the future."

AJ looked directly into the Director's eyes. "I was the person in charge of collecting the video footage, under cover of being a wine and spirits distributor for the Caribbean. I kept copies of some of them, with records of where and when they were taken, and who the subjects were. I left these with trusted friends, to be released to the news media this evening, for the 6 o'clock news, in case we can't come to an agreement, or in case..." AJ looked directly at Bedrosian, "...some unfortunate accident should befall Leah and me."

David looked at the Director. "No offense meant to you, of course, John," he said.

"No offense taken," the Director mumbled. He looked like his mind was racing furiously.

David waved his arms in the direction of Washington, DC, across the Potomac. They could see the Washington Monument in the distance.

"You know the Washington culture, John," he said. "They're willing to forgive little things like getting dozens or even thousands of people killed, lying to allies, things like that. But anything to do with sex...is the kiss of death." He paused for dramatic effect.

"And hiring hookers—including male hookers—and shooting pornos of prominent people, quite a few of whom have been photographed with their arms around the President, would make you, Director, the Chief National Pimp." He smiled. "In fact, 'Chief National Pimp' is the term I used in writing up the report I left to be released to news sources."

Bedrosian was gasping for air, barely able to speak. "He's bluffing," he said.

AJ took out his cell phone, pushed a speed dial button, and then pushed the speakerphone button. "S'up?" came a voice with a deep Jamaican accent.

"Hi, Jimal," AJ said cheerfully. "This is me, AJ. I'm with a couple of gentlemen here in the US. Could you tell us who you are?"

"Yah. I'm a news anchor on Kingston's CVM-TV channel."

"And did you get my email?"

"Yah, mon, I'm to get a package from our friend if I don' hear from you by 6:00 tonight."

"Thank you, Jimal. I'll call you back," AJ replied.

He turned to the Director. "Any questions? Would you like time to check out this source?"

"No, that won't be necessary," Whelan replied. He shook his head. "I've been called a lot of things in this town, but Chief National Pimp..." He shook his head again, and smiled ruefully.

"Nothing personal," AJ said. "Nothing personal—to you, Director," he amended himself.

Whelan looked at his hands for a moment, and then back up at David, AJ and Leah. "All right, I take all your points. But I'm not going to demote Bedrosian."

He turned to his Assistant Director of Operations for the Caribbean. "You're fired! Turn in your ID card and get out. Don't go to your office. It'll be sealed."

The ADO Caribbean opened his mouth, but no sound came out.

"Now, I said!" intoned the Director.

Bedrosian gathered his papers, got up and walked out the door. He seemed to have visibly shrunk in size.

Whelan turned to David. "I'll do the other things you suggested. Not because of anything you might have to release to the media, but because it's the right thing to do." He beamed at him.

David replied enthusiastically, "I would never think anything different, John." He pushed papers at the Director. "Please sign here. And here. And here." He counter-signed and pulled back his copies. "You should have your docs from the general within a couple of days." He motioned toward AJ and Leah. "You're losing two valuable employees. You might think about..."

"Great idea!" the Director said. "Your severance checks will be ready for you by tomorrow. But instead of reading you out, how about we make both of you consultants?" He hastened to add, "No need to do any of the, er, undesirable projects you might have done before."

AJ looked at Leah, who nodded. "OK. Consultants. And Leah no longer works for me."

"Glad to hear it," Whelan said. "I have your first assignment. After you take some time off. I'd like you to read the documents we got from the U-Boat, and do a report on Operation Electric Blue. We might learn something we can use in the modern day."

AJ hooked a thumb at David. "Sign him up, too. He can translate, and he's the history buff."

The Director said, "Done." He took a black Amex credit card out of his wallet, and handed it to AJ. "Dinner tonight is on me. You might want to take Leah to a really nice place, to discuss, er, the future."

AJ looked at the card and accepted it. "We'll do that, thanks."

They all shook hands, gathered their briefcases and left the conference room. David looked back to see the Director talking on his cell phone. He turned and stuck his head back into the room.

"By the way," he said. "At least one folder will stay in the safe of a very close friend. To use in case anything ever happens to us." He smiled grimly. "We all know how dangerous Caribbean roads can be. Fatal accidents happen all the time."

The Director terminated the call on his cell phone. "Of course," he said. "Please—for the sake of the Agency—all of you, please drive carefully."

David smiled at him, and joined Leah and AJ in the hallway. They signed out and got into the elevator.

They did not speak until they were on the sidewalk. AJ let out a whoosh of air.

"Well, that went well," he said.

"No kidding," David replied. "I was holding my breath there, at times."

"I don't know how I can ever thank you," AJ said, with feeling.

"You saved Erika and me," was the reply. "I was already pre-thanked for today!" He hugged both of them, and said, "I've got calls to make. Have a great evening!"

Leah waved farewell to him, and then looked at AJ, her eyes shining. "You came for me against direct orders?" she asked.

AJ took both of her hands in his. "I had to. Else I could never have done this."

He looked her directly in the eye. "I want to, er, I..." He swallowed as his throat went dry.

She looked at him encouragingly. "Yes. You want to..."

He looked desperate. He took out his cell phone and thumbed various buttons on its dial. "Wait a minute. I recorded this."

He grew frustrated. "I'm trying to find the right video clip. It's about..."

She smiled as she touched his face softly with her fingers. "You want us to be together as a couple?"

He nodded.

Her smile grew broader, and she flashed her teeth, which gleamed in the sunlight. "And you'd like me to come to Anguilla, and help pick out a house, and move in together?"

He nodded nonstop.

She took both of his hands in hers. "Thank you for asking me. What a wonderful surprise!"

He smiled nervously. "I was going to discuss it over dinner. But I can't wait any longer. I almost lost you once. I know we don't know each other that well yet. We haven't really even kissed each other properly."

Leah laughed softly and put her arms around his neck. "Let's get that handled right away. I won't even tell you how often I've dreamed about this."

They held each other tightly, their lips meeting gently with little kisses that slowly grew more meaningful, as the busy flow of pedestrians swirled around them. A few paused to look at them, and smiled at the sight.

Chapter 69

David pulled his wheeled suitcase behind him as he walked up to the impressive formal building next to Central Park. He was frustrated that his flight of the night before had been canceled after a two-hour wait, and he'd had to catch an early-morning plane instead.

He looked up and smiled ruefully as his eyes fixed on the floor where he used to own a condominium. That seemed like another lifetime. He walked in, and the guard in the lobby recognized him immediately.

"Hello, Mr. Kilmer," he said. "Nice to see you again. We miss having you live here."

David shook his hand. "Hello, Hank. I'm glad you still remember me. I'm afraid I'm a few million short to be living here right now."

The guard seemed embarrassed for him, David sensed, and didn't know what to say in return, so he simply said, "I'm here to see Mrs. Weinstock. Could you call her to admit me in?"

The guard was solicitous. "No need to do that, Mr. Kilmer. You go right on up. She's been expecting you."

David was about to ring the bell at 21A when the door opened, and a smiling, elderly face appeared. It was attached to a bent but spry figure holding a walking cane.

"Hello, Nana," David said.

"David!" Emma Weinstock shrieked, and rushed forward to embrace him, dropping her cane in the process. "I was so worried about you!"

David embraced her, which took some effort, as he had to bend over to accommodate the much shorter woman, and said, "No, Nana, I cheated death once more. Let's go inside, and I'll tell you all about it. And I have something for you that I hope you like."

He picked up both her cane and the handle of his wheelie and held her hand as he escorted her back into the apartment and to an overstuffed couch.

They sat down, and Emma indicated a tea service on the low coffee table in front of them.

"Ready for some tea?" she inquired, joy radiating from her face as she pushed a giant plate full of cookies toward him. "Here, have something. They're fresh baked. Eat, eat!"

David smiled, and took a sip of tea. "Anything warm sounds good right now. It's a lot colder up here than in the islands, and I don't travel by heated limousine these days."

"Oh, David," Emma said, concern evident in her voice. "I heard a lot of people got killed down there!"

David smiled weakly. "There were some exciting moments. But all's well that ends well. The only really sad thing is...Bucky is... dead."

"Oh!" Emma's penciled-in eyebrows shot up. "I'm so sorry about Bucky. I know what he meant to you." She touched his hand. "But, hand me my cane and stay on the couch. I'll be right back."

He settled on the couch and refilled his teacup. Emma reentered the room with a dark red cat carrier, and placed it on the coffee table. She opened its front door. For a moment, nothing happened.

David's jaw went slack. "You don't mean..." he started to say, when suddenly a small gray head appeared from out of the door. Rather than emit a customary *Meow*, it tried its best attempt at a guttural growl, but sounded like a sparrow gargling.

David smiled, but shook his head. "Nana, I appreciate it, but I can't replace Bucky. No cat will ever be like him again. When I first saw him, he ran right across some boxes straight toward me, eyes fixed, not noticing he'd suddenly run out of boxes, and—"

As he spoke, the smoky-gray kitten emerged from the cat carrier. Rather than glance around, it took one look at David and made a beeline for him. David stared as the kitten ran over the table, still staring intently, and then, like a cartoon character, kept right on running when it ran out of table. It landed on its head on the carpet, where it lay for a moment, stunned.

David's jaw dropped. He pointed at it. "That. That's what he did." He looked down at the kitten, which appeared dazed as it slowly got up.

"My God, it's the spitting image of Bucky," he said.

Emma smiled. "It should be. It's his brother."

"Wha-a-t?"

"Your friends Leah and Marie checked Bucky's body at the graveyard, and found he had a chip implanted in him, something that's commonly done with valuable purebred cats. They got a scanner and read the ID in his body and called me. I found out he was a champion Maine Coon Cat that had escaped from his breeder at a cat show here. His registered name was Champion Roland, Prince of Maine."

"Bucky? Champion Roland?"

Emma continued. "His parents produced another litter about two months ago. This kitten had been sold already, long before birth, but I have my connections. Favors were called in. Threats were made. Money changed hands. And here you are."

David noticed a letter attached to the cat carrier, and set the kitten in his lap while he opened it.

"It's from Aunt Marie," he said, and read it.

My beloved David,

The spirit of Bucky was strong, and stayed on the hilltop where you two spent so much time together. I asked that he remain with us for another lifetime, in this kitten, and he said yes.

Captain Baisley flew up to New York to pick up the kitten and bring it down here. Bucky's spirit merged with that of his brother, and then he flew back to New York. The whole island chipped in to pay for the travel. We are all hoping to see both of you again soon.

All my love,
Marie

David's eyes moistened. He held up the purring kitten to speak to it. "Well, I would never call Auntie Marie a liar. If she says you're the genuine article, that's who you are."

The kitten unceremoniously licked David's nose. He laughed. "I guess...I guess we get a second chance." He looked at Emma. "You were the one who first told me that, Nana." He gave her a hug. "Thank you."

She smiled. "I was happy to do it. What will you name him?"

David laughed as the little cat crawled up his chest and settled onto his shoulder.

"What else? He acts just like him. It has to be Bucky, Junior."

His eyes grew moist as he stroked the little cat. "I thought I had lost you, forever."

Emma patted his arm with one of her frail old hands. "It looks like he's taken you on again."

David smiled ruefully. "Yeah, except I'm sitting in a Park Avenue apartment right now, instead of lying drunk next to JJ Sullivan's Pub in the rain."

He turned to her. "Now, it's your turn to sit. I can't wait any longer."

David parked the kitten on the couch, to a protest of "Urk-urk," and opened the zippers on his suitcase as Emma refilled his tea. "Here it is," he said proudly, as he presented her with a package wrapped in a silk cloth. "I'm afraid I don't have the fancy wrappings this box originally came in. The best I could do was to buy a silk scarf from a street vendor."

He beamed at her as she slowly unwrapped the package. "A friend of mine smuggled it into the country. Not that it matters, since there's a law that allows property of Holocaust survivors to be returned to them without paying any taxes or duty."

David involuntarily glanced at Emma's forearm. For a moment, he imagined he could see faint blue numbers on the wrinkled, parchment-thin skin.

Emma's eyes shone as she peeled aside the final layer of silk to reveal an inlaid walnut box with a glass front door, behind which rested the coronet, a magnificent tiara-like crown studded with precious stones that immediately started flashing, reflecting the ceiling lights by projecting bright white and blue and red stars.

David gingerly opened the glass door, extracted the coronet and proudly presented it to her. "This is for you."

"Oh, my!" she said, holding it in one hand and touching the other one reflexively to her lips. "The last time I saw this was 1942. It's my princess crown. I can still remember after all these years."

She clasped the coronet to her breast and closed her eyes a few moments. When she re-opened her eyelids, she had a faraway expression, and a tear emerged.

"When I was eight, we lived in Rome, in a large apartment not unlike this one. One week I was sick, and home from school, and Papa came home that night. I didn't get to see him often, because he was always traveling for work—he was in the jewelry business, and had stores and clients all over the continent. He told me I was his little princess, and that he had gotten me this as my crown. He told me stories about every stone set in here."

She touched a large, faceted red stone that flashed bright fire, as if it had glowing magma inside it. "This ruby used to belong to a maharajah in Bangalore, he told me," she said. "I remember..."

Emma drifted off for a few minutes, and David quietly sipped his tea, content to let her reminisce.

She suddenly came back to the present. "Like I said, Papa wasn't home a lot, and when he was, he seldom spoke. My mother was very religious. She was usually in her room reading or praying, and they said almost nothing to each other. The only things he really loved, I think, were fine jewelry—and me. So it was a special treat when he came home, and sat on my bed at night, and told me stories about every stone in this crown. It was like my very own Andersen's Fairy Tales."

She took both of David's strong brown hands into her pale, frail ones. "Thank you so much, David. I know what you must have gone through to find this. You've brought back my childhood!"

David held on to her hands and slowly lifted her to her feet and walked her over to a full-length ornate mirror on the wall. As she faced the mirror, he carefully lifted up the coronet and placed it on her head, brushing a few gray hairs aside. He bit his lip for a moment, took a deep breath, and said, grandly, "I now crown you—princess—of Park Avenue!"

He released the coronet and stepped back, looking at her blissful image in the mirror. "I just realized. I brought back the treasure, after all." His throat was dry. "For all the kindness you showed me over the years. I'm so glad I was able to...that you believed in me..."

Emma turned around and placed a finger on his lips. "Sh-h-h. It's my place to thank you."

She turned back to the mirror, and her face took on a faraway look. "Oh, my," she said slowly as she stroked the coronet, touching one jewel after the other.

"The last time I saw this was over 70 years ago." She spoke slowly. "Papa was home. That night he told me about this green sapphire"—she pointed to a large stone on the front of the crown—"and this ruby." She gingerly touched a large red stone that seemed to burn and fling sparks into the room. "He told me a red sapphire was called a ruby. Then he put me to bed and kissed me good night. He turned at the door and said, 'Sweet dreams, princess.' That was the last time he ever spoke to me. The next morning, men in dark uniforms came and took him away, and this box and the crown with it."

She held the coronet up to the light, which reflected off the intricately carved gold and danced within the embedded jewels. "I never thought I'd see it again."

She looked at the box. "This even has a secret compartment," she said. "Papa and I would hide notes for each other in it." She twisted one of the carved pieces of wood, and a drawer sprang forward. "Look, there's a large envelope in it."

"And that envelope belongs to me, thank you," intoned a voice behind them.

Chapter 70

They whirled around to see Fowler and two other men standing in the apartment. Both of his companions had the look of bodyguards, with broad shoulders and built-in facial scowls. One wore a long brown leather coat, the other an identical one in black. Fowler and the brown-coated man both had guns in their hands. David and Emma had been so entranced by the box and its contents that they had not noticed them entering.

"Fowler!" David spat out the name.

Emma frowned, "How did you get in here?"

Fowler looked smug. "We duct-taped your guard downstairs and helped ourselves to his keys," he said.

"You son of a bitch!" David snarled.

"Now, now, be nice, and I might let the two of you live," Fowler said as he moved toward them. His eyes glittered as he snatched the box.

"You came all this way—and spent all that time torturing me—just to get this coronet?" David asked. "Why? It can't be that valuable."

"Actually," said Fowler, waving his gun to make his point, "I don't really care about the coronet." His eyes shone as he examined the container. "I want the box it was in."

"What? What's so valuable about the box?" David asked, puzzled.

"I think I can show you in a minute," Fowler replied, putting his gun down on a side table, after checking to make sure his companions had them both covered. He set the box back down on the coffee table, and extracted the envelope from the drawer.

"Weinstock stole not just the crown, but the baronial lands of my family—and the title that went with it, Baron of Glenbourne, in Scotland. Noble titles were usually associated with land, and up until recently could be bought and sold. My family went from having a noble title to being commoners—and the shame was handed down to the son and grandson and great-grandson."

He grinned malevolently as he unfolded and read a document that had been stored in the envelope. "And this is the title to nobility, with ownership of the land attached to it."

"That's why your grandfather wanted this thing in payment for being a spy in 1942. To get his title and lands back," David said.

"Spy is such a harsh word," said Fowler, sneezing suddenly. "Yes, in addition to a cash payment in gold, my grandfather asked the Germans to get his rightful property back. They told him they had seized it and it was on its way to him, when the U-boat mysteriously sank. Imagine how happy I was when you showed up and told me you were going after a sunken U-boat in the vicinity of Anguilla."

"There's a handwritten note along with the deed," Fowler continued, digging another sheet of paper out of the envelope, and unfolding it. "It seems to be for you," he said, handing it to Emma. "Tell me what it says. I can't read German."

Emma put on her reading glasses, which were attached to a chain around her neck, and started to read, pausing now and then to work out the translation.

> My darling Emmachen,
>
> In addition to the coronet, which you have been playing with, I also bought you the land and title that go with it. The income from the land will be held in trust with my attorney in London, and you will get annual payments from it. When you reach 18, you can put your name on the deed and claim the title of nobility, which I have signed over and had notarized.
>
> You will then legally be a Baroness. That's as high a title as I could buy for you. But in my heart, you will always be my princess.
> All my love,
>
> Papa

Emma sniffled, then wept, as she gently placed the paper onto the coffee table. She rose and started walking to a desk at the opposite corner of the room. The brown-coated companion scowled and swung his gun on her.

"What do you think you're doing?" Fowler snarled irritably.

"Can't you see I'm crying?" Emma sniffled. "I'm going to get the Kleenex on my desk." She pointed to a box sitting on top of the old wooden office desk in the corner.

"All right, all right," Fowler said, irritated.

"What are you going to do with us?" David asked him, and Fowler swung to face him.

"We need her to sign over the deed and title to me. I have a Notary who'll stamp it and witness that he saw her sign it. But as for you..."

He sat on the couch and idly waved his gun in the air. "I really don't have much use for you any more."

He reached for the box. The kitten, which had been circling on the coffee table, ran over and raked his hand with its paw, hissing. Fowler yelped and snatched his hand away, jumping back from the couch.

"You little rat," he shouted. "I'll blow you away. Just like I did that stupid cat on the ship." He turned to the brown-coated man behind him. "Actually, you do it. You've got the gun with the silencer."

As the man lowered his Beretta P92F 9mm with its obscene-looking silencer onto Bucky Jr., David shouted, "No!" He ripped the Glock pistol AJ had given him out of its concealed holster and fired three times so rapidly it sounded like a single shot. The .40 caliber slugs knocked the man back against the wall, and he released his Beretta, which fell with a thump and skidded along the floor. David whirled in the direction of the second guard just as the man dove headfirst into him, knocking him over.

They wrestled over the gun. David was strong, but his opponent was a bull of a man. He held onto the gun with his left hand while sinking rapid body blows into David's midsection. Even worse, he started to turn the Glock slowly, agonizingly, in David's direction. In desperation, David released one hand and jammed his thumb into the man's left eye, evincing a howl of pain and the release of the pistol, which slid under a couch.

David dove for the Beretta, grabbed it and swung it toward the man. He pulled the trigger, with no result. Near total panic, he looked down, realized the safety was engaged, and flipped it up with his thumb just as the man lunged toward him. He pulled the trigger twice. He thought for a moment that nothing had happened, though the man stopped moving toward him. He pulled the trigger once more, aiming carefully, and this time heard the *PFFFT* of the silencer. He saw the man's head jerking backward, as a hole unfolded like a red rose in the middle of his forehead.

David heard a click behind him, and turned his head while still kneeling on the floor. He saw Fowler pointing a nickel-plated S&W .357 magnum at him, hammer pulled back.

"You can say good-bye now," Fowler said, smiling as he started to pull the trigger.

David winced as he heard *Blam!* And again, *Blam!*

He looked down at his chest, but could see no evidence of having been hit.

Fowler, on the other hand, showed considerable surprise on his face, as he slowly turned, to see Emma standing behind him, holding a smoking Walther PPK, which erupted a third time, *Blam!*

Fowler slowly sank to the floor. David stood up, and carefully approached the body, kicking the Smith & Wesson to one side. He waited a moment, and then gingerly dug the toe of his shoe into the side of the body.

"He looks like he's gone," he said, "But it doesn't hurt to be sure." He retrieved his Glock from under the couch. "Besides, AJ got me a license for this," he noted as he emptied another four shots into the body, seeing it jerk with each hit.

He bent over the bodies of the companions to search for a pulse. He shook his head briefly, and rose to face Emma, who was still holding the Walther.

"Nana?" he asked inquiringly.

She smiled grimly. "While they were distracted with you, I pulled this out of one of the drawers in the desk. I learned how to shoot in the kibbutz where I grew up."

She looked disdainfully at Fowler and his companions. "Papa used to tell me that not all Nazis wear uniforms."

She motioned proudly with the PPK. "This is like the James Bond gun. I got him! With every shot!"

David gently took the pistol from her and hugged her tightly. "Yes, Nana. I'm so proud of you." He looked down as he felt a tug on his pants leg. It was the kitten, standing on its hind feet, begging to be picked up.

He stooped to scoop him up and touched noses. "You did good, too, Bucky."

He led Emma to the couch, handed her the coronet, and then went to fetch the box of Kleenex. "OK, Annie Oakley. How about you sit down and rest for a while. I have a few calls to make."

Chapter 71

It took David a few minutes to figure out where he was. Every bone and nerve in his body screamed from the beating he had taken the night before. He looked at his Rolex Mariner to check the time, and saw that it was already late in the morning. Bright sunlight streamed in on him in one of Nana's guest rooms. He looked down to see Bucky splayed on his chest, snoring softly. He stroked him gently, and he woke, yawning to reveal a bright pink mouth and the sharp little teeth he'd bared the night before. He was allowed to ride on David's shoulder as he went about his ablutions.

David marched into the breakfast nook of the kitchen to see that Emma had already prepared coffee, English muffins, eggs, toast, bagels, fruit, jams and other goodies in a variety of containers, next to a can of cat food. He opened the can, put a little on a plate in front of Bucky, filled a small bowl with milk for him, and then dug into the homemade feast.

Emma entered, wearing an embroidered black and gold house coat, smiling brightly. He rose to kiss her on the forehead, and grinned as he realized she was still wearing her coronet.

"That looks good on you," he said. "How are you this morning?"

"Much better than last night," she answered back. "I was so tired. Just filling out those police reports was bad enough, but then having the detectives and the coroner tramp all over the unit was awful. I had to keep watching to make sure they didn't break anything."

She touched his cheek. "I'm so glad to have you here." She nodded to the cat. "I see you two have bonded already."

David shook his head from side to side. "I'm still pinching myself to see whether I'm dreaming." He looked at the coronet. "When I first saw it, I tried to figure out the value of the stones, to see whether you got a decent return on your investment. I thought I'd pay you from the sale of the coins if you didn't."

Emma shook her head. "I don't care if they're all made out of glass. This is priceless. I would never sell it, for anything!"

He nodded. "I understand that, now. Like I said, I got the treasure, after all."

She nodded. "I went to sleep dreaming of all the stories Papa told me about it, like the *1001 Nights*."

David smiled. "I would love to hear them. Would you write them down? I'll get it published, so your grandkids will have something from your Papa!"

She looked at her hands. "I'm afraid these old hands can't do much typing."

David took her hands in his. "They won't have to. I'll get you a laptop with a microphone and software by a company named Dragon. You just talk, the computer types. I'll edit."

She smiled. "I'll get started this afternoon!" She reached for a pocket and produced an envelope. "Speaking of this afternoon, that reminds me. This came for you by messenger a few days ago. I had forgotten all about it."

David opened the envelope. "It's an invitation to the Paleontological Convention, which features Dr. Erika Bettelman speaking...at 1:30 p.m. today."

He looked at his watch. "I'd better get showered and dressed." He added wryly, "Although almost anything would be an improvement on how I showed up for the first one." He looked at Emma. "Would you like to come?"

She shook her head. "Normally, I'd say yes. I have friends on the board, so I'm sure I could get a ticket. But I'm exhausted. You go ahead, and have fun."

"OK, Nana," David said. "I'd better take off really early. I have a feeling—if I trained her right—this might be quite a production."

He looked at his watch as the taxi pulled up in front of the Museum of Natural History. It was 12:15 p.m. He paid the driver and crawled out of the cab, pulling the small cat carrier off the seat behind him. "I'm sorry you can't come out yet," David told the protesting feline. "Later, OK?"

He trotted up the stairs of the museum and went to a table under a sign that read, "Preregistered H-K." He showed his invitation, and took the pre-printed badge and stuck it onto his jacket. "Where's the Speakers' Room?" he asked the white-haired lady behind the table.

"Upstairs in Room 210," she answered, and he trotted in that direction.

He entered a large meeting room and saw Erika sitting at a corner table. There were three other speakers working at laptops nearby. She wore the outfit he had gotten her in St. Martin, together with a cream-colored blouse with ruffles. He came up behind her, put his hands around her eyes, and asked, "Guess who?"

She jumped slightly, and turned to look at him and ask, "David! What are you doing here?"

"I'm glad to see you, too!" he replied. He looked at her screen. "Still working on your PowerPoint slides?"

She shook her head. "Not really. I'm just trying to remember it all. And what you told me."

He smiled at her. "Just talk directly to your fan club. We'll be in the front row, like I promised."

"That's nice," she said quickly. She lowered her voice. "But the whole Society will be looking at me, and the President has all these expectations..."

"You're still worried because you want the acknowledgment of...a bunch of old men who...what was it you said—fart dust?"

She looked around. "Shh! Not so loud! Well, when you put it like that..."

David smiled grimly. "Aunt Marie has this saying: You never get enough of what you don't really want."

Erika nodded. "I'll keep it in mind." She glanced toward the cat carrier. "Is that a new kitty?"

He shook his head. "No. This is the old one in a new body, according to Aunt Marie." He let the kitten out of the container, and it looked shyly up at Erika. "Rika, meet Bucky, Junior."

"He's gorgeous," she laughed. She picked up the kitten and stood, holding it up and twirling around. She looked at David, showing off her outfit. "What do you think? Tell me the truth—is this the best I've ever looked?"

He thought a moment. "You want the truth?" She nodded, and he said, "The truth is the best you've ever looked was that evening in my cabin, after you had sifted through Bucky's sand. The moonlight was shining on your hair, and you had this huge smile, like a 5-year old. You lit up the room. And took my breath away."

She looked at him with a crooked half-smile. "You mean I spent a whole afternoon shopping for this blouse and getting makeup and hair done, and all I really needed was a plastic scoop with some cat shit?"

He nodded emphatically. "Oh, yeah!"

She shook her head and laughed. "Bloody men!" She handed him the kitten and sat down again. Her smile faded as she turned to her laptop, noticed something, and started tapping at the keyboard.

David looked at her and tilted his head, frowning. "You know, this isn't exactly the warmest greeting I've ever gotten."

She gave him a nervous smile. "I'm sorry. We need to talk. Soon."

He looked at his watch. "OK. Your presentation is from 1:30 to 2, and I'm sure you'll have questions after. How about 4, in Central Park, at the Merry-go-round? It's about 10 minutes away." He sketched a quick map on a nearby sheet of paper.

She nodded. "I know where that is. We'll catch up then." She glanced toward the door. "I'm afraid I've got to get back to my briefing right now."

"All right," David said cheerfully. "I'll let you go." He bent to kiss her, and she turned her head to present her cheek. He walked backwards a few feet and gave her a thumbs-up sign. "Go get 'em. Take no prisoners!"

She nodded and gave him a fleeting smile before she turned back to her screen.

He left the room, feeling vaguely disappointed. As he walked down the hall, he passed a tall, handsome man in a snugly fitted suit carrying a bunch of long-stemmed red roses, who hurried into the room he had just come from. "Strange," he thought. "Doesn't seem like a typical professor."

Chapter 72

David entered the presentation hall, and noticed that every seat appeared to be filled. The back was lined with TV camera crews. He walked authoritatively up to the middle seat in the first row, and told its occupant, "Sorry. Reserved for Society Board members." The man looked at him, confused, and got up and left. David sat down, and removed Bucky from his carrier. He whispered in his ear, "Note that I didn't say I actually *was* a Board member."

To David's right, Lord Shrewesbury was sitting near the middle of the second row, his ample body spilling over the arm rests of his seat like a giant muffin. One of his usual sycophants, a Master's Degree student, asked him, "Where in the world are all these people coming from? And TV camera crews! We've never had TV camera crews!"

Shrewesbury nodded his head, activating several layers of chins. "They probably heard about my presentation later this afternoon." He waved a red folder with the title *Velociraptor Nest Building Behaviors: An Analysis of New Nesting Groups Found in the Gobi Desert.* "This might cause a bit of a sensation when I release it today. And you will be among the first to hear it. The general public knows Velociraptors, since they were made famous by the *Jurassic Park* movies."

He looked back at the camera teams. "They might even be making a new movie, and want me to consult on it." He set off on one of his belly-shaking laughs, and the student watched anxiously to avoid any spittle that might suddenly spray out from the swollen, liver-colored lips.

"It won't be cheap, though. I'm going to charge them a pretty penny, I can tell you that," Shrewesbury chortled, basking in the admiring glow of the graduate students on both sides. He knew they would give anything to get a chance to do a thesis with him.

He looked to his right at a red-headed young student he had started to fancy. He leaned forward dramatically and whispered to her, "I can tell you in confidence that the director of the museum told me they are making an announcement for a major new show. I take that to mean that they may feature my Velociraptor nests in a special exhibit. Did I tell you that we have three fossilized eggs in one of the nests? Three!" He chortled again as he pushed his bulk suddenly back into his seat, causing the whole row to shake.

The lights started flashing to indicate that the lunch break was over, and the program was about to begin. Shrewesbury looked at the program and harrumphed. "I cannot believe they're letting that charlatan back onto the stage. Oh, well, we'll just have to suffer through her presentation and..." he looked at the program, "...two others before they finally get to us and we all can hear something worthwhile."

A slight and bespectacled man took the podium up front, brushing a shock of white hair out of his eyes. "Members of the Society, ladies and gentlemen, and..." he nodded toward the back, "...members of the Press, we welcome you to our program this afternoon. We have a very full schedule, so I won't delay this any more. Our first presentation will be by Dr. Erika Bettelman, entitled, *New Evidence of Mosasaur Survival Adaptations in the Western Hemisphere*. After this presentation, I will have an announcement of some import, about a major new exhibition in the museum, something the whole world will want to see, with a Grand Opening this week."

"You see, you see?" Shrewesbury whispered to the student next to him, jabbing him with his elbow in his excitement and nearly knocking him out of his seat. "I told you that he was giving a special exhibition for my dinosaur egg fossils!"

The lights dimmed and a spotlight shone on Erika as she came on stage and walked to the podium. David smiled at the stagecraft. He noted that she was wearing the electric blue suit with the short skirt that he had bought her, together with the wedge sandals with multiple layers of leather straps. He detected a sway to her hips as she approached the podium. The audience seemed to murmur its approval, all except for one hiss of "Strumpet!" from the second row.

A video played on the giant screens that had been set up around the stage. David recognized some of the pictures that he had seen previously of fossilized Mosasaur remains. Erika scanned the audience. She looked in his direction, and smiled as he grasped one of Bucky's paws and waved it at her. He scratched the kitten behind one ear as they looked up at the stage expectantly.

"Good afternoon, members of the Academy, ladies and gentlemen. I hope to have something different to show you today. As you may know, I theorized that one of the most remarkable animals to ever inhabit this planet, the Mosasaur, continued to exist for some time past the 65 million year extinction period. My team discovered fossils in the Anguilla area of the Caribbean, and evidence that the animal had electric organs, like the Amazonian electric eel, that allowed it to find prey deep in the ocean in absolute darkness."

She paused to let this sink in. David noted with satisfaction that she did not look down at her notes or out at the great mass of the audience, but was fixed on two or three friendly faces in the front row, just as he had taught her.

"To dive to great depths and hunt prey such as giant squid and sharks, the Mosasaur would have had to grow to rather large size, like this," she flicked a red laser pointer onto a 3D model of a Mosasaur swimming on the center screen behind her. "In fact, we believe it could have been over 70 feet long, and might have looked like this." She turned to look at the central screen directly behind her. An animated Mosasaur was swimming through a 3D Computer-Generated image of a lagoon at great speed. It suddenly rose out of the water, and streams of spindrift cascaded from it as it became airborne. The animation froze in mid-air for a moment, and then repeated from the beginning of the clip.

"We will demonstrate today," she continued, facing her audience squarely, "that the animal behind me did not die 65 million years ago, not 60 million years ago, not 50 million years ago, but survived until less than 30..." she let the word hang in the air.

Lord Shrewesbury could contain himself no longer. He propelled himself to his feet, sending his vast belly into undulations. "Poppycock!" he shouted. "Absolute poppycock!" His face had turned sunburn-red. "You are insulting this entire Academy with such..." he sputtered, unable to find a word condemnatory enough for a breach of this magnitude, "...nonsense!" He looked around at his fan club, each member of which nodded his or her head in earnest assent.

Erika's eyes narrowed as she looked at Shrewesbury. "Lord Shrewesbury," she said sweetly. "I'd like to see whether you mean any of that, or are just blowing hot air."

His lordship's skin color became even ruddier, and the chins started to wag from side-to-side, setting up a complex, wavelike motion as he sputtered his protest.

"If I could demonstrate beyond doubt that Mosasaurs lived more recently than, say, 30 million years ago, would you be willing to give up your seat on the Governor's Board, and remove your presence from this hall right now?"

Shrewesbury continued sputtering, too angry to formulate a reply.

"I can't hear you," Erika said loudly and directly. "Tell you what. If I lose, I'll give you a quarter million dollar grant that I recently received. Every penny. Now, do you accept the challenge, or was it just hot air?"

"You, you, you..." Shrewesbury was trying to catch his breath in great gulps. Suddenly he realized what she had said. "A quarter million dollars?" he asked, incredulous.

"Yes, that's what I said. 250,000 US if I can't demonstrate what I just said. If you lose, you agree to honor your verbal contract to give up your Board seat and immediately leave this hall."

"The woman is mad. Utterly mad," Shrewesbury said, turning to the audience around him. "Of course I'll take your money," he said.

"The question was, do you accept the agreement," she went on, relentless.

"Yes, yes, yes," he replied, waving one arm in the air. "I accept. I accept."

"Very well," she replied. "We have a contract." She moved across the stage, taking the wireless microphone with her. There was a shuffling sound across the audience, as if all of its members were sliding to the edges of their seats. Hundreds of pairs of eyes were totally riveted on her.

David grinned from ear to ear. "She has them eating out of her hand," he whispered into the kitten's ear.

"As I was about to say," Erika continued, "before I was so rudely interrupted. We have absolute proof that this species of Mosasaur continued to exist less than 30..." she let the word hang in the air once more. The hall held its breath, except for the snorts and snuffles from the second row.

She continued triumphantly, "...*days* ago! This Mosasaur was witnessed and photographed less than two weeks ago!" Behind her the 3-dimensional animated model of the monster morphed into a videotape of the actual animal itself, swimming from the middle of the lagoon until launching the spectacular leap into the air, where the video froze for a minute and then repeated itself.

There was a collective gasp, as if from one throat. A low roar started to build in the hall. Banks of lights came on along the auditorium walls as every camera crew came on full alert and started filming. Erika held up both arms like an Olympian crossing the finish line, and pointed at the side screens, which started to display:

THE LIVING MOSASAUR
The T. Rex of the Seas
A Major New Exhibition
Exclusive videos of a Live Mosasaur Family!
Grand Opening Sept. 1!

Erika moved to two large glass cabinets that were being wheeled in, and pointed at their frost-covered contents. "We have video and photos of the animals. We have dozens of witnesses. We also have ten kilos of frozen tissue—bones and muscle tissue taken from a living animal just weeks ago—in these refrigerated cabinet displays," she said. "The Academy President confirms their authenticity."

"However," she went on, adamantly, "before I can continue, we have something we have to take care of first." She looked down at the middle of the second row. "Don't you have somewhere else to go, Lord Shrewesbury?" she asked.

Shrewesbury's mouth hung open, his tongue lolling to one side. He looked desperately up at the President of the Academy, who stood at the left side of the stage. His expression fell as the President's face lit up excitedly as he pointed at the announcement and the two cabinets and nodded his head, giving a "thumbs up" with both hands.

"We're waiting," Erika said pointedly, staring at his Lordship.

Shrewesbury looked around him, his breath coming in short gasps. He turned to the red-headed coed nearby with a pleading look on his face. He took hope as she opened her mouth to say something. His multilayered face fell as she yelled, "Come on! I want to see this! Hurry the fuck out of here!"

He moved his bulk down the row with some difficulty and staggered toward the back of the hall, his eyes unfocused. Eager hands opened the door for him and guided him through it, slamming it closed behind him. As if by a signal, dozens of cameras flashes started strobing around the room.

Erika nodded to Moshe in the front row, and video segments started appearing behind her. "We observed four of the animals," she started. "A male, a female, and two juveniles."

David started to grin from ear to ear as the opening music of the film *2001: A Space Odyssey* started playing in the background, accompanying the main points of her presentation.

"We have said before that this was an apex predator, the most dangerous animal there's ever been, the Tyrannosaurus rex of the

Seas," she intoned. "These four appeared for a couple of hours in human company, at the end of which over 120 people lay dead and dying."

She paused as dozens of journalists scribbled, "Killed a person a minute!" in their notebooks.

David chuckled. "She's leaving out a few details, but that's probably for the sequel," he whispered to the cat.

A new video clip started on the screens behind her, edited from footage captured by Resort vidcams. It showed the female Mosasaur grasping two men from the front seats of an approaching ATV; David recognized it as the one that Morrison had piloted from the back. Erika pointed at the animal with a laser, and said, "Here's the mature female. You can get an idea of her size and power when you see her snatch two men and swallow them—at the same time!"

The audience members were now fully on the edge of their seats. She continued, "You may remember that I spoke of possible electric powers of these animals, and what they might be capable of. There was some skepticism at the time." She paused.

"Here's an illustration of what they can do. Note how far away the animal is, over 100 feet." A second video came on, showing a man trying to run away from the monster on the roof. David remembered seeing the man from AJ's ATV. The crowd gasped as the man stopped and jerked up suddenly as a blue-white bolt traveled over the wet road and hit him. Several people cried out as his face melted and he crumpled into a puddle of grease and bones and charred clothing on the roadway.

The video on the screens behind her faded to show the Great Seal of the Academy. "Before we carry on with the presentation, I'd like to tell you some further news. The President of our Academy has done me the great honor of making me a member of the Board of Directors, since there is now an opening on it." She glanced briefly at Shrewesbury's empty seat as the audience erupted in applause.

After a few minutes, she held up a hand to halt the applause, and continued. "The President also bestowed an extraordinarily generous award on me," she continued, "the honor of naming this new species—this 'new' species that is tens of millions of years old."

She turned her head to look directly at David, and smiled. "With the help of a colleague, I chose to call it *Mosasaurus Maximus*."

"That's what I first called it," David whispered to the kitten. "Big Mo to you and me—without the Latin."

A roar erupted from the crowd as the new name of the ancient monster went up in animated lettering on the screens, to the accompaniment of the drumbeats from *Also Sprach Zarathustra*. The place fell into pandemonium as people rose up and even stood on their seats to get a better view, and broke into thunderous applause and shouts of approval. The camera crews in back found their views blocked and started moving toward the front, fighting for space.

David looked around him at the surging crowd. He saw that the kitten had become frightened by the noise, and was digging its claws into his neck in terror.

"OK," he said. "Let's go."

He extricated the kitten's claws from his suit with difficulty, and placed it into its cat carrier. He slowly got out of his seat, walked crouched-over to the aisle, and made his way to the exit, holding onto the carrier with one arm and elbowing his way through the tumultuous crowd with the other.

He turned at the door for one last look at the stage. Erika was looking in his direction, though it seemed impossible that she could see him in the banks of bright TV lights surrounding him.

"Well played, Rika," He said softly. "Good on ya." He gave her a small salute with his right hand, then turned and pushed his way out through the exit. He closed the doors behind him and hurried past the puzzled people in the hallways, who wondered about the pandemonium inside the auditorium.

Chapter 73

David walked down the steps of the Museum of Natural History and caught a cab to Central Park. After he exited the taxi, he called Emma on his cell phone.

"Hi, Nana. Erika was terrific. What a production! You'll see it in the news. I am so proud of her. Not one nervous twitch. She was awesome."

"I'm happy to hear that," Emma said. "Are you two getting together?"

"Yes, she's meeting me at 4 o'clock in Central Park, next to the Merry-go-round. Bucky and I just got here, and are having some ice cream. Do you want to join us?"

"No, you go ahead. I'm still a little tired. I haven't shot anyone in a very long time. I'm still getting over it. And I'm having the carpet replaced."

"You may want them to fill up a few holes in the floor, here and there, also, Nana. OK. I'll talk to you later."

He reached the park and walked slowly around the area, eventually arriving at the Merry-Go-Round Building. He smiled as the music and hubbub brought back fond memories of coming there with Nana. He bought an ice cream cone from the vendor, sat down on a bench, and released the kitten from its cat carrier. It promptly marched onto his arm and started licking at the cone with its tiny pink tongue.

"Oh, you think you're entitled to that, do you?" he said in mock severity. He looked around at a gorgeous day, with everything in extra-sharp focus. Trees rustled overhead, and golden dots of sunshine spilled through their leafy veils. He took a deep breath. "I don't know why, but I have a funny feeling in my stomach. Let's go for a walk," he told the kitten.

He arrived back at the meeting place a few minutes before the hour, and settled down on a bench attached to a picnic table. He played with the kitten as he waited. He left several voice mails, and checked his iPhone repeatedly for messages, but found none. He texted the location, to make sure she knew where to meet.

"She'll probably be here soon," he told the kitten. "We could take a quick nap." He lowered himself onto the bench.

"Meek-eek," was the reply, as Bucky settled onto his chest and got comfortable.

Chapter 74

David woke with a start. He rose slowly, holding onto the kitten on his chest. The sun was setting, and a chill was setting in. He glanced at the Merry-Go-Round Building, and saw that the doors were locked. He looked around to see what had woken him. The voice repeated itself.

"Can you spare a dollar?" A sad-eyed old lady held her hand out in front of him. Her other hand leaned on a Safeway shopping cart, which held a tall pile of ballooned-up trash bags bulging with items of clothing.

He hesitated a moment, and then said, "Sure." He handed her a five dollar bill. She remained a moment longer, staring at the bill as if to make sure it was genuine, and then shuffled off.

David looked at his watch. "Seven o'clock," he told the kitten. "It looks like we've been stood up."

Bucky replied, "Eeep."

David sighed, and headed for a taxi stand.

Chapter 75

David walked into the apartment and stooped to kiss Emma, carefully balancing the kitten on his shoulder.

"How did it go?" she asked, sensing his disappointment.

"I was stood up. We agreed to meet in the Park at 4. I finally left at 7. I guess I've been replaced."

"Oh, David," she replied, holding his hand. "I'm sorry." She waved at a couch. "Sit down. I'll bring you coffee and *Buntkuchen.*

"I'm OK, really, Nana."

"Sit, sit." She waved her hand, and he rolled his eyes upwards in resignation as he sat and she carved him a massive slice of cake and placed it on a blue-and-white Meissen china plate. She handed him a steaming cup and sat close by.

"You'll meet someone else really nice," she said as she patted his hand.

He chortled as the kitten licked his ear.

"Are you OK?" she asked. "You're not..."

"...going off the deep end, like last time?" he asked. "No. My life is different. I finally accomplished something...useful." He looked up at the coronet, and they both smiled. "And I have you, and Bucky, Jr. I have AJ and Leah, and a whole island full of family. I have a lot to be grateful for."

She brightened. "I just had an idea. The owner of that Italian family-style restaurant we like has a daughter that just got divorced. Her name is Susan, and she works as the hostess. You should go have dinner there."

He grinned as he stood up. "OK. I'm starving. Want to come?"

She shooed him out the door with fluttering fingers. "No, no. Go and have fun."

He exited the elevator and exchanged a few words with the doorman. They heard car doors slamming outside, and caught a glimpse of two stretch limos in front of the building. The revolving door whooshed and Erika entered, trailed by a dozen formally dressed people, all buzzing excitedly.

"Hello, David," she said.

His face brightened, and he replied, "Hi, Rika," as he moved to embrace her. He was stopped by her right hand, which she reached out. It hung in space in front of him.

He looked at it, and then back at her. She wore an off-white silk pants suit. He noticed with annoyance that a suntanned young man with an immaculate hairdo and a finely tailored dark mohair suit with matching tie and pocket kerchief was resting his hand on her right shoulder. He recognized him as the man in the hallway outside the Speaker's Room.

David shook her hand stiffly. "Good *evening*," he said pointedly, looking at his watch and back up at her, his eyebrows lowering.

"I'm sorry. I've been really busy. It's been a madhouse," she replied.

The tanned man next to her pulled an envelope out of an aluminum briefcase. "In fact, we're in a rush. It seems you've watermarked and copyrighted all the photos and videos of the Mosasaurs, preventing commercial usage. We could challenge that in court, of course, but it would be much simpler if you would just sign over the rights to Dr. Bettelman." He pulled out a sterling Mont Blanc pen and offered it to David.

David's expression darkened as he looked from the man to Erika. "And who might this be?"

"This is Roy Fenneman, my attorney," she replied. "And these others are my PR and management team. Roy's drawn up some papers, and..."

David spat out the words. "So that's why the fuck you finally showed up! Because you and this yo-yo want the rights to the pictures from the lagoon?"

The man stepped forward to confront David. "You can't talk to Dr. Bettelman like that. I, that is, we..."

David spoke with growing anger. "*We* can kiss my ass!"

Fenneman puffed up his chest. "I'm warning you. I'm trained in martial arts. One more word from you, and..."

David's face reddened, and his nostrils flared. He leaned forward, and his voice dripped venom. "All right. Let's go outside. I've killed about 23 people in the last two weeks. I'd love to make it an even two dozen!"

Fenneman stared at him, taken aback, and muttered, "You're crazy!"

"Oh, no, he's not," the doorman chimed in cheerfully. "He killed three of them yesterday, right in this building. I saw what was left of them carried out of the lobby."

The lawyer turned back to David. "You can't," he said, shaking his head. "You'd wind up in jail!"

David smiled grimly. "No I wouldn't." He handed Fenneman one of his old business cards. "You can check on me. I've never lost a major case. I'll get off *and* get a half million from your estate."

The lawyer stared at the card, and then at David. "Oh, my God! I've heard of you. Your nickname was 'Killer' Killmer."

David chose that moment to pull his jacket back slightly.

Fenneman stepped back in horror as he saw the butt of a black .40 cal. Glock peeking out from a shoulder holster with an official-looking star clipped to it. He quickly melted into the back of the crowd.

David turned back to Erika, his anger still rising. "So that's the only reason you finally came?"

"Why, were you planning on keeping them and getting rich?" she asked.

"It wouldn't be a bad idea to pay the medical bills of the rescue team. A bunch of them got beaten up and wounded, and were lying in hospitals. Did you visit them?"

She reddened. "I've been really busy, getting ready for..."

"Have you called them? *Any* of them?"

She faltered. "I've been busy..."

"They weren't too busy to save *your* sorry ass!" David growled. "Did you take a moment to visit Bucky's grave? The one you were so fond of?"

"I didn't have the time..."

"Why?" he shouted. "Because he and the others were no longer useful?"

The PR lady standing next to Erika opened her mouth to say something, but shut it quickly as he glared at her.

"I don't have to answer to you," Erika said angrily, a flush of scarlet rising in her cheeks.

"No. Not any more," he growled. "You're off and running. We got rid of that stage fright thing, but now uncovered a real mean streak in you. I didn't see that coming."

"What are you on about?" she shouted back. "You're the one who left!"

He looked puzzled. "What? I never left you."

"When I woke up, I was told you left. It sure looked like that's what you really wanted to do. I've been through that before, over and over, and..."

He held up one hand. "Ah. I see what's really bugging you. OK, I'll give you what you want."

The lawyer emerged from the pack, pulling his document out with a hopeful expression, but faded back again when he saw David shoot him a look of pure hatred.

Erika stared at the dimple in David's chin as the trace of a sad smile played around his face.

"You were expecting it so much, but I never intended to do it. I never said good-bye," he said firmly.

She opened her mouth to speak, but he held up his hand.

"I'm saying it...now. Good-bye! Erika!"

He marched toward the door. The crowd parted in front of him like the Red Sea in front of Moses.

A blonde, bright-eyed PR lady tapped on her watch and whispered urgently into Erika's ear. "The mayor! We're late for the mayor!"

Erika ignored her, and called out, "David!"

He turned, with one hand on the revolving door, and raised an eyebrow.

"Um. Have a nice evening," she said.

He shook his head. "Afraid not. I have to pay Leah 20 bucks."

"Why?" she asked.

"She bet me that you'd break my heart."

Erika shot back, "You know that thing with Fowler wasn't true!"

David glanced at the floor, then back again. The fire in his voice was replaced by a deep sadness. "She was talking about... today."

The anger returned as he started through the exit and hissed, "Wuss!"

He moved through the revolving door with such force that it kept spinning even after he was outside.

Chapter 76

No one moved for a moment. The PR lady took a firm hold of Erika's arm and led her out the door to the waiting limousine. Erika took one last look at the departing David, who was walking briskly down the block, talking on his cell phone. She started to call out, but was pulled into the car by several pairs of hands.

"OK, AJ," David spoke into his phone. "Tell Leah I owe her 20 bucks. I'll send a check."

"I have a better idea," AJ replied. "You can take us both out to dinner at Cap de Luca this Saturday."

David laughed. "You know I don't have that kind of money."

AJ replied. "Ah, but you will. We confirmed the coordinates of where Fowler's chopper went down. You found that gold the first time when you had 100 square miles to look in. Do you think you can find it in one or two square miles?"

David gripped his cell phone tightly. "Really?" he asked excitedly. "That's wonderful news."

"But you need to get going. Some of Fowler's men that escaped from the chopper will know where it crashed, and they'll be going after it."

"I'll book a flight in the morning," David replied. "I'm pretty wiped out right now."

"And I wouldn't worry about cash flow. A Japanese restaurant owner found out you have Mosasaur meat in a freezer, and sent an offer for $10,000 a pound, payable up front. I'll give you the details over dinner. They want to call it 'the world's rarest meal.'"

"That's pretty funny," David laughed. "Good thing I hung on to most of it. That'll also pay off any outstanding hospital bills. And here we are at our restaurant. Bucky and I are dining family-style Italian tonight."

"Hold on a minute, bud," AJ said. "Leah wants to talk to you."

Her honeyed voice came on the line. "Hi, David. You OK? Feeling lonely?"

"No, I'm good. I have Bucky again, and I just need to think of you and AJ and Anguilla to feel part of a family. I learned you don't find home, you bring it."

There was a chuckle from the other end of the line. "Aunt Marie will be proud of you. See you this weekend. Bring a suit, the governor wants to make a big fuss over all of you. Love ya," she said, and clicked off.

Chapter 77

David stopped in front of the restaurant door, and looked up at a sign that announced *The Colibri* in flowery red swirls, flanked by two of its namesake hummingbirds. He opened the door, and was met by a beaming hostess with large brown eyes framed by long, curly lashes, who wore a low-cut dark blue dress with spaghetti straps.

"Hi," David said, grinning. "Are you Susan, my Internet date?"

She laughed, shook her long auburn hair, and winked. "Afraid not, but we can talk later." She gave him a friendly hug, and kissed him on both cheeks. Warmth radiated from her skin, along with the scent of freshly-applied, musky perfume. "Emma called to tell us you were coming. My mom is making you the 'Heartbreak Special' dinner, a lot of great food with two bottles of Brunello from Tuscany."

David's smile grew broader. "Sounds great."

She stepped back and gave him an appraising look. "It's an honor to meet you, Lord David. And this must be Bucky."

"Huh?" David replied, confused. "You've mistaken me for somebody else."

She smiled. "Emma told my mom she had this title of nobility that she's giving you. She said she didn't need it, and her two daughters are already too stuck up."

"What?" he stammered.

She snorted. "Whichever one she gave the title to would become impossible to live with, and the other one would hate her the rest of her life. And if she kept it, they would hound her about it every day."

She added, "I know both daughters. Real snobs. And cheap tippers."

"But I haven't heard...I can't..."

She smiled at his confusion. "Apparently the paperwork's already started. A lawyer from London will be contacting you." She took his hand and pulled him along. "You're getting the royal setting by the window."

She took him to a table next to a stained glass window that had sinuous green vines with broad leaves framing the sides. Two iridescent blue-green hummingbirds hovered before bright red flowers along the top. She pulled out a chair, and told him, "It's on the house. It's not often we see royalty." She laughed at his open-mouthed expression. "Or a lawyer that's speechless."

She pulled something out of a pocket in her apron, and placed it on the table as she leaned in close to him and whispered warm breath into his ear. "Speaking of the law, keep this close, so we don't get busted."

He didn't fully understand what she said, as her lips lightly brushed against his ear, and he was already occupied staring down the gap between her breasts. He looked at this hand, and saw a small jacket with "Therapy Animal in Training" printed on the sides. He grinned as he slipped it over Bucky and closed it with Velcro fasteners.

Susan stood back and winked at him before she left.

David started in on his first dish, which appeared in front of him like magic. He dangled a strand of angel hair pasta in front of the kitten, which jumped at it when he pulled it out of reach. A voice spoke from behind him.

"Is this a closed party, or can anyone join in?"

He turned to see Erika standing there, shifting from one foot to the other.

His reply was cold. "It's invite-only. Shouldn't you be with your crowd of ass kissers?"

She tried looking stern. "You're just envious because I'm having dinner with the mayor."

He snorted. "I used to go hunting with him when I was a campaign contributor. Someday, all your new friends will turn on you, and you'll know the real meaning of feeling alone."

She hesitated. "Do you think I'm a total bitch?"

He shook his head firmly. "No. You're a powerful, gorgeous, smart lady who has issues. As I do."

Susan appeared with a bottle of Brunello. She uncorked it and then leaned far forward to pour a glass, revealing a generous amount of tanned skin. She smiled at David and left, hips swaying from side to side. Erika cut her a look as she passed by.

She sighed. "I really miss our evenings on board ship."

"Uh-huh."

She tilted her head. "And I need your help. I'm smart enough to know when I'm in over my head."

He scowled. "You can get your fancy lawyer to do that for you!"

She snorted. "That wimp? He almost peed his pants. He's history. I fired him."

His face relaxed visibly. "So, you want to work together, as professionals?"

Her expression was guarded. "Could it be more? I'm being asked to go back and search for Mosasaurs, and to do films and God knows what. I need a partner, in more ways than one."

He bit his lip. "It's too late for us to 'just be friends.' And I'm hesitant to get intimate with a chainsaw."

Her cheeks colored. "I think I lost the chainsaw part of me in the caves." She grabbed his wine glass and drained it in one gulp. She took a deep breath. "Don't make this so hard for me. The reason I didn't visit the team members in hospital, or Bucky's grave..." She stopped, and started again. "I was afraid I'd start crying, and never stop."

He said, "Hm-m."

Susan returned to refill the wineglass. She smiled at David and pointed the bottle of Brunello di Montalcino at the hummingbirds along the top of the window. "Did you know that *Colibri* is Italian for hummingbird? Native Americans believed they had magic powers to make you forget bad events from the past, and replace them with joy and celebration."

David feigned surprise, with a wide smile. "Really? How interesting!"

Susan gave a slight bow and replied, "You're welcome, my lord."

Erika frowned as Susan left and asked, "Are you two an item?"

He shook his head. "Not that I know of. I just met her, ten minutes ago."

Her jaw dropped. "And what—she thinks you're God?"

He nodded, a smile curling the edges of his lips. "I guess *some* people can see the good in me."

She changed direction. "You called me a wuss. In the lobby."

He blinked his eyelids. "You were running away and hiding. That's what wusses do."

She stared intently into his eyes. "You think I wanted to push you away?"

"What do *you* think?"

She did not reply.

David glanced at the two stained-glass birds overhead, and said, "I don't want to go through this, again. I said, 'Good-bye.' Let's leave it at that."

She pulled out a chair, and sat down. She grasped one of his hands and stared into his eyes. "Take back the 'good-bye' and I'll give it all up. I'll call them and tell them all to bugger off."

He looked at her in surprise. "You really mean that?"

In reply, she pulled her cell phone out and started initiating a call.

He held up his hand. "Hang on. If I take it back, what's next?"

She glanced at his bowl of pasta and said, "Next, I'm ordering some of that, to make up for the dinner with the mayor I'm missing." She looked down and laughed at the kitten, who was licking her thumb. "Look, you. I've got one vote of approval, already."

David blinked several times. "My God. You really do mean it. All right. I'll take it back. We can start over. Now, go on out there and give 'em hell, and make us proud. Give me a shout when you come up for air."

She chewed her lower lip. "Maybe we could go out to dinner. What are you doing Saturday night?"

David picked up the kitten to keep it from climbing into his bowl of pasta. "I'm having dinner with AJ and Leah, in Anguilla."

"OK. I'll fly down and go visit everybody, to thank them. And Bucky's grave. I won't wear any eye makeup. And I'll get a nice place for us. Maybe put some rocks in the bedroom, to remind us of the caves. And I'll pick up the cost of dinner. And bring a six-pack of your favorite wines."

He hesitated a moment, and then grinned. "You should have been a lawyer. That was the best closing argument, ever."

She exhaled. "OK, then, it's a date." She looked at him closely, and suddenly changed to a stern expression. "You were fu..." she noticed the people at an adjoining table, and quickly changed to, "You were messing with me, weren't you?" She hit him on the arm. "Wanker! I know you too well!"

She glanced at her watch. "All right, then. I'll get back to my arse kissers." She turned to leave, but spun in place and quickly sat down in David's lap. She put one hand on his cheek and the other firmly behind his head, and gave him a full kiss on the lips. She rose and beamed, "I'll see you two on Saturday."

She had almost reached the door when David called out, "By the way. You were magnificent."

She turned and grinned. "Thanks. I had all that help from you, and the presentation..."

"I didn't mean that," he replied. "When you flashed DuBois. If you hadn't done that, none of us would be here now. That was a magnificent flash."

The corners of her lips curled up into a full dolphin smile. His heart squeezed almost painfully at the memory. Her eyes shone, and her radiance seemed to fill the room. For a moment, all the tension and tiredness in her face melted away, and she said, "Hold that thought! Until Saturday night!"

She was still smiling as she closed the door behind her.

Chapter 78

A few feet away, passersby outside the restaurant could see David and Bucky framed by the stained glass window. Several laughed at the image of the playful kitten lunging for a strand of pasta held above its nose.

A few dozen feet away, a dark window in a long white limo rolled down silently. An iPhone emerged and clicked twice before the window turned dark again.

A few hundred feet away, special edition papers were being delivered onto the sidewalk next to a news kiosk. "Ancient Monsters Found in Caribbean," blasted the *New York Times*. "Monsters Caused Curse of the Bermuda Triangle," screamed the *Post*. "Dinosaurs from Space Kill Hundreds," posited the *Enquirer*.

A few miles away, Lord Shrewesbury started his presentation, which had been postponed to the evening. The auditorium was almost empty. He tried to cover up his humiliation by being even more pedantic and dramatic than usual with his text, shouting out some of the points and braying explosively at others. This combined to form a veritable cloud of spittle suspended in front of the podium. Later that night, he would be somewhat mollified when he received a note in his hotel room, which read:

> *Dear Lord Shrewesbury,*
> *Thursday at 6 p.m. is the Grand Opening for the new "The Living Mosasaur" exhibit at the Museum. We would appreciate your presence there, along with your insights. It would not be the same without you.*
> *Cordially,*
>
> *Erika Bettelman*

A few hundred miles away, AJ and Leah had spent the day packing up his Washington, DC apartment. They finished taping up boxes to get them ready for the moving van. They were as excited as children about their new future together in Anguilla. Both of them were taking a short break from the packing chores, sitting on the balcony and alternating between typing on their laptops and watching the moonshine sparkle on the majestically flowing Potomac below them. She held AJ's hand with her left, while using her right hand to search for "House to Rent" in Anguilla. AJ was smiling as he used his left hand to Google for "Maine Coon Cats for Sale."

A few thousand miles away, the huge female Mosasaur pushed sand and rocks to the side, widening her nest to assure space for her and her two offspring. She looked around in the new and unfamiliar cavern, recognizing other members of her new pod.

She had traveled for days, frantically trying to find another entrance to the tunnel system that had been their home. It had been difficult to hunt, because her youngsters could not yet descend into the depths of the ocean to hunt the giant squid that were a mainstay of her diet.

Finally, her keen sense of smell had caught the scent of her own kind, almost a mile away, and she had approached the group, hesitantly at first. Fortunately, two of the Mosasaurs had been members of her old pod, also cut off from the old nests, and she had been accepted. She had gone with them into a different tunnel system that was new to her, but had also been fashioned by volcanoes eons ago. She had hunted with the group that night, and now she and her offspring had full bellies.

She turned her head to look at them. One, the young male, was already asleep, making little grunting and snuffling noises. The young female had placed her head onto her mother's tail, and her eyes were starting to close. The Mosasaur mother felt herself relaxing. At some level she missed her mate, but she heard the roar of the pod's enormous alpha male further down the cavern, and she felt safe. She let her massive head sink slowly into the sand, and gradually closed her eyes. She was home.

The End

Hopefully, you really enjoyed **Electric Blue**! Please watch for the sequel, **Electric Blue: Battle Primeval**, available soon. The first chapter follows.

Chapter One

The majestic silver bird shuddered as it hit a sudden downdraft, but shook it off with a slight tip of its shiny wings. David glanced out the window of seat 4A of the United Boeing 777, bound for Miami. He noticed his Bloody Mary had slopped over, and wiped it up. He took another spicy sip, and returned to his email.

The first one was from Erika. He smiled at her enumerated points, typical for a post-doctoral paleontologist with a (mostly) organized mind.

Dearest David,

1. The meeting with the mayor of New York was fantastic. He brought his two young sons, who are huge dinosaur fans. They'd seen the TV coverage of my presentation on Mosasaurs to the Paleontological Society. We had a Press conference in the restaurant. The place was jammed with news media—they all want to find out more about how you and I discovered what they're calling "the T. rex of the Ocean" alive in the Caribbean.

2. The mayor wants me to repeat my presentation—in Madison Square Garden! This Sunday afternoon! No paleontologist has ever been on stage there; it's beyond my wildest dreams. Even the White House is sending someone—they want to make this part of a national campaign about kids learning science.

3. My PR lady is getting swamped with requests. We're showing only a selection of the video and photos you took of the monsters in the lagoon. I heard that you have more videos, and even a huge chunk of Mosasaur in a freezer, which you never told me about. Wanker! Not that I can blame you.

4. That brings me to my bad news. I'll miss meeting you for dinner on Anguilla this Saturday night. I am so sorry—you have no idea. But this is an honor I can't refuse. I'll do my best to get to the island as soon as I can. Please don't leave!

5. In other news, I got a visit from a Chinese billionaire's attorney. He offered me $10 million and the use of his yacht, to capture a Mosasaur for him, perhaps a juvenile. He wants to put it in a theme park. Can you imagine: the world's most dangerous animal in an amusement park. What a bloodbath that would turn into! I told this guy he

was nuts, but he said his client won't take "No" for an answer, and always gets what he wants.
Look forward to seeing you soon.
Love, Rika

David stirred the clinking ice cubes in his drink. He looked down when he heard a "Meep" from below. He reached under his seat and opened a small cat carrier. He extracted its furry content and held it up to his face. He immediately got a lick from a bright-pink tongue with the texture of sandpaper, and smiled as he said softly, "I'm sorry, I couldn't take you out sooner." He looked around at the plush cabin, and added, "You should be grateful I've sprung for a first class ticket, so you could be up here." He set the kitten on the arm rest, from where it started to nibble on the drink's celery stalk.

He sighed, and said, "Bucky, I was afraid of this. Erika's gotten seduced by the bright lights. Well, she had her chance. Though, I can't really be mad at her—this was her lifelong dream."

The kitten continued to chew on the drink's celery stalk. David was interrupted by a female voice.

"He's so cute!"

David looked up to see an elegantly dressed young Asian woman standing next to the empty 4B seat.

"May I pet him? What's his name?"

David smiled and nodded. She swung smoothly into the dark leather seat next to him, and petted the kitten with two fingers. David noticed they were immaculately manicured. He also noticed that her red wine-colored skirt rode high on tanned thighs.

"I have a gray cat at home in Singapore with similar coloring. Smoky gray, like a snow leopard. With faint stripes, like a snow tiger, if there were such a thing." She held out her hand to David. "Nice to meet you two. I'm Sunny Lee."

David took the hand, enjoying its silky smooth texture as he replied, "His name is Bucky, and I'm David. How far are you going today?"

She gave him a bright smile with two rows of perfect teeth as she replied, "To St. Martin. I'm going to a convention there, with my sister." She gave a slight wave to the passenger in 2D, a young woman with a strong resemblance to her. "We're staying for the weekend in some place called Anguilla. I understand it's an island next to St. Martin."

He nodded. "I know both islands well. I lived there for two years, and will be staying on Anguilla with friends."

She brightened. "Really? Could you possibly...maybe show my sister and me around a little? We'll gladly take you out to lunch, or whatever you'd like." She pulled a card out of her pocket. "Here's my cell phone and email address."

He handed her his card. "Here's mine."

She looked at it. "David Killmer. Didn't I see you on the news recently?"

He shrugged his shoulders. "Maybe someone who looked like me."

She smiled again. "Well, until we meet up, then." She patted Bucky on the head once more, and returned to her seat.

David read his second email, from his friend AJ, a former Marine Corps buddy who now consulted to the CIA.

David,

> We're looking forward to seeing you tonight. We got you a room in a hotel; our place is being remodeled, and is a mess.
> I got a report from the Joint Interagency Task Force, South. We've got the coordinates of where the helicopter with your packages went down, give or take a couple of kilometers. It's near a group of small islands.
> You have to hurry. We know there are at least a dozen of DuBois's henchmen left, and they'll be looking for it, also. A hundred million is sure to attract a lot of sharks.
> Leah and I bought a dive shop here in Anguilla, so we can help get you outfitted.
> We also got a report that there's a mole in the Agency, who may be tracking our movements. Watch your back, my friend.
> See you soon, AJ

David glanced around. A thin, bearded man looked at him from seat 4D, but quickly pulled his eyes away. Farther up the aisle, both young women were intently working on their laptops. He told the kitten, "You and I are going to have some great adventures together. But, the hardest thing in this world, Bucky, is knowing whom you can trust." His face softened as the kitten rubbed its chin against his hand and purred. "On the other hand, it's like Aunt Marie says, 'You gotta trust somebody.'"

www.ingramcontent.com/pod-product-compliance
Lightning Source LLC
Chambersburg PA
CBHW062011170626
46813CB00001B/112